CW01151226

STONE COLD WITCH

STONE COLD WITCH

NEXUS WITCH
BOOK ONE

PATRICK DUGAN

DISTRACTED DRAGON PRESS

Copyright © 2024 by Patrick Dugan

Cover Design by Natania Barron

All rights reserved.

No part of this book may be reproduced in any form or by any electronic or mechanical means, including information storage and retrieval systems, without written permission from the author, except for the use of brief quotations in a book review.

To the wonderful people who backed the New Year, New Books Kickstarter so this book could be published.

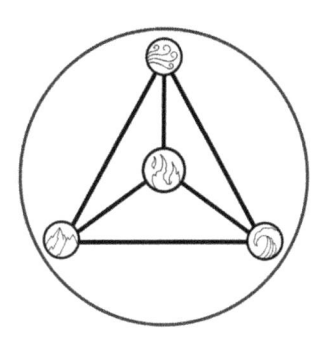

Excerpt from *Adrianne McDonald's Grimoire of Mystical and Arcane Symbols*
Circa 1640

Symbol: Mytorian Circle
Culture of Origin: Unknown
Era First Seen: pre-dates written history.

The Mytorian Circle is unique in my research. While the origins are unknown, covens around the known world all share this as a symbol of their connection to the universe.

Over the centuries, scholars have pieced together the supposed meaning of the circle. The outer ring symbolizes the universe while the triangle and orbs designate the dimensions that are connected by the mystical doorways that dot our world.

Each orb denotes an aspect of the witch's magick. The above is an example of an elemental witch whose power flows from the four elements. Other symbols include death markings, spiritual insignia et al. to correspond with one of the nine paths of magick that make up a coven.

In this researcher's opinion, this symbol is far more than a way to denote witchcraft. According to the coven members I've spoken to the symbols act as a focus to concentrate one's magick. It is far more powerful than I ever expected and will require significant study.

1

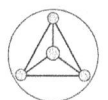

The room spun as I fought to regain my equilibrium. Strange faces blurred around me. I took a deep breath and steadied myself against the bar. The spinning lessened and then settled into a slight rocking motion. How much had I had to drink? "I'm done."

Basil put his hand on my shoulder. Tonight he wore green slacks with a yellow button down and cap. He looked more like a parrot than angelic being. "Jessica Flood, it is barely midnight. We have several more hours before we turn into pumpkins."

I shrugged off his hand. Basil was my best friend and a disgraced seraphim angel, so he didn't actually have a job. Not to mention his husband, Chip, made more than enough to support them both. "Unlike you, I have to work in the morning. The brew tours don't run themselves."

"Noon is not morning."

"It is to me." I decided not to complain to him, again, that Magdalene, the coven mother, was on the rampage, also again, about my "lack of dedication" to learning my magick. She frowned upon my young-person-from-this-century partying ways.

But I had earned my fire sigil on the first try. I'd mastered loads of useful cantrips, the smaller spells that took almost no magick. The earth sigil would be just as easy when I decided to go for it. Mags needed to relax. I had hundreds of years to perfect my craft, and it wasn't like the world depended on it. In my six years as an official coven witch, we'd only encountered a handful of issues, and the more experienced members of the coven had handled them.

Well, except for that one time, but that had been an accident, not an indication of my talent.

"At least let me drive you home," Basil said. The slight slur in his words told me he was in no better shape than I was. You'd think being an ex-angel would make you alcohol-resistant, but it absolutely did not.

"I've got Nao's insta-sober token in the car. I'll be fine." At least I hope I did. Last week I'd left the magical coin in my other pants and had been forced to responsibly sleep in my tiny car. "I'll see you tomorrow."

"Yes, you will, my dear," he said with a big wink.

I rolled my eyes and stumbled toward the door, nearly connecting with the door frame. How much had I had? The August night hadn't cooled much, but it was better than the oppressive heat of the day. I took a deep breath and steadied myself. I'd find my car, use Nao's magickal cure-all, and get back to the coven house before one AM. That would leave me with ample time to sleep before work.

The cracked concrete sidewalk made getting to my car harder than it should have been, but after the day I'd had, I deserved to blow off some steam. I stopped and put my hand against the brick wall on my left. A tingling in the back of my head that wasn't alcohol induced caught my attention. I was being followed.

I took out my phone and swiped on the camera. At first, I didn't see anything until I focused downward. Behind me a midnight black creature strolled along the sidewalk.

I pushed my cell back into my overly small back pocket and turned to look at the cat. It was as large as a border collie with mangy fur that stuck out at all sorts of angles. Its eyes looked red in the streetlights. Its tail whipped back and forth like it was ready to fight.

"Go on." I shooed it away.

In response, it crouched and snarled at me. Leave it to me to run into a feral cat. I guess it could be worse. A bear had been meandering down the streets a few weeks ago. "Get lost!" I shouted at it.

That was when I noticed the fangs.

"*Scutum*," I stuttered just as the cat leapt at me. The red gold shield materialized between me and the feral whatever it was. It shrieked as it struck the fiery barrier. It landed on all fours and leapt again, but this time it sailed over my head.

Could cats jump all the way over a human? I whipped around to face it, but my shield stayed behind me. Fuck.

"*Punus*," I said.

The cat sprang at my head. I clumsily swung my fist at the beast, clipping it on the leg. It was enough to knock it off target and it struck my shoulder instead of my face. It also unbalanced me, so I fell flat on my ass.

I swear the cat laughed at me.

"You want some more?" I said, pushing myself to my feet. "Come on."

It did. This time I connected more solidly and drove the thing into the wall. While it was stunned, I kicked it in the head, my combat boot doing some definite damage.

With a sickening snap, the thing's vaguely feline body fell to the ground. I pulled out my phone and used the flashlight to see what the fuck this thing was. A bobcat? But weren't bobcats…spotted? How much had I had tonight? I should tell the other coven members about this. I probably want to skip the massive drinking part.

With a shake of my head, I headed for my car. Inside the Honda it smelled like old McDonalds and beer. I really needed to clean my ride. I leaned over, ignoring the lurch in my stomach, and rifled through the glovebox. Registration, fast food napkins, straws, and other accumulated debris fell onto the passenger side floor.

The silver coin finally appeared. I placed it over my heart. "*Purgo.*"

The effect was instantaneous. My head cleared, the car stopped spinning, and sobriety hit like a freight train. Sometimes the slam of the magick was so intense that some details of my overindulgence bounced right out of my brain. I'd pay for it later with a headache, but better that than a full-fledged hangover. Nao worked miracles with her talisman spells.

I pushed the ignition and drove home, Godsmack playing on the radio. I headed out of Asheville toward Blue Mountain Parkway. After a short drive through the mountainous terrain, I reached the gravel driveway of home. The coven house glowed in the darkness, though only the sisters who lived here could find it. I cruised around the house and pulled into my space in the garage.

For a long minute, I considered sneaking in, but in the end it would only make it worse. I got out of the car. Maybe Mag was asleep already.

"You going in?" a deep voice said from behind me.

I nearly jumped out of my skin. Gareth, our handyman/weapons master, stood next to his truck a few bays down from mine. He wore a black T-shirt and jeans that reminded me I should work out more. I had no idea if all the other covens across the world had a Gareth, but from what I could glean based on observing his and our coven mother's relationship, theirs was a unique bond, and I don't think she wanted to share. "Was thinking about it."

He laughed. "Mags giving you a hard time again?"

I nodded and looked at my feet. Gareth was one of the few people I wanted to impress, but I often failed miserably, though my combat training had been admittedly more effective than my magick training.

"She's tough on you cause you can handle it. If you wash out as a witch, you'd make an excellent soldier."

"Thanks," I said and rolled my eyes. "I'm sure I'd do great in the military."

"True, they frown on disrespecting authority figures. Have a good night sleep, Jess."

"You too." I pretended to be sorting through trash in my car so I could watch him leave the garage. It doesn't hurt to look. Once the show was over, I headed for the backdoor. I hung my keys in their appointed space. Everything had to be just so at the coven house.

I should hydrate before I crashed, so I stepped into the kitchen. My sister Heather sat at the island drinking a cup of tea. A huge smile broke across her face when she saw me, and she pushed a lock of dark hair off her forehead. The locket her grandmother had left her caught the light. She never took it off. "Good morning. How's my favorite sister?"

I leaned on the island across from her. "Bad day at work with a tour full of frat boys and idiots, but it's over. What are you drinking? Something weird happened earlier." I tried to focus on the memory of that weird bobcat thing, but it slipped away from me like a dream.

"EnchantMint tea. Would you like a cup and to tell me about it?"

Before I could answer, Magdalene entered the room from the foyer. "Jessica. We had planned to work on your earth magick spells tonight. Would you like to inform me why you chose to not attend our session?"

Fuck, I had totally forgotten and gone drinking with Basil instead. "Mother, I am so sorry. I—"

"Save me your excuses." she said. "I hope the day never comes when the coven must rely on your strength in a crisis. I do not understand why you refuse to apply yourself. You have more power than anyone I have ever met, yet you squander it. You would rather gallivant around with the heretic than take your place as a member of this coven."

And here I thought I *was* a member of this coven. A girl couldn't learn a lifetime's worth of magic in six years. "Why do you insist on calling him a heretic? He's my friend," I said, trying to keep the anger out of my voice and failing miserably.

"He is a bad influence, is that better?" Mother crossed her arms and regarded me in a way that roused all my worst impulses. "You are out drinking and partying instead of learning your craft."

"Nao goes out more than I do." I hated that I sounded like a sullen child, but Magdalene's lectures triggered me. The thing she absolutely had in common with my biological mother was disappointment. I could hear my mom saying the same things to me growing up. I was a useless burden, I'd always be a failure, and she'd be better off if I was gone. When the pull of my magick came, I ran to escape that life, only to deal with the same issues here.

"Nao has had many years to perfect her craft. She is an expert in crafting magickal talismans. She has earned the right to do as she pleases," Mother said.

"I thought my magick was what earned me the right to be here. Maybe I'd be better off somewhere else."

Magdalene shook her head. "You would have felt the pull if you belonged elsewhere. It is up to me to bring out your potential. Tomorrow we will continue your lessons."

I tried very hard not to pout openly. "I have to work." Coven members were provided with food and shelter, all basic needs met thanks to long-lived witches and careful investments, but if a girl wanted anything else, like beer and spare combat boots, we had standard human jobs, too.

"Mother," Heather interjected from her seat. I'd forgotten she was bearing witness to my latest argument with Magdalene. "You have always said we need to be part of the real world and Jess's job keeps her grounded."

Magdalene's eyes narrowed. "Heather, you are correct. Maintaining employment demonstrates a good work ethic. Fine. We will resume training on Wednesday morning. I will expect you to be ready to learn."

I lowered my head, more to cover my anger than out of any shame. "I will be ready, Mother."

"See to it you are," Magdalene said. "Good night to you both."

"Good night," we echoed as she departed.

Once she was gone, I turned to Heather. "Thank you."

"While her approach is all wrong," Heather said, pausing for a long sip of tea. "She is correct. You are the strongest witch here. If you spend the time mastering your magick, you will have plenty of years to have fun without all the strife."

Heather's way of expressing it got through in a way Mother's did not. To change the subject and avoid admitting the error of my ways, I opened the fridge and grabbed a Bed of Nails. I poured it into a pint glass and took a seat. There had been something I wanted to tell Heather, something about my night. Was it about Basil and his long-suffering husband? Or something at one of the breweries I'd led my tours on today? "I have lots of gossip, if you are interested."

Heather's eyes sparkled with mischief. "Only if it's juicy."

"Oh, just wait."

Heather never failed to make me feel better, whether I'd had a bad day in the human world or the magickal one. What would I do without her?

2

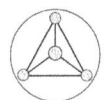

An insistent pounding at the door roused me from my slumber. I always slept very soundly after a Basil-and-Nao-talisman night. "I'm coming."

"Hurry up!" Lucia's voice came from the other side.

I pulled the door open and was greeted by the glowing smile of my sister Lucia, who had been with the coven far longer than I. She wore a Warcraft T-shirt and leggings. Her phone flew toward my face. "Check this out. We killed the final expansion boss last night. It was epic."

Lucia's technically advanced age had not stopped her from embracing all modern technology. "What time is it?"

"Just after eleven." Her face was firmly planted in her screen. "Oh, this is the good part."

"Eleven! Fuck, I'm late." I dashed into my bathroom and ripped off the clothes I'd slept in. I needed to meet my tour group at Hi-Wire Brewery at noon. If I drove like hell I could make it in time, barely. I threw on the clothes closest to me, pulled on my blue suede Vans, and ran past a distracted Lucia toward the main floor.

I thundered down the stairs and into the kitchen and right into Pallavi. The ebony goddess that was my sister Pallavi, or Vi as I called her, caught me by the shoulders.

"Slow down, little one. What is the rush?" Her words carried a hint of her West African heritage even after a century of living in the United

States. She had on a sleeveless light green top and jeans and carried herself like a fashion model. No matter what she wore, she pulled it off effortlessly.

"I'm late for work." I tried to sidestep her, but she blocked my path.

"I had a dream last night about you."

That stopped me in my tracks. When a divination witch dreams about you, you listen. "What did you see?"

Vi pulled a face. "I saw you alone and searching for something, but whatever you found upset you. I couldn't see past that, but I am worried for you. Fear and sadness were what I experienced during my time in the dream state."

Even in a rush, I wasn't about to ignore Vi's warning. I wasn't a stranger to fear and sadness, but it had been from before my time with the coven. "What should I do?"

"Go to work but be careful. I don't know why, but danger could be imminent and we must be prepared."

"Prepared for what?" Heather said as she entered the kitchen.

"Vi was sharing a dream." I tried not to freak out, but I spotted the microwave clock clicking closer to me being late. "I'll be careful, but I am late for work."

"Can I ride with you?" Heather asked. "I'm meeting Vada in town and I can ride back with her."

Vada and Heather often ran errands together. Dropping her off wouldn't slow me down. "Sure. Let's go."

I grabbed my keys from the board and Heather drifted after me to the garage. Once we were buckled up, I pulled out and headed toward Asheville. "What's up? You normally go with Vada instead of meeting her."

"I wanted to talk away from the house," Heather said, her gaze focused out the passenger window. "Mother was hard on you last night. Are you all right?"

I shrugged. By now, I was used to being considered a failure. I'd gained my fire sigil in the first year, but it hadn't been that much of a challenge. I had three more sigils to go to become a full elemental witch. But given my apparently deep well of strength, I figured I was far more useful as a member of a circle than controlling my own magick. Sharing my power with my sisters meant they could accomplish far more than they were able to alone, and that had to count for something. No matter what Magdalene said, I didn't see any reason to push myself. I had a century or more ahead of me. What was a few wasted years? "Mother is always on my case."

"Jess, we all know you are very strong." Heather held up a hand as I opened my mouth to answer her. "But you don't have any control. You don't have any magick outside of fire. What makes an elemental witch formidable in a fight isn't one element. It is the combination of all your skills."

"So now you are going to ride my ass?" I tried and failed to tamp down my temper. "You and Vi are my closest friends. We sit around doing nothing but study and practice. For what? Other than the one incident with the hellhound, we've easily stopped anything that has tried to come through the portal. The last time, Belinda did it by herself and we're still listening to her tell that story."

Heather laughed. "You aren't wrong on Belinda. She has a very high self-worth. May I tell you a story? I promise it will be better than Belinda's."

"As long as it's done by the time I reach the brewery."

"I'll be brief." Heather paused for a moment to stare out the window again before beginning in a musing tone. "My first coven was in upstate New York in a small town called Lillydale. A creature—"

"Creature?"

"I don't know how else to describe it other than it was something out of a horror movie. It had thrashing tentacles and a huge mouth full of razor sharp teeth. Mother of our coven was an elemental witch. We lost six sisters before she crafted a spell that combined all four elements and smashed it to bits. If she hadn't, that thing would have been unleashed to kill far more people than it did."

A full coven generally had nine sisters, so the death of six of them would be a huge catastrophe. I shuddered. "Sounds awful."

"It was. Shortly thereafter, I used the portal to take my place here with this coven." The sun coming through the windshield sparkled on a small tear rolling down her cheek. Heather was definitely the softest, sweetest coven member, which was why it was so safe to love her.

"What happened after?"

"It's not unusual for a coven that has several losses in a short time to regroup," Heather said. "But my point is just because it has been quiet here doesn't mean we can relax. Portals are always active. At any time, a truly horrible creature could push through into our world to wreak chaos. The portal is connected to all dimensions, so you don't ever know what will arrive."

I'd heard other stories from my sisters, but Heather never talked about her previous coven. Now I knew why. "But if all the Nexus Portals are guarded by a coven, how did you travel here?"

"When you feel the pull the next time, you will know where to go and you'll use our portal to arrive with your new sisters. The covens are older than mankind and we must guard them, but they have a variety of uses."

Seemed like instant transportation would happen a lot more if it was that simple. "So why don't we travel the world through the portals? I had to hitchhike to Asheville. Would have been nice to use a portal."

She laughed. "I walked from Iowa to Buffalo in the nineteen twenties to get to my first coven. Once you are established in your coven, it is much easier to answer the pull of the universe. But casual use of the portals isn't recommended. It attracts the wrong kind of attention."

I scored a parking spot two doors down from Hi-Wire Brewing just as the clock hit noon. The rainbow facade made the place hard to miss. Once we got out of the car and locked up, I hugged Heather. "Thank you for telling me your story. It means a lot to me."

"Jess, I love you as I would my own kin. Think about what I said. I would hate for you to reach a place where the coven needs you and you aren't ready."

As much as I wanted to scream at her, everything she was saying about the portals that dotted our dimension was true, at least as far as I'd been taught in the past six years. And what was also true was that I wasn't ready. The hellhound incident had certainly proven that. If something truly awful came through the Nexus Portal, I wouldn't be much more than a battery. Heather didn't ever side with Mother, so it must be important for her to broach the subject. "I will work harder. I promise."

She kissed my cheek. "I'll see you at home."

Shaking off the thoughts of things I wasn't good at to slip into entertainer mode—which I was good at—I strode into the brewery like I owned the place. The Captain Fantastic pinball machine sat silent this early. A group of people milled around the taproom, like a herd of sheep in need of a shepherd.

I pinned on my best tour guide smile. "HI, I'm Jess Flood. I'm a certified Cicerone, which is like a sommelier is for wine, but I just know beer. If you can hand me your tickets, we can get started."

An older couple approached, and the wife handed me their tickets. I checked their names off on my phone and did the same for the other three groups for a total of eight tourists. I was missing one pair. Before I could say anything, two younger guys stormed in from the street. "Sorry, we got lost."

I smiled at them and accepted their tickets. From the smell, they'd either already started drinking or they were still going from last night. Great. "Hi, fellas. I'm Jess and I'll be running the tour."

The second guy winked. He wore oversized jeans and a backwards baseball cap. The height of fashion. "You can tour anything you want, babe."

I resisted the urge to puke and turned my attention to the other members of my flock. "Please follow me and we'll discuss the amazing beers you'll be trying today."

"When do we get to drink?" the first dude said. His jeans fit better, and his shirt boasted some Greek frat letters I probably should recognize by now, but I was always confusing the fraternity and sorority letters, and magick was all in Latin, not Greek.

"This is a learning tour," I explained, pouring on a little company patter. "You'll get to sample some beers, but the point is to educate yourself on how beer is made and all the flavors you can achieve from just malt, hops, water, and yeast."

"Screw that, I want a beer," the second guy slurred.

It was going to be a long day.

3

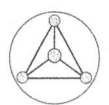

After eight hundred years of the two jackasses drinking and belching and holding everyone up while they used every restroom in the city, the final stop on the tour was the Funkatorium to sample sours. My problem clients didn't like those, but the rest of the group found the beer brewing process interesting and asked some good questions. The tour finished with a flurry of applause and a few generous tips. I collected the surveys and cash so I could meet up with Nao before I went out with Basil tonight. One last hoorah before I started hitting the spellbooks and studying for my earth elemental test.

I used the bathroom since the frat twins were parked by the exit. I didn't want any hassles after dealing with their bullshit all day, though they were wasted to the point I could knock them over with a stiff breeze. I wondered what air spell would do that. Another reason to get back to learning. Air usually came after a witch mastered water which was after earth. I was never going to get all my sigils.

When I emerged, they were gone. Finally, a bit of luck.

Nao strolled into the Funkatorium as if summoned. She wore a club dress and heels. She knew how to rock the ensemble. With her was my sister Belinda, our death witch. Unlike Nao, her pink and purple getup made unicorns want to barf, but I supposed the two of them were an interesting contrast. Sort of like Scary Spice Witch and Baby Spice Witch.

The minute Belinda spotted me, she frowned. She and I did not get along.

"Ladies," I said as I approached them. "You both look amazing. Big plans?"

Nao twirled to show off the backless portion of her dress. "I'm ready to meet some boys and have some fun."

Belinda laughed. "Jessica, it is so good to see your dedication to your unique style. It must have taken you two whole minutes to pull off that look."

Belinda and I traded insults like it was a game. Childish, but since we both did it, we could pretend it was "our thing" when in reality we simply didn't like each other. Plus, it had taken me three minutes to pull off this look because one of my Vans had been under the dresser. "Willy Wonka wants you back at the factory."

Nao snorted but covered it with a cough. "I brought you the trinket you asked for."

She produced a necklace with a crafted stone that resembled an angel. It didn't have any magickal properties, but Basil wanted a gift for Chip, and Nao was an amazing artisan. The eyes were so well crafted they almost looked alive. "Thank you. Basil will love this."

"You know Mother doesn't want you hanging around with the heretic," Belinda said with a sneer.

"Fuck off, Belinda." I turned back to Nao. "Seriously, this is beautiful."

"You're welcome." She hugged me and I returned the embrace.

"I'll let you know what he says."

"Mother's going to be disappointed in you. Aren't you supposed to go home and study? Or maybe you're going for the coven record of longest time in elementary school." Belinda gave a mean little smile and flipped one of her ponytails to the side. "Nao, we have a party to attend. Let's stop wasting time with the rabble."

"Belinda, I'm speaking to Jess," Nao scolded.

"It's fine, Nao. Have a great evening. I'll see you at home." I pushed past Belinda and exited into the warmth of the night. I took my time walking to the Twin Leaf Brewery. I was looking forward to a Ninja Porter or two. I'd promised Mother I'd be up to work on my earth sigil tomorrow, so it would have to be an early night. I guess it wouldn't hurt to study a few days a week instead of a few days a month.

Maybe if I'd paid attention more, I'd have known what to say to Heather when she told me about her first coven instead of saying stupid things about nexus travel. At the same time, her story reinforced the fact that being a coven witch wasn't exactly a constant battle to save the world or something. It was a lot more mundane, like we were on the world's longest stakeout spying on a portal that hardly ever did anything.

Case in point, Heather had been a witch for almost a hundred years and only once had something terrible come through the Nexus Portal. In six years, we'd only had the hellhound, and it did not compare with whatever the creature was Heather had described. And I wasn't useless. By adding my strength to the circle, I did contribute to defending the innocents of Asheville, though I could see my way clear to losing a few of them. Frat boys who nearly ruined my tour and lost me my tips, for starters.

But was a power cell all I was meant to be? I wondered, not for the first, or even the hundredth time, why I had been called to the coven. My magic would have manifested regardless, but without training I would have become a hedge witch, a healer, or a fire mage who had no other responsibilities than to myself. Unseers knew nothing of the magickal world so I would have been on my own to learn, but others had managed it, and I guess I would have, too.

I was suffocating in the expectations of others, and there was no air to breathe. Just like it had always been with my biological mother. Instead of trying and failing, I guess I'd just decided not to put myself in a situation to let anyone down. Or use my magick too much, or the wrong way. When the hellhound had emerged from the portal, people had died because of my magick. Even though it had been an accident, it still left a mark.

My thoughts were interrupted by my phone chirping at me. I opened the message from Sasha who needed a couple things from the grocery store. While Magdalene was the mother of the coven, Sasha was the mom. She was warm and caring and almost as sweet as Heather whereas Magdalene was cold and stern. I texted her a thumbs up and continued on my way to meet Basil at Twin Leaf.

I reached the front door and a nice, gray-haired gentleman held it for me. I thanked him and reminded myself that not all guys were jerks, just most of them. The taproom was deserted this early in the evening. The long rows of tables sat mostly empty except for Basil and my sister Vada. I waved and headed to the bar, more to process why Vada was here when Basil hadn't said anything about her being a part of our evening. She had already been friends with Basil when I showed up six years ago, which chapped my ass because she never got lectures about the heretic. Maybe Mother didn't know, though that seemed unlikely.

Dale approached with his ready smile and a friendly hello. I knew most of the bartenders in town since I did tours through all of the breweries. "Mexican lager, please."

He poured a pint and waved off the twenty I held out. He slid the beer across and I took a sip. That was a good beer. "Your money's no good here, Flood."

"Thanks, Dale." With a grin, I shoved the twenty in the tip jar headed for the table. He sighed behind me, but I ignored it. Dale was a student at The University of North Carolina at Asheville or UNCA for short, and the extra would help.

"Hello, Jessica," Vada said as she stood to hug me. Our invocation witch had long, dark hair that hung down her back. I swear she used magick on to keep it looking so tangle-free. Her figure was straight off an old 50s pin-up calendar. Her creamy, tan skin spoke to her Middle Eastern heritage. I felt like a fourteen year old boy standing next to her. She returned to her seat and I sat across from her and next to Basil, whose blue dress shirt intensified the blue of his eyes.

"What brings you out?" I asked, taking a sip of beer to cover my interest in the answer. "I thought you and Heather were spending the day together."

"Heather and I finished, and she had some other things to do. I ran into Basil, so I invited myself along." She took a drink from the wine glass in front of her. "I hope it isn't a problem."

"Not one bit. I was surprised to see you is all." I pulled out the bag with the angel necklace that Nao had made for him and handed it over. "Nao sends her regards."

Basil opened the bag and gasped as he saw the beautiful rendition Nao had crafted. "It's wonderful."

"Nao is brilliant," Vada said before returning her gaze to me. "Basil and I were catching up. It's been a long while since we've chatted."

"Vada, your beauty and grace are wonderful to behold after such a long drought," he said with a playful half bow. Though he was in a chair, he managed to make it look elegant. "You are always welcome."

"Mother doesn't approve of me spending time with Basil." I plunked my elbows on the table and looked straight at Vada. "Does it make her angry that you are friends with Basil?"

"Am I still the heretic?" he asked with a laugh.

"Yes," Vada and I answered at the same time.

"Mother has her own views on the world. I feel she is more concerned that Jessica isn't reaching her full potential as a member of the coven, rather than any true issue with Basil." Vada ran her hands through her hair and it still looked perfect. It had to be magick.

"And you?" I asked pointedly.

"I agree that you have not mastered your craft, though you've done well for the minimal time you've invested." Vada rotated the glass of wine in her hands. The red liquid reminded me of blood. "I would love to see you obtain your sigils and step to the front of the coven as our elemental witch. You certainly have the strength to do so."

First Heather and now Vada. Mother had infected everyone with her criticism of me. "I get enough lectures at home."

Vada tsked. "Jessica, I am speaking the truth, not attempting to shame you. We all travel our own paths at the pace we are meant to. You are still my sister and I love you and want the best for you."

"If that were the case, you would be sticking up for me, not guilt tripping me while I'm out with my friend. One who doesn't constantly make me feel like a failure." I stood and pushed my chair in.

Vada arched her elegant eyebrows. "I am not trying to do any such thing. You asked a question and I answered it."

I could see the upset in Vada's eyes and knew she meant it, but I'd had enough. "I have to go the grocery store for Sasha. I'll see you at home."

4

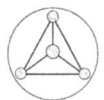

The demon's presence tore at me as I maneuvered my shopping cart through the human herd crowding the Harris Teeter. They milled about, bleating over trivial concerns, unaware that the ultimate predator was in their midst, waiting to kill. From the intensity of its effect on me, it might even be a demon in the flesh instead of a possessed person, which is what our coven normally dealt with.

In between frantically dialing everyone in the coven, I searched up and down the aisles, staring at every person's face. My skin burned with the demon's hellfire. But as hard as I tried, I couldn't locate its point of origin. I needed help.

I took out my cell and called the coven house one more time. Nothing. I tried each sisters and nobody picked up. I got worried anytime Magdalene in particular didn't answer her phone.

If I couldn't get help from my fellow witches, that left one person. Desperate, I called Basil, knowing I'd hear about it later. He was probably still drinking at Twin Leaf.

He picked up on the second ring.

"Daah-ling, are you all right? I didn't know Vada was coming but she's gone now. Come back and we'll have a few nightcaps."

I'd have to deal with that situation later, but for now, the demon took precedence.

"Basil, I need a seraphim ass-kicker, not RuPaul. I'm at the Teeter on Merrimon and there's a demon here. I think it might be a full one."

His tone changed in an instant. "I'll be there in ten. Don't do anything stupid."

"When have I ever done anything stupid?"

A barked laugh preceded the line going dead. One fuck-up and I was going to be listening to it forever.

I shoved up the sleeves of my flannel shirt to make sure the mytorian circle tattoo on my right forearm was visible. I knew my magick would work regardless, but superstition won out over cool logic this time. Each of my tattoos linked me to a certain aspect of my magick, helping me focus it, making me far stronger than I'd ever been without it.

I pushed my empty cart around the periphery of the store, looking for signs of the hell born. Possessed people had a certain smell to them. A sulfuric scent mixed with brimstone and shit. The demonic energy set every hair on my body on end. Magdalene had trained me on that within my first six months at the house, or I would have thought the way I felt right now meant I was going crazy. And this was certainly the first time I'd ever felt it when I was alone. Was that true? That bobcat the other night might have been possessed, but I was too drunk to sense it.

The demon's power pulsed through the magickal flow in a rhythm that echoed my increasing heart rate. The mytorian circle glowed to my eyes, though the magick-blind around me saw it as three black-inked, intertwined leaves and a circle on my right wrist.

I caught a whiff of sulfur through the double doors set in the back wall. Bad sign. Demons inhabited two types of people, either a practitioner who invited them in, in exchange for power, or a truly evil person whose deeds left them open to possession. But this smell, this was stronger. Different. *Fuck*. The reek of brimstone and flame meant one must have slipped through a nexus, maybe even ours, and was physically on this plane.

All my training, such as it was, had prepared me for this moment.

I left the basket in the aisle, hearing a squawk from a soccer mom in yoga pants and an extra-large top as my cart was blocking hers. Quickly, I stepped through the swinging double doors into the storage area. Rows of shelving stood like mute sentinels to my incursion. I was sworn to protect the people of Asheville from anything coming through the portal. A little trespassing was nothing.

I crept down the first aisle between pallets of toilet paper and canned goods. Ahead, one of the loading bay doors stood open to the night. The stench increased as I closed in on the loading docks. No trucks were parked nearby, nor were there people moving around the door. The demon's pulsing energy deafened me in the warehouse's silence.

"Hey! What are you doing back here?"

I spun to find an employee decked out in the familiar green vest and nametag identifying him as Todd. Was it the demon? It would pretend to be human at first, so I had to act like I thought it was human. I closed the distance between us with a big smile on my face. He smelled normal so I relaxed, a bit.

"I need to pee. Where's the bathroom... Todd?"

His eyes narrowed as he studied me. At five foot two and one hundred fifteen, I wasn't exactly a threat, but my neo-grunge look didn't seem to be reassuring Todd, either. If Belinda were here, with her southern charms, blond hair, and a big, fake smile, he'd have been falling all over himself. I was a different story.

"It's in the store. You can follow me." He pointed back the way I'd come. When I didn't move, his frown deepened. "Do I need to call security?"

I didn't have time for this crap. Stepping toward Todd, I made a quick hand gesture and said, "*Sopor.*" A spark of magick flew from my hand, and his eyes closed when it struck him. I caught the lanky guy as he collapsed, sound asleep. Magdalene frowned on using cantrips, especially on the unseers, but ridding the world of a demon took precedence over everything else.

I settled the poor guy on his side, his head resting on his arm. I returned to the task at hand, hoping no one, demon or otherwise, would stumble across Todd in the meantime. Stalking to the open door, I peered out.

With only a few streetlights illuminating the deserted loading dock, I saw outlines, but no details. A large, misshapen creature stood over a small body. Suddenly, I didn't have time to wait for Basil.

"Hey, get away from that person!" I yelled as I ran across the concrete dock. The figure turned as I leaped down to the pavement below.

A low, menacing growl came from the demon as I approached. It stood over seven feet tall. A goat face with curling horns and flaming, red eyes focused on me as it snorted a gust of brimstone and sulfur. It stepped forward and its hoof cracked the pavement.

"Oh, fuck." I'd been right that it wasn't just a possessed person. I'd never seen an actual manifested demon before aside from the hellhound, and nobody could have prepared me for the fear. I wanted to run, but somehow held my ground.

It lifted its head and roared, a sound somewhere between a lion and a Mack truck revving its engine. I backed up, wondering how long it would be until Basil arrived. Before I could finish wondering, it lowered its head and charged, plumes of asphalt erupting around the churning hooves.

I spun, but not fast enough. The horns caught my shoulder, throwing me against the red brick of the grocery store. The building rattled as the beast struck the loading dock.

The demon staggered a bit as it rebounded. The force of the blow had cracked the building's reinforced concrete. Pieces of twisted rebar hung where the cement had crumbled.

I shook my head to clear it. My stomach protested as vertigo played around the edges of my perception, but I climbed to my feet. The phoenix tattoo on my left shoulder flared to life as I summoned the element of fire to me. I might be the youngest witch in the coven, but I'd learned enough to be dangerous.

"*Sphaera.*"

I concentrated as a ball of fire formed in my hand.

The goat demon roared again and lowered his head. I threw the ball of flame as I pivoted out of his way, striking him between the horns. The fiery orb splashed off him, setting small fires on the pavement, but did nothing to the bleating trash-eater from Hell.

He pulled up this time, avoiding the building. One, two, three more fireballs struck him in various parts of his body to no effect. My first solo fight was not going well.

I backed up hastily as the demon tracked my movement, but I tripped and landed hard on my ass. My hand accidentally smacked the back of the demon's prey. I fought the need to vomit when I saw her face. It was… Oh, God.

It was Heather. My friend. How could this have happened? Her glasses still clung, askew, to her nose.

The demon's roar broke my fixation on Heather's body. I scrambled back, gaining my footing once more. The brute pawed at the ground, rending it like it was Play-Doh.

"*Ignis!*" I shouted into the night as tears welled in my eyes. A steady stream of flame shot from my hands. However, instead of aiming for the beast, I concentrated on the asphalt between it and Heather's corpse. That monster would not touch my sister, not again. I would retrieve her body so the coven could release her soul into the cosmos.

The oil-based asphalt melted under the searing heat. When the goat demon charged, his hooves sank into the sticky tar and slowed him. Not good enough, but I still had a few tricks for goat boy.

"Conglacior."

I used the spell to pull all the heat from the pavement and channel it behind me to dissipate in the cool evening air, solidifying it around the demon's feet.

I heard a car door slam and footfalls came up behind me. I didn't turn to look but knew who it had to be.

"It's about time you got here, Basil. I need some help."

A female voice with a familiar Greek accent boomed behind me. *"Apstergo."*

I almost lost control of the spell at that point. Magdalene? She hadn't even answered the phone. How had she known where to come? When this was over, I'd be in some serious shit, but I couldn't dwell on that now. We had bigger problems.

The demon twitched before he tore into the pavement to free himself. Magdalene gasped. Without the coven's power, her spell hadn't been strong enough to banish the creature back to hell. I stopped channeling and raced back, grabbing Magdalene's hands in mine.

The older woman looked shocked but understanding dawned quickly. I opened myself, allowing my magick to flow into her. I couldn't replace nine sisters locked in a circle, but it was all we had.

Magdalene seized my power, adding it to hers. *"Apstergo."* The parking lot vibrated with the strength of her word. I slumped as magick left me, draining my reserves. The demon stiffened, going transparent as the spell took effect. Then it solidified and went back to breaking free.

"Kolos," Magdalene swore in her native tongue. Even after two hundred years in America, she cursed in Greek. "Are you up to one more try?"

I nodded, though I wasn't sure how much oomph I had left. I opened myself to her, felt the rough embrace as she took control of my power, and readied a strike that never came.

A blaze of light crashed into the parking lot. Basil, wings fully extended, holding a two-handed sword of gold over his head, flew across the intervening space. As he plummeted, he swung the sword in a wide arc. The demon bleated in fear and tried to run, but he hadn't yet broken free of the tar. A shower of sparks erupted as the mighty sword cleaved through the monster, leaving nothing behind.

Basil slammed to the pavement. He staggered about before collapsing to the ground. His sword and wings disappeared, leaving his Dockers and light blue shirt with a sweater tied around his shoulders. My own private Gap model had arrived.

I pulled away from Magdalene's grasp and ran to Basil's side. He pushed himself up as I arrived, shaking his head as he fought to get to his feet.

"You okay?" I asked, though what could hurt a seraph?

"Fine. God takes personal offense when I use his gear. Takes a minute to pull myself together, is all." He glanced at the approaching Mama Magdalene. "Ah, the battle ax is here. Wonderful."

"Why is the traitor here? The fallen do not help with God's true work." Her eyes traveled past us to Heather's corpse. "Oh, no." She ran to our sister, gathering her up in her arms and rocking her gently.

Sirens sounded in the distance. Asheville's finest would be here momentarily. A lump tried to form in my throat when I let myself think about Heather, how I'd seen her only a few hours ago, how I'd been the one to drive her to Asheville. To this. "Mother, we have to go."

She didn't answer. Basil moved faster than I thought possible in his condition. He scooped up Heather's lifeless body like she was a child and strode to Magdalene's Beemer.

I helped Magdalene to her feet; she looked every day of the two hundred plus years she was. Basil set Heather in the back seat before he vanished. We hopped in the car and left the scene.

As we drove home, I realized I hadn't even gotten Sasha's groceries.

5

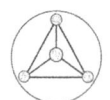

Neither of us spoke as Magdalene maneuvered through Route 25 traffic and Blue Mountain Parkway. The cars thinned out the closer we got to the address where the coven's house had stood for over two hundred years. I kept my eyes locked straight ahead, not wanting to glimpse Heather's lifeless body in the back seat.

Magdalene's seven series was immaculate. You could eat off the floor mats, they were so clean. Every few months she would come home with a new car, dealer plates, and that signature smell. Most of us had jobs and bills, but being older had its perks when it came to money. Alt-Nation played on the satellite radio, some indie band I'd never heard of. Mother always said you had to keep discovering new things since boredom killed more witches than hunters ever had.

At last Magdalene broke the strained silence. "Care to inform me why you were battling a demon in the Harris Teeter parking lot?" The tension in her voice could have cut through titanium. Losing a sister was devastating. Losing a sister you'd known most of your life had to be magnitudes worse.

"I stopped to grab a couple of things. At first, I thought a possessed person was in the store, but then I caught the reek of sulfur and hellfire. I tracked it to the goat demon in the parking lot."

Magdalene nodded. "And you found our sister."

I said nothing, instead trying to mop up the tears with my sleeve. The song on the radio changed to a new band I didn't know. Asheville flew by as Magdalene drove us toward home.

"It's not your fault, Jessica."

"I know, but what if I'd found the demon faster? Could I have saved Heather? It was like that weird bobcat the other night."

Mag's head turned toward me. "What weird bobcat?"

I closed my eyes and firmly kicked myself for having a big mouth. "It was nothing. A feral bobcat attacked me the other night."

"Feral? Did it have any other characteristics?"

"Its eyes looked strange, but it was dark and…"

"You'd been drinking?"

I sighed. This was the last thing I wanted to talk about with my dead sister in the backseat, but here we are. "Yes. I left the bar and a bobcat attacked me. I meant to tell you, but I forgot when we were arguing."

"I am not upset as I own half the blame, but knowing a possessed animal was in Asheville could have stopped this tragedy from occurring."

"So this really is all my fault. If I had told you…"

"This is a game for the weak. Second-guessing your decisions is a fool's errand at best and suicidal at worst. You can only work with the tools at hand. For all you know, had you been earlier, I'd have two corpses in the backseat."

She had a point, even though I hated to agree with her. Magdalene was the mother of our coven, but we were polar opposites. "What does it mean that there was an actual demon here? How did it get past us?"

"I do not know yet. We will inspect the nexus as soon as possible."

"Do you think Heather felt it and that's why she…" I couldn't even finish the sentence.

"I don't know that, either." She glanced at me and frowned. "Why did you not call when you discovered the demon?"

Did she think I was stupid in addition to lazy and untrained? "I called all of you and got no answer. Do you want to check my phone logs or are you going to ground me like a fucking teenager?"

One thing Magdalene hated more than anything was cursing, especially from a woman and me in particular. Her back stiffened. "Perhaps you should act your age and then I won't treat you like a child. Continue the story."

I bit back an angry reply. We'd fallen back into an old argument rather than facing the fact that our circle had been broken and Heather was dead. My emotions were all over the place, but I couldn't help it. Heather was gone. Heather. "Fine. No one answered their phone but Basil, I investigated. When I reached the parking lot, I saw the demon and a motionless body on the ground and the demon promptly attacked me. I was too late..." Tears leaked down my cheeks as I spoke.

Magdalene sighed. "I am distraught about the outcome of tonight's mishap. We will convene the coven to discuss how we are to go forward and thoroughly investigate any traces of this at the nexus."

I scrubbed at my wet cheeks. The sisters would need to prepare the ceremonies that accompanied a witch passing into the nether. It would be the first time I experienced the holy rite. An odd thought crossed my mind and came directly out of my mouth, as usual. "Mother, how did you find me? I tried to call, but no one answered."

Her cheeks flushed. "I am a spiritualistic witch. I felt Heather's panic and pain until I lost her. Soon after, I knew you were using your magick and realized something was wrong. I came as fast as possible to assist in any way I could."

It was common knowledge that Magdalene sensed our emotions, but she'd never located one of us that way before. Cross-training me in other witch abilities hadn't been anyone's priority. "That doesn't explain how you found me so fast."

"I used Find My Phone to pinpoint your location." She at least had the decency to look embarrassed.

I laughed despite the situation. "You hacked my phone so you could track me? That's it, I'm buying an Android."

She waved me off. "Technically, Lucia modified your phone so I could always find you. It turned out to be a prudent plan." A slight pause. "Jessica, we need to discuss the fallen angel."

"You mean the guy who saved our lives?" I asked, muffling the urge to scream. Was this a good time to ask if she cared that Vada was friends with Basil?

When Magdaline did nothing but pinch her lips together, I continued. "Basil is not a fallen angel. He turned his back on God. They did not cast him out of Heaven as Lucifer was. Basil is a good man and a great friend."

"He is a heretic. Whether or not the Almighty threw him out is irrelevant. He has more in common with Satan than God. He practices unnatural activities, just like the Father of Lies. Since we are the protectors of God's children, that makes him our enemy. It is not that I am ungrateful for his assistance tonight, but he is not on our side. Furthermore—"

I cut her off before the full sermon started. "Magdalene, he's gay, not a demon lord or a fallen angel. He saved our asses tonight at great personal expense. He can still wield the sword of righteousness and use his wings. Do you think God would allow him access to those if he were evil?"

"I don't care who he sleeps with. As you said, they punished him for using the weapons. That is my issue, not his orientation."

"Yes, because God wants him to return to his service, not because he's evil. You refuse to see what is before your eyes."

This brought her up short. She slowed the car, pulling into the coven's driveway. "No, child. I worry about your safety, is all." She placed her hand on mine. "I've seen evil in my time on Earth that I would protect you from, but as all parents must, I will let you make your own choices and your own mistakes and pray that God keeps you safe."

"Thank you, Mother."

She nodded curtly. "You are welcome, and we are home. Let us set to our grim task."

An awful task indeed. Never were truer words spoken.

I shivered as we drove through the protection wards that kept the coven invisible to normal people. Those without magical ability didn't see the house, just more impassable forest. We pulled down the long, winding driveway to our home. They had built it in the late 1800s, but the coven kept it up-to-date and well maintained. The Biltmore House architect built our house as a prototype which Magdalene purchased as soon as he finished. Then erased his memory of having done it. It had the same peaked roofline and brownstone facade. Behind the grand house stood a ten-car garage. Each sister had a bay, and we all had a vehicle, including Gareth's truck. The Beemer halted at the back door of the house.

The door opened, and Gareth approached. His wide shoulders slumped as he opened the back door. I got out of the car while he gently lifted Heather from the back seat. Anguish raged in his dark eyes, a storm waiting to break. It was completely inappropriate for me to want to hug him, and I wondered if it was for his comfort or for my own.

A moment later, Lucia appeared. She wore oversized horn-rimmed glasses and a Warcraft T-shirt. Our Mistress of Ceremonial magick spent more time in online gaming than anything. "Mother, Jess," she said, averting her gaze from Heather's lifeless body as Gareth carried her into the house. Lines of grief bracketed her lips. "Vi sensed a disturbance at the nexus. Belinda took the rest with her to investigate. They've requested our assistance. They haven't heard about Heather yet."

Was it connected to the goat demon? It had to be. Magdalane handed me her keys. "Jess, take my car and join them. Lucia and I have rites to perform before the moon reaches its apex."

I shook my head. "Mother, I would like to stay with Heather—"

"Heather is dead, but your sisters are not, and they may need your strength to protect this realm. It should have partly rebounded by now."

I bit back my response. "Yes, Mother."

She looked relieved. I cursed myself for being an ass. While she'd seen more years than I ever expected to, she wore the pain of Heather's death on her sleeve. She tossed me her keys and headed into the house.

"You okay?" Lucia asked.

I forced a grin onto my face. "I will be." I didn't add "unlike Heather" to the end.

She rubbed my arm. Lucia appeared to be in her early twenties with shoulder-length brown hair that went blond at the tips. You'd never expect her to be in her sixties. Of course, Magdalene was over two hundred, though she'd never admitted her actual age. At twenty-six, I had a long way to go before I was an experienced witch. "Jess, you are strong. You'll make it through this."

I hugged her and then jumped into the beemer. The engine purred to life. I adjusted the wheel and mirrors and headed to meet the rest of my sisters at the nexus. A simple trip to the grocery store had turned into a major incident.

As I drove, the tears flowed freely as I said a silent goodbye to my sister.

6

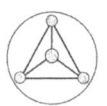

The gravel road that led up to the nexus had the same magicks as our house to prevent the unseers from finding it. I turned the car, slowing down to avoid the worst of the ruts. No matter how many times we smoothed out the gravel, nature brought back the potholes.

After a bumpy ride up the side of Mt. Pisgah, I arrived at the nexus. I parked between Vi's monster SUV and Nao's jag. I got out of the car and headed to the dirt path where it met the tree line of the small clearing. "*Sentio*," I whispered, and the night became day, sort of. I picked up the pace, following the path through the trees, around a couple boulders, and over a dead fall branch.

After a couple of hundred yards, the path widened out to expose the nexus in all its glory. The structure that Lucia dubbed "The Dark Portal" after one of her favorite video games had been crafted from the solid rock face behind it. The supports were thick hewn rock with larger pieces above and below forming a frame around the shimmering surface of the portal itself..

Pallavi turned to face me. Her dark skin blended into the night. "Jess, where are the others?"

"They sent me to assist." Now wasn't the time to reveal the fact Heather was dead. We needed to focus on the nexus, not grieve our fallen. Well, until later.

"Who in the hell called for the B-team?" An angry voice pierced the silence of the moonlit night. Belinda stomped over to join us, no longer in her pink and purple outfit. "Pallavi, I told you we have this under control. We don't need anyone to interfere with closing the portal."

"I did not call," Vi said with an elegant calm I'd never master in a thousand years. "Mother must have sent Jess to lend us her strength."

"Then who called Mother?"

"I did." Vada crossed from where she'd been standing near the portal. Had she been the last one of us to see Heather alive? She adjusted her glasses and patted the pocket on her sleek black skirt where she tucked her phone. "We are a coven, and we protect the people together."

Belinda practically huffed in annoyance. "We have the situation under control. We do this all the time. We don't need the klutz to help."

Little did she know that this was a bit above and beyond the usual nexus disturbance. What could I tell them without telling them about Heather?

"It does not matter," Vada said smoothly. "Mother sent Jessica to assist."

I saw Nao, who was still in her backless club dress, and Sasha, gray hair shimmering in the moonlight, working on either side of the portal. "What are they doing?"

Looking for goat hoofprints, maybe?

"They are setting up protection wards," Belinda said, her words dripping with acid. "If anything breaks through, the wards will hold them until we can banish them back."

"Something may already have come through," I said. "Tonight at the Harris Teeter there was a demon. A real one."

The others looked at each other before Belinda answered. "It happens. These wards will stop anything else," she snapped.

"Don't you need all nine of us for it to work?" I asked, hating myself for holding back on Heather's death. This had to take priority or more of us might die. I wanted to kick myself for thinking that way, but when you are the sword to protect this dimension, you do what you have to do.

Or perhaps the coven in Fiji needed an elemental witch with only one sigil?

Pallavi held up her hand to forestall Belinda's onslaught. "Jess, we would be better off with all nine, but this close to the nexus, we should be able to shove anything back through."

The word *should* sent a cold chill down my back. Could the goat demon have a buddy? In my limited time in the coven, we'd only had one situation that hadn't gone to plan, and now this one. Given that no one knew all the dimensions that were hooked together through the nexus, You never knew what to expect.

A loud growl filled the air, sending chills down my spine. It had taken Basil to banish the goat demon, and he wasn't here. All attention moved to the nexus which had changed to a dark red and black swirl pattern.

"Let me out," a deep, gravelly voice said from beyond the portal. "The words have been uttered and I am here to claim the souls I was promised."

"Wonderful," Sasha said from where she was completing her ritual. "Some *cpaka* summons up a being from hell and we are the ones who have to clean up the mess."

"Everything comes with a price," Nao said from the other side of the standing stones. "I'll trade unlimited partying and youth for cleaning up an occasional mess."

They seemed to have no idea of the gravity of the situation. Was the goat demon not actually that much of a threat? Maybe I was just too weak to fight the thing. But it had murdered our sister. I dug my fingernails into my palm and waited for the others to tell me what to do.

Sasha huffed. "You might think different in a hundred years. You will get old, even if it doesn't feel that way. I was young and beautiful. I danced away the nights with the Russian Czars before I came here."

"Enough," Vada said, her tone stern. She was Mother's right-hand witch and nominally in charge with Magdalene not here. "The wards will do their job and we'll all be home shortly."

"I'm not going home," Nao said under her breath, "I'm meeting James back at The Underground as soon as we are done."

"I think Vada is right and we should return home ASAP. We have things to discuss, according to Mother." Vi straightened to her full height, towering over the rest.

"Party pooper," Nao grumbled.

"I agree with Vi and Vada," I said, but whatever was on the other side of the portal interrupted the rest of my explanation.

"Release me!" the voice commanded, louder and more forcefully than before. "The contracts been made and signed in blood. I demand it!"

"Someone has an over-inflated sense of self," Nao sniffed.

This night kept getting worse. First a full-fledged goat demon in the Harris Teeter parking lot, and now a grumpy entity trying to push their way into our dimension. Imagine being an innocent normal human and having no idea what actually stood between Earth and destruction. Those stupid frat boys would have pissed themselves by now. I wouldn't be at full strength until I slept, but I had a fast rebound time and should have enough to close the portal.

I also had a lot of rage and grief to spare. "I want to force it back."

Vada considered for a second. "Go ahead, Jess. See if you can close the nexus."

"Are you kidding me?" Belinda said at a pitch only meant for dogs. "She has zero control. She'll release whatever it is before she closes the portal."

"Enough, Belinda," Vada said, irritation creeping into that cool, controlled tone I envied so much. "Jess is a member of the coven and is valued for her abilities."

"Thank you."

"When she fucks it up, I'm not dealing with the consequences." Blinda turned and huffed off into the night.

"Understood," Vada said, though the glare she shot Belinda could have destroyed the nexus. "Jess, begin when you are ready."

I nodded, pulling my magick through the phoenix tattoo on my right shoulder. I added what little trickle of earth magick I could currently manage to the mix to solidify the fire. I focused on the fiery outline of the massive creature who was trying to force itself into our dimension. I fed the anger and pain of losing Heather into my magick until it felt like a living entity in my hands. *"Propello!"*

A mass of flame coalesced around my hands and flew off like a streaking meteor on a clear night. It hit the nexus and pierced the veil. A scream of agony flooded the clearing. The nexus shimmered, then returned to its normal blue glow.

"There," I said. I shot Belinda a nasty glare but resisted sticking out my tongue. "That should take care of that."

"Nicely done, Jess," Vada said. "Sisters, we will return home to discuss this with Mother."

"What?" Nao said. "I have a date."

Before Vada could reply, the nexus flared red, the membrane of the portal stretching into the clearing. What the fuck? I'd never seen that before. Something was holding whatever it was back, but not for long as the monster pushed closer to us.

"The deal has been struck. Free me, now!"

The outline of the form continued to take shape as the nexus extended like cheap taffy. It was one thing for a spirit or the goat demon to sneak through, but this was something else entirely. According to the grimoires, if the nexus barrier broke, the resulting release of energy would kill us all and leave no one to stop whatever was on the other side. Not something I really wanted to experience firsthand.

"Sisters, to me!" Vada summoned her magick as we all ran to join her.

"Where is Mother?" Sasha said as she grabbed Nao's hand to start the circle.

"Focus," Pallavi said, grabbing the older witch's arm. I took Vi's arm and sensed our energy connect and multiply. As the circle closed with Vada, the power surged, amplified by the combined strength of the six of us. I opened myself up to the circle, my magick mixing with my sisters. A faint scent of rot filled my nose for a second before vanishing.

"Jess, send this being back to where they belong. I know you can do this."

I pulled on the strength of my sisters, feeling a tidal wave of magick flood through me. I worried the intensity would wash me away, but now I felt like I'd leveled up. I focused the power load and honed it with my own magic. *"Propello!"*

If the first strike had been a meteor, this one lit up like the asteroid that killed the dinosaurs. The spell streaked across the clearing toward the intruder. It was a clean shot that should have incinerated anything in its path, but at the last second a shimmer surrounded the form and the flaming ball winked out of existence.

"What did you do?" Belinda screamed. "I'll handle this."

"No!" multiple voices yelled, but it was too late.

Belinda yelled *"Morior!"* An inky sphere shot across the intervening space, impacting the being on the other side of the nexus.

It laughed. "Thank you, little one."

That was when everything went black.

7

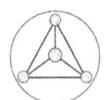

I glanced around, but I was alone. The darkness concealed every detail of the world. The ever-present hum of life had vanished along with all other sensations. My heart pounded a steady rhythm that flowed through me like a marching band on New Year's Day. I waited for my eyes to adjust, but nothing changed. Limbo had claimed me.

Slowly, flickers of motion caught the periphery of my vision. It was like one of those rides where you don't move, but the scenery flows around you. "Hello!" I shouted, but the sound died as soon it left my mouth.

Memories flooded through me. My time as a child, high school, the loss of my grandmother, all filled my head. The call of my magick came next, flickers of the journey to Asheville to find the coven I knew nothing about. The long hours of practice with my sisters, the physical exertion of training with bare hands, knives, bows, swords, guns, and all the rest. Gareth's voice, stern and penetrating, teaching me each weapon as if my life depended on it, which it had on multiple occasions. Heather's kindness, Nao's spunk, Vada's soothing voice, Gareth's loyalty, and all the rest spoke to me, but were nowhere to be seen. Finally, the parking lot and the goat demon played out. If I'd been a book, someone had just riffled through my life.

Dim lights rose around me. The first thing I saw were the twinkling stars above. The scene slowly came into view. Ahead of me, I picked out the familiar figures of Magdalene, Vada, Pallavi, and, what the fuck, Heather. Well, hell, was I dead now, too? Because here she stood, seemingly alive and surrounded by the magick she was casting.

Things moved beyond them in the darkness, illuminated by the magick my sisters threw at them. Heather used her spells to destroy the invaders. The wax in her hands formed into the creatures we fought before she broke them in two. Spirits flew from Magdalene, and Vada wielded a shimmering silver sword.

Belinda bumped my elbow. "Pay attention. Mother left us to defend the farmer's house. If anything gets through, I will handle it. You watch and learn from your betters."

I started to respond, but my tongue wouldn't move. Behind Belinda stood an old farmhouse and my soul froze solid. The faded white house with the one broken shutter stared back at me. I knew what was coming, but how did we end up back here?

Heather's magick flared, showing the hellhound charging at her. "*Apscindo!*" she said, twisting the writhing lump of wax in her hand. The demon in front of her squealed in pain as the spell took hold. Cracks appeared down the flanks of the hound, leaking flames and molten plasma. With a solid cracking noise, the hellhound tore in half, falling to the ground.

Vada skewered another and Magdalene's spell shattered a third. All those years ago, I'd relaxed at this point. Now, knowing what would come, I fought the urge to run back to the beemer and fly out of here. But there wasn't a car. Worse, the symbols that joined me to my magic weren't inked into my skin, tingling in anticipation of their use. Ice water ran through my veins. I couldn't stop what was coming now, any more than I could then.

"What are you doing?" Belinda said. Her tone held the harsh notes I'd grown to loathe over the ensuing years. Her blond hair stood out in the starlit night. Now, I knew her magick created the aura of light around her, but that night I thought she was powerful and my friend.

Fifty percent correct wasn't too bad. I steeled myself for what was about to happen.

"Jess, Belinda," Magdalene said with no panic or fear, only calm reassurance. "Two have flanked us. Protect the family in the farmhouse."

My mind clicked off and the memory took over. I ran toward the nearest hound, and my magick flowed within me, triggered by my fear.

Adrenaline surged through me, pushing me. My magick burst into being as I yelled, *"Ignis!"*

A blast of flame shot from my outstretched hand to the nearest hellhound. The heat and fire consumed the beast in moments, leaving a snowstorm of fiery motes in its wake.

"I told you to leave them to me," Belinda said in her normal, nasty tone. "You got lucky."

Her aura coalesced around her. It was so black I couldn't see where she left off and the night began. Shapes writhed within the darkness, shrieking in wordless tunes of agony. The release of energy pulsed with an eerie sensation that set my teeth on edge.

The second hound charged into the swirling maelstrom of Belinda's magick and tore through it like it was wet tissue paper. The hound grew as it ripped away the spell meant to destroy it. Instead of a small pony, we now faced a rhino-sized beast.

I heard Belinda gasp but didn't have time to worry about it. I ran to her side, summoned my power, screamed, *"Ignis!"* and hurled the spell with every ounce of magick I could muster.

The world tipped on its side and everything went wonky.

"No!" Belinda pushed me aside just as my spell finished. My aim, which had been dead-on, now went askew and the fire streaked across the darkened field to strike the farmhouse instead of the hound. The explosion filled the field with noise and light. In one second the house stood there, and in the next it flew into a million pieces, taking the unsuspecting family with it. They never stood a chance.

"Get out of my way, plebe," Belinda said, glancing to where I laid on the ground.

I couldn't take my eyes off the burning farmhouse. Magdalene had told us a family of seven lived there and now they were dead and it was all my fault. Damn Belinda for her pushy attitude and need to be the best at everything.

The giant hound bounded toward us. Belinda cast another spell but it was as useless as the first. I could see its great glowing red eyes and the spittle of flames dripping from its fangs. I hadn't been a witch long enough to die, but here we were.

A cascade of pure white drifted down, surrounding the rampaging hound and holding it still. The motes of light dissolved through the beast like sugar dropped into hot water. A few seconds later, Magdalene approached us.

"What happened?" Magdalene asked. Her face did a great impression of a thunderstorm about to burst. "You were supposed to protect the farmhouse, not destroy it."

"Mother," Belinda said. "I told Jess to leave it to me, but she threw fire that hit the house. She should be expelled from the coven for negligence."

What the fuck happened? How could I have missed? If I'd destroyed the hellhound, the family would still be alive.

"Why is Jess on the ground?" Vada asked as she approached. Not a touch of sweat touched her warm olive skin. "It seems there is more to the story."

"I'm sure there is," Magdalene said. "We'll sort it out at the coven house."

I shook my head. This had happened years ago. We were at the nexus, denying something from entry. This wasn't real. I concentrated and the edges of the memory frayed like old denim. I kept it up and suddenly, I was back at the nexus. I reached out and shook Vada whose eyes had glossed over.

"What is going on? Where are we?"

"The nexus, and something is breaking through the portal."

Vada's head whipped around and her eyes grew wide. "Sisters, we must fight back."

The others emerged from whatever memory had consumed them. In a moment we had joined hands and set the circle. Vada took the lead.

"Belinda, lock the portal," Vada said.

Belinda nodded and did as she was told, for once. The magick I held evaporated as Belinda took the accumulated power and sealed the nexus from the intruder.

"It won't last more than a day, but by then whatever was on the other side will have gone," Belinda said with a self-satisfied smirk.

Was nobody worried that we'd all been caught in a dream state for who knows how long? Surely it couldn't be this easy.

"What just happened to us?" I asked. I didn't want to share what I'd just seen, but the fact that we'd all been in a trance had to mean something. "How long were we out?"

No one answered. My temper exploded. "SOMEONE NEEDS TO EXPLAIN WHAT THE FUCK JUST HAPPENED, WHY IT ISN'T A PROBLEM, AND DID WE GIVE THE MONSTER ON THE OTHER SIDE A CHANCE TO ESCAPE"

Once everything was explained by Vada, I settled down, it was time for what I'd been dreading. "We need to return to the house."

"We will," Pallavi said. "We need to ensure we are finished here first."

"I know, but Heather is dead."

No one ever accused me of an overabundance of tact. And tonight was no exception.

⁂

The witch motorcade arrived back at the coven house shortly after midnight. We parked and entered the house. Sorrow consumed the joy in the place. My sisters and I filed into the meeting room. There on an altar at the back of the room lay Heather's lifeless form. A shimmering field of light surrounded her, keeping time from decaying her body further. I choked back an ugly sob, though the tears streamed down my cheeks. It seemed Vi's vision for me had come true already, because I was experiencing great sadness and fear.

"Oh, Heather," Vada said. Her voice cracked with sorrow. "Why did this happen?"

Magdalene approached the assembled coven. "We will mourn our fallen tonight. I wish it could be more, but it seems that we are under attack. The presence of a fully present demon in Asheville today and the manifestation at the portal confirm that it has entered an active phase."

"How are we to go forward without Heather?" Nao asked. Her mascara trailed down her face. "Without nine of us, we can't wield our full power."

"Nonsense." Sasha's gray hair stood out in the dimness of the meeting room. "We can't quit because we aren't at full strength. We can't sit around and wait for our new witch after what has happened.."

"Sasha is correct." Magdalene's demeanor hadn't changed a bit. She might as well be talking about the weather. "We loved Heather and will release her spirit on the full moon, but we would be doing her a disservice to not protect the people she gave her life to defend. I trust you are all with me on this?"

Seven heads nodded in unison like a bobblehead parade. My sisters were hurt and angry. Not the mixture you want when dealing with a coven of witches.

"Excellent," Mother said simply. "I will leave you to mourn, while I make preparations and Gareth will prepare a meal. Belinda, Vada, I have need of you both."

Belinda looked so smug, I'd normally want to smack her, but all I could think of was Heather laid out on the altar. She'd died and now there would never be another night of hot chocolate and bad eighties movies. No more sisterly talks about guys, work, or magick. Other than Pallavi, I'd been closest to Heather. She'd guided me through my early days in the coven and now she was gone. I fell into a chair. My sisters did the same and then the tears burst loose.

8

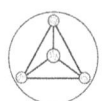

"Magdalene wants to see you in her room," Belinda said in her nasty, tattletale way which I so needed after a long night of mourning Heather. She wore a bright pink sweatshirt with Pink spelled out in sequins. She looked more cheerleader than death witch with her hair in two ponytails. "I'm sure it's about earlier."

Vada shot her a dirty look. She wore a simple black robe tied with a silver and black sash. It might as well be a formal gown the way she wore it. "Mother has asked to speak to you is all. It's been a trying night for all of us." Vada's smooth, sultry voice melted men's hearts. Nothing rattled her, though the petty squabbles among the younger members had been known to test that. "She's asked Belinda and me to accompany you."

Great. I avoided Belinda as much as she did me. I nodded. "Thank you, Vada. I guess we should go talk to Magdalene."

Vada surprised me. Instead of heading to the main staircase that led to the living quarters, she led us down the basement stairs to the working rooms. Magdalene was an early to bed, early to rise type, a trait we didn't share. I'm more the stay up all night, sleep all day sort. We passed by the alchemist laboratory, the gym, training, and the storerooms that held food and supplies for the house. I practiced my elemental magicks in the training rooms that were warded against everything. No sense burning down the house.

Vada stopped before a set of doors that had been taken from a mausoleum in Ireland, according to the lore of the house. The Celtic cross design had been carved into the patina over wooden doors. Antique pulls graced the front of the relic. Belinda set her hand on the door and I felt a tingle as her magick allowed us entrance.

The rock floor had been cut into a pentagram design, with different types of stone making up the points of the stars and the center. Metal glyphs and runes were inlaid around the circle to reinforce the protections of the pentagram. The walls were solid stone blocks taken from graveyards all over the world. Wards had been etched into each block. Nothing from the other realms could escape this room. In theory, at least.

Magdalene sat in a high-backed chair at the small wooden desk in the corner. Deep, dark circles ringed her eyes like a raccoon. "Thank you, Vada. You may stay if you'd like."

Vada inclined her head before moving into the room to take the other chair by the desk. She crossed her legs, ever the observer.

"Mother," Belinda whined like a spoiled child. "I've scyred the Halls of the Dead and Heather isn't there. I don't need—"

Magdalene arched one finely shaped eyebrow at her, cutting off the flow of protests. "I understand, child, and appreciate your efforts, but one of our coven has been murdered and we must know how the goat demon managed to get past our wards and if it is connected to the continued disturbance at the nexus. Tonight, you and Jess must both enter the Halls and find your lost sister."

I gasped in shock. Belinda paled as her mouth dropped open. Only the gravest of danger warranted physically stepping into the realm of death. There were no guarantees that you could get back depending on what waited for you on the other side.

"I know I ask much of you both, but we need information."

"Both?" Belinda stammered. "You expect me to take grunge girl with me? I've only done this twice. I can't protect a noob."

Mother's eyes flashed with anger. "You will keep a civil tongue. Jessica is your sister and a member of the coven. She risked her life tonight fighting a demon that even I couldn't banish. This is not an accident, and we must know what happened."

Belinda's gaze hit the floor. "I'm sorry. I don't understand why you think I need help in this matter. Have I done something wrong?"

"No, Belinda." Magdalene stood and placed her hand gently on Belinda's chin, raising it until their eyes met. "I am worried for your safety as well as for all the members of the coven. Go get changed and we will begin."

Belinda left the room without a sound. Magdalene studied me for a moment, but Vada broke the silence. "You are right to send Jessica with her. She is the strongest in her magick, even if her training isn't complete."

"Well, let us hope it is enough," Mother said, returning to her seat. "Great evil is coalescing around the nexus to a degree which we haven't experienced in decades. I will reach out to my sisters in other covens to see if their portals have likewise been affected, but this has every indication of a pinpoint incursion. Jessica, that is when a particularly strong entity focuses on the nexus it thinks is the weakest in order to gain admittance to this plane."

"I know what a pinpoint incursion is," I said. "That entity on the other side—it was talking about how words had been said and it was promised souls. What's up with that?"

"Demons lie," Vada said. "We don't know if a person on this plane is involved yet."

A few minutes later, I sat on the left side of the star. Nao sat in a gray tracksuit on my right, her long black hair pulled back in a ponytail. Vada sat on my left. A lock of Heather's hair sat in the middle segment of the pentagram. The five of us held hands, opening the flow of magick to merge us.

Magdalene's voice came through our bond strong and clear. "Belinda will open the portal into the Halls of the Dead. Once it is stabilized, Belinda will take Jessica through, find Heather, and ask her what happened. Do not linger. We will keep the portal active from our side. If there is any trouble, run."

Nervous energy poured off Mother, which set my palms to sweating. Belinda's spell started, the magick rising at her urging. She used words and images, building a structure to force the raw power to take the shape she needed. A portal to the waystation. Once a soul passed out of the Halls of the Dead, they were beyond our reach even when using death magick.

Voices I'd long forgotten came to me. My grandmother from when I was a child, whispering warnings. "This land is not for you, sweetheart. Do not cross the veil. Please, listen to me." Unbidden memories of cookies, Christmas in front of her fireplace, and finally her funeral. Her body, ravaged by cancer, had withered away to nothing, leaving a virtual skeleton in place of my loving Grammy.

"Focus, Jess. Do not allow the spirits to distract you from our mission." Magdalene's voice banished the images, and the voices stopped, though I longed to speak with my grandmother one last time.

I returned to my breathing, and the power swelled in response. A shimmer appeared at the center of the circle as Belinda constructed the spell, giving it shape and life. After a few moments, an ancient-looking structure of white columns with a massive stone lintel wavered before us. A hazy, green-gray membrane formed over the open doorway.

Horrible shrieks erupted from the edifice as shapes pushed at the membrane, stretching it into our world as they fought to return to the land of the living. It wasn't unlike the gravel-voiced entity at the portal last night, but we had full control over this one, or, in theory, Belinda did.

I closed my eyes and maintained my concentration. I'd take channeling the elements of earth, air, fire, and water any day over plying my trade in the land of the dead. The noise rose and fell as Belinda controlled our combined power to create a safe passage across the veil.

With an audible click, the noise stopped, and the doorway stood tall and solid. Belinda rose, and I followed her lead. We joined hands and stepped through from our world to the next. A faint oily sensation washed over me. I shuddered at the cold of it.

I'd never seen, let alone been in, the nether realms. My skin crawled, and I wanted to run screaming, but I refused to give Belinda the satisfaction. A mammoth room the size of a small city stretched out all around us. Columns rose to a darkened ceiling far above. Creatures were carved into the stone, some beautiful, some so awful I couldn't make them out. The distant walls were lost in the gloom of the place which existed in a perpetual twilight of the moment the sun has set, but night hasn't established itself.

People, their eyes closed and heads bowed, stood in all directions. Belinda, now dressed all in black, including the ribbons that held her pigtails, studied me. "And the first time I came here it was on accident when my mother died, before the call of the nexus. But the second time I had mastered my magick, and I have studied the realm for decades. Heather should be here."

I gawked at the enormity of it all. There were more dead here than I'd ever seen in one place. "How will we find her in this crowd?"

"We used her hair to anchor the portal to her. She should be close."

Belinda tugged on my hand and we started walking in a circle around the shimmering opening that floated in midair. On this side, the structure was gone, leaving an empty space. I examined the people as we hurried, and none of them were Heather. We searched for a few minutes with nothing to show for it.

"What now?" I asked a bit more harshly than I intended. The absolute silence of the place unnerved me. All the souls of the dead ignored our passing. They felt solid and would open their eyes to stare at you, but the light was gone. Acid pushed its way up into my throat. I swallowed hard to keep from vomiting.

Belinda shook her head slowly, pigtails swaying with the motion. "I'll have to call to her. It's dangerous, so be on guard."

"Okay." Be on guard? Seriously? We were standing in the land of the dead trying to find our murdered sister in the middle of millions of souls. On guard was an understatement for what I felt. A quick snap of my fingers brought up a small flame that guttered like it was in a strong wind.

"What are you doing?" Belinda hissed. "Are you trying to attract attention?"

I dismissed the flame. "Just wanted to make sure my magick still works."

"Magick attracts the barrow wraiths, especially magick that isn't death magick. They sort the souls for judgment. Having them remove your soul while you're still alive can't be pleasant, and I don't want to find out. Keep yourself under control, Wednesday Addams."

Leave it to the prom queen to get nasty while I was guarding her sorry ass. Motes swarmed around her as she prepared herself. The gentlest breeze touched me when she released Heather's name into the void. Tingles cascade down my spine as the spell spread out across the hall. After a long moment, Belinda's eyes lit up. "I've got her."

I followed Miss Priss through the throng of bodies that parted before us as the Red Sea had for Moses. Ahead stood Heather, her glasses gone, but she still wore the sweater, jeans, and white Keds she'd had on when she died. Belinda placed her hands on either side of our sister's face and blew a breath at her.

Her eyes flickered open as she returned to a lifelike state. She glanced around, confusion etched on her features. When she fixed her gaze on Belinda, her eyes grew wide with shock. "What are you doing here?"

"Magdalene sent us to find out what happened to you. Jess found you in the parking lot after a demon had killed you," Belinda said, her tone soft and reassuring like dealing with a friend who'd been sick for a long time.

Heather's face took on a puzzled expression as she cocked her head. "The demon didn't kill me. I'd gone to Vortex Donuts to talk to Esther about a charm I'd found."

I butted in. "What charm? You had nothing on you." Belinda glared at me. Heather just smiled her ever-patient smile. I shut up.

With an extra dirty look, Belinda asked, "What type of charm?"

Heather shook her head as if trying to clear it. "I don't know. I met with Esther then I remember nothing else."

My heart tore apart watching my sister and friend as she struggled to recall her own death. I rubbed her arm. "We tried to save you but failed. I'm so sorry."

"Um, I think I was dead before you got there..." Her eyes began to close as she stilled.

Belinda puffed air at her again and she revived. "I know it's hard, but anything you remember might help us figure out why you were murdered."

"You've got to go." Heather's eyes darted around as if seeking an escape. "This is a trap. I can hear them. They are coming for you. Run!"

I whirled to see the goat demon knocking bodies out of his way. What in the world? Basil had destroyed that bastard, and as far as I knew, the Halls of the Dead were only for humans.

I braced myself and started a spell when Belinda slapped me. "No magick in here."

Heather's eyes were closing again. "Love you both. Run..." She faded back to the lifeless soul we'd first encountered.

"Where is the crossing?" I shouted at Belinda, whose head looked like it was on a swivel as she searched for our way home. The demon bore down on us, closing the distance quickly. I noticed a man behind him, dark hair in a black suit, who stood watching us. He was in vivid color while everything around him were muted and bland. His eyes bored through me to my soul. Belinda's panicked yell broke my reverie.

"This way." She took off at a dead run.

I charged after her encouraged by the loud grunts that followed us. My magick beckoned to me, but I refused to make things worse than they already were. Belinda stopped suddenly, frantically turning in a circle. "It's here, I can feel it, but I can't access it."

The monster slowed as it came closer. It snorted in what I took to be laughter. That just pissed me off. "Find it, I'll delay goat boy."

I knew fire wouldn't help, so I gathered my magick and cast *"Robur."* A faint trickle of power flowed into me. Normally, it would make me stronger and tougher than a heavyweight brawler. Not so much in the Halls of the Dead. But I had to buy Belinda time.

I dove at the demon, startling him with the sudden attack. My blow landed on his stomach, knocking him back from the force of the punch. My knuckles flared with pain. I couldn't worry about it now or we'd be stuck here. He swung his clawed hand at my head. I gracefully dropped to the ground like a bag of trash after a rave. His massive hoof rose over me. I rolled to the side, avoiding the strike, and smiled to myself.

Demons don't wear pants, so his balls hung low like dual punching bags. I kicked for all I was worth and struck gold. The steel toe of my combat boot took him full in the balls and drove them up into his crotch. The thing bellowed in pain as it grabbed its damaged organ and sank to the ground, bleating.

I got to my feet and ran to Belinda who had her hand over her mouth, eyes wide with terror. "Without a restoring spell, I can't open the gate again, but a spell will bring the wraiths."

I saw shapes flying over the crowds of waiting souls. "Do it. They are already on their way."

The nearest one flew in a zig-zag pattern. Long bony arms stretched out before it, jagged nails glinting in the soft light. A skeletal face screamed. Rotten cloth and pieces of flesh fluttered off the decayed corpse.

Belinda spoke the ritual words and I realized she needed more time. Leaping into the air, I slammed into the wraith, sending it into a column. Another soared into its wake, raking my arm as it went by. The leather of my jacket shredded from the nails. A burning sensation lanced across my arm as the leather began to rot.

More wraiths flew toward Belinda who stood still casting the spell. If they broke her concentration, we'd never get home. I summoned fire and got nothing but more of the keepers heading toward me. If we quit using magick, they'd go away, but magick was our only hope.

Even more fun, the goat demon had regained its composure and was coming after me again.

It took everything I had to run as my arm was now fully engulfed and painfully burning. My magick is derived from the elements which weren't prevalent in the Halls of the Dead, but magick flowed freely. I gathered all the energy I could together, forcing it into a glowing sphere. All the keepers were drawn like flies to shit. As I reached the demon, I shoved the ball of magick into his chest and dropped to the ground.

The wraiths swarmed the monster who fought with a terrified strength. He batted his attackers away only to have more set on him. I crawled away from the fiasco and got to Belinda in time to watch the gate reopen.

I turned back to the fight and saw the demon would lose eventually. Served the motherfucker right. Right before we left, I noticed the oddly vivid man from earlier staring at me from just beyond the melee. He nodded to me, a small smile on his eerily handsome face.

Belinda said something I didn't hear. She grabbed me by the shoulders and pulled me through the gate and back into reality.

It never failed, Belinda always ruined a good party.

9

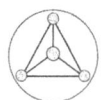

The shock of cold hit me like a hammer as hands dragged me free from the Halls of the Dead and back to the world of the extremely snarky. Belinda let go and dropped me straight on my ass. "Ow, take it easy, will ya?"

"What do you think you were doing? I told you magick attracted the wraiths. You could have gotten us killed." Belinda's ponytails bobbed in time with her pointed finger.

"Listen, Malibu Barbie. If I hadn't taken care of the goat demon, he'd have—"

Magdalene's voice was like a shot across the room. "Stop. The demon we fought earlier was in the Halls of the Dead?"

Vada groaned. *"Zayy iz-zift."* She rubbed her face with both hands. "Mother, this is troubling."

"Jessica, tell us what happened," Magdalene said, holding up her hand to Belinda. "I have no doubt you did everything correctly, *tékno*. Jessica saw the demon and now I need more information."

Belinda shot me a sour glance but said nothing, for once. I wanted to stick my tongue out at her. Instead, I told the waiting witches the details of the fight. When I got to the part about kicking the goat in the testicles, Nao giggled only to be silenced by Mother's glare. I finished the rest of the story uninterrupted.

"It sounds like the same demon. The heretic's blade should have returned it to the pits, not the Halls. This is troubling. It also hints this might be more than a pinpoint incursion." Magdalene exchanged glances with Vada. The other witch shrugged and shook her head in response.

"Jessica, quick thinking on your part. Due to the risks you and Belinda took, you've gone a long way toward protecting the nexus and our coven. Get some sleep, as the next few days will be trying. Nao, remain behind a minute if you would."

I nodded to the older witches before leaving the summoning room. My wounded arm ached. Belinda stood in the hall waiting for me, a thundercloud of anger floating around her. You'd think after seventy years she'd have better control over herself.

She confronted me, hands on hips and a sneer on her normally perfect features. "You were reckless in there. You could have gotten us killed."

"Pound salt, prom queen. I'm tired and I've lost a sister that I actually cared about. If you want to fight, go find somebody who gives a fuck." I pushed past her hard enough that she hit the wall. After the day I'd had, I was done. I glanced over my shoulder to see Blondie staring at my back. I kept walking until I got to the garage. Garreth had brought my car back from the Harris Teeter. I could kiss him for that.

I needed to clear my head, and I knew just the place.

Well, right after I got my arm healed.

❧

A short time later I entered Green Man Brewery, my home away from home. The brown brick building had huge windows and a massive wooden door. It was a Tuesday night, so the tourists had gone back to Charlotte or wherever they came from. I entered, greeted by the mosaic Green Man on the wall.

Basil sat at the farthest bar stool to the right talking with Oak, the bartender. The TV flashed a red banner with the words *Meteor Strikes Parking Lot* all in white. The on-site reporter was interviewing a man who swore he saw a huge ball of light impact the ground near the grocery store. What else could it be but a meteor? I hopped up onto the stool next to Basil.

"Hey, Jess, what'll it be?" Oak must have been six and a half feet tall, with a long beard down to his waist and hair in the back to match. Dressed all in green, he looked like a mossy tree. In reality, Brad "Oak" Night was Bredbeddle, the Green Knight of lore and about the nicest guy you'd want to meet. The nexus attracted people with magickal sensitivity as well as adepts. While Oak couldn't wield magick, he'd lived for centuries under his 'bonds of servitude' as he called them. It never pays to piss off Merlin.

"Do you have any Green Man and the Chocolate Factory left? It's been a tough week."

He lifted his chin in Basil's direction, who nursed a large amber beer. "So I can see." He filled a large mug with dark foamy beer and set it in front of me.

"Thanks," I said before taking a long pull from the glass, savoring how the chocolate played across my palette. Best stuff around. I took another swallow; the alcohol hit my empty stomach, suffusing me with warmth. Probably should have eaten first.

As if he read my mind, Basil said, "I ordered a pizza. Got to build your strength back up." He chugged the last half of his beer, set it down with a thud. A new one appeared in its place. Oak put the dirty glass away before joining us.

"What kind of mischief did you two stir up? I assume the light show from last night was Wings here?" Oak said as he cleaned the taps set into a wide iron pipe that rose out of the bar. He did each tap in turn, ensuring they were clean and poured well. A true professional at work.

"Missy here decided to play with a major demon by herself. If I hadn't shown up on time, there'd be two dead witches last night."

I kicked Basil hard, but not as hard as I should have. Oak's eyes went wide with shock. "One of the coven died?"

Basil's hand started for his mouth, but he restrained it, realizing his mistake. All that stood between Asheville and the nexus was the coven's power. If word got out we couldn't handle the situation as we had so many times over the centuries, panic would ensue in the magickal community.

Compounding the issue, if we couldn't keep the nexus capped, the unseers would pretty quickly have a crash course on demons, witches, seraphim, ancient knights, and other magical entities. While the nexus was open and spewing demons, they would be busy freaking out and trying to take us back to Salem and the trials. Humans never focus on the thing that really matters.

I gave a sigh like I was simply exasperated instead of tired, grieving, and anxious as crap. "No one died, Oak. The demon knocked out Heather, but Mother Mags arrived in time to set things straight. Basil just decided to showboat. Probably figured Vada was around and wanted to impress her."

Oak eyed me suspiciously, stroking his beard. "You're sure Heather is safe?" I fought back the urge to cry, but I had to stay strong for my sisters. Heather with her North Dakotan accent and soft nature was Oak's favorite sister by a country mile, as the saying goes. I hated to lie, but the protection of the coven far outweighed any falsehoods I'd tell the big man.

Basil rolled his eyes. "You cut a demon in two and then they get upset when you embellish a little. It's so annoying."

Oak grunted. "I'll keep my mouth shut. Hell, I'd pull out the old sword if Vada was around to see it. People panic if they think even a small demon could break through, especially after what happened at Breeson's farm."

My lips tightened and I hid my response with a vigorous nod. That was the fire I'd caused when Belinda knocked me aside so she'd be the hero. Seven people had died in that fire. "Yeah, I'm sure they would." I covered my irritation with another sip of beer. Man, was it good. Oak moved off to the other end of the bar to clean the taps there.

I hissed at Basil. "What the fuck are you thinking? You can't divulge coven secrets like that. Are you trying to get people killed?"

He lowered his eyes. "I'm sorry," he said in his clipped accent. "Using the sword took more out of me than before. One time I'm going to use it and I won't be able to resist His command to return to my place."

I didn't know what to say. It wasn't every day you counseled a seraph on his dysfunctional family. "I'd miss you for sure, but would it be so bad to return?"

He studied his beer for a long while. "Yes and no," he said softly. "Being in His presence fills you with love and joy, but it also makes you a slave. No free will, no independent thought. There is no Basil if I return." A sad smile blossomed. "Plus, what would Chip do without me? He can't even turn on the stove. He'd starve."

I laughed. Chip was Basil's husband. He was a lawyer and did a lot of pro bono work for kids. Sweet man, but a major klutz. "Is that why you left?"

Basil looked at me oddly. "Because I'm gay? No, God doesn't care who you love as long as you love someone. No, I left because bad things happen to good people, and I refuse to stand by and do nothing. Someone has to protect those that can't protect themselves."

"I actually meant because you fell in love in general, but that works, too." I took another swig of beer, intent on our conversation, when the door opened and the aroma of pizza hit me.

Dominic strode over and dropped it on the counter. "Boss said this one's on the house."

"Thanks, Dom," Basil said as he slid him a ten for tip.

"You betcha." Dom spoke to Oak for a minute before he left.

As usual, the pizza was cold. Dom—good guy, bad delivery dude. I snapped my fingers and mumbled, *"Calefacio,"* triggering the cantrip. Even after my magickal expenditures today, I always maintained enough juice that I could cast such a simple spell. Steam rose from the pizza as I winked at Basil.

We dug into the now hot pizza. Oak came over and grabbed a slice. We all munched away like contented cows left in the pasture. I finished off two pieces, and the boys took care of the rest. Hell, Oak would probably have done the honors solo.

"Basil, you're looking better," Oak noted as he cleaned pizza crumbs from his massive beard. "I told you long ago, my friend, to get rid of the sword."

"Have you gotten rid of yours, oh Green Knight?" Basil asked, eyebrows arched.

Oak glared at him. "No, but they have chained me to this reality. I'd gladly take up my sword again and fight against the oppressors. My sword is the only scrap of honor I've retained throughout the long centuries of servitude."

Wow, we were a morose bunch. I heard laughter coming from the upstairs bar. Maybe I should drown my sorrows up there. I finished my beer while Oak filled us in on the local news before I begged off, refusing Basil's offer to talk more elsewhere. It had been a truly shitty week, and the sooner I went to sleep, the sooner it would be over.

10

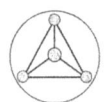

The surrounding room was one I didn't know. I wore a long, off-the-shoulder gown of teal and silver. My reflection was distorted in a myriad of mirrors that hung at odd angles on the surrounding walls. Each image seemed to depict a different version of me, though none showed me as I thought of myself.

A door opened where there'd been no door moments before. Dream logic kicked in, explaining that it had been there the whole time. I relaxed and let the dream continue. Witches knew dreams to hold a power that the conscious mind could not fully fathom. The analytical part of me recorded the details for later reflection.

A small woman scampered in, wringing her hands as she came. She wore a blue dress and white bonnet that hid her face. "Oh, my. His majesty is waiting on you and we don't want to make him wait." With the frenetic energy usually reserved for children and meth addicts, she skittered around me, adjusting my hair and jewelry.

"Best we can do on short notice," she whispered, shaking her head. "You need to eat, you're all skin and bones. A woman needs curves."

I opened my mouth to respond, but she snatched my hand and pulled me through the door and down a long corridor. Chandeliers of gold and diamonds hung from the ceilings, casting a dappled light across the blood-red carpet. More mirrors covered the walls, continuing the parade of Jessicas that ever were or possibly would be: a short-haired version sitting at a computer; a serious one in a doctor's coat, stethoscope around her neck; a third on the ground, a needle sticking out of her arm. My guide kept up a constant stream of babble that I tuned out as we walked.

The hall ended in a gilded door large enough to drive a semi through. As the doors swung open, they revealed a grand ballroom. The floor glittered with inlaid gold, gems, and pearls in an intricate pattern that defied logic. Walls shimmered with a reddish-gold light as did the faceted illumination of the chandeliers. An arching ceiling rose upward into a spire, every inch covered in a massive mural that refused to come into focus no matter how hard I stared at it.

A raised dais dominated the far end of the room. My guide bowed to the figure that lounged upon the gilded throne before she scampered out and closed the doors with a hollow boom behind her. I stood like a statue in the center of the room.

The figure descended the stairs, striding across the intervening space between us. My conscious mind screamed a warning, but my dream self stood still. The man I'd seen in the Halls of the Dead was before me, dressed in the same dark suit. His dark hair, perfectly ruffled, and the open neck of his shirt gave the impression of impertinence. His eyes were black as night and reflected distorted images of me. I disliked him already, no matter how attractive I found him.

He took my hand and kissed it, burning my skin. I yanked my hand back at the pain. He smiled as he straightened. "You are far lovelier now that you are properly dressed. I'll never understand why men allow their women to wear pants." He shook his head, his lips pursed. "It is a shame to hide the feminine form. Alas, we are not here to discuss fashion, are we, my lady Jessica?"

"Why am I here?" I asked in a deadpan tone. This was not one of those occasionally prophetic witch dreams of omens and foresight. This was something else entirely. What it was exactly, I didn't know. I wanted to wake up, break the nightmare, and get Magdalene to ward my sleep. None of that happened.

The throne from the dais appeared behind him. He dropped into it, throwing a casual leg over the armrest. "Why indeed?" He smirked. I wanted to slap it off his face. His full lips pouted at me like a sullen schoolboy. "First, I must say, you impressed me in dealing with my pet. I expected him to dispatch you and the annoying shadow walker with ease. Quite clever using the wights to do your dirty work."

I struggled to get words out of my dream self. "Who are you?" I wish I had Vi's dreamer abilities. Since I didn't, I was a passenger on this ill-fated trip.

He swept an arm before him. "As you are well aware, knowing someone's name, especially if you are a witch, gives you power over them. But we can't just go on not calling each other anything. You may refer to me as Lord Zental. My realm connects to the X'thante nexus in what you call Asheville. The nexus that your dreary coven has guarded since its founding."

I fought for control of the dream, but Zental was too strong and my skills lay in other areas. This only made me fight harder to break his grip on me. "What do you want?" I wanted to scratch the eyes out of his pretty face.

"Straight to the heart of the matter. Excellent." He swiveled until he faced me, leaning toward me with elbows on his knees. "I like a direct woman. A deal. That is what I'd like." He stood, hands behind his back, and paced. "After your display earlier, I admit to being vexed, if I'm being honest. My first thought was to destroy you, though killing a pretty little thing like yourself seemed such a waste. I could strip you of your magick and make you serve me, but where's the fun in that? No, I'd like to make a deal. You will assist me in opening the portal from my realm to your world."

"What?" I gasped.

He held up a finger to forestall further interruptions. "In return, we will subjugate your dimension and you will be left to rule over whatever you choose. You will live forever, young and beautiful. All will bend to your every whim and all you must do is secure the nexus at the appointed time."

I finally managed a few choice words. "You've got to be fucking kidding me."

"Such a shame. The others will have to do it without you. I'm very disappointed. He stopped slowly, eyeing me as he approached. "Reconsider before I do something you'll regret forever."

"Shove it." I used what little magick I could gather as a pry bar, searching for a crack I could widen. It slid off the barrier Zental erected around me. I was truly fucked.

He stabbed a finger into my midsection. Heat flared as the skin singed at his touch. I screamed both in the dream and in my bedroom. My body convulsed with pain as it spread outward. "You would have been my favorite, I'm sure. No sense wasting a quick death on you."

The pain cracked the barrier as I gasped for breath. In response to my anger and fear, magick surged through me. The chandeliers swung wildly in the dream room, causing Zental to spin in circles. I struck my prison with a sledgehammer of magick. My body registered a coolness flowing through me, taking away the pain and the burning.

Magdalene appeared at my side, eyes blazing with a fury like I'd never seen before. The room began to tear apart. "I abjure you, demon." Her voice echoed like a struck gong in a library. Sounds of shattering glass and metal striking the floor replaced the silence. Zental backed away, confusion painted across his handsome face.

"You," he hissed from between clenched teeth. "I'll see you dead."

"I've dealt with your kind for a long time and I've not died yet. You harm any more of my coven and I'll remove you. Understood?" Magdalene blazed with power that illuminated the area around us, destroying the lies of Zental's magick. He fled.

"Wake up, Jess." With an invisible push to the shoulders, I fell backward and sat up in my bed. My mytorian circle blazed blue with power as I returned to consciousness. My coven sisters ringed my bed, worry evident on all their faces, even Belinda's.

Magdalene stood, rising from where she'd been seated on the bed. Behind her and the others, it looked like a whirlwind had torn through my room, but it smelled like burnt fabric. Had I done that while in the dream?

"Ladies, the wards will hold now. We will discuss this in the morning." She touched each of them between the eyes and wished them a peaceful sleep. After Sasha left, the two of us were alone in my room.

The older witch examined the room, noting the damage I'd done to the walls and my possessions. "You certainly are strong, child." She leaned over and kissed my forehead.

"Magdalene, what was all that? I have so many questions…" The last thing I heard as I slid off into sleep was a soft goodnight from Mother.

The asshole had slipped me a magickal roofie.

11

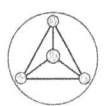

I awoke to an ungodly amount of light in my room. The morning sun forced me to blink hard to get the sleep from my eyes. After a minute I realized why. During the fight with Zental, when I'd unleashed magick in my room as well as the dream, I'd taken out my window coverings. The blinds and curtains, both of the expensive blackout variety, lay ripped into pieces on the floor. "What a shitshow."

The door opened, and Sasha stuck her head in. Her long gray hair had been pulled back except for a couple of artfully loose pieces that made her look sensual, not sloppy. "Good morning. You worried us last night." Her Russian accent hung heavy on her words, even after all the years in America. "You slept well?"

I frowned, which may have been a full-on pout, but I was irritated. "Not like I had a choice."

A rich, strong laugh followed my statement. "Mother's not known for asking permission when it's her children. I've brought you this."

She handed me a small onyx talisman carved in the shape of a scorpion. Its eyes glittered against the polished darkness of its body. A thin silver chain looped through the jump ring at the top of the scorpion's head. "I had Nao make for you, will protect from evil. You should wear it next to skin to keep you safe."

I fastened the amulet around my neck. The cold of it against my skin lasted for an instant before it settled into place. "It's beautiful. Thank you and Nao both for thinking of me, Sasha."

She nodded curtly, but her eyes studied my face. "Will you tell me what happened?"

"Of course." I tapped the bed and the older woman perched on the edge. "I'd just gone to sleep when I started—"

Vada stepped into the room. Even this early in the morning the woman looked stunning. She wore a black tank top under a beige sweater, while I looked like a teenage boy in my sweats. "You're awake, though it is a bit early for you?"

I gestured to the windows and their lack of coverings. "My blinds didn't hold up very well. I guess I'll head to the hardware store today." While Gareth did a lot of cooking and odd jobs around the house in addition to weapons training, I never felt comfortable asking him to handle any of my personal errands like some of the others did.

"Ah. Mother wants to see you in the training room." When I didn't get up, she raised her eyebrows at me. "Now."

Sasha chuckled. "We talk later?"

"Absolutely, Sasha." I climbed out of bed, checking with Vada. "Can I take a second to change?"

She smiled her impish grin. "Of course, you've got at least a whole minute, take your time." She closed the door with a soft bump. I hopped into the bathroom, threw on jeans, a Halestorm tee, and my tie-dye Vans. After pulling back my hair, I ran a toothbrush over my teeth before leaving the junkyard of a room behind. I met Vada in the hall. "Ready."

She pretended to look at her watch. "I guess it will do." Her eyes twinkled with mirth. At least somebody thought she was funny. Vada had a strange sense of humor and was usually in a good mood.

We trod the same path we'd taken hundreds of other times. I entered the training room in front of her. Magdalene paced back and forth across the center of the room. Her head came up, her eyes catching Vada's. I glanced at the invocation witch who nodded and backed out of the room, closing the door on her way out.

"Mother—"

Her hand came up, silencing me. She cast a spell I didn't recognize. Spiritualists used different methods to wield their magick than my elemental magick. A tingle passed over me as the spell completed.

"I've sealed the room as we need to speak in private." Her voice took on a stern note as she addressed me. "Jessica, the coven is in grave danger, and I need your help if we are to survive the coming storm."

My eyes widened at that. We'd always faced trouble as a unified coven in the past. Even with the pinpoint incursion and the demon guy showing up in my dreams, why was this so much more a threat to our very survival? "Don't we stand a better chance together?"

"Sit down and let us speak." Mother sat easily on the floor, cross-legged. I hoped I could still do that at two hundred. "The demon lord you faced in your dream last night is real and extremely powerful. None of the Lords of Hell have ever been able to penetrate the nexus before and I fear he has help from someone inside the coven."

I thought back to the dream, running it back through my mind, and cursed. "He said that the others would proceed without me. Just like the entity at the nexus was running its mouth about souls being promised. But none of us would do such a thing."

"Heather's neck had been broken, but there was a faint residue of magick left on her body. But here is my concern. A demon like the one we thought the heretic banished would not have killed her in that fashion. That type is physical and brutish, not magickal."

My brain couldn't keep up with Mother before any caffeine. "Meaning what?"

"Meaning the goat demon was not the murderer. Heather's death was caused by magick. Lucia's ritual magick flared against it, but there weren't any magickal fingerprints to be found."

The only thing Lucia excelled at as much as magick was technology. She'd be a hacker if she hadn't been called to serve like the rest of us. "Lucia is safe, then?"

She shook her head. "We can trust none of them until the traitor, if there is one, is found. The only way Zental could have invaded your dreams was if he had help from someone inside this house. If we don't stop Zental, he will destroy our very existence."

I scoffed. "Surely, Sasha and Vada are safe, they've been—"

"No one," she snapped. I could see the anguish in her eyes. She'd known them both for a long time. "I can only trust you because the demon lord chose to attack you. All of your sisters are suspect until we find the truth."

"But wouldn't a traitor realize we would know Zental had to have help from inside?" Mother was inside the coven and had more knowledge than any of them. No that was crazy. She had fought the goat demon and her spell was full powered, No it couldn't be her, but I'd keep my eyes open.

"Not if we appear that we do not realize it," she said.

I opened my mouth to argue more but shut it firmly. A slight smile crept on to Mother's face. "Good. You understand."

I did, and I didn't, but I trusted Magdalene more than anyone except Basil. "What about Gareth?" Not that I planned to drag the guy into this, but I had to know.

"He has no magick," Magdalene answered. "And he would never harm someone in the coven. He is not involved in this." Her certainty brooked no argument.

"Okay. What do you need from me?"

She sighed. "Jessica, you are strong in the power, but you are so undisciplined. I've been lax in your training. By now you should have mastered more than the basic fire evocation."

My hand touched the phoenix tattoo on my left shoulder. "I've earned my sigil of flame and used it to fight the demon. A few more minutes—"

"And you'd have been dead, like Heather." She let the words hang between us. Our gazes locked, but I averted my eyes after a long moment. "Raw power will not be enough to defeat a demon lord. You should have mastered all four elements by now, but you are too distractible to dedicate yourself to your calling."

I couldn't have been more shocked if she'd slapped my face. I knew she thought I fucked around too much, but to claim that I was basically a remedial witch was a whole other insult. "I have worked hard at my craft."

"No, you have not. After six years you should be an initiate in all the elements. You've but one. You still rely on vocal casting. Have you mastered your spellcraft without using words? No, you refuse to practice. Talent and strength, you have. Discipline and drive, you do not. This will have to change, for our very survival is on the line."

I had nearly died so many times in the past twenty-four hours, and all I heard from Magdalene was basically it was my own fault. I felt I was a disappointment. That I was not holding up my end of the bargain.

That the coven might be better off without me.

I stood up and went to the door. "I'll be back later."

"You will sit down and we will devise a plan to get you to your true potential."

I didn't answer as I exited the room and closed the door with a bit more force than necessary. Stomping up the stairs, I grabbed my car keys and left the coven grounds. I cranked the stereo up as Seether's "Same Damn Life" came on. The car flew down the road as I raced to get away from Magdalene's words.

I ended up at Vortex Donuts, since I hadn't had breakfast and my stomach had taken to gnawing on my spine as a reminder. Being Wednesday morning there wasn't a crowd, so I parked in front of the shop. April Lyn smiled as I entered and before I could order, two turtle donuts appeared on the counter. Now that's service. Unfortunately, Esther was nowhere to be found.

"Thanks. You know how to make a person feel special." I caught the coffee cup she tossed to me.

"My boyfriend would agree…usually," she said, rolling her eyes. "You leave one sink full of dishes and suddenly you're a bad person. I wash dishes all day, geez."

I laughed. "Have you seen Esther around?"

April Lyn shook her head. "She quit with no notice the other day. Took off like the devil's own were chasing her."

I thanked her, wondering if hell's minions were actually chasing her or if she was on their side. I filled my cup and sat at a table by the window. People watching was better on the weekends for sure. I devoured my donuts in record time. My phone chirped, but I ignored it. I needed to cool off before facing the wrath I had coming. Magdalene's words had hurt me, yes, but one did not simply walk out on the mother of your coven. Especially when that same mother has just told you that you're the only one she can trust. How unfortunate that the coven's biggest disappointment was her best chance at stopping whatever was happening to our nexus.

And sadly, she wasn't wrong. I couldn't yet cast spells without a verbal element, though I had been working on it. I just hadn't succeeded so I hadn't informed anyone of my efforts.

To while away the time while I sulked, I sipped my coffee and crafted *Ignis* in my head, attempting to light the decorative candle in the center of the table.

I had succeeded in turning the wick black and was celebrating with a second cup of coffee when Arty sat down at the table. He wore a colorful apron over the beginnings of a beer belly, or maybe a donut one. His long, tousled hair was more gray than black, but his face looked much younger than his fifty-odd years. He and Lucia had an on-again off-again thing, and I made a lot of jokes about her robbing the cradle until she threatened to hex my mouth shut.

"Wanna talk about it?" he said as he cleaned the table with one of my napkins. "Heard there was a commotion at the sorority this morning."

Wonderful. Magdalene must be tracking me again. I really needed to switch to Android. "Not really."

He checked the store but there weren't any unseers present. He held out his hand and a globe of swirling blue energy appeared above his palm. "Order and chaos are in a never-ending battle, but you can't have one without the other." Ribbons of dark and light rippled through the sphere. "Chaos magick teaches us that you can't control anything absolutely and to try is to know failure."

"Are you getting to a point anytime soon, Arty, or is this a metaphysical lecture?" I cocked my head.

He stared into the glowing ball as if transfixed by the patterns. "Nah, just some advice from an old mage. You've got to be yourself—"

"Exactly," I proclaimed a bit louder than necessary. I heard April Lyn laugh behind the counter. "Magdalene thinks I'm lazy, but I'm farther along than she's aware of. If she'd pay attention instead of making assumptions, we'd get along a lot better."

I wasn't even sure if that was true at this point, but the sympathy from Arty had me feeling the feels. How far along should I truly be? How much more powerful could I be if I applied myself? How close was I to getting my next sigil?

Arty stared at me and I realized I'd cut him off. My cheeks flushed pink.

"Like I was saying. You have to be yourself, but when the universe picks you to wield its power, you've got to be prepared."

"Oh, so Mag told you."

He shrugged. "She called to check that you were okay. I figured the rest out." The orb popped and was gone in a shower of motes. "My first master thought beating me would teach me best. Didn't work out so well for him. My next locked me in a room with my books."

So chaos mages didn't figure out their magic on their own. They too had teachers. "I can't see you being happy like that."

He winked at me. "I wasn't. I escaped and wandered. When I asked my final master how he taught, he said the universe had already done it for him. His job was to clean up my bad habits."

"Did he?" I asked, though I was pretty sure I knew the answer.

"Yep." He sat back in his chair and folded his arms. "Chaos magick is a fickle beast. You can guide it but never control it. Gives you a different perspective on the world."

I nodded. Arty was a great guy, but a bit absentminded. Working with the underpinnings of the universe had strange effects on the wielder. He pulsed with a random magickal pattern as if in tune with some unheard song.

"Anywho, Mags asked me to tell you to return home." Arty shrugged. "So, I told you. Question is what is Jess going to do?"

Good point. He studied me as I thought about the situation at hand. Running away like a spoiled child proved nothing but Magdalen's point. Nevertheless, the accusation that I didn't work hard enough rankled me. I understood a lot more than she realized about all the elements, just by using what wisps of them I could without my sigils. Why did she have to sound so much like my mother?

Arty leaned forward and produced a small vial of pulsing blue. It swirled like the globe he'd held earlier. I took it; energy tingled my fingers as I held it. "What is it?"

He smiled. "Pure chaos. It is a good reminder that the universe is entropy and even the most rigid systems rely on chaos to offset it. Everything ends in chaos." He patted me on the shoulder as he left me pondering the tube. Suddenly, I knew what I had to do.

I put the vial in the pocket of my flannel, then shot a text to Magdalene. "Meet me at the cavern." It was time to set the record straight or die trying.

12

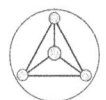

I leaned against my trusty Honda, waiting on Magdalene's arrival. Today would be the day I proved myself to everyone or they'd be looking for a new elemental witch. The cave opening led into the heart of Mount Pisgah. I readied myself to take the test of earth.

The BMW rolled up the gravel road faster than I'd have expected. Stones flew as the car slid to a stop. The driver's door opened and Mother climbed out. Her oversized shades reflected the sun at me. She strode across the space that separated us. "What do you think you're doing? You are nowhere near ready to face the earth test."

I formally bowed my head to her. "Mother, I am ready to face the challenges of my path. I intend to master the earth element and claim my sigil."

She blew out harshly. "Jessica, I know I stung your pride earlier, but more experienced witches have died during this test. Return to the coven now and we will ensure you are ready for your sigil."

I shook my head. "I need to prove myself to you. If I fail, then a new witch will come to take my place. My mind is made up."

Her face flushed red. "Child, we've lost Heather to the enemy. If you fail, you will die, and I'll have lost the only person I trust, as well as someone I love." She took a deep breath. "Please, Jessica. Come home. I can't lose you."

The words struck me like a hammer. For an instant I doubted myself, but I needed to do this. "Mother, I am ready. The coven needs me to be strong with what lays ahead. I will do my part."

Magdalene switched into coven leader as she pulled herself erect. Her hands clasped before her, though I saw them shake. "Jessica Flood, initiate of the elements and beloved daughter. Go forth and discover your destiny in the cave of the earth elements. May they find you worthy and return you to us."

I wanted to say something but didn't want my voice to crack. The darkness of the cave beckoned. While I had learned a lot from the rest of the coven, witches don't train with a master as mages do. The covens have grimoires each witch adds to as she learns and grows in power, but since covens do not duplicate skills, each witch learns alone. Elemental witches harness the power of nature for their spells. I'd have to rely on my skills of earth to pass this test.

Stepping into the cave, I plunged into darkness. With a snap of my fingers, I cast my *Sentio* cantrip. A soft glow emanated from the floor, walls, and ceiling, allowing me to see well enough to follow the trail deeper into the depths. It smelled slightly of mold with a touch of stagnant water. An air freshener spell would have gone a long way in here.

The path curved downward as I descended. Nothing moved, no bats, no monsters, nothing. The silence was oppressive as I traversed the darkened space. I saw an old wooden bridge that crossed a deep rent in the earth. It appeared to be stable enough, but if I fell, no one would ever find my body.

A loud grinding noise greeted me as I approached the bridge. I covered my ears that had grown used to the absolute silence of this place. A stone golem grew out of the floor, pieces twisting into place. Dust and salt drifted down as it stood, barring my path. "Who are you to disturb Pentral Lapis?"

The words flowed from me like I'd been born to them. "I am Jessica, daughter of earth and stone. I seek dominion with the elemental Pentral Lapis to further my knowledge and serve the earth."

"Welcome, daughter. Best me and you will be granted passage."

I bent my head, keeping my eyes on my opponent like Gareth had taught me. "I welcome the challenge."

Earth golems should be slow and ponderous, but not this one. The floor beneath my feet burst upward, forcing me to jump back or be propelled into the chasm.

"*Robur.*" Strength swelled in me as the earth elements lent me their power. I grabbed a piece of the jutting stone, snapped it off, and hurled the twenty-pound boulder at my opponent. It hit dead center in its chest and did nothing except disintegrate into gravel. My foe advanced and swung his club arm at my head. I ducked as it whistled by, faster than expected.

Quickly I summoned my power and channeled it. *"Rima."* I slapped my hand on its chest as the spell flowed out of my arm. A sharp crack sounded, but no visible sign of any damage. I needed to dig deeper into my knowledge; simple spells weren't going to stop a golem any more than a whiffle ball bat would stop a train.

A downward strike clipped my shoulder when I dodged too slowly. My left arm went numb from the blow. Without the extra strength I held, it would have ripped my arm clean off. *Focus, Jess.*

"Testa," I called, releasing a volley of stone projectiles at my opponent. They struck with a rapid series of thuds. Debris rained down as parts of its arms and chest pitted from the impact. It started toward me, each step booming as it struck the floor. I backed up, thinking frantically as to what I could use to stop the stone guard.

"Veni." A rock jutted up from the ground, but behind the golem. I ran and launched myself feet first into its chest. It stumbled a bit on the piece of rock that struck the back of the golem's legs. It maintained its balance and resumed its progress toward me.

I wish I'd been so lucky. As I landed from the kick, my sneaker slipped on a loose piece of stone and I fell, twisting my left ankle in the process. Pain shot up my leg as my muscles seized. I pushed myself to my knees. The golem loomed over me, arm raised to strike.

"Nivis Casus Ignis," I screamed as the arm descended toward my unprotected head. I tumbled to the side, rolling away as the first rock struck the stone guardian. A waterfall of lava and rock rained down, striking the golem with savage force. The heated lava cracked its head and body as the stones struck over and over. When the spell died it left a ruined, smoking pile of rubble in its wake.

Forcing myself to my feet took a bit, but I managed. I hobbled to the bridge and crossed it, using the rope handrails to support myself as my right leg wasn't up to the job. Lucia would fix the damage if I made it out of here. Doubt flared in my brain as I limped. I'd barely beaten the golem, and it was just the first obstacle. I could turn back and try again.

No, I needed to see this through. Leaving would prove Magdalene right, and I refused to do that.

I reached the far end of the bridge, sweating and panting like I'd run a marathon. A marathon would be an oasis compared to this challenge. I took a deep breath and focused on the task at hand. The cave ended before me. Dark walls closed into a perfectly formed semi-circle of stone.

Before me lay a square slab of white marble, etched with the earth symbol. The downward-facing triangle surrounded by a circle with the bisecting lines of power. It was an ancient symbol for which the meaning had been lost in the past. I limped over and knelt in the center. White light rose from the surrounding symbol.

A figure flowed out of the wall in front of me, running together like mercury pooling on a mirror. Her features were beautiful, composed of various stones, as was her flowing robe that rippled in an unseen wind. No human hands could have created such perfection.

"Speak the words." Her voice came from all sides like a surround-sound theater. The echoes ran through the cave.

"Earth Mother, I, Jessica, submit myself to be an initiate of the earth." I held out my hand and spoke the word. Flame leaped from my palm. "I wear the sigil of your brother fire and he has found me worthy. I beseech you to accept me and teach me of the earth."

Cutting off the flame, I bowed my head. Gaining my sigil of fire had been an ordeal, and the burns had taken weeks to heal, but I'd done it. I didn't even want to think about what water would be like. I snapped out of wondering, forcing my attention back to the present.

"You speak the words and have defeated the golem in combat." A piece of solid black rock the size of a golf ball appeared before me. "Take the stone and sunder it."

I picked up the piece and turned it over in my hands. It was smooth to the touch, and a coldness radiated from it. This was easy. *Rima* would crack just about any stone.

But something nagged at my mind. I flipped the stone over in my hands again, allowing my senses to penetrate the material.

"Hematite," I whispered. Using *Rima* on it would have backfired on me. The ore reflected magick back at the user if you weren't paying attention. I studied it carefully, finding a faint seam that ran through it. I concentrated on the flaw until it became laser-focused in my mind. "*Disrumpam.*" The stone split neatly in two.

"Very good."

I set the stones on the marble before me. They turned liquid and flowed into the ground. That had been close. *Rima* might have ripped me in half given the size of the hematite. Jumping at the obvious answer could have gotten me killed.

"What do we learn from stone, daughter of mine?" she asked, her voice soft as a whisper though it reverberated with unseen power.

I looked up into her onyx eyes, sure I'd never read a passage that answered that question. Searching my memory, I failed to recall anything. "I've not come across an answer to that question, Earth Mother."

"Only here will you find answers. My child, the lesson of stone is patience and persistence. Rock is hard and unyielding, but even when it is broken down, it is still hard. When it is ground to dust, it will still bind together to form anew. Patience is the key to unlocking the power of the earth. Do you understand?"

"Yes, I understand." I studied her black eyes that hid a depth of knowledge I wanted to explore. I was holding my own so far.

"Daughter, stand to accept my blessing."

I rose to my feet; I'd passed the trials. The sigil of earth was mine. I could pursue more learning in the ways of the earth. I'd done it.

The sound of clapping interrupted my celebration. Demon Lord Zental stepped from the shadows, red eyes glowing in the dim light of the cavern. "Jessica, did you think I'd let you go so easily?"

"How did you get here? This is a holy place, demon." I clenched my fists, held ready at my sides. He'd had a part in Heather's murder and attacked me in my dreams. I'd put an end to him here, where I was strongest.

He looked around, amusement playing over his features. "Holy? This dreary pit barely qualifies as a dump."

The Earth Mother held one hand out before her. "Begone, foul intruder. Your kind is not welcome in the realm of stone."

He dismissed her with a flippant wave of his hand. She reached for him. A loud crack and then another and another. They grew louder and faster as the Earth Mother shattered into pebbles.

"No," I screamed as I charged at the demon lord, my twisted ankle forgotten in my rage. I cast *Robur* and felt a surge of strength. I threw a punch at the hated demon while he smiled at me. My fist connected with his face.

The world went white as Zental exploded under the impact. The explosion propelled me backward into the chasm I'd crossed. I fell for a long time until I landed hard on my back, knocking the breath out of me.

My eyes opened and everything swam in front of them. I shook my head as I lay there, trying to clear my vision. Light surrounded me as I realized I was outside the cave; a sharp pain stabbed into my back.

"Patience and persistence, my child, is what makes an earth witch. Come back when you've learned this lesson and I will embrace you as my own." Her words echoed inside my head and faded.

"Yes, Earth Mother," I whispered as hands grasped my shoulders.

"Jessica, child, are you all right?" Magdalene asked, helping me sit up.

My head ached, my back was sore, and my pride was severely bruised. Blood dripped from where my forehead had been sliced open. A gash on my right arm dripped as I tried to wipe the blood off my face. "I'm fine. I should have listened to you, Mother."

She hugged me tight, which didn't help my aches but did make me feel better all the same. She held me at arm's length, examining me for a moment. Her face took on her normal business as usual look. "Good. We've got things to discuss."

I groaned as I rubbed the sore spot on my back. It would end up being a nasty bruise. As I rolled to my feet, I saw what I had landed on. Half of the hematite stone I'd split lay on the ground. I picked it up and limped back to Mag's car, my ankle swollen and painful. Mother helped me into the front seat.

Patience and persistence were the last things I thought before I passed out.

13

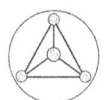

Gareth carried me into the house where Lucia had set up her apparatus. The summoning room had been adorned with the tools of her magic. Normally, the meeting room worked for healing, but with Heather's corpse preserved on the altar, other arrangements had been made.

Candles had been lit at the intersections of the circle and the pentagram. Gareth set me in the center and left the room with Magdalene. I settled my head on the small pillow Lucia handed me. She wore her large horn-rimmed glasses, as always, but had on a purple robe with gold embroidery along the edges of the cuffs. She knelt near my head as she murmured the spell that would heal my wounds. Sasha and Vi knelt on my left, Vada on my right, and Belinda at my feet. All wore purple robes, though not as ornate as Lucia's.

She picked up a small bell and rang it three times. A faint humming filled the room. Bouncing off the warded walls, the candles flickered fitfully. I relaxed and emptied my mind as she started chanting. The pentagram glowed as warmth spread itself across me like a blanket fresh from the dryer. My ankle stopped aching as the magick healed the damage.

The change in Lucia's cadence was the first sign that something was wrong. A note of panic crept into her voice. Darkness slithered up from the floor like a snake made of an oil spill. Tendrils lashed around me as I tried to pull free, and another shot into my mouth. I started to scream and choked; hot bile rose into my throat. I struggled to breathe. The lack of air took its toll.

"*Absisto.*" Lucia's voice was strong and clear. Light flared around me, clearing my throat of foul magick. Air surged into my lungs as I coughed. The tendrils withdrew for a moment then attacked again. A patch of darkness again settled over my nose and mouth, cutting off my air.

A low, menacing laugh filled the room as the tendrils became thicker. My ankle swelled under the pressure. Blood spurted from the wounds on my forehead and arm. My eyes flickered to each of my sisters who lent their power to Lucia. Pallavi swayed dangerously. Sasha looked pale as a ghost. Belinda's eyes bore down on me as she watched me struggle, unable to help.

"*Dea,*" Lucinda cried out as she rang the bell one time. The room stilled as the power of the spell struck. The tendrils withered and died. Golden light filled the room. Lucia's goddess formed over me. The wave of pure light flowed into me, healing my ankle. The gashes I'd suffered closed, returning to unblemished skin.

The goddess faded from the room. Lucia slumped, obviously exhausted. I climbed to my feet and stepped to her side. "Thank you."

She nodded slowly. "I thought I'd lost you, Jess." Her head leaned against me. "Never before have I encountered such evil in all my years as a witch. I don't understand what happened."

I did. While my vision of Zental in the Earth Mother's cave had been a test, this invasion had been very, very real. The demon had forced his way into the healing ceremony and almost killed me in the process. Between the wards and four witches, there was no way he should have been able to breach the room, but he did. A few more moments and he would have suffocated me. What the fuck was going on? My world had been beer tours, partying, and occasional rites with the coven. Now I had a demon trying to kill me, and all I wanted to do was go back to bed for a month.

"It had the feel of the spirit that tried to break through the nexus and that Jess saw in the Halls of the Dead with the goat demon," Belinda guessed. "I recognize his ick."

"Yes," I agreed, wondering what I could share without betraying that Mother thought one of my sisters might be a traitor. "And from my dream. He calls himself Zental."

Sasha came over, her color returned to her cheeks. "That was very powerful magick. You did well to stop it." Her pronunciation of very sounded more like wary with her Russian accent.

Pallavi and Belinda joined us. "My friends, that was bloody intense," Vi said in her British accent, a remnant from her years growing up in Kenya and reinforced in the London boarding school her parents sent her to. "I've never experienced anything like that."

Sasha stiffened. "It felt like death magicks." Her eyes swung to Belinda, accusation in them.

Belinda tugged a ponytail in irritation as she returned Sasha's gaze. "That wasn't death, or I'd have been able to control it."

"Hmmph. This makes no sense." The older woman stood, straightening her robe. "I discuss with Magdalene." With that she left the room.

Belinda flushed with anger, adding another tug to her ponytail for good measure. "I didn't do anything wrong. You should know I'd never hurt any of you."

"I know you didn't and appreciate you fighting to save me." I was not sure what to believe, but after the painful lesson of this afternoon, I wanted to see how things played out before deciding. Belinda and I didn't get along, true, but that didn't mean she would try to kill me. I helped Lucia up. "Let's see what's for lunch. I don't know about you guys, but I'm famished."

Gareth had lunch on the table when we arrived in the kitchen. Platters of roast beef, ham, turkey, and every vegetable known to man sat on the island with home-baked bread. I stopped at the roast beef, my bread ready to receive its meaty goodness.

"The raw stuff is still in the refrigerator, Jess," he said as he added a fresh loaf of bread to the basket. "How you can eat it like that I'll never understand, it still mooing and all."

For some reason, we elemental witches tended to like raw meat. I'm not sure why, but my sisters said all the elemental witches ate the same way. I grabbed the wrapped package, opened it, and piled the contents on my bread. A couple of tomatoes and pickles and I was ready to eat. Lucia shuddered as I took my first bite. Some blood may have run down my chin, but she didn't realize what she was missing.

"Jess, I'm really sorry. I don't understand what happened. It was like a virus infected the spell and antivirus wouldn't clear it. I finally went full rootkit and blew it out of the system. The energy flow got really jacked right before it attacked. The last burst shoved Zental out of the room, but I don't know how he penetrated the wards."

Ahh, my geek sister. She'd be as much at home in Silicon Valley writing software as she was in Asheville fighting off demons. "No worries, Lucia. It's been one of those days. Zental is strong and crafty."

She glanced around, making sure no one was listening. "Did you really challenge for your sigil?"

I nodded, not trusting myself to speak. Having failed was embarrassing, though most failures ended up far worse than being ejected like a pilot from a crashing plane. Patience and perseverance echoed through my head. I wished I was the patient type, but I might as well wish to be taller. I'd have to work harder than I had been if I was going to gain my earth sigil.

It was clear that my strength was needed. But it was too late to regret the past six years. I could only focus on what I could do now.

"She failed from what I heard," Belinda stated as she sat down with us. "She wouldn't have needed the healing ritual if she'd passed. Must be nice to be an elemental. Screw up with death magick and you're dead."

"Hmmm. I guess the healing ritual agreed with you since it tried to kill me, or is that a coincidence?" Just as the words left my mouth, I wanted them back. Patience zero, mouth one. "Sorry—"

Belinda's glare could have cut glass. "Believe me, grunge girl. When I want you dead, you'll be dead." She grabbed her plate and lemonade and left the kitchen. Everyone stared at me, not saying anything, but their looks said I'd fucked up.

Gareth cleared his throat. "Finish your sandwich and let's go work off some of that attitude."

Sounded good to me. Hand-to-hand combat drills with Gareth. There were worse ways to spend an afternoon than playing with the weapons master.

An hour later, as I landed flat on my back for the third time in as many rounds, I realized it could get worse. I rolled over on the mat and pushed myself up. He stood stock-still, waiting. We were out beyond the garage in the gym where Gareth trained us in everything from knives to automatic weapons. He was proficient with any weapon I'd ever heard of and a lot more.

"You'd think a southern gentleman wouldn't hit a lady," I said as I got into my fighting stance.

"Well, darlin,' when we've got a lady livin' in the house, I might have to reconsider." His fake southern accent dripped with sugar right along with his smile. In the six years he'd been training me, I'd never hit him. Not once. Fucking annoying is what that was.

I stepped in, throwing a quick jab. He caught my wrist. Our eyes locked as he held on to me. Damn, he was a fine-looking man. "Jess, you've gotta keep your wrist straight. You're losing all your power with it twisted like that. Again."

I threw another punch that he dodged. "Much better. You want to tell me what's bothering you?"

I lowered my fist and jumped back, but he didn't sweep my legs, just stood there waiting. He was a bit over six feet tall and muscular like a panther, not bulky like the brawlers in the movies. His blond hair was short, and he sported a goatee. I guessed he was in his late thirties.

"I failed to obtain my sigil just like Mags said I would. The worst part is I passed the initial challenge, but when I should have waited, I charged in. It was a stupid mistake."

"Sit down." When I hesitated, he bowed, signaling the end of training. I returned the bow and sat. He dropped to a crouch. "One of the hardest parts of being a warrior is knowing when to strike and when to wait. It is very easy to solve your problems with a weapon, be it fists, guns, or magick."

"How do you learn patience, when waiting could get someone killed? Worse yet, what if you wait and a demon gets free and kills a lot of people? We're charged with protecting people from whatever lies on the other side of the nexus." I rubbed my forehead, willing away the headache that threatened to launch into a migraine. Magdalene trusted Gareth, so I felt safe around him, but couldn't just spill everything as much as I wanted to.

"Good question. If I had an easy answer, I'd be president." He chuckled. "I've spent a lot of time around covens and the sisters. I think there is a reason that you are drawn to the nexus you are. Each sister fills a need in each coven."

I frowned. "Did this coven need a screwup?"

One eyebrow shot up, a gesture he reserved for stupid statements. "No, they needed a warrior. The sisters here have not faced a major challenge in many years, and you showed up in time to be trained before the nexus became more active. Before what is happening now started happening. On the new moon, the nexus will be the easiest to cross and you'll be in for a fight. They needed a magickal bruiser to anchor their circle. The rest are talented, but they aren't going to throw down with a demon. You will."

"And if I fail?" I had already failed between not telling the coven about the bobcat demon and the goat demon at the Teeter.

"Then you fail. Hopefully, your sacrifice buys the coven enough time to stop the breach with their talents. I expect once the nexus returns to normal, you'll be pulled to a new coven. Probably one that is gonna face some serious shit."

I shook my head in amazement. "How do you know so much about the covens?"

He smiled. "I've been following Magdalene around for a while. She's been at a few different nexus. She has her part to play, just like the rest of you."

"I thought she'd been here since the coven began?" My first day, Magdalene had told me that she had helped found the coven here in Asheville.

"As you were supposed to, but Gareth has a soft spot for his fighters and a big mouth." Magdalene approached us from the doorway. Gareth laughed.

"I guess I do at that. You know she's on the level, and more information is a good thing. Now, I've got to go finish up my super-secret project." He tipped an imaginary hat in our direction. "Afternoon, ladies."

When the door closed behind him, Magdalene scowled. "That man is incorrigible. I should have left him in England."

"England?"

She smoothed the front of her red dress which her shawl complemented perfectly. "Let's sit someplace comfortable. We've got things to discuss, Jessica."

I now knew how the frog with the scorpion on his back felt.

14

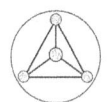

Back in the house, we adjourned to the library with a pot of tea between us. The large, overstuffed leather chairs were antiques but still comfortable. The room was lined floor-to-ceiling with bookcases holding histories, magickal theory, and just about any other supernatural resource material you could want. Our collection was impressive, though I'd heard the Alexandria coven had catacombs full of magickal tomes dating back to the first witches on record.

She set wards around the room to ensure privacy as I poured us each a cup of tea, placing two cubes of sugar in Magdalene's. Taking her seat, she lifted her cup, purring as the steam rose around her face. "The colder climes take their toll on this old body of mine." She sipped her tea, regarding me over the lip. "How long have you been with us, Jessica?"

A jag of panic shot through me. Was I being dismissed for failing my test? "Six years."

She nodded, taking another sip. "When a woman arrives at the coven house, we ask no questions and most of us keep our secrets. There comes a time when all the secrets weaken a coven and isolate us."

Had she found out I'd been arrested before I came here? I stilled myself as I waited for the next question. How would I explain it to this prim woman? I didn't answer, just stared at her.

"Jessica, I'm not inquiring into your past, child," she said quickly. "You'll have to excuse an old woman her foibles."

Sinking back into my chair, my stomach unknotted. I'd tried to bury my past and had no intentions of opening up that chapter of my life. An abusive parent and a life of crime that had landed me in juvenile detention were best forgotten. "I'm not sure I understand."

Her teacup clinked as she set it on the small table between us. "There is so much that a young witch must assimilate that we don't speak about the process of becoming a practitioner of magick."

I knew how to be a witch, not a good one for sure, but I was determined not to be the fuck up everyone thought I was. I'd learned magick, passed my first sigil test, and almost my second. "Am I doing something wrong?" I felt the edges of my anger flaring as I spoke. I stamped down on it hard. My new mantra, patience and perseverance, repeated through my thoughts.

"Not at all." She sighed, taking another sip of tea. "I am making a disaster of this, I'm afraid." She rubbed her temples as I waited.

"Jessica, I need to explain a few things that I will require you to maintain in full confidence. My spirit guides have become insistent that I share this information with you. I've learned to follow their lead, though had I done so sooner, Heather may have been spared."

I swallowed hard. Magdalene and I had never shared secrets. She might with Sasha or Vada, but none with the younger members of the coven.

"Best to start at the beginning. I was born in Athens just over four hundred and fifty years ago."

"What?" slipped out of my mouth before I could stop it. "I thought you were two hundred or so." A sly grin crossed her face. I saw she was pleased by my reaction. She might be wise, but she still held a touch of vanity about her looks. "Sorry."

She chuckled, her eyes twinkling with mirth. "I'll take the compliment." Her expression turned serious. "I was sold to a brothel by my mother before the nexus in the South of France called me. This I tell you, so you understand that I lived through bad times, not to gain your sympathy."

I nodded, unable to stop the picture of a young girl being sold by her own mother from intruding on my consciousness. I had thought my mother was bad, but I'd stolen some things and ended up in juvenile detention, not in a brothel. How had she survived such events?

"After a number of years, I made my way to England, a horrible trip that took months. By then I had full use of my magick so I could defend myself and was forced to frequently. Dealing death does not come easily to those of us that wield the spirit magick."

I reached over and refilled her teacup from the pot. After a couple of sips, she continued. "I met Gareth in the town of York. He was a soldier in a lot of trouble due to his temper. I relieved the military of their problem, and after many years I bound us together."

"You're married to Gareth?" Today had certainly been an eye-opener. Both Magdalane and Gareth were much, much older than I realized. I wasn't sure if I wanted to understand all the things she told me or how I felt about them, but I damn sure wasn't getting out of this chair until she finished.

She laughed, a throaty sound that made my eyes widen in shock. "No, dear. I'll not discuss Gareth's story; that is his to tell. The binding allows him to better protect me. A few paths of magick can do such things."

I frowned, curiosity eating away at me, though part of me was relieved to find out they weren't together. Gareth had been a weapon's master, not a warrior from long ago. I asked a different question than the one I really wanted an answer to. I had no right to pry into their relationship "Can elemental witches bond another?"

She shook her head. "I'd think not, but I fathom little of the elemental arts. You may discover a way in your studies." She adjusted her shawl around her shoulders. "Where were we..." She pursed her lips as she thought. "Ah, yes. England. Every forty to fifty years, I would feel the pull and go searching for the next coven. Sometimes they needed a leader; sometimes they fought demons so strong they needed my spiritual magick. A few I never knew the reason, but I'm sure there was a good one."

I understood from my single experience the power of the call. An itch began between your shoulder blades and grew until you were dreaming of the journey. The day I arrived at the front door, a drowned rat standing in the pouring rain, I knew I had arrived home. Belinda had been the one to greet me, all smiles and caring. Too bad it hadn't lasted.

"The reason I need to tell you these things is the demon you fought wasn't like anything I've ever seen. The nexus barrier in our portal is collapsing and forces from this world are responsible. Zental is one of the seven lords of hell. We are facing more danger than I've ever known."

It seemed like such a rapid turnaround, for us to go six years without much disturbance and then suddenly our portal out of all the portals in the world was the one that a demon lord picked to try to come through?

The books agreed that the seven lords were bound to hell and only their minions had the ability to enter the world. Minions like the goat demon, for example, or the wretched spirits that slipped through and possessed innocent humans. Also an agreed-upon fact, if a demon lord were to breach the nexus and physically enter this plane, humanity would quickly become extinct. "What can I do to help?"

Worry creased her brow. "We need to find the people that are trying to open a way for the demon lord. They are dangerous, Jess, and we must stop them, but we have to find the right way to do so."

"Could it be a possessed person?" I didn't know what would be involved in helping a demon lord through a nexus, but I did know that humans who got possessed by spirits did a lot of awful things. Surely a person would have to be possessed to willingly help cause the destruction of humankind.

"No, it has to be a person on this plane in full control of their faculties or it wouldn't work. You have to knowingly sell your soul for that kind of power. It will be someone close to the nexus but not someone who would have any obvious indications of demonic influence."

"So it could be anyone."

Face drawn, she inclined her head. "It will not be easy to find them."

Patience. It came back to the same lesson, over and over again. I'd always gone with my instincts, fought hard, and dirty if need be. Now, she was asking me to watch and wait. Life was never easy.

I picked up the pot of tepid tea and cast *Calefacio*. Steam whispered from the spout as the tea warmed. I poured another cup for Magdalene. "Mother, why me? Vada or Sasha are much more experienced. Why not one of them?"

She set the cup back down. "I've known them for a long time, but I know you are true, or the demon wouldn't have attacked you."

I groaned internally, hating what I was about to say. "The wraiths attacked Belinda in the Halls of the Dead and Zental confronted both of us."

A slight smile played across her tired features. "Zental did not invade her dreams, and the wraiths attack any use of magick, not good or evil. I know what it costs you to suggest she is innocent, but I need more proof before we bring any of our sisters in."

It made sense to me, but I felt very alone. The coven was family, even Belinda, I grudgingly admitted to myself. I'd been with them every day for over six years. They'd been my teachers, my friends, and my confidants.

Was one of them secretly trying to kill us and bring a demon lord through the nexus? My head swam with the implications. The millions that would die. Would the other covens be able to help? What about the hedge witches and other magickal beings? Would the seraphim emerge from Heaven to fight for us, since this was presumably the plane they cared most about?

Too many questions and no answers. Patience and perseverance.

"Tomorrow, go to the Unseen Eye. I left instructions with Cam for a new design I think you'll like."

"Certainly." The Unseen Eye was a tattoo shop where the magickal community went for bodywork. Cam was the owner and head artist. She created the sigils which helped us channel our magick. The phoenix on my shoulder held the fire sigil in the design. Most of my sisters opted for small tattoos on their backs where they couldn't be seen. I reveled in them, so mine were on display. Only another witch would be able to identify what they truly were.

"I have two things for you." She reached under the table and pulled out a dark wooden box. It was inlaid with mother-of-pearl in a symbol I wasn't familiar with. The box clicked as it unlocked. She produced a vial with a reddish liquid in it and offered it to me.

I felt the power immediately as my fingers closed around it. "What is it?"

"That is Elixir of Theron. It works as a truth serum and will expel a demon if it is possessing a person. I only have enough for one use, so it's a last resort. The vial is warded and will not break."

Good to know. I couldn't be walking around with a piece of glass that would shatter the first time I had to fight. "Thank you, Mother. I will do my best."

Second, she conjured a coin the size of a silver dollar. Gold on one side, platinum on the other. She flipped it over and I caught it easily. A dragon's head was inscribed on one side and an angel on the other. I probed it with my magick. I should get a feeling for it if it were an artifact or another talisman. "There's no aura around this."

"Correct." She sighed deeply. "If the nexus is torn, throw the coin into the breach. It will close any tear."

Something struck me as wrong; there had to be more to it. "What aren't you telling me?"

"If you use the coin, it will close the tear and destroy everything within a hundred-mile radius."

"Like a nuclear bomb? Drop it and kill lots of innocents?" I'd taken a vow to protect the people of this world, not kill them.

"If the demons inhabit this plane, all life will end eventually. It is your decision whether it is better to sacrifice yourself and those around you or let everyone perish."

As long as the fate of the world wasn't on my shoulders. Oh, wait it was. Man, I needed a beer.

15

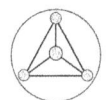

It was midafternoon when I emerged from the library. The house was quiet which was a bit unusual but not unheard of. I walked through the kitchen, stopping to grab another slice of roast beef. I munched on it on the way up to my room. Between the healing and the workout, exhaustion took its toll.

I removed the wards and entered into the blast zone. My magick had done a number on my room during my dream fight with Zental. Where to start?

I tossed my jacket onto my desk chair, then righted the toppled LED monitor. The edges had some damage but the screen wasn't cracked. I switched on the PC and watched as Windows booted. The start screen appeared, and I logged in. Miracles do happen. Lucia would be happy not to have to play tech support tonight.

I removed the broken blinds, putting them to the side. The windowpanes were spelled to resist just about anything. I added a ripped-up pillow and two cracked frames, after removing the pictures, to the growing pile. I'd have to grab a couple of extra brew tours at work to replace all the broken items.

I took the opportunity to shove my dirty clothes in the hamper and tidy up the remaining clutter. Might as well have a clean room to start with. I found a photo of Basil and me sitting outside at Sierra Nevada.

Chip had taken it while we weren't paying attention. It shocked me to see how happy I looked.

A soft knock on the door roused me. "Come in, the wards are down."

Gareth entered the room, two sets of blinds under his arm and his drill in the other hand. "Thought you'd like to return to your nocturnal ways," he said with a grin. "Can't have you up early, messes up the rhythms of the house."

"Thanks." It was hard to believe that Gareth, who looked in his mid-thirties, was almost as old as Magdalene. I studied his face for a moment longer than I probably should have.

He closed the door. "So, Maggie told you?" His amused expression that said to me this had probably happened before. "Every time she blabs to one of her covens, I get that look of, 'How do you look so young?' Witches are allowed to not age, but guys are supposed to wither and die. Maybe I'm a male witch, ever think of that?"

That was the last thing I was thinking about. "No, not at all."

"Do you know how sexist that is?"

My cheeks warmed as I blushed. "Sorry. It's not that. I haven't been here long and didn't realize it, is all."

He sighed louder than necessary, signaling the start of him teasing me. "She told you she bound me?"

"Yeah, I thought she meant married."

He snorted. "Marry Maggie? Interesting. Is that all she told you?"

"Yep, and that your secrets are your own." I put my hand over my heart. "I swear never to repeat any of it. Though I might have to ask the coven, you know, theoretically, what happens to a man's...parts when he's so old. It might be a good dinner conversation, now that I think of it."

"Wow," he said, awe in his voice. "You play rough. I knew you'd be a good…" His eyes went from mine to being trained on the floor for a second which felt like an hour. "Student for me. Do you want the blinds up?"

"Yes, please." I dropped onto my desk chair as he got to work installing the blinds. I'd offer to help, but the view was better from here. "I made sure to get blackout shades, so the light doesn't burn my precious vampire."

"Aww, you're so sweet," I said, mimicking Belinda's favorite phrase for wheedling things out of boys. Gareth guffawed at the imitation.

When he finished the job, he stood back, admiring his handiwork. "Not too bad for an old man." He reached into his boot and tossed me a sheath. "That's a dragon claw karambit. Keep it handy; there is some weird shit going down, and sometimes cold steel trumps magick."

"Thanks. She's a beauty." I examined the knife. The carbon fiber handle would hold up to anything, and the blade had an elegant curve for slashing. I slid the dagger from its sheath to examine it. I removed my flannel shirt, thankful I had a T-shirt underneath, but still very aware of Gareth's eyes on me, and put the underarm holster on. If you needed the knife, it was nice to know you could get it quick. I decided to put my flannel back on, given the circumstances.

"I had David make it special for you." I'd never heard Gareth so unsure of himself. This was uncharted territory for me.

"Umm, thanks. It's beautiful." I slid the dagger back in the sheath and moved to hug Gareth, until he extended his fist for bumping. I stepped back to fist bump him. Of course, he extended his arms for a hug.

He flushed a bit as he bumped my fist quickly. "Try to get some sleep." He headed out the door, closing it firmly behind him.

Pulling the knife out, I turned it in my hands, marveling at the craftsmanship. David made knives and implements for the magickal community as well as for locals and tourists. Gareth knew weapons, and this one was amazing. Perfect balance, not a nick or crack in the steel. The handle fit seamlessly into the guard. If it was a piece of art, it'd be the Venus de Milo.

I lay back on my bed, thinking of the day and all I'd learned, as well as everything I needed to learn. I *would* earn my earth sigil soon. I had to. If things went south, I'd need all the magick I could muster.

༄

The ringing of my phone woke me from a sound sleep. I hadn't even changed before going to bed I was so tired. On the third ring, I answered it. "Yeah?"

"Jess, It's Cam. Are you coming in for your appointment or what? Magdalene told me you'd be here."

I had completely forgotten about seeing Cam today for a new symbol. "Sorry, I overslept. I'll be there in twenty."

"Fine. I'm gonna get a donut and I'll meet you here." The phone clicked off. I ran into the bathroom, gargled some mouthwash, pulled a brush through my hair, and headed for the garage. Fuck, I'd parked my car at the cave and Magdalene had driven me back. I hit the door and there dangled my keys in their appointed place.

"Gareth drove it back yesterday," Vi's voice came from the kitchen. The man was an angel.

"Awesome. I'll be back later so we can catch up." I didn't hear her response as I dashed to my car. "Invincible," by Skillet blared out of the speakers as I drove into town. Luck was on my side and I found a parking space near the Unseen Eye.

The brick exterior of the tattoo parlor blended in with all the rest of the shops, though the blinking eye above the door stood out. A banner below the eye proclaimed, "Tattoos so good they're magical." To the rest of the world, witches lived in Oz, and demons were only found in video games. A belief that the magickal community wanted to maintain. When normal people discovered witches in their midst, bad things happened.

The door weighed a ton as I pushed against it. One of these days, I'd magick myself strong enough to tear the door off its hinges, just to see what everyone did. Silvi sat behind the front desk, reading a book on medieval history.

"Test coming up?" I asked as I let the door slam shut behind me.

She looked over her horn-rimmed glasses at me. "Yeah, the professor is a dick. Cam's waiting in the back."

I nodded. A couple of girls, holding hands as they flipped through a book of designs, sat on the black leather sofa against the left wall. The four bays that the artists used were empty. New artwork decorated the chalkboard painted walls. I headed to the rear of the store, exiting through an opaque glass door.

Another two bays were back here, but the walls were covered with occult symbols and runes of power. Cam, her flame-red hair loose all the way to her butt today, stood over a slight figure who lay on the table. The back tattoo was extremely intricate, depicting a dragon fighting a hippogriff.

"It's healing fine," she said. "Just don't scratch at it, or you'll make it bleed."

A sullen okay was her only answer. Her client got up, pulling their button-up shirt back into place. I stepped into the other bay to wait for Cam. She rolled in, long legs displayed by the shorts she wore and a sleeveless shirt showing off her ink, which included a dragon that coiled from the back of her hand up to her shoulder.

"Nice to see you, Jessica," she said with a hint of sarcasm. "Late night?"

I sat on the adjustable chair in the center of the bay. "Long day. Sorry for being late."

"Apology accepted. I had a turtle donut to bide the time." She retrieved a folder from her tool stand. "You want to see what we're doing?"

"Of course." All witches used symbols to help focus energy. I always thought of it as a shortcut to accessing my magick. The tattoo acted like a conduit to the source where your magick flowed from. My phoenix held the symbol of fire in the center of its chest. "I can't believe Magdalene set this up. She's not a fan of my excessive ink."

Her eyes raised to Heaven as she adopted Mama's Greek accent. "Spiritual magick doesn't require ornate symbols, child." She smirked at me as I laughed. "She's one of the few I've not done work for. Here's the design."

The paper held a drawing that looked like a blueprint more than a drawing. Lengths and widths were marked all over the page. The tattoo would be beautiful. A waxing crescent moon hung over a series of lines connecting it to another downward-facing crescent below. The lines created a pattern that drew the eye. "Wow. That will be amazing on my right arm."

Cam shook her head. "No, darlin', it has to be over your spine. I have exacting specifications on this one and can't change a thing. Sounds like some higher-level hoodoo to me."

Down the spine was going to hurt. Anytime you inked over bony parts, it was painful, and with all the crossing lines, doubly so. "I guess we better get started."

Cam handed me a wrap to cover myself before adjusting the chair so I could lay on my stomach. I got as comfortable as I could while Cam flicked on her machine, set out needles and the ink she'd need. She pulled on her gloves as she got ready to start.

"What colors are we using?" I asked, still curious as to why I was getting this specific design. I'd have to research in my grimoires to see if it was referenced.

"All black, no color. Lay still. Like I said, this has to be exact." She produced a ruler and a pen and set to outlining the design over my spine. I waited as she drew, mumbling to herself as she etched out each line in turn. After forty-five minutes she finished. "You might want to use the bathroom now. I'm supposed to finish this tonight without stopping, once I open the ink she gave me."

Special ink, exact design. What was Magdalene up to? I made a quick trip to relieve myself. I climbed back on the table, situating myself so Cam could work on my back.

She made her final preparations, and I drifted into my zone. I loved having tattoos, getting them wasn't my favorite. I'd heard some people become addicted to getting them. Not me. Cam had the touch, so they didn't hurt the way a rough tattoo artist did, but it still stung like a mother when she crossed bone.

Her hands settled on my back as I felt the needle start. I tried to relax as she worked, reciting the earth spells I could remember in my head as a distraction. Too bad the grimoires didn't come as audiobooks, or I could have studied for my next test. She moved away from me, sorting through a drawer for something. She returned, taking a drink from a plastic water bottle. The work resumed. "I've been meaning to ask you. I haven't seen Heather for a few days. Is she okay? I've heard a few rumors from the community."

I flinched.

"Don't move," Cam almost shouted. "I can't erase mistakes."

"Sorry." My mind whirled around the question. Oak must have told someone about what Basil said. "She's fine. I saw her working out with Gareth yesterday."

She whistled. "I'd like to do some working out with Gareth." She then went on to detail just what she'd do with him. At least we weren't talking about Heather.

I'd have to take care of the Heather rumor soon before it got out of hand. Lucky me.

16

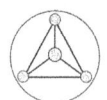

I arrived back at the coven house after dinner. It had taken far longer than expected to finish. Vada had left me a plate of lemon chicken, mashed potatoes, and asparagus which I happily reduced to nothing. My back ached from the tattoo, but my evening's work wasn't finished.

After cleaning up my dishes, I made my way into the library which had become the parlor for the next two days while Heather's corpse waited for the new moon. We would say farewell to our sister under the darkened sky of our grief, but until then we would pay our respects as a group. Pallavi and Vada played cards at the table where I'd met with Magdalene yesterday. Sasha, Belinda, Lucia, and Nao had a board game at a folding table. Mother sat in the corner reading a book.

I cleared my throat as I entered. "While I was in Asheville today, a bunch of people from the community asked about Heather. It seems there is a rumor that she's dead."

Vada folded her hand and set the cards on the table. "This is not good. If the coven is seen as broken, we will have panic."

"Agreed," Magdalene said as she closed the book in her lap. "Ideas?"

Might as well plunge right in. "I think Sasha should disguise me as Heather and I'll go into town, hit Malaprops and the relic warehouse at Willow's Dream so I'm seen. That should put the rumor to rest."

Sasha frowned. "You expect to walk into a relic safehouse and not have illusion dispelled? That place is locked down tighter than a Siberian prison."

Belinda chimed in. "Plus, it's closed."

I ignored the jab and kept going. "Then we pick another place. The point is to be seen."

"Jessica, if Sasha will cloak me in Heather's guise, I will accompany you," Vada said with a sidelong glance at Belinda. "We can go to Malaprops and then meet Basil for a drink."

I nodded. "That'll work. Is everyone in agreement?" Nods from around the room. Even Belinda couldn't argue with Vada's plan.

I called Basil and told him to meet us at Green Man in an hour while Vada got her jacket. That would give Oak a good look at the fake Heather, since he was the one Basil had fucked up in front of. Sasha prepared, using a lock of Heather's hair for the spell.

Pallavi came over as I studied Sasha. The two exchanged a look that I didn't understand. What did they know that I didn't? They'd been with the coven much longer than I had and had probably lost sisters before. Worse, Magdalene didn't currently trust anyone in the coven besides me. Any strange behavior from my sisters right now was bound to get my attention.

"You've had an eventful week. How are you holding up, luv?" Vi asked.

I could see the worry in her eyes. I'd been close with Heather, but Vi was my true sister. Magdalene was wrong to suspect all of the others equally. "It's all good. Even though I'd rather be chilling with you in front of *Project Runway* and eating popcorn."

"You are stronger than you know, plus there isn't a new episode this week." She hugged me and I did my best not to wince as she put pressure on my freshly tattooed skin. "Trouble is coming. I see it in all my readings, and the augury I cast earlier turned to blood. Be careful."

"I'm always careful." That got a good laugh out of her. Where I was reckless, Pallavi was meticulous in her planning. Vada returned, her long brown hair bound up in a bun.

Sasha cast her spell and Vada transformed into Heather before our eyes. Dressed in a sweater set, capris, and her white Keds, just like the night she was killed. I pushed back the tears that threatened to spill down my cheeks. Vada slid on the purple framed glasses, completing the image. "How do I look?" she asked, all traces of her accent gone, replaced with a mid-western one.

"Perfect. You expect less?" Sasha said, throwing up her hands. She glanced over at Vi again before addressing me. "You think I'm some hack?"

"Of course not," I interjected. "Her own mother wouldn't suspect it wasn't her."

"Thank you, Sasha." Vada looked at me. "I turn into a pumpkin at midnight, so we should skedaddle."

Sasha grinned. "I used a babble spell so she sounds right. Can't have Vada's husky voice coming out of a little girl."

"All the details are perfection. Let's go." I followed Vada out to the garage to my car. I turned down the radio before I pressed the ignition button. No sense deafening her.

"Jess, this has gotta be hard fer ya. The coven can't thank you enough," Vada said in Heather's voice, her intonations, even her choices of words. Sasha did good work.

"It is, but whatever is happening, we need to face it together." I turned onto the interstate, heading toward the bookstore. Heather loved to read more than anyone I'd ever met. Her room had books on every surface that would hold them. I'm sure she'd have stacked them in the bathtub if she could have.

"Vada, can I ask you a question? It may sound disrespectful but I hope you'll realize it is just curiosity."

"With an intro like that, who could pass? Shoot." Vada shook her head. "I'll be glad to talk like me again."

Me too. The whole thing creeped me out. "How long will it take for a new witch to appear to replace Heather? I realize we haven't even returned her body yet, but I haven't been through this before." The time between when I'd first felt the call and I'd arrived at the coven house had been a few months because I had no money, no car, and no help. I'd been told that the elemental witch before me had been named Jennifer Adelman and had died due to natural causes.

"It depends on where she is. My first coven was a week or so from my home, don't cha know. Didn't take me long at all."

I stifled a laugh. The expression on Vada's face was priceless. Vada had a cool, cultured accent and now she sounded like Heather who'd grown up in Fargo, North Dakota.

"Don't you go laughin' at me, girl. I'll get you good after, you betcha."

The conversation came to a close as we parked near Malaprops. "Heather had two books ordered so we can pick them up and then go meet Basil."

Vada nodded. I locked the car, and we strolled past the three metal lady statues and into Malaprop's Bookstore. From behind the register, Greg greeted us by name.

"Hiya, Greg. Good ta' see ya," Vada replied.

Being Thursday, there were more people out and about. Fall in Asheville is peak fall color season. Leaf peepers come in from all over the world to hike through the natural areas, admiring nature's beauty. We call it the onslaught. The café held three couples drinking coffee and chatting about whatever normal people chat about. The businesses and craftsmen of the area profited from these people, but the crowds made me uneasy. If another demon appeared on Patton Street, would the unseers write it off as a gas main explosion or an environmental accident of some kind?

Various people strolled the aisles, picking up books from local authors or grabbing an old favorite from the stacks. The best part about readers is they don't watch their surroundings as much when there are so many books around.

I made my way through the racks to a door marked fire escape with a large alarm attached to it, Vada following behind me. A quick check confirmed that none of the unseeing customers watched us, so we deactivated the alarm and slipped through the door, descending the metal spiral staircase to the real bookstore.

Shelves in the basement were crammed with ancient texts in every language known to man, and a few from other realms, cases with scrolls covered the far wall, a magickal field protecting the delicate materials. Cullen and Dennis stood in front of a case having a whispered argument. Cullen, a Druid and head chef at Non-Grata, gestured frantically while Dennis Meyer, a weather mage, frowned.

We stepped over to the Archivist's mahogany desk. Behind it stood a case with demonic writings that seemed to pulse with malice as we approached. Books were piled all over the desk framing a young woman reading an oversized text, thick glasses perched on her nose. The name plate on the desk read Katherine Christensen, but we all called her Katy. Her cats Kitnit and Walter laid on the file cabinets behind her, like her own personal bodyguards.

"Hey there, Katy," Heather said as she stood in front of the desk. "Have the two books I requested come in yet?"

She blinked as she realized we were standing there. "Hello, ladies. No, I'm afraid they've been difficult to find. Let me check on their progress." Her eyes glowed a soft blue as she looked into the ether. All the Archivists

STONE COLD WITCH

connected to a central entity they called the repository. According to legend, the magickal world's knowledge was housed there. Her eyes returned to normal. "Bella thinks she's got a lead on where the books are being kept. Hopefully, another week or two and we'll have them."

"Shoot. I was hopin' fer them sooner."

She nodded knowingly. "The quest for knowledge can be frustrating at times. Any information you'd like to sell or barter for?"

Archivists were info junkies, the magical world's equivalent to Google. Given permission, they burrowed into your brain and copied any information you were willing to share. The fight with the demon would fetch a huge amount of credit but given the circumstances, it would stay safely locked in my brain. Maybe later I'd barter for some upper-level elemental grimoires.

"We are meeting Basil at Green Man for a brew. No time to wait," I interjected more from nerves than anything. I glanced over to see Cullen and Dennis watching us dubiously. Had the rumor of Heather's death had spread far wider than a few people Oak knew? Basil and his big mouth.

The two approached us, Dennis in the lead. "How are my two favorite witches?" he asked conversationally, but his eyes were locked on Heather. Now we'd see how good Sasha's illusion really was.

"Hey there. Sorry, I missed ya' on Monday, Dennis. Coven business had me away for a couple of days, don't cha know. Can we reschedule?"

Dennis exhaled sharply. "Of course. I'd heard . . . umm . . ."

Heather smiled. "That I died? Yeah, took me a minute to figure out why everyone was starin' at me."

"We're glad you're okay," Cullen said with a smile. "I've got a new trout dish I'd love for you to try at the restaurant."

Heather cocked her head, a puzzled look on her face. "Why, you really want to kill me? You know I'm allergic to fish."

His smile widened. "Sorry, been a long day. I'd have Jess try it, but she eats her meat raw."

I gasped, feigning indignation. "Not raw, just rare."

"Rare. That's the word for it." He chuckled.

The sound of footfalls on the stairs attracted my attention. A pair of expensive black leather shoes came down the treads. As the person came into view, my heart sank. It was Gerwin Aaker, the local eccentric millionaire, and an Oracle of Menestheus.

He wore a custom-tailored suit that cost more than my car. His tan skin and perfectly coiffed hair set him apart from a lot of the Asheville natives. Making money was easy when you could glimpse the future, though he fancied himself a savant when it came to finances and he let everyone know it. How hard was it to notice everyone wearing Nikes in your visions, buy low, sell high?

He surveyed the room as if he were the king. His eyes fell upon us last. "Everyone out," he announced in his penetrating voice. "I need to speak with the witch sisters in private."

Cullen and Dennis fled, as did two others I hadn't spotted in the stacks. Katy cleared her throat.

Aaker rolled his eyes. "Obviously, you can stay, Katy, though what transpires here is not for sale, understood?"

Katy nodded rapidly. "I'll put the credit on your account for when you give permission to release the information."

I wanted to set his expensive suit pants on fire for being such a pompous ass, but I was told to play nice with others.

He flipped his hand dismissively. "Very well." He turned his gaze on us. "We need to speak of the impending nexus collapse and how your coven is going to stop it."

As if this week wasn't bad enough, now the fucking oracle was giving me a hard time. Just what I needed.

"Jessica Flood, I saw you die."

17

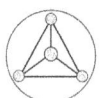

L earning you are about to die at twenty-six when you should live a couple of hundred years is eye-opening, to say the least. Hell, I can't think of a good day to find that out. I blurted out the first thing that crossed my mind. "Are you fucking kidding me?"

"Now that I have your attention." Gerwin Acker pushed a stack of books aside, causing Katy to squawk in alarm. He leaned on the clean edge of the desk as Katy relocated the books before they fell. "Something monumental is in motion and I am blind to it." He sounded annoyed. Surprises for an oracle must be a rare occurrence. "Forces are aligning against me, clouding my vision, limiting me to shadows of the events to come."

"So how does that lead to me dying?"

"The only image I see clearly is one of you lying bloodied on an altar. I see a knife penetrate your chest and then all is dark. With that single event, I feel all is lost. Past that point is only nothingness. None of my brethren have encountered such until now. None of us can pierce the shroud that lays over the future."

What do you say to that? Could this all be interrelated. The bobcat and goat demons, and all the rest. "Well, I'll try not to let anyone kill me. Any more details that might help?"

A quick shake of his head. "None. The Oracles are vastly powerful, so whatever is blocking our visions is immense in scope."

"I've never heard of such a thing." Vada stared at Aaker in disbelief which looked especially funny since she was still wearing Heather's face. "Couldn't you all pull together to pierce it?"

"We've tried and failed." An embarrassed look crept across his face. Oracles are smug to the extreme. "Vada, however lovely Heather was, I do prefer your normal countenance."

"So Heather is dead." Katy poked her head over the pile of books in front of her, tears welling in her eyes. "I just saw her last week."

"That information is covered by our deal, Mr. Thackery." Aaker faced us again. "Jessica, you seem to be the lynchpin in the events that are unfolding, and I have naught to offer but my support."

"And the price?" I asked cautiously. Oracles are stingy with the future and the cost is outrageous. If you are desperate enough, then you'll pay for it. Not that I could trust any of these people, especially Vada, until I found the traitor.

"None. I stand to lose as much as any if the future we can't glimpse comes to pass. There is hardly a market for blind Oracles."

"Good point. Thanks, Gerwin," I said with a big grin on my face. Oh, how he hates being called by his first name. Pompous through and through.

With a curt nod to me, he took Vada's hand and kissed it. "As the end draws ever nearer, would you do me the pleasure of dinner tomorrow night, my lady Vada?"

Normally, Vada offered polite refusals to her many invitations. But with Vada rocking Heather's persona, she scoffed. "Nooooooo."

He nodded. "If you change your mind, please let me know."

"Will do, bucko."

With a shiver, Gerwin stalked back up the stairs, mumbling to himself.

"I've gotta say, that was fun." Vada beamed ear-to-ear. "He is such a bore."

I checked my phone. "We're going to be late to meet Basil."

୧

Green Man Brewery was hopping by the time we get there, most of the crowd upstairs in the larger space. Basil occupied a table in view of the tile mosaic that took up an entire wall. A pint glass of what looked like the lager sat in front of him. It's a good beer and a favorite when I brought people on the tour.

I waved to Oak and he half-heartedly returned the gesture. He flinched when Heather came into view, but it was gone in an instant. Had he not believed my fumbling explanation the other day? Part of my reason for wanting to come here was for Oak to see Heather supposedly alive. He might be the legendary Green Knight, but he'd always been sweet on Heather. I'm not sure if he ever got up the nerve to ask her out.

We took seats at the table. Basil wore a blue sweater with brown suede patches on the shoulders and berry colored pants. I don't know how he pulls off such a singular style. I'd worn my Sex Pistols shirt under my leather jacket, jeans, and boots. Comfortable and ready for a fight if need be.

Oak wandered over with two beers in his hand. "ESB for Jess. IPA for Heather." He set the glasses on the table. "Glad to see you here, Heather. I'd heard you'd been injured." He shot Basil a nasty look. His giant beard made it all the more menacing.

This was probably a test like Cullen had done. How would Vada do? I held my breath.

"Don't cha know, rumors are usually wrong?" She took a sip of the IPA. "How's my favorite maple tree?"

Oak's smile broadened. Heather always said that he was too pretty to be an oak tree, so she called him a maple tree because he was so sweet. I swear he blushed under all that hair but who could tell? It seemed he was buying it. "I'm good. Just worried about you."

"Well, here I am, Maple." She paused to take another sip of beer. I could sense Vada's discomfort over lying to the big man, and I shared it. "We're going to have a beer and then go eat."

"Yeah, Tupelo Honey has a new menu that I'm dying to try," Basil said, a bit too excited.

Oak laughed. "You're more interested in the new kid at the hostess booth."

Basil shrugged. "I'm married, not dead, and he's certainly nice to look at." At that, Oak returned to the bar to pour for a couple of tourists who had just come in.

Vada whispered, "How does she drink this stuff? It's awful."

I switched glasses with her. "IPAs aren't for everyone." I took a deep swallow and savored the bitterness of the brew.

Vada smiled as she sipped her ESB. "Much better."

Basil kept an eye on Oak as he spoke. "He's been out telling anyone that will listen that Heather was killed. According to Anne, he's grief-stricken and upset that he isn't being allowed to say goodbye. Who knew the old knight was so sentimental?"

I took another pull on my beer. "He worshipped Heather and would kill anyone that hurt her. It's got to be tough on him."

"Well, now he can see I'm all right," Vada said. "At least it'll stop the rumors."

We finished our beers, paid the tab, and headed out. After thanking Basil for helping us pretend everything was normal, I dropped him at home before we returned to the coven house. I needed to speak with Magdalene about the Oracles. If Gerwin and his peers couldn't pierce the barrier around the future, we were in serious trouble.

I took Route 197, the twisted road that led up into the Pisgah National Forest back to the coven. The way was dark. As we drove, Linkin Park "Numb" played on the radio. I kept to the speed limit since deer tended to bound across the road at the worst times.

"I feel bad fer Oak," Vada said as she peered out her window into the night. "You know how special Heather was to him."

I sighed. It was probably okay to discuss the situation with any of my sisters, since we all knew about the goat demon and the other demon guy who had tried to kill me in the dream. Being reluctant to discuss the trouble might tip the traitor off, if the traitor was indeed one of my sisters. The very thought of it soured the nice beer in my stomach.

"Sounds like if we don't stop whatever is happening, none of us will be around to feel bad for him," I said. Not technically true since Aaker hadn't mentioned all the sisters dying, just me. But I couldn't treat Vada or any of the coven as if I suspected them of anything, like when I'd gotten salty with Belinda after the healing ritual tried to kill me.

Vada's head turned to face me. "It was ominous, but it got me thinking."

I glanced at her as her eyes widened.

"Watch out, Jess."

My eyes snapped back to the road. A deer sprawled in the middle of the road, blood all around it. Something crouched over the carcass. I swerved, hitting the gravel shoulder. The car slid as the tires fought to stop our motion. A tree did a much better job. The airbags burst out of the steering wheel, striking me in the face.

It took a minute to clear my head. Blood trickled out of my nose, splattering the deflated airbag. "Vada?"

"I'm all right. What happened?" Her words held a dreamy tone to them. She must have hit her head, too. I saw blood on Vada's hands, but the illusion covered wherever she'd been hurt. Sasha's magick kept her looking like Heather, but it made checking her impossible.

The car jolted as something landed on the hood of the car, spraying blood from the deer head hanging from its mouth all over the windshield. Its frog face was accompanied by bright red coloration, with spines protruding from its head and back. Two spindly arms ended in webbed hands and long talons. The thing's long pink tongue flashed out, cracking the windshield.

"We've got to move," I said.

Vada pulled at her seat belt, but the roller had locked in place, restraining her. I slipped the dragon's tooth from my underarm holster. The steel shone in the dim overhead light. It cut through the belt on the first pass.

I unlatched myself and found the door handle. "One, two, three." I opened the door and rolled away from the car, the demon's tongue slashing through where I should have been. Vada's door wouldn't budge. She crawled across my seat as the frog beast moved to intercept her.

"*Ignis.*" The phoenix on my shoulder flared to life as the flame spell activated. A gout of fire shot across the intervening space. The hellspawn leaped to my left. Good—it put me between it and Vada as she clambered out of the car.

A loud croak preceded another tongue attack. It reminded me of fending off boys in high school.

I was ready this time. "*Murus.*" A wall of flame flared up between the beast and me. A squeal of pain came as the beast's tongue burned on the barrier. I dropped the spell, the scent of seared flesh permeating the air. I hadn't fully recovered from the fight with the goat demon, and now I was locked in another brawl.

Vada stood next to me. Her outstretched hand before her, she said, "*Ensis.*" A sword made of light burst into being. The frog shied away from it. Vada advanced, sword held in the exacting way Gareth taught us. The demon croaked as it circled away from the weapon.

A shot rang out from the forest. The sword flew from Vada's hand, winking out of existence and plunging the area back into night, the single unbroken headlight now the only source of light. Vada collapsed in front of me. The demon jumped, literally, at the chance to kill the fallen witch.

"*Veni,*" I shouted as I pointed to the ground under the demon. A spear of rock shot up, impaling the frog. Ichor spurted from the huge wound.

At last the thing shuddered and went still.

Before I could check on Vada, a second shot whistled past me. I ducked, scrambling behind the car. A third shattered the windshield, cubes of glass skittering everywhere. I kept my head down, visualizing a rock wall protecting Vada's prone form. *"Rima."* The stone reached out to shield Vada with a muffled cracking sound. She crawled behind the shelter, so she was still alive.

A bullet hit the stone and ricocheted away from my sister. I crawled to the trunk, peering into the blackness of the forest. Another shot rang out.

I pointed to where I'd seen the muzzle flash. *"Ignis."* I cast the flame into a tight spiral that arced into the forest. I spotted a figure dressed all in black dive as the flame struck a couple of feet to the side, igniting the undergrowth in the process. Now was my chance.

"Robur." The strength of the earth flooded into my system as I ran toward the assassin. Ahead of me, I heard my prey running from the scene. I could make out the movements as our assailant fled.

I increased my pace, practically flying over the shoulder, but by the time I hit the line of trees, there was no more sign of the sniper. If I couldn't actually see them, I supposed I shouldn't leave Vada. Plus Gareth would skin me alive if I ran into the dark forest after an armed shooter, so I would restrain myself to a search for clues.

I picked up a piece of burning tree branch, using its light to survey the area. Nothing. No footprints, left behind cups of takeout coffee, or maps to the secret hideout of the gun toting bad guys.

I didn't have the kind of magic that could help here, so it was time to check on Vada. As I turned, a reflection caught my eye. Hanging from the bottom of a bush was a gaudy blue teardrop on a leather cord. I retrieved it before extinguishing the flames. No sense in causing a forest fire.

Whoever the assassin was I knew one thing about them. They had terrible taste in jewelry.

18

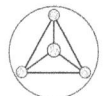

Tow trucks are a lot slower than Gareth. He pulled up in his pickup, helped Vada, who had been shot in the shoulder, and left with no one the wiser. I used a spell to open a hole under the frog demon and closed it over top of it. I really didn't want to answer questions about a giant red bipedal frog on top of everything else. Since we were using the whole hit a deer excuse, I stayed with the car to wait for the tow truck as any normal person would. I sat on the ground next to my wrecked car, with it between me and the woods as a safety precaution. The lack of bullet holes in the chassis made the story of the deer, whose carcass now sat on the side of the road, all the more believable.

The windshield could be explained away by the crash.

Twenty minutes later, I saw headlights and climbed to my feet, hoping the tow truck had finally arrived. No such luck. Belinda's black SUV parked next to me. "Seems you need a ride home." The smug look of satisfaction made me want to slap her.

"I'll wait for the tow truck. Thanks." I leaned against the car and crossed my arms.

"Change of plans. Mother wants you home and I'm supposed to bring you. Stop being a baby and get in."

Great. Mother summoned me like a wayward child. I'm sure she had her reasons. How it must steam Belinda to be her errand girl. I hopped in the front seat and buckled in. I used a healing cantrip to stop my nosebleed and lessen the swelling around my face.

"Wow, you look rough," Belinda said as she pulled away from my dead car. "I didn't realize the wreck was that bad. We thought you'd had a fender bender or something."

I nodded, slightly concerned that my brain was sloshing in motion with the nod. Many more concussions and I'd be a vegetable. "Yeah, it was bad. And there was a frog demon, as I'm sure you've heard, plus some jackass in the woods taking potshots at us."

She squirmed in her seat for a moment. "I'm glad you're okay."

This was new. Compassion from the cheerleader of the dead. Maybe things were changing.

"If somebody is going to mess you up, I want it to be me." She smirked as she said it, and I realized she was joking.

"You'll have to wait until I'm healed. Not sure I can tangle with your death fire in this state." I watched to make sure understood I was playing along. From her smile, she got it. Taking the win where I could, I changed the subject to something more standard between us.

"How can you listen to this garbage?" Some hillbilly twanger was going on about his truck. Hadn't I suffered enough for one night?

"Garbage? You listen to all that depressing crap. At least country is upbeat."

"Did he just say he loved his truck more than his girl? Seriously?"

"The truck is probably more dependable. At least they aren't crying over spilled lattes."

We bantered back and forth as we headed home. I doubted it fixed anything between us, but it was better than open warfare.

After we arrived, I jumped out of the SUV and waited for Belinda. Today she wore a bright pink and yellow dress and matching shoes. She pulled a duffel bag from the back seat. Magdalene greeted us as we entered the kitchen. Belinda set the bag on the island while she retrieved a bottle of juice from the refrigerator.

The bag wasn't zipped shut. I glanced inside— balled up black cloth. Odd. "What's the bag for?"

She took the top off the bottle. "I went climbing this morning with this new guy, Reg. We met online and have been dating. He's been teaching me to climb over at the old quarry. I have to wear that god-awful suit. They don't even come in colors."

Interesting. "Doesn't it mess up your manicure?"

Her head whipped around, ponytails flicking like an angry horse. "I wear gloves. It's not like I'm some hot-house flower, you know?"

I held up my hands in surrender. Way to wreck a good thing, Jess. "I was being serious. I would think rock climbing would wreck your nails. No insult, honest."

Her eyes were still narrowed. "I found a set of gloves with reinforced finger pads. Nao crafted inserts that protect my nails and help with my grip since it's not as strong as Reg's."

"It's good to learn new things. As the years pass by it helps to keep you sharp," Magdalene said as Belinda retrieved her bag.

"I'm going to study before bed. Goodnight." With that Belinda bounced out of the kitchen.

Magdalene watched her go, an unreadable expression on her face. "Shall we discuss the day in the library?"

"Yep. I'm getting a beer." I saw the frown before it even formed. "I've had a horrible ass week and I'm entitled." I fetched a pint glass from the cabinet. Gareth stocked ten different types of glasses since different beers required different shapes. I'd never developed the taste for wine but working on the brew tours had taught me a ton about beer. I snagged a Hi-Wire Bed of Nails from the beer fridge and poured it, placing the empty in recycling before going to the library.

Mother was establishing the wards as I entered, closing the door and locking it. Wards were more effective than locks but I wanted the added security. Magdalene didn't say anything about it.

We returned to the same chairs as our last chat. I took a large swig, enjoying the mellow flavor of the beer. I started talking, telling her about Malaprops and meeting with Aaker. Then I told her about Oak's reaction to seeing Heather and how I felt like we'd convinced him Heather was fine. I ended up with the demon frog and the shooter in the forest. In all the excitement, I'd almost forgotten the pendant I'd found.

I produced the necklace, an unusual blue teardrop, and handed it to Magdalene to examine. The older witch closed her eyes as she spoke her spells, examining it. I drank my beer, feeling the bruises and scrapes from the car wreck asserting themselves.

Magdalene opened her eyes, lips pursed in contemplation. "It has residual magick, but I cannot fathom the original purpose of the item. Nao might have better luck but…"

"I'll take it to Anne at Willow's Dream tomorrow and let her see it." The relic hunter specialized in magickal artifacts, antiquities, and devices from all over the world. Plus, she was the best hairstylist in the magickal community. Not that you could tell from my hair which desperately needed a trim.

She handed me the teardrop, and I stowed it in my jacket pocket. I finished my beer and was about to say goodnight.

"Jessica, I can imagine how difficult this is for you. You have not been here long and now you are at the center of all this. I want you to know, I believe in you. If you take nothing else from me, believe in yourself as strongly as I believe in you."

I bowed my head. Partly in embarrassment from being complimented. Partly from the way I've treated Magdalene at times. Authority figures and I don't mesh well. "Thank you, Mother. Goodnight."

"Goodnight, my child."

I woke in the morning-ish with a swollen face, a split lip, and burning down my back from my healing tattoo. I texted a picture of my face to my boss at Brew Tours and he kindly gave me the day off, with pay. No tips but what can you expect? We agreed I'd take the weekend so I could heal. Everything had been done, so I rolled over for a couple more hours of rest.

My second attempt at getting up went better but included a general aching in all my muscles from the wreck and subsequent fight. I hobbled my way to the bathroom and started the water, only to turn it off again. The tattoo still had the membrane that Cam had used to seal it. I couldn't shower until it healed. I used the toilet, washed up, and brushed my teeth while thinking about changing into real clothes, not that there was anything wrong with my Thor nightshirt.

Someone knocked at the door while I was perusing my extensive wardrobe for a baggy shirt. I pulled down the wards. "Enter at your own risk."

Lucia stuck her head around the door. "Hiya. I thought you might need some TLC from your favorite witch." She grinned. My techno-wizard strolled into the room.

I realized I hadn't seen Vada since arriving home last night. "How is Vada?"

Lucia grimaced. "She'll be fine. Nasty shot to the shoulder. The bullets were hexed. Even with Nao's help, it took me a while to break it. The girl is a wiz at hexes. Uses them in her talisman crafting. After all that, we healed her. If she'd been shot in a more vital place, I doubt we could have saved her."

Anger poured over me at the thought that someone could have killed Vada. After losing Heather, my emotions were as frayed as an old rope. I choked down my feelings and tried to calm myself. "I'm glad she's okay. You would have found a way to save her."

Lucia's cheeks flushed pink while she produced a small white bottle. "Anywho, I brought you something to try."

"What is it?"

"This is my own concoction. I used it on Gareth after his accident last year, I just cooked up and bottled a fresh batch."

"No healing circle?" I asked.

"Nope. It's for small injuries like, say, a fat lip. Can I show you?"

I grabbed my hand mirror from the bathroom and flopped on my bed. Lucia plopped next to me and dabbed a bit on my swollen lip with her finger. The swelling went down after a few seconds and the split mostly healed over.

"That's amazing, Lucia."

She threw back her head in what I think was a fashion pose that failed miserably. "I know. I'm incredible." She handed me the bottle. "Put a little more on and the damage will be gone. Keep the bottle with you."

I thought about it, but if I went downtown and saw any of my coworkers giving a tour, I needed to look as if I'd been in a car crash. I set the bottle down next to me. "Will do. Any other tips?"

"Well, you might need to reapply every so often. When I was testing it on a bruise, the bruise went away, but a few hours later it reappeared in a lesser version. It's more like a band-aid than a healing spell, but it does speed up the process."

"I'll keep that in mind. I'm going to get dressed. I need to run a couple of errands."

"If you don't wreck it, you can take my car. I'm meeting Jose in Azeroth for a raid in Warcraft." Her eyes twinkled with delight. It was easy to forget that she was a powerful witch at times.

I laughed. "I hadn't planned on hitting that stupid deer. I'll be as safe as possible."

"Great." She bounced up. "Gotta run. Keys are in the usual spot. Could you bring me back a chocolate milkshake?"

"Of course."

"See ya on the flipside." And out she went. I'd never had that much energy and Lucia was at least fifty years older than me. I set to making myself look as presentable as possible. I'd stop and have Cam clean my back since no one but Magdalene knew about the sigil and it needed to stay that way.

I decided on a vintage Ramones tee and a flannel shirt. The weight of my jacket wouldn't be comfortable and it wasn't that cold yet. October would be a different story. I put the teardrop necklace and the bottle in my pocket. I stopped and grabbed the blue chaos energy Arty had given me just as a reminder. Tonight was also the full moon and the ceremony to commit Heather to her final resting place.

After brushing out my hair and deciding a ponytail would do better, I left my room and was setting the wards when the screaming started.

I raced for the stairs, ready for anything. At least I thought I was.

19

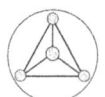

I ran to the top of the stairs, though my legs protested the whole way. Lucia stood at the banister staring down into the foyer. I could smell smoke coming from below as the shouting intensified. I arrived at the landing and gaped. A pentagram surrounding Zental burned in the center of the room. The wards should have kept him far from here. This was truly bad.

Five of my sisters, hands linked, stood facing the demon lord. Belinda chanted a spell, drawing power from the coven. Beads of sweat ran down her face from the effort.

"Ladies, I've come with an offer." He glanced up at me at the top of the stairs. "Welcome, Jessica. I hoped you'd be here."

"You can take your offer and shove it up your demon ass, Zental." I shook with fury seeing him invade the one safe place I'd ever known. Every nerve in my body screamed at me to charge, call my magick, and strike him down. But the earth spirit whispered in my mind. Patience and perseverance.

"Now, now. Remember your manners." A sudden pressure encased my chest, squeezing slowly, forcing the air from my lungs. I gasped, trying in vain to pull in oxygen as the invisible fist constricted. This would be a super handy time to have completely mastered nonverbal spellcasting so I could smash Zental with a fireball, but no such luck.

Lucia knelt in front of me, holding my hands as I sank to the floor, unable to hold myself up. She screamed over her shoulder. "Leave her alone, you're killing her."

His voice reached my ears. "Consider this an object lesson for the price of defying me. As easy as that, I kill your strongest, leaving you in an increasingly precarious situation. Kneel before me and I will see you exalted above all others. Use your power to serve me."

I saw Lucia's mouth moving, but the words were fuzzy as my brain seized up. Magick stabbed into the vice grip that crushed me to no avail. My vision grew dim as my body slumped to the floor completely out of oxygen.

Just as suddenly as the attack had started, it disappeared. My lungs expanded, greedily gulping down air as I struggled to breathe. Lucia held me as I convulsed and came back to myself. She muttered a spell and energy flowed through me.

"Enough." Magdalene's voice stormed through the room. I didn't hear the spell she used, but Zental laughed at her efforts.

"You don't have the power to stand against me, old woman."

Lucia helped as I pulled myself up to the landing's metal railing. Zental flicked his wrist, sending a black orb directly at Magdalene. White light flared around her as the ball dissipated. A look of shock filled his eyes.

"You'll have to do better than that, motherfucker." Power radiated off Magdaline like the rays from the sun.

He straightened his gray morning coat. "As I was saying, I have an offer. Any of you that swear allegiance to me will be given immense power over the human rabble. Refuse me, and you seal your own fate."

I couldn't use *Ignis* in this close of space unless I wanted to burn the house down or fry one of my sisters. "*Proluit*." The flames at each intersection of the pentacle flared to life, sending streams of fire to crash against Zental, doing absolutely nothing to him.

I ran down the stairs buoyed by the energy Lucia's spell had given me. *Robur* worked better when in direct contact with the earth, but as I reached the main floor, I cast it.

Zental's eyes gleamed as I charged toward him, only to stop short. I'd done the same thing in the cave. Patience and perseverance. If I struck the demon lord, I made the same mistake as earlier. I understood his game and wouldn't give him the satisfaction of winning this time.

"We don't bargain with demons." I concentrated with every fiber of my being. "*Conglacior*." As the spell took hold, the heat surged away from the fires dotting the pentacle, extinguishing the flames instantly.

A loud cracking sound filled the room as the pentacle shattered. The floorboard buckled as the spell summoning the demon lord broke down. Zental's mouth O'ed in surprise before the pentagram sucked him back to hell.

"Man, what a dick," I said. Laughter came from around the foyer, a reassuring sound after such an awful event. Even Magdalene looked amused. "How the hell did he get in here?"

Belinda crossed into the flame-etched pentagram and picked something off the ground. A metallic goat's head. Parts of the horns had melted, but it was still recognizable. All the attention shifted to Nao.

"I don't know where that came from." Her eyes darted around the room in a panic.

Magdalene held out her hand for the talisman. Belinda obliged, dropping it into her outstretched palm. The older witch closed her hand around it, eyes shut, speaking a spell we couldn't hear. "There is magick here, but it is of a hellspawn variety, not witchcraft."

"It's not unheard of for witches to use hell's power," Vi said quietly. "But there's never been an attack inside a coven house before now."

No one else said a word as the accusation hovered over the coven. I expected Nao to run, but she held her ground. "I did not create that obscenity, nor will I stand by and be accused of such."

Sasha broke the tension. "A witch might use that power, but she cannot touch hell's evil and remain unmarked. Must be some other explanation."

"Nao helped me last night and there's no taint of hell-born spirit on her. It's like a virus on a computer and my magick would detect it," Lucia said, putting her arm around the talismanic witch's shoulders.

Magdalene nodded. "I'll ask Gareth to see to the floor. The rest of you, keep your eyes open."

I didn't miss the fact that she looked straight at me as she said it.

An hour later I'd parked Lucia's Tesla at a charging station and walked the rest of the way to Willow's Dream. Downtown was crowded with tourists which did nothing to brighten my mood.

One of the pub-cycles sped by full of half blasted yuppies and college kids led by Sal, who barked encouragement for them to keep pedaling as they did the brewery circuit. On my tours, people learned about beer and the history of Asheville. Those pub-cycles were nothing more than self-powered Ubers with an attached bar. I guess people thought the exercise offset all the drinking. To each their own.

I shook my head as I watched them go. This wasn't getting me any answers as to what the fuck was going on. A hand grabbed my shoulder and I flinched in shock. I spun, knocking the arm away, to find two guys, one rubbing his forearm.

"Hey, babe. Just wanted to know if you wanna party with me and Seth?"

"No." I turned on my heel and resumed my mission. The sound of rapid footfalls announced the boys weren't taking no for an answer.

"Come on," the one called Seth whined at me. "Tyler and I in town for the weekend and you look like fun. We love the Ramones. Let's get a couple of brewskis and have a good time."

Seth made the mistake of putting his hand on my arm. I removed it, hitting his brachial plexus with a quick jab of my finger. His arm dangled as it went dead. Thank you, Gareth. "Look, boys. I'm not a party girl, and I'm not your babe. Next time either of you touch me, I'll stick my foot so far up your ass it will come out your fucking nose. Got it?"

Two sets of wide eyes answered my question. They backed away cautiously before running like Satan was on their tails.

"And you wonder why you don't have a boyfriend." Basil's voice came from over my shoulder.

"You saw that?" I asked as I fell in step with him.

He clapped theatrically. "It was a masterpiece of feminine wiles, I assure you." He glanced over his shoulder. "Too bad. Tyler's got a great ass."

I shot him a dirty look. "Yeah, unfortunately it's on his shoulders." I decided it was time to change the topic. "What are you doing?"

"I'm shopping for an anniversary present for Chip. Thought I'd go see what Willow's Dream has on hand for the non-magickal husband who has everything."

"You just gave him an angel necklace that Nao made." Should I tell him what had happened at the coven house or was that coven business? I knew I could trust Basil, even if Magdalene disagreed.

"I like to spoil him."

"Then let's go together. You can keep me company." I grinned at him as he put his arm through mine.

He smirked. "Am I allowed to touch you?"

I slapped him a bit harder than I should have. "Why of course, Basil."

Before long we saw the baby blue exterior of the store, a collection of merchandise set outside to lure the tourists. We entered Willow's Dream,

Basil holding the door for me, always the gentleman. A few people wandered the racks of jewelry, cards, and assorted clothing. Anne stood talking with Elaine, a Chrono-mage with long silver hair. The Chrono-magi don't live in one timeline but shift constantly between many realities and times. Conversations with her gave me a headache.

"I can't fix what another hairdresser hasn't done yet. Plus, that will teach you to let just anyone cut your hair," Anne said to a distraught looking Elaine. I elbowed Basil.

"I had to. You were an accountant in the timeline I was in." Tears streaked down Elaine's face.

Basil swooped in to intervene. "Elaine, I've got the perfect solution. Come and we'll design a fierce new look for you."

Given that Basil wore lime green pants and a pink button-down, I wasn't sure if I'd be excited by the prospect of him designing anything for me, but Elaine babbled excitedly as they climbed the crooked staircase to the upstairs salon.

Anne shuddered. "An accountant? What was my other self thinking?" She shook her head. "Chronos are so difficult to work with sometimes. What brings you in? New style maybe? Unicorn hair is all the rage and it'd match your Vans."

"What's wrong with my style?" I asked, more defensively than necessary. "I look good. Two guys just asked me to party with them."

"The 90s called and they want their stuff back." She smiled at me, and I laughed. "Seriously, business or pleasure?"

"Coven business, I'm afraid."

Anne nodded and led me up the stairs and through the hanging sheet of corrugated tin that disguised the door into the relics room. Anne was a psychometer and a really powerful one. All magickal items gave off energy that Anne could use to determine what it did and, if I was lucky, who crafted it. I produced the teardrop necklace and handed it over. She took a seat in a leather chair next to the oaken desk she always did business at and closed her eyes.

I loved this place. Magickal objects and artifacts were displayed in glass cases around the room. The walls were covered in runes and sigils, warding it from outside forces and a variety of other things. I didn't recognize half of the writing. A silver dagger gleamed in a case behind Anne. A blood-red ruby was attached to the pommel with a dark material woven around the handle. It was a beautiful piece.

Anne opened her eyes and followed my gaze. "Nice, isn't it? Recovered from a serial killer in Columbia. The handle is wrapped in human intestines. Rubies store life energy. Lucky that he wasn't a practitioner, or they'd never have stopped him."

"Wow. So, what about the necklace?" I asked, eager to drop the topic of intestine-wrapped knives. "Can you get a reading on it?"

"It's got traces of power, but somebody went to a lot of trouble to hide what it's for." She studied the teardrop with a jeweler's loop. "Craftsmanship is outstanding. Can I hold on to it for a couple of days?"

It wasn't like anyone else could do better. "Sure. Anything you can find out would be greatly appreciated."

She set it on the desk. "Rough night, I hear."

"Stupid deer jumped in front of me, and I hit it and then a tree. It hasn't been my week."

She handed me a tissue. "Your lip is bleeding."

I pressed the tissue to my lip, wincing. "Call me if you find out anything." Once out on the sidewalk, I fished Lucia's potion from my pocket. I guess it had worn off. I popped the cap so I could rub some on my lip.

A hand struck mine, and the bottle went flying, shattering against the wall. Basil, his face red with anger, stood in front of me. "What are you doing with that?"

Oh shit, I'd pissed off the wrong seraphim.

20

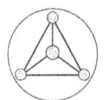

I stared at Basil, my mouth hanging open. In all the time I'd known him he'd never struck me, not even in jest. Now, he glared daggers and had his arms crossed, confronting me as if I'd just committed high crimes.

"Where did you get that?"

His angry tone unsettled me, and I'd faced down demons. "Lucia gave it to me to heal my bruises. What the fuck is wrong with you?"

He pointed in the direction the bottle had flown. I followed his outstretched finger.

On the ground, a mass of black tar bubbled, eating into the pavement as I watched. What the fuck? Lucia had given me the potion to help heal my injuries, but the substance eating away at the pavement didn't look overly friendly…or like what I had put on my lip earlier today. "What is that?"

"That's hellspawn serum. It would have addicted you and only death would release you."

"Oh," I said meekly. Basil's face resumed its normal shade as we stood there. Luckily, none of the tourists had noticed the disturbance. The tar melted into the cement, leaving only shards of the bottle behind.

He cleared his throat. "I couldn't let you touch it. I've seen what it does to people. It's horrific." He shuddered, wrapping his arms around himself.

"No problem," I said, still in shock.

He flashed a quick grin and picked up a piece of the broken bottle. "Strong magick. Some kind of shield, or a stealth ward. That's why you didn't feel the wrongness."

I cocked my head, thinking back to Lucia giving me the bottle. "Lucia put some on my lip and it healed. Shouldn't it have addicted me then?" I thought some more. "She put her finger in it, so wouldn't she have been risking addiction herself?"

Basil didn't answer right away. "You shouldn't have been able to touch the serum without it taking over. What color was it?"

"White. It took down the swelling in my lip." I stuck it out at him like a puppy dog pout.

Basil rolled his eyes. "We're discussing serious business and I get the pouty face?" He rubbed his forehead for a moment before he knelt next to where the serum had melted the concrete.

He stood up and walked. I ran to catch up. "Where are you going?"

"We need to talk to an alchemist about this one. Talos should be able to figure out what's going on."

Great, just great. Could my week get any worse? Frank Talos, one of the town's alchemists, was a pain in the ass. He thought the sun rose and set in his pants and every woman should sample said delight. I routinely wanted to kick his ass. Not that it would do much good. "And why do we need to see the West Texas Casanova?"

Basil's eyebrows rose. "Casanova? You've been around the old ladies too much."

"Vada is one of those old ladies."

He flushed pink. "She's different." He changed the subject. "Anyway, I want him to determine what was in the bottle. There is some stuck to the glass."

I swerved away from him as we quick-stepped down the sidewalk. I don't like snakes or potions that will turn you into a junkie. For all my faults, stupid isn't one of them. "I'll let you handle the sample."

"Good idea."

We traveled down the side streets until we came to White Labs. They produced most of the yeast for the breweries in Asheville and across the nation. There is an adjoining restaurant where they use the yeast to create works of culinary art, including amazing pizza, but we needed the production facility. We entered the foyer: polished concrete floors with the bright white emblem set into the center. A couple of chairs and a small table sitting under a poster of replicating yeast cells were the only furniture outside the reception desk. A few people milled around, waiting on the tour.

Behind the reception desk sat a woman about my age, clicking away at her keyboard. Basil smiled at her, which she returned tenfold. "Can I help you?"

"Yes, we're here to meet with Frank Talos. Basil Dove and Jessica Flood are here to see him?"

Her smile retreated. "Yes, sir." She dialed an extension, and after a few words, she set the receiver down. "He said he'll meet you in the outer courtyard."

"Thank you." Basil headed toward the side door that led out to the courtyard. We took a seat at a picnic table. The building blocked the wind that had a faint chill to it. Another month or so and it would be cold again.

A few minutes passed before Frank emerged in his white lab coat. At least he'd taken his hairnet and booties off. His face split into a wide grin as he saw us. "Look what the cat dragged in." His black hair poked out in every direction, distracting from the tan skin and rough good looks. The collar of his blue checkered shirt sat over this lab coat lapels. He swung a leg over and sat across from me. "Hello, Jess. You are looking particularly fine today."

I looked down at my Ramones T-shirt and purple and red flannel, no makeup on and my hair pulled back into a rough ponytail. "Yeah, right. Can we get down to business?"

His smile dimmed, but never had a dose of discouragement stopped his relentless come-ons. "I'd sure like to handle your business."

Basil had the decency to groan, loudly. "Are you going to hit on Jess all day or do we need to head over to Lamsil's place to get what I need?"

Talos stiffened. "You'd go to that CBD dealing hack? Most you'd get off him is a contact high. Whatcha 'ya got?"

Basil held out the piece of glass; a drop of the black liquid still clung to it. "I think it's hellspawn serum, but I'm not sure."

The alchemist whistled. "Boy howdy, that's some nasty shit." He pulled on a pair of latex gloves before taking the sample from Basil. "It looks like the stuff."

"Jess touched it earlier in the day and it healed her, but now it's polluted. How would somebody do that?" Basil asked, watching Talos closely as he did.

"Come on." Frank stood and walked toward the far end of the building to an empty spot at the corner. We followed along, watching over our shoulders for onlookers.

"We're clear," I said to the alchemist as he drew a rectangle of light in midair. A door solidified, replacing the light. He opened it and motioned us inside. The huge lab stretched out well past the empty spot next to White Labs. "Gotta love these pocket dimensions. Cuts down on the real estate taxes for sure."

Rows of long tables held all matter of devices. Some were made of surgical steel, others brass, and one particularly gruesome machine, bone. I decided I didn't want to know what type of bones they were.

Talos trotted to a large machine that took up at least ten feet per side. After flipping a few switches, a light came to life and the hum of power filled the air. A second later a bestial roar shook the room from outside. "Sorry, noisy neighbors. They can't get in… usually." He slid a glass panel back on the top of the machine, revealing a golden basket. The sample went in and then he pushed the glass back into place.

Vibrations came through the soles of my Vans as the machine whirled to life. The humming intensified as did the shaking. I put my hand over the vial of chaos energy that Arty had given me. Releasing chaos magick in this place sounded like a really bad idea. Sounds of clanking glass, pinging metals, and the groan of the machine blotted out any chance to speak.

What would happen if the place shook apart? I had no desire to come face-to-face with whatever was roaming around roaring in the pocket dimension outside the lab.

A loud ping announced the processing had completed. A panel rose from the top of the machine. Angelic script conveyed with LEDs scrolled across. "According to this," Talos said, pausing to read more. "It's hellspawn serum, but there are traces of something else that isn't from the divine planes."

"I dabbed a portion on my lip and it healed it for a while." I didn't mention Lucia for two reasons. One, it was none of his business, and two, I didn't want to listen to how hot my coven sister was. I had to be honest with myself that any of my sisters could be the traitor, but why had Lucia stopped Zental from suffocating me just to kill me in a different gruesome manner? Maybe it was a bluff to get me to trust her more or to throw me off the real traitor.

"That would seem to explain it. Can I keep this so I can look at it more after work?"

Another mystery item I would have to wait to learn more about, even as someone had managed to help Zental get into our coven house and then try to shoot me last night. Which would run out first—my patience or the time I had left to live? There were far more questions than answers and it fucking pissed me off.

"Of course," Basil said. "This needs to stay between us. No one else, not the other alchemists, the coven sisters, and especially not whatever women you are trying to pick up. Understood?"

I'd gotten used to Basil over the time we'd been friends, but today reminded me how intimidating an angry seraphim was. Talos, however, only saw Basil as an avenging angel and that had to scare the fuck out of him. He nodded so fast I thought his head might break off his neck and bounce across the lab.

"Good."

We followed Talos back out into the courtyard. "I'll call you, Basil, since I don't have Jess's number."

Before I could answer, Basil cut in. "Thank you, Frank. I owe you one."

Talos blanched. "Seriously?"

"Yes, within reason. There are limits to the favors I can grant."

We left with Talos gawking after us, his mouth hanging slightly open.

After we were out of earshot, I asked, "Are you sure you want to owe Talos a favor?"

Basil chuckled. "His imagination will run wild for a while until he realizes all the favors he wants wouldn't come from an angel. He'll end up asking for help with a parking ticket or maybe your phone number."

"If you give that creep my phone number..."

"I told him there were limits, and incurring your wrath is definitely a limit for me."

We walked together in silence before Basil asked, "Is tonight the ceremony?"

I nodded, not trusting myself to speak. For an hour I could get busy with everything that was happening and forget that Heather was gone and then something would remind me, and I'd lose my cool. Hot tears pushed at my eyes, trying to force themselves out. I refused to cry in public. As it was, tourists stared at me as we passed them. I sniffled loudly and rubbed my eyes. "Yeah, I need to head back."

Basil put his arm around my shoulders and squeezed. "As your friend, I'd like to remind you I'm always here for you. I know a thing or two."

I snorted. My archangel buddy "knew" a thing or two. He'd lived in the presence of the divine creator himself. "I doubt you know more than me."

He scoffed in feigned indignation. "I most certainly do. Like how the Ramones clash terribly with tie-dyed Vans. Your purple ones would work much better, especially given the lilac tones of your flannel."

Basil could make anything ridiculous. "Thanks, Tim Gunn. I'll start calling you before getting dressed."

He shrugged. "You could do much worse." He stepped in front of me, putting his hands on my shoulders. "Tonight is a time to grieve, but Heather was a joy, and she will be going to a better place where she can rest until the next time she is needed. Remember that. Life and love are eternal."

Staring into his eyes, the image of Heaven lingered still, though he refused to call it that. I felt a warm, peaceful sensation in my chest that spread outward. His gaze held the promise of redemption, and I longed for it, but for now, I'd fight with everything I had to stop whatever was coming, even if it cost me my soul in the process.

"Thanks, Basil." I hugged him and left for the car. Tonight, we'd release Heather into the hereafter. Tomorrow, there'd be hell to pay for whoever did this.

21

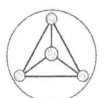

Silence assaulted me as I walked into the house. A cold, unnerving quiet that amplified the feelings of loss I'd been suppressing since Heather's death. I hung Lucia's keys on their hook and listened to my footfalls as they echoed through the space. The coven house wasn't some magickal sorority with pillow fights and loud arguments over who stole whose boyfriend or lip liner, but at any given time my sisters would be in the kitchen conversing or discussing various issues that faced the house. Today, they were all absent.

I stopped to examine the scorched remains of the pentagram that Zental had used to invade our home. The fire had dug into the two-hundred-year-old oak boards, leaving only ash behind in the grooves. He had openly attacked the coven in our own home, yet we were blind to who was helping the demon lord.

A light step from behind made me spin to face it, fists raised to fight. Magdalene stepped back, surprise on her features. "Sorry, Mother. You startled me."

"It's all right, Jessica," Magdalene said as she composed herself. "All of us are jumpy with recent events. Might we speak for a minute about your role in tonight's ceremonies?"

I nodded. "Of course, Mother." I followed her into the library where she closed the doors and renewed the wards she'd placed earlier. I took the seat I'd been in the last time we talked. As always, a pot of tea sat on the table with a cup, saucer, and folded linen napkin. Such a small thing, but it comforted me that not everything had changed.

Magdalene took the chair across from me. "I've spoken to all the sisters about the ceremony tonight, so they won't find it odd we are speaking."

"Makes sense. This is my first returning ceremony as a sister." I fought the urge to crack my knuckles. Stress brought out my bad habits in droves. "Is it complicated?"

"No, Belinda will lead the ceremony, but I'd ask you not to fully commit your power to the circle. I want you to hold back enough in case we need to defend ourselves. You can't do that if you're fully engaged."

"What?" I asked. "Why?"

For a moment I saw the old woman that led our coven. She'd been a witch for over four centuries, and tonight the responsibility hung on her like the stench of Sunday morning stale beer. She rubbed her eyes before she answered. "Jessica, you understand little about spiritual magick."

I agreed. Spiritual spellcasting was directly opposite to my elemental ones. Magdalene channeled the magick of the Almighty whereas I pulled my power from the basic elements of nature. My magick must look coarse and unwieldy to a spiritualistic witch. "I've not yet mastered the four elements, let alone learned how the rest of you use your power."

"To put it simply, I can speak with spirits of all kinds. They come when I summon, but occasionally, they seek me out to deliver warnings. The last time this happened, Hitler captured half of the coven in Poland because I did not react fast enough."

How do you carry something like that around with you for a lifetime? There were layers of Magdalene I'd never seen and might never have known about if not for this attack. Shame boiled within me as I thought of all our arguments over the last six years as she tried to turn me from an undisciplined brawler into a proper witch.

"Three days ago, another spirit delivered a dire warning. Even the spirit world is blind to what is happening. This time, however, they gave me the sigil you now wear on your back."

She had my full attention at that. "What does it represent?"

Magdalene shrugged. "The spirit warned me that a great evil sought to consume the coven and then the world. I slid into a trance, and when I awoke I'd drawn out the design with your name written under it. I don't know what it does, though I would like to see it."

"Of course." I stood up and pulled my shirt up so that my back was to her. A light touch slid over the tattoo as she traced the healing skin.

"Cam does beautiful work," she murmured as she continued her examination of the tattoo. A finger firmly pushed in the center of my back, and a burning sensation took hold. I tried to pull away, but I was locked in place. The pain increased, causing my back to arch in an attempt to stop it. The fire spread across my shoulders, down my back, and into my legs. Soon my whole body seared with burning pain. My mind emptied of all thought as I bucked against the agony. I'm not sure how long it lasted but as the pain fled, a soothing coolness rushed in behind it, banishing the pain as if it had never been.

Magdalene slumped into her chair. I pulled down my shirt and pivoted to confront her. Rage filled me. How dare she do that…

The words died on my lips. A trickle of blood ran from the corners of her eyes and from both nostrils. I plucked up a napkin from the table and cleaned up her face.

Her eyes focused on me. "What happened?"

I did the best I could to clear all the blood away before I took my seat again. How do you explain something when you have no idea what happened yourself? I sorted through the blur of my memory and only found pain. "You touched the sigil Cam tattooed on me. Then I swear I was being burned from the inside out. Now I'm fine."

She straightened herself. "I remember touching the tattoo and then everything went blank. May I see it again?"

"Maybe don't touch it this time?" I suggested before pulling up the back of my shirt to reveal the sigil.

"How fascinating. It's glowing."

"Glowing?" I asked incredulously, trying to peer over my shoulder. Why was there never a mirror when you needed one? I pulled down my shirt and dropped back into my chair. "How exactly does a tattoo glow?"

"I know not, but I heard a voice. 'As were the pieces scattered.' That's all I remember of what was said."

What the hell does that mean? Pieces? Pieces of what and where were they scattered? Being a Brew Tour guide sounded like a better career choice right about now. "Is my tattoo some kind of puzzle that has pieces? Or is it the piece of a puzzle itself?"

She shook her head. "I don't know. Be on guard tonight. Even though it is a full moon, evil is stirring and accomplices are assisting Zental in his plans."

I told her about Lucia's healing potion turning into a hellspawn serum and the trip to talk with Talos. She listened patiently, interjecting questions for clarification. "It would take great skill and power to craft such a potion. Of our coven, three besides you have the power to accomplish this, though power and knowledge are not always paired."

There was no part of me that wanted her to answer the obvious question, but I asked anyway. "Who?"

"I would judge Vada, Lucia, and Nao strong enough in the craft to do such as you describe."

Wonderful. At least Vi wasn't on the list. I tried to imagine reasons for any of them to be in league with Zental. Lucia was a geek and a softy, could she be in league with demons? Really, why would any of the sisters ever side with hell against their own?

"Jessica, I realize I've placed a huge burden on your shoulders, but if we are to stop this atrocity from happening, we must be strong."

I stored the pity party for after this was all over. "I will do my best, Mother."

"Of this, I have no doubt. Go ready yourself for tonight. I hope that all is well, but we must be prepared."

I left Magdalene sitting in the library. As I climbed the steps, I realized there was another sister who had the power but wasn't on the list. Magdalene herself.

※

At eleven-thirty we gathered by the front doors. Both were open wide, allowing the cool night breeze to ruffle our hair and robes as we stood in the foyer. I was glad I'd worn my flannel under the robe. Gareth had moved Heather's body to the wooden stretcher we all carried by the eight handles. The runes etched into the carrier protected the body and lightened the weight enough so it could be carried easily.

Magdalene and Sasha were at the front where Heather's feet now rested. Lucia and Vada were next in line with Nao and Belinda behind them. Vi and I carried the end where Heather's head lay. Her face had ritual runes and sigils drawn on it as did her hands and bare feet.

A deep sense of loss rolled through me as I looked at Heather's face. Not a mark was visible, though I knew her neck was a mass of bruises where it'd been snapped. I pulled Mr. Bear out from my sleeve where I'd concealed him. Nothing magickal about him, but he'd been with her since she was little and it felt wrong for him not to move on with her. I kissed the stuffed animal on his forehead, then leaned close and kissed Heather's. I placed him with his head on her shoulder, tucking him in between her arm and chest so he wouldn't fall. I straightened to find the coven staring at me. Each nodded my way before taking their appointed places.

I studied my sisters for anything out of the ordinary, focusing the most attention on the sisters Magdalene had mentioned. I hated myself, but I watched her as well. Circumstantial evidence is a funny thing. You can spin it different ways to get different results. Lucia might have tainted the potion, just as Nao had the ability to craft the talisman that opened the pentacle for Zental. But both of them seemed like such obvious culprits, and I refused to believe they were both attempting to kill me and take down the coven.

But after over four hundred years, you collected things. Could those items have been in Magdalene's possession and she pointed me at the coven to cover her tracks? It would be too outrageous if Magdalene had pulled me aside and told me she feared one of our sisters was a traitor while herself being that traitor. Why would she fight the goat demon? This logic puzzle of who's the traitor was a Gordian knot.

The perfect way to distract me from wondering if it was her, though.

The moon rose in the east, bathing the courtyard in front of the house in a soft glow. Heather's skin reflected the light, so she shimmered as we waited. Gareth stood off to the side dressed in a black and blue sweater and dark slacks that hugged his ass perfectly.

I hadn't gotten a good look at the shooter, but if anyone could give me the slip in the woods, it was him. If Magdalene was orchestrating the attacks, then Gareth would be a part of the plan.

While I stared at him, he checked his watch before nodding to Magdalene. "Sisters, peace be with you." Gareth walked past us as he returned to the house.

In unison we pulled up our hoods, covering our faces from death, a tradition so old Magdalene didn't know its origins. "Tonight, we begin our lost sister's final journey. Does anyone have a reason not to proceed?" Magdalene's voice was smooth as glass as she spoke. No one answered her. "Let us begin."

In measured steps, we carried Heather to where she would be returned to the universe. With a second between steps, we took ten minutes to follow the trail to the coven alter beneath the tree of life. Trees blotted out the full moon, leaving us in darkness. Gareth had cleared the trail so we didn't trip while walking. The urge to summon my night vision warred with the sanctity of the ritual. My better self won out, and I remained magick free as per the dictates of the ceremony.

We turned right into the moonlit clearing. An altar built from stone rose at the far end of the space. The first Elementalist, a man named Gentry Blalock, had summoned the stone edifice in the first year of the coven's existence. I'd been shocked to realize that men could be witches as well as women. Normal people thought them to be Warlocks, but those people didn't understand much about the magickal arts. I wondered idly as we crossed to the altar what Gentry would think of the current coven.

Behind the massive rock structure stood the widest tree I'd ever seen. Its canopy must have covered two hundred feet in all directions. All the sisters combined couldn't reach around it. Each coven house grew a piece of the original tree and maintained it with their craft. Talos would give his left arm for a piece of the bark or a single leaf. Quiet power radiated off the tree like the warmth of a radiator.

We placed Heather on the lowest portion of the altar. Carved angels and seraphim silently watched as she slid into place on the rock bed. The board drifted back the way we'd come to be stored for the next occasion we needed it. I hoped that day was a long way off.

We arranged ourselves in a semicircle in front of the altar. Magdalene stood at the end where Heather's head lay, I at the other end of the semicircle near her feet. With hoods up, it was difficult to pick out individual sisters, though Pallavi's height made it easy to identify her.

Belinda, in the center of the arc, raised her hands to the night sky. "Tonight, we return our beloved sister to the universe and the Almighty." She began to chant as she summoned her magick to begin the ritual.

The ceremony began as I watched for trouble.

22

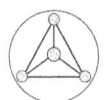

Belinda's chanting increased in pace as she worked the magick of the dead. A stream of blackness, like smoke from a tar fire, arced from the death witch to the corpse on the altar. The runes on Heather's skin shed a soft blue glow as the magick flowed into her. I imagined that she slumbered on the bed of rock that held her. The light from the full moon crept into the glade, a hesitant spectator to our night's work.

Memories of our time together unfurled in my mind, a slow progression of images. Some comical, some sweet, all very much Heather. I could hear her laugh as she found something funny, or a cut off swear words when she was pissed. Doubts presented themselves around her death, but they would have to wait until later; tonight was about saying goodbye.

Lucia's voice joined Belinda's as she set her spell in play. The hair on my arms stood on end. Power filled the clearing. Motes of light fell like snow as the spells gained intensity. A pale orange ribbon of her magick looped and twisted before connecting to Heather.

Stories Heather had told me about accidents with magick and boys returned to me, long forgotten in the recesses of my brain. It's funny the things you think of at a time like this. I'd been to funerals before, but they were for people I didn't much care for or didn't know well.

A pure white trail of magick left Magdalene and spun into the mix of energies. Images moved inside the white light, flickering to life and then gone again before I could focus on them. The black ribbon flowed around the white and combined into a yin-yang of magicks before Lucia's strands joined the dance. A pillar of light emerged from Heather's corpse, so fragile it barely held together as it rose.

Spirits soared in the sky above us or at least I wanted to believe they did. Magdalene's magick opened a gap in the veil between us and what the unseers call purgatory. Angels would escort our beloved sister to her next adventure. Basil would probably scoff at all the drama around releasing Heather fully from this life, but this wasn't his coven sister. Even in the Halls of the Dead, she'd been tied to our realm, tethered to a body that no longer needed her.

Vi's fierce tones joined the others as a verdant green flowed from the divination witch's hands. Thin tendrils from each of her fingers braided themselves into an elaborate pattern. No dancing or spiraling around for our Nubian priestess; it was a bold and shamelessly beautiful weaving. An elegant lace made of the stuff of pure magick.

The structure flared as Vi's energy entered, growing with new life, pushing toward the sky. As Sasha's deep violet strand interwove with the construct, it solidified. The form shifted through millions of people's faces as it continued to take shape. Witches that had gone before flickered into existence and were gone again in a blink of an eye.

The lights swirling above Heather illuminated her body, including Mr. Bear, who turned his head to look at me. He blew me a kiss off his padded paw before snuggling back against his person. Tears resumed as I fought back a hard sob. The magick had given the little bear life for a few moments, and I hoped he traveled with Heather to her next station.

Vada's sultry voice came on strong and sure. Silver light sparkled from her hands, joining our sisters in crafting our final farewell. The chanting had become a song in a way. Each voice filled its own space and enhanced those around it.

I waited for Nao to begin. My magick came last, the fire that would bind all the individual strands together like a forge binds steel into a solid piece. I glanced over at the talisman maker. Her hands hung at her sides, no chanting, no magick. Her hood swiveled back and forth rapidly as if she were panicking. With all the motion, it fell back, revealing her brightly dyed hair and her enormous, frightened eyes. Fear had taken hold of her and I thought she might bolt. I pulled down my hood and caught her eye, willing her to be strong and finish out the ceremony.

Nao's eyes widened as we stared at each other silently across the clearing. Her chin dropped to her chest. I worried she might pass out, but after a moment, her head came up and she nodded once in my direction. Vibrant nails emerged from her sleeves, arcs of blue magick rippling across her knuckles before they leaped to join the other flows.

I left my hood down, not wanting it to obstruct my view of the spectacle before us. The construct stood about five feet high and bore the shape of a human form in flux. I thought about Heather and pushed my love for her into my magick. Not all of it, since Magdalene had warned me to hold back, but enough to do Heather honor. Tendrils of red smoke flowed serpent-like to touch her. Mr. Bear slid, so he hugged Heather's neck, ready to be with her forever. The construct collapsed into Heather's body.

Bright ribbons of light from eight witches' magick swirled around Heather's corpse. They pulsed like a heartbeat as the glow gained strength, intertwining in a dance both beautiful and intricate. The pace increased, more colors merging into the twisting maelstrom of magickal power. Faster and faster it spun, imprinting my retinas with the shape of the shifting light sculpture. The amazing beauty stood in stark contrast to the death of my sister. Tears ran down my face as I watched, feeling the energy flowing among my sisters as we crafted this illuminated structure.

Just as the brightness reached a point of being uncomfortable, it vanished. In its place stood Heather, a spirit made of magickal energy, her feet resting gently on her former body. Pinpoints of light spun in unison to create her spectral form as perfect in detail as if she was standing before them.

Magdalene's voice broke the silence. "Sister, we are gathered together to return you to the magickal vortex. The coven thanks you for your service, love, and sisterhood. We will cherish our memories of you for eternity."

The hard truth that I'd never see Heather again gut punched me. I wanted to rage against the unfairness of it all but knew no one promised fairness, honor, or kindness in this lifetime. Kindness was rare enough that instances of it shone in my memory like stars against a pitch-black sky.

The specter reached down and retrieved her bear, hugging him against her chest. "Jess, thank you for bringing Mr. Bear," she whispered in my ear. "I've missed him so."

"You're welcome and I'm so sorry I failed you."

"My last memory was outside Malaprops. Jess, you could never fail me."

"Thank you, Heather. I love you."

Heather's head came up sharply as she turned to face Magdalene.

"Thank you, Mother." Heather's words echoed in the open area. "I miss you all and will await our reunion in the future, but it is not safe for you to tread this close to the spiritual veil. Even now it tears beneath the claws of the demon lord. Release me before he comes. Release me now!"

My eyes shot to Magdalene whose face was hidden by the hood of her robe. Her hands flashed. "Thank you, Heather. We love you."

"And I you, now go. He nears." Heather's form blurred as if it was an unfocused movie. Her face distorted as she mouthed words we no longer heard.

"Dirimo," Belinda shouted, panic thick in her voice. Heather's body burst into a white-hot flame that stunned me with its brilliance. I blinked my eyes hard, trying to remove the afterburn images. Heather's magickal form struggled as parts dissipated while others returned to full solidity.

Black tendrils oozed up from the stone, extinguishing the flames as they rolled over Heather's corpse. I slammed down hard, breaking my connection with Heather's body. My sisters screamed in agony as the black tar corrupted their magick, the flows turning gray under the touch of the foul presence.

Without thinking I yelled *"Ignis"* and shot a solid stream of fire at Heather's corpse. The ooze retreated slightly then attacked the fire. I cut the flow before it was tainted like the others. The rest of the coven lay on the ground writhing and screaming as the gray pushed closer and closer to them.

How do you beat something you can't attack? I needed to protect my sisters before the whatever-the-fuck goo reached to them.

"Veni," I yelled, forming the image of a coffin in my mind. The stone altar flexed as it folded the edges around the corpse. Would that break the demon lord's hold?

It broke something, all right. A loud cracking sound pierced my ears as the granite slab blew apart. A jagged piece struck me beneath the eye. I wiped away the blood. I needed help.

Magdalene. I raced around the outside of the circle and found Mother curled in a ball. The grey evil magick had nearly reached her, her pure white power only two inches from her hands where it was anchored. I pulled at her but couldn't move her, her body tied to the earth as if she'd been set in cement.

What the hell could I do? The howls rose from my sisters as the corruption closed in on them. They couldn't stop the magick draining from them and they couldn't stop the evil that had nearly reached them. No doubt it would kill them or worse, control them.

I did the only thing I could think of. I pulled the karambit from the sheath and slashed across the white part of the magick inches from Mother's fingers. Sparks flew like from a welder joining hot metal together.

Magdalene stopped screaming. The knife dripped as it melted, and I threw it away from me. I'd deal with that later.

"Magdalene, we have to stop this before it kills the others."

Her eyes opened, blazing with fury. I helped her to her feet. She clamped onto my hand. "Child, open yourself to me."

Raw power surged toward Magdalene as I opened the flood gates. The older witch glowed as my power filled her.

"*Concalo Ruina!*" she screamed into the night sky. The glade went from night to day in an instant. An inhuman shriek rose from the altar as the tendrils of black goo burst into flames. The magick that had connected my sisters to Heather burst like fireworks on the Fourth of July.

Mother released my hand. "Burn it, now," she barked at me, her voice unrecognizable under the strain.

"*Ignis,*" I shouted, pushing both hands toward the body of my fallen sister. A gout of flame flared so hotly that the granite and body both melted as it was all consumed. I released the flow and slumped to the ground.

My sisters were in various stages of unfolding from their fetal positions and cursing the demon lord's attack or complaining about the pain. Magdalene spoke into the tumult of voices. "It is over. Let us return to the house."

The sound of falling tree branches and booming footfalls came toward us from the direction of the house. An echoing roar announced that we weren't done yet.

Magdalene had spoken too soon. I rose to my feet, tired, upset, and pissed off.

Whatever they sent at us was in for a fucking bad night.

23

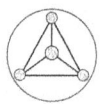

Magdalene and I helped our sisters regain their footing. The trees on either side of the trail rocked precariously from the thundering footfalls. The crashing closed in as we got everyone ready.

"Sisters, close the circle. We need to fight as one," Magdalene called as we gathered. I stood facing the trail with Belinda on one side and Vada on the other. Magdalene stood directly behind me as the three of us faced out of the circle. Who would want to have some hellspawn attacking with your back presented as the prime target?

Two trees toppled away from the trail as the demon pushed through into the clearing. The largest spider I'd ever seen reared back to roar its challenge. Six of the legs ended in sharpened spines that stabbed into the earth, while the front two boasted giant human hands. The head elongated, displaying rows of shark-like teeth and long black fangs on either side of its mouth. It swung its enormous head back and forth, glaring at us with the many eyes on each side.

My grip tightened on my sisters' hands as they did the same. Another roar sent tremors through me. It was all I could do not to shit my pants. I wanted to run, but that would be death for sure.

"*Clypeus*," Magdalene intoned as the spider leaped in an arc toward us. A bright light enveloped the coven, causing the demon to bounce like it had hit a windshield at eighty. The thing screamed in either pain or rage, I didn't much care which.

As soon as the legs touched the ground, the demon launched itself at the shield again, rearing back so it could slam the long jagged second set of legs down into the shield. The legs flashed in a staccato rhythm as it sought to break the egg we sheltered in.

"*Telum.*" A black bolt as thick as my arm shot out and struck the creature in the exposed abdomen. Belinda's spell impacted with a dull thud, forcing the demon back, but not doing much damage.

The shield fractured under the spider's renewed attacks.

"*Exancio.*" The death witch cast again. Whips of dark magick flashed out, wrapping around the back four legs.

The spider bucked like a horse, fighting to free itself from the power that held it tight. It fell forward toward the dome of light, but instead of striking the dome, it landed on its hands. The second pair of legs flashed in the moonlight as it destroyed the tendrils of magick that held it.

Belinda's hand loosened from mine slightly, then let go completely. I glanced over to see her stagger. She'd overextended instead of pulling from the communal pool of magick.

"Belinda's going down," I shouted. She sank to her knees and a second later Sasha's hand was in mine. We were two down including our lost sister Heather and still hadn't done anything to hurt the demon.

"I'm fine," Belinda's slurred voice came from behind me.

I couldn't be worried about her now. If we didn't find a way to banish this thing, we would all be dead or worse. As the spider charged again, I cast my spell. "*Robur.*" Strength flowed into me and around the circle. We'd already been in one fight tonight and needed all the help we could get.

"The shield will not withstand another assault," Magdalene said as the spider sped toward us "When it strikes, we must disperse and attack from all sides."

Sasha squeezed my hand twice. "Thank you."

I winked at our illusionist as we prepared for the charge. I summoned my power, wishing I'd earned my earth sigil. My spells lacked their full strength without it.

The demon leaped, striking the dome with a massive crash. I let go of my sisters, turned, and hoisted Belinda up from the ground. Without the extra strength from my spell, I'd never have been able to pull off such a stunt. As it was, a slashing talon clipped my leg and sent me and Belinda tumbling. I climbed to my feet and tossed off the robe. I didn't need the heavy thing tripping me up.

Magdalene had cast a white beam of light directly into the demon's face. Smoke poured off it as the holy power struck the hellspawn beast. The thing shrieked in agony as it backed away from Mother. "I abjure you back to the pits of hell." Her voice carried a raw power to it. She advanced the light, brightening as it went.

Thicker plumes of smoke rose from the spider as it tried to shield itself. The terrible sounds it made curled my stomach into a ball. Just as I thought the demon was done, Magdalene tripped. She fell face-first onto the ground. The light snapped off as if a switch had been thrown.

Faster than I'd ever believed possible, the demon spit a web at the downed woman. The web stuck to her as Magdalene screamed for help. Fangs pulled her in like a fish on a line.

"*Ignis*," I screamed as I launched a blast of flame at the webbing, hoping to break it. The flames scattered across the webbing as if they were harmless sparks. Magdalene fought to pull away from the demon.

From the right, Vada ran in wielding a glowing blade. She hacked at the silken line in a smooth overhead chop. The blade bit into the silk and clung to it. A spidery leg slashed out and threw her back from the demon's prey. Pallavi and Nao reached Mother, tugging her away from the gaping maw of the beast. It skittered forward and knocked them away.

I grabbed Sasha and Nao by the arms. "Sasha, throw images of me around that thing." She stared at me blankly. "Now! We have to save Mother."

Sasha dropped her chin, grabbed Nao's outstretched hand, and six of me appeared arranged in front of the demon. I channeled fire through Sasha so it flared to life from each of the illusionist's hands. It wasn't accurate, but the thing reared back.

Nao screamed to the others. "Get her while Jess holds it off."

Vada, Lucia, and Pallavi ran to Magdalene's side. Lucia threw powder onto the webbing and they pulled Mother free. Pallavi and Vada dragged her away from the demon.

Lucia stood her ground, lacing the surrounding ground with the same substance that had freed Mother. She chanted as the demon recovered from the flames and attacked again. Its hands reached out to grab the nerd queen. They stopped just shy of her as she continued her spell. A streak of white smashed into the demon, hurling it across the clearing into trees that dropped like bowling pins under a fifty-pound ball.

I cut off the flames and ran to Lucia. Nao and Sasha followed me. "That was amazing," I said to Lucia as her shoulders drooped with exhaustion.

"I do more than play Warcraft, you know."

The loud crashing of the demon righting itself broke off the conversation. It launched into the air, landing hard among us, scattering Sasha, Nao, and me. The second set of legs stabbed at Lucia but didn't touch her. A nimbus of orange light surrounded her.

"Not today," Lucia growled at the beast.

A string of webbing shot out, wrapping around the shield until Lucia couldn't be seen. Shit, what else could cut that web? Nao lay on the ground, her head against the remains of the stone altar. Sasha had fallen on the far side of her, not moving. We were losing fast.

Though Lucia was the one wrapped in webbing, the demon resumed its pursuit of Magdalene. Vada barred the way, an ax made of light held in her hands. She swung, striking the beast in the face as it tried to bowl her over. It flinched back as she struck again and again until one of the demon's hands grabbed her and tossed her away like old trash.

Pallavi still supported Magdalene while our coven leader tried to use her magick. The spider pounced, both hands grabbing her away from Pallavi.

"*Veni*," I called out as my magick responded. Large spears of stone shot up, piercing the belly of the beast. The tips of the shafts erupted out through its back, spewing the area with ichor. It thrashed as it tried to flee with our leader but the stalagmites of doom held it fast.

Pallavi rushed in, attempting to pull her free of the monster's grip, but it batted her away. It might be pinned in place for now, but it still had all those legs. She crumpled to the ground and stayed there. We were running out of witches.

I grabbed Magdalene and reached for my knife. Then I realized it had melted before the demon had arrived.

Knives weren't my only weapon. Gareth had taught me how to fight and I used everything I knew. Aided by the earth's strength, I slammed my fist into the demon's body as it tried to hoist itself off the stone spear. The chitinous plate cracked from the blow, but the beast moved forward unrelenting, pulling the spike out of the ground as it went.

"Jessica!" Vada yelled. "Catch."

I pivoted, caught the glowing blade, and slashed the leg nearest to me. The blade tore through it like a metalhead on speed. I sprinted through the space where the leg had been, avoiding the worst of the spraying ichor. The demon spun, forcing me to dive aside or be impaled by its fangs.

I moved in, swinging at the elongated head. A sharp impact in the back hurled me across the clearing. I crashed to the ground and heard my jeans tear as I slid. My head banged against a jagged piece of rock. Warm blood dripped down my face as I wobbled to my feet. An impossibly blue light lit the darkened clearing as the vial of chaos magick dropped from my flannel's torn pocket. I stooped to pick it up, staring into the depths of the light.

A scream from behind broke my trance. I stumbled as my knee started to give way, but caught my balance and lurched back into the fight, or what was left of it. Pallavi and Vada were down, trapped in gobs of webbing. Magdalene screamed as the monster pulled her in on the end of a long strand.

I pushed my abused body as fast as it would go. My magick was exhausted along with my strength as I floundered toward Magdalene.

"Jess, run," she screamed as she pulled away from the demon with all her might. "Save yourself."

"No," I shouted as I forced my body to accelerate. My vision narrowed to Magdalene and the need to save her. I grabbed her outstretched hand and pulled. The demon tugged hard, and I stumbled back as it yanked her away from me. Diving, I reached her, grabbing her hand again. Spittle from the gaping maw of the hell-spawned beast showered me.

"Let me go," she said.

"Never."

A sickening scream filled the air. The spider's mandibles wrapped around and pierced Magdalene's body. It pulled her to the awaiting mass of teeth. I lunged, pulling at her arm. The vial of chaos in my left hand slipped as I struggled to release Mother from the monster. Blue light blossomed from the magick contained within. The spider shrieked in rage.

Magdalene's eyes opened, and she grasped the vial, freeing it from my hand. "You're our only hope." She jerked her arm free of my weakened grasp right before the demon dragged her into its mouth. When the teeth crunched down on Magdalene, a blue light supernova exploded, turning the darkness into daylight. The impact of the explosion tumbled me across the ground like a piece of trash in a hurricane.

I opened my eyes to see the blasted body of the demon evaporate back into the ether. Nothing of Magdalene remained. I let my head fall back to the earth, beaten but alive.

This is a war, we were losing, badly.

24

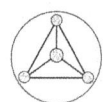

Pallavi and Vada appeared out of the swirling ether of the blast. "Jess, by the beautiful lady, I believed you were consumed by the explosion," Vi said as she helped me to my feet.

I gratefully took her hand and got vertical. The clearing might have been straight out of a war movie. The altar lay in pieces, broken beyond repair. Pallavi walked with a limp. Vada's face showed bruises. What the fuck just happened? I'd seen some weird shit, but that took the cake.

"What is going on? Where is everyone?" Lucia said as she approached us. "I couldn't see anything through the spiderwebs."

"Mother is gone." Vada's head sank as she said the words. They were like a knife through my heart. I pushed the thoughts away. Focus on the living, not the dead.

"Where are Sasha, Belinda, and Nao?" I asked. We'd all been knocked down during the fight, but I hadn't seen what happened to them after.

Sasha's words floated to us. "They have fled the scene." The older witch staggered into view, a large gash across her forehead. "When the spider lost, the two ran from here. They must work with hell-born."

"What?" As much as I didn't get along with Belinda, I had a hard time believing she'd side with the demons. Death witches knew better than anyone what waited in hell for those who were sent there. And Nao? The coven wild child? What could they offer her that would bring her to their side? She was blissfully happy as a coven witch and great admirer of the world just the way it was. None of it made sense, but if Sasha saw them run, who was I to question it?

"Nao would never betray us," Lucia said, anger thick in her voice. She stifled a cry. "I can't believe Mother's gone. I did everything I knew to stop that horror."

I put my arm around her shoulders. "We all did, but the demon was too strong."

"What the fuck happened here?" Gareth said as he entered the glade. He carried a shotgun in his hands and a sword sheathed over his right shoulder. "An explosion rocked the house, and I smelled the smoke." He stopped, looking at each of us as his face paled. "Where's Maggie?"

Vada went to him. "Gone. She killed the demon with her magick at the end, but sacrificed herself in doing so."

I stayed quiet. The others hadn't seen the vial of chaos magick. It didn't look good that I'd handed Magdalene the item that killed her. I'd lost two sisters and two more were missing. I wouldn't chance the others turning on me.

Gareth shook his head, tears dripping down his chiseled face. "Not Maggie."

"We are all so sorry," Vada said rubbing Gareth on the back. I wanted to comfort him, but it wasn't the right time. All of us were suffering from the loss of Magdalene and the rest of what had happened here tonight.

"I figured something was wrong, but I..." He looked at each of us. "Where are Belinda and Nao? They aren't dead?"

"No," I said. "Sasha saw them run off."

"Why would they do that?" He held up his hand. "I know, coven business, but they are part of us."

"We should get everyone home," Vada said, as she guided Gareth along. "We need to sleep and discuss what we will do in the morning."

The silent procession stumbled along the trail back to the house. I heard Lucia's sobs and Vi's gentle voice soothing her. How could we be a coven with only five sisters? Eight hadn't been enough to stop the spider. What would come next? If Zental pierced the nexus and stepped fully into our realm, all was lost. It wasn't like the witch cavalry could come to save us. If the nexus was under siege here, if we were the weak link, who knew what was happening at all the covens around the world?

Bruised, bloody, and defeated, we entered the house. I'd torn my jeans and my left sneaker had been scorched. I'd have to throw them out which pissed me off since they were my Donkey Kong pair that they didn't make anymore. And what did it say about me that I was focused more on my ruined shoe than the sisters we'd lost tonight?

I headed for the kitchen, but Gareth had beaten me there. A pint glass of Lemon Space Dog sat on the island matched by one of his own. I picked the glass up and we clinked them together. "To Maggie," he said quietly. I echoed his toast and sat on a stool as we both drank in silence for a minute.

He didn't ask, but he didn't have to. I started with the ceremony and Heather's return to the universe and then moved into the attack. Though I tried to summarize, tried not to dwell on all the horror and the things I'd done right, I mentioned cutting the spell with the karambit he'd given me.

He raised his hand to stop me. "Can I see the knife?"

"It melted when I cut through the tendrils."

"Impossible," he stated matter-of-factly. "That was a dragon's claw. Nothing I know should damage it."

"I don't care what name you give it, it melted like a honeycomb on a hot day." I took another drink as his mouth worked soundlessly.

"Jess, that's not its name, that was what it was made from, a dragon's claw." His eyes had a bit of wildness to them.

"Holy fuck, seriously?" I blurted out, instantly embarrassed since Magdalene didn't approve of such language.

He shook his head. Pain shone in his eyes as he dealt with losing Magdalene. "I had it made special for you. Tell me the rest."

I did while finishing a second beer. I reached the end of the parts I was willing to share and waited for him to comment.

"That is some messed up shit." He took a large swallow of beer. "We'll have to go scout the glade tomorrow and see if we can turn up anything. You should get some sleep."

"Yeah, I should." I stood and started for the stairwell but turned back. I needed to say more, tell him how sorry I was. Magdalene's words about my lack of discipline rang in my ears. With four sigils I might have saved her. "Gareth, I failed her. I wasn't strong enough."

Gareth crossed the room and hugged me. After a minute, he held me at arm's length and said, "Magdalene loved you, even though you drove her crazy. She hounded you because she knew how powerful you are. If you weren't strong enough, no one was."

"I wish that were true," I said and returned to my room, tired and defeated. I got ready for bed, bandaged my assorted wounds, and huddled into my bed. Sleep didn't come for a long time as I played the scene over and over in my head, looking at all the things I'd done wrong. When the clock read six, I got up and dressed, tossing my ruined Vans in the trash and pulled out my pair of blue skateboard shoes. I slipped in the metal toe caps and headed down to the training rooms.

Gareth sat in his meditation pose as I entered. Part of me wanted him to be here; the rest felt guilty for feeling that way. What kind of person crushes on a guy who just lost the most important woman in his life? For that matter, what kind of person crushes on a guy when she just lost the most important woman in her own life?

I sat across from him, wrestling my mind into submission, allowing my breathing to slow and my pulse to lower. Meditation didn't come naturally to my swirling vortex of a brain. One day I'd master it. but not today.

"That was longer than usual," Gareth said, a slight smile on his lips. "Let's go see what we can find."

I followed him out and down the trail to the clearing. It looked worse in the daylight. The altar was just so much rubble strewn across the clearing. A patch of dirt fifteen feet in diameter was all that remained of the spider and Magdalene. Gareth crouched to study it, held the dirt to his nose after rubbing it between his fingers. He scowled as he stood. "It smells wrong. Witch magick has a different scent."

I glanced around, making sure we were alone. "Arty gave me a vial of chaos magick the other day to remind me about how the universe works. Magdalene pulled it out of my hand last night while…"

He put his hands on my shoulders. After all the fighting and loss, it felt good to have his reassuring presence around. No wonder Magdalene was with him for so long. "The spider had her?"

"Yeah." I took a deep breath and kept going. "The chaos magick detonated and killed them both. This is all that's left."

He didn't say anything as he processed what I'd told him. "Walk me through the fight."

I did, to the best of how I remembered it. Being in the clearing made it both easier and harder to share, so this time I withheld no details, no matter how small or insignificant.

He studied the ground where Sasha, Nao, and Belinda had fallen with me. We found the remains of the webbing from Lucia's entanglement and where Vada and Pallavi had been dropped. Being careful not to trample anything, we stepped lightly around the areas.

"You know what gets me?" Gareth asked as he rubbed his chin. "No footprints. You can see where the four of you fell and there's crushed grass where you ran back to the fight, but none headed away from here in any other direction."

"If Sasha said they ran for the house, there should be something." I traced the imaginary line they would have taken. There were a couple of places that might have been prints but not a trail of them.

Gareth huffed. "If they are working with the demons, they could have been given something to disguise their path. Neither of them works magick in a way to allow them to pass unseen."

There were so many possibilities with magick that it was impossible to tell. End of the day, they were gone. "I still can't believe I didn't see them."

"You were a bit busy, Jess." Gareth went over the ground one last time but shrugged after a half an hour. "I give up. None of this makes sense."

"Agreed." I started back to the house with Gareth in tow. "I'm sure Vada will want to convene the coven so we can pick the new leader."

Gareth barked a harsh laugh. "I think I'll head to town for groceries. When the coven chose Maggie, I thought there'd be a duel to resolve it. Some of the others thought she was too bossy. Can you imagine?"

"Mother? Bossy? Never." We both chuckled though the wounds were still too fresh to truly rejoice in her memory.

"You ready for this gathering?"

"I doubt anyone will argue about it. We're all too tired." We finished our walk in silence, both lost in our own thoughts. I had fought as hard as I could and still crashed. Patience and perseverance led to the same place that charging in did—failure. With only five of us left, we were in serious trouble. Hopefully, one of the older witches had a plan for how to deal with this. I certainly didn't.

I entered through the front door as Gareth walked to the garage. The reduced coven sat in the meeting room; an empty chair sat open for me. Vada indicated I should take it. "Jessica, we have assembled to select our new leader. Usually, we would wait until after Magdalene was returned to the universe, but times are dire and we must act as one."

Lucia spoke next. She looked exhausted, dark circles under her eyes and her hair a mess. "Vada worked with Magdalene the most. Maybe she should lead the coven?"

"I think Sasha should take the lead as she is the elder among us," Pallavi's said, the cool tones of her voice taking the edge off her words. Vi seemed to be struggling with exhaustion as she continued. "We are facing a terrible enemy that we must stop."

Sasha nodded to her. She stood and glanced at each of us before addressing Vada. "I'd be honored to be Mother if you want me."

"I am not sure that is our best chance." Vada's gaze flickered to me for a second. "We are at war and need our strongest at the forefront of the battle. You all know Magdalene considered Jess as the protector of the coven and she showed that in the battle last night."

"But we lost," Sasha said simply. Her eyes held mine as she continued. "She is strong, but youngest here. You know my affection for her, but leadership requires experience."

"I agree with Sasha," I said, nodding to the older woman, understanding it wasn't personal. "I don't have the first clue about leading a coven. My track record is terrible. I tried to save Heather and Mother and failed both times."

Vada shook her head, her long hair swaying with the motion. "No, Heather was dead before you arrived and we failed you last night. We weren't strong enough as a coven to defend our own. Magdalene would have chosen you, as do I."

"I'm not fit to lead this coven." How could Vada even suggest I replace Magdalene? I had none of the skills she had. Try as I might, I failed at being patient and persevering as the earth spirit told me to be. This was a joke.

"Vada is right, Jess. We need you," Lucia said. "I failed you last night, but I will follow you until the very end."

"Lucia, this isn't a Warcraft raid. People have died because of me." I wanted to shake her to bring her to her senses. I looked imploringly at Pallavi. She would back me up and insist Vada or Sasha lead.

"I agree," my best friend said as we locked gazes. "I will follow you to the end. My strength is your strength to wield."

Sasha chimed in. "Perhaps Jessica's unique viewpoint will be a secret weapon for us in the war to come. Jessica, I will follow as well, no matter how crazy this is."

Vada stood. "Sisters, it is agreed, Jessica Flood is the new leader of the coven and our new Mother. Lucia and I will move your things to Magdalene's room."

I started to object, but was cut off by Vi. "Mother has the main room. We will uphold tradition while we are still a coven."

I threw my hands up in surrender. I guess I was moving rooms and the Mother of the coven.

My sisters had lost their fucking minds.

25

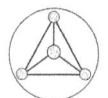

My first official act as coven leader was to run away as fast as possible. I headed to Green Man after a quick call to Basil from my ugly rental. Things were spiraling out of control, and I needed his firm grip on reality to set the course straight. Like that would happen. Really, I needed to vent and have someone that knew when to listen and when to kick me in the ass. It was a skill Basil had to use many times over the years.

I'd met Basil shortly after I'd arrived in Asheville, dust still on my shoes and stars in my eyes, as he told anyone who would listen. We'd become fast friends, and once he revealed who he really was, I owned up to being a witch. Of course, with his connections, he'd already known. Gossip travels fast in the magickal community of Asheville.

Oak wasn't on duty, so I grabbed a table in the corner upstairs overlooking the bottling machines and conveyor belts they used to package products for retail. Being Sunday, the crowd was light and entirely local. I had a full view of the taproom, so no unwelcome surprises. Suzie brought me an ESB while I waited. My internal compass was MIA and I had no idea of where to go next.

Basil strolled across the room, a hello for everyone he knew. Suzie had a Trickster poured and ready as he stopped at the bar. He wore a pair of red pants and a crazy, multicolored shirt that gave off a hip celebrity vibe. I'd look like a thrift store cowgirl in that outfit.

He slid into the seat across from me. I retrieved a small white rock from the pocket of my hoodie and set it in the middle of the table. Basil cocked an eyebrow at me. "Is that a silence stone?"

I nodded. "I have bad news and don't want anyone eavesdropping on our conversation."

That brought him up short. "What happened?" No flippant comments, no jesting or playful banter. Basil the seraphim was at full attention.

I ran him through the events of the last twenty-four hours. His face blanched as I told him about Mag dying and our missing sisters. I went over searching the area this morning and the sisters choosing me as the coven leader. Then I just talked like someone had wound me up tight and let me go. I let it all out, pausing only when Suzie brought us fresh beer. For over an hour, I vented my sorrow, frustration, and pain to Basil and all he did was listen. No questions, no how to fix it, he just listened, and I felt heard. It was the nicest gift I'd ever gotten.

Suzie brought over two more beers and retrieved the empties. I just stared into the golden liquid and watched the bubbles as they rose to the surface. I didn't have anything else to say.

"When you have bad news, you really have BAD news," Basil said once he realized I was empty. "My only question is what are you going to do?"

I shook my head. "What can I do? I'm going back to the coven to wait for the demon lord's next move."

"That isn't a very Jess thing to do," he noted, his normal sarcastic tone returning. "Usually, you're all about taking the fight to the enemy."

"Patience and persistence." I sipped my beer, enjoying the flavor. "My way hasn't worked so far, so I thought I'd listen to the earth spirit. I have to prepare the coven to fight back, but against who? And how? Belinda and Nao are gone. Heather and Magdalene are dead. I'm open to any advice you have for me."

He shrugged. "Run. As far and as fast as you can."

"You know I won't," I said, feeling more tired than I ever had before. "I swore to protect the innocent from the danger of the nexus and that includes the demon lords."

He leaned across the table toward me. "Jess, this is bad. I asked a few of my sources and there is no demon named Zental. I thought it was some low-level hack trying to make a name in the pit, but it's not. My guess is it's one of the major lords, even Lucifer himself. If that happens, all is lost."

I drank my beer in silence. What could I and my four remaining sisters do to stop that? If Lucifer broke through the nexus, he could take control of Earth and all the people in this dimension. Even if, and that was a major if, we could stop him, I still had two rogue witches working against us, assuming they really did run. Again, so many questions and no answers. I wanted to bang my head on the table. "Will the Almighty lend us help?"

Basil looked everywhere but at me. "No, the pact with Lucifer keeps him from interfering directly. If Lucifer does claim the mortal realm, then he might."

"Might?"

"Jess, the first war almost destroyed the universe. I'm not sure which would be worse for humanity. I wish I could say differently, but other than me, you're on your own."

"Wonderful. My options are being ruled by demons or absolute destruction. I'm thinking doing nothing is better than bowing to the Prince of Lies."

"Agreed." He shot a sickly grin at me. "The good news is they can only pierce the nexus on the new moon which gives you two weeks to prepare. I have faith that you'll stop them."

I finished my beer, grabbed up the rock, and dropped a twenty on the table. "Since I've got to save humanity, I'd better get started."

Two weeks to stop a horde of demons from flooding the earth. Great way to start a Sunday.

❦

I arrived back at the coven house with Blink-182 playing on the radio. After parking, I entered the house and called a meeting. I took my seat in the circle and waited. The table Heather had been laid out on still had the remnants of the candles and flowers Lucia had used in the preservation ceremony.

This room held a lot of memories for me. I'd been here for over six years and spent countless hours in this room listening to the business of the coven, learning the theory of magick, and being surrounded by my sisters. While not everything that happened here had been happy, I belonged here. I'd never belonged anywhere until I'd walked through those doors and left the "real" world behind.

Pallavi arrived first wearing a rainbow dress that went to her ankles. I guess I'd missed the color memo. Sasha entered on her heels. The older witch's long white hair hadn't been styled and looked windswept. I'd never seen her wear it that way before. Dark circles clung to the bottom of her eyes. Today the weight of her two hundred years was upon her.

Vada strode into the hall and took her seat to my left. She gripped my hand and shot me a smile. Lucia, wearing her Dalaran University T-shirt, ran into the room at full speed.

"Sorry." She gasped for breath. "I was finishing a raid when you called. I was the number one DPS and didn't want to leave them hanging."

"You play games at a time like this?" Sasha snapped at her. "Magdalene is dead and you waste your time on that?"

"Sasha." I kept my tone even and met her gaze with what I hoped read as a serene appearance. "Each of us deals with tragedy in a different way. We need to be kind to each other if we are to stand against the hellspawn."

Lucia's eyes were fixed firmly on the ground. I could see her bottom lip trembling. "Lucia, I'm glad you could find some comfort after all you've been through. Each of us needs that."

"That why you went off drinking like a sailor, I suppose?" Sasha sneered at me. Sasha never took the lead in anything, so why all the venom now? Was she punishing me for being elected leader instead of her or was this her response to tragedy?

"None of this bullshit gets us ready for what's coming." Screw the serene act. If we didn't find a way out of this disaster, hurt feelings were the last of our concerns. "You can help us or go sit in a corner and stew for all I care."

I caught Pallavi and Vada grinning before returning to their normal cool expressions. "Mother, do you have a plan?" Pallavi asked. The way she stressed *mother* was a dig at Sasha, who deserved it.

"No." I held up a hand as Sasha began to speak. "But we will come up with one as a coven. First off, we need information. Basil reminded me that the nexus can only be pierced on a new moon. That gives us thirteen days to be ready, and we will be ready, sisters."

Vada stood up and faced me. "Mother… Jessica, we have faith in you. Regardless of the outcome, I am proud to be your sister." She returned to her seat.

"Thank you." My voice came out like a cough. Since I'd run out of tears and serenity would never be my style, action was going to be my answer to the grieving. Patience was going to have to wait. I nearly laughed out loud at the thought. "Lucia, I need you to dig into the archives and find any reference to Zental or piercing the nexus. Any information would be helpful."

"On it, Jess. Sorry, Mother." Lucia's cheeks blushed which almost made me laugh.

"Until further notice, can the title. I'm Jess and that's how you'll talk to me. When we are back to full strength, we'll pick a new leader." I faced Pallavi. "Can you divine anything around what is going on?"

Pallavi shook her head slowly. "I've been trying, but I'm unable to gain any insight into the events that are unfolding."

"Just like the oracle told you," Sasha interjected. "Divining is touchy art."

Yeah, the oracle had said that. Something about what else he'd said scratched at the back of my brain, besides the seeing me dead part. I pushed it aside to concentrate on the task at hand. "Try to ask about things near the new moon. Ask about Nao and Belinda; there has to be a loophole in the curtain they are pulling across our eyes."

"I will continue to try, Jess," Vi said.

"Sasha, I need you to assume Magdalene's guise and drive around town. Take Gareth with you for protection. Do the same as Nao and Belinda. Call me if you see anything strange. Anything at all."

"I will do as asked, Jessica." As Sasha leaned back in her chair, I saw her wince.

"Are you feeling well?" Sasha looked to be in her late seventies, where Magdalene had appeared to be in her early fifties.

She chuckled. "I'm not young like you girls. Getting hit by demon hurt me and it takes a bit to get going again. One day you too will understand this."

At the rate we were going, I didn't think I'd make twenty-seven, let alone two hundred. "If you need healing, we can convene the ritual."

"No, I am old, not hurt."

I nodded. "Vada, I need you to come with me to the vault. We have a lot of research to do if we're going to be ready."

In the movies, this was where the spunky leader gave the pep talk. Not my style. "They messed with the wrong coven, and we owe them for our losses. Let me know what you find and stay safe."

Time to give Lucifer a black eye.

26

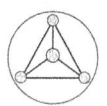

For the next four days, I lived in the vault with Vada. In our basement was the accumulated magickal knowledge of the coven. Grimoires, scrolls, lore, and every other piece of historical fact were stored in perfect condition. Stasis fields kept the pieces as new as the day the coven had acquired them. The vault ran hundreds of feet underground. It would take a nuclear bomb to damage this place.

I tore into the Elementalist magick. Spells, theory, and practical applications were all examined for any bit of usefulness. My fiery phoenix sigil gave me access to more power from the fire elements. I needed more, and I needed it fast, but fast had led to a whole lot of issues, including failing to earn my earth sigil. As Magdalene had told me before, I needed to focus and learn anything that would help me protect my coven, Asheville, and the world.

As I pulled down Livithican's Mastery of the Elements, I wondered how much more powerful I'd already be if I'd shown this kind of dedication since I'd arrived at the house. Magdalene had hinted at the benefits of study, and I'd resisted even more every time she pushed me. I'd gotten my fire sigil to prove to her I could do it, not out of any joy or sense of accomplishment. Running loose with the rules was fun, but I'd seen firsthand how unprepared I was.

My phone rang, showing Anne's smiling face on the display. "Hey, Anne."

"Hi, Jess." Her voice sounded weird, like she was holding back being upset or hurt. "Can you come down to Willow's Dream? We need to discuss the necklace you left with me."

"Sure. Give me twenty." I hung up after she said goodbye. "Vada, I'll be back in a while. I'm headed over to see Anne about the necklace I found."

Vada frowned. "I should come with you, Mother. It isn't safe for us to travel alone."

I groaned. "Vada, I'm Jess. When this whole thing is over, I'll be back to being Jess. You know, beer tour, loud music Jess."

"Jessica, you must move past your former self if you are ever to become the witch that the world needs." She cleared her throat. "Here you've gone and got me sounding like Magdalene. You are the strongest of us and we need you, not irresponsible, rebellious Jessica. We need the real you that you keep behind the falsehood of your younger self."

That stopped me cold. Vada never spoke out about anything I did and often defended me. "I'll be quick, and I'll be careful. I've got to chase down this lead while you keep researching. It might be the difference between survival and death." I left the room, her words following me down the hall like a bloodhound on the scent. Grabbing my keys, I got in the rental and pulled out of the garage. Hardwired by Metallica came on the radio and I winced. "Hardwired to self-destruct" hit a little too close to home at the moment.

I headed into Asheville, windows down, enjoying the wind in my hair. The Pretty Reckless replaced Metallica, but Going to Hell wasn't any more reassuring. For the first time in forever, I turned off the music and drove.

I pulled into a metered space in front of the shop. With a tap on the meter as I walked by, two hours of parking time flashed on. I entered Willow's Dream and headed up the stairs after waving to Marcy at the register. I climbed the switchback stairs, stepping through the tin panel that covered the entrance to the magickal store. Anne's bodyguard, Drew, sat by the door, small jets of steam venting from his nostrils. He was a squat man with heavy layers of muscles bulking out his frame. I'd seen Drew transform once, and it hadn't been good for the mage that pissed him off.

Anne sat behind her desk and waved me over. I took the seat in front of her. "Jess, you need to tell me where you got this."

"I found it." Anne's eyes narrowed as she watched me. "I can't tell you everything, coven business. What I can tell you is it was near where I hit the deer the other night. I saw somebody in the woods, and when I investigated, I found the necklace."

I could see the wheels turning as she processed the information. The coven was famous for being secretive, so me not telling her the full story shouldn't have shocked her, but whatever she'd found out about the necklace had freaked her the fuck out. If push came to shove, I'd tell her everything to get the information I needed. If the necklace had clues as who had unleashed that frog demon at us and then taken pot shots at us while we dealt with it, it would be worth violating secrecy for sure.

She rubbed her face before sitting straighter at the desk. "When whatever is going on is over, I want a full rundown."

"Agreed. I will tell you everything once it is safe for you to know." Things like, the world may be about to end and there are only five of us left to protect you.

A shadow of worry crossed her face. "I wish I was an accountant in this timeline." Drew chuckled behind me which was a good sign.

Anne leaned to the side to look at the animagus. "You should probably tell her your part first."

Drew settled into the chair next to me. You'd never guess from the stylish hair and clothes that he could turn into just about any animal. He wore a silver necklace with a stylized lion head pendant. "I had a client's hair appointment run late, so I volunteered to lock up the shop. Once Mr. Winhall left, I locked the front door and came in here to set the wards and —"

Anne held up her hand. "The coven has their secrets and we have ours. Drew turned on the security system for the relic hall."

I'd heard rumors around the community that Marcy and Anne employed extra-dimensional help in protecting the hall. Everything from djinn to aliens had been bantered around. Though my curiosity was piqued, I didn't ask.

He grimaced before continuing. "Ah, I set the security system. As I was getting ready to leave, the relic hall door alarms went off. Something big was trying to breach the defenses. After a few minutes, it stopped. When I left, the upper floor, the shop looked like a tornado had hit it. A couple windows were broken. The chair at my station had been ripped from the floor. Whatever attacked the door was big and strong."

"Did you get any video of the attack?" Why attack the relic hall? Was it a coincidence that I'd dropped off the necklace and someone wanted it back or was there something else they wanted?

Anne opened her top drawer, removing a laptop she then set up. A couple of minutes later I watched the parking lot camera. "All the interior cameras were hexed so nothing recorded. All we got was the outside camera."

The video showed the empty lot until a blur appeared from the lower right corner at the front of the store. A figure emerged. Two long blond ponytails bounced as Belinda strolled across the parking lot and vanished behind the shop next door.

"That is Belinda?" Anne asked, her mouth pursed in concern.

I nodded. "It looks like her, but…"

"Anyone could use a glamour to make it look like her, I know." Anne snapped the lid shut. "Why would a witch from your coven want to break in here?"

"I don't know. You have a lot of powerful artifacts in here. Anything new that would draw attention?" The whole thing felt off. Belinda was strong in the ways of the dead, but a full assault on a defended portal wasn't her style. Brute force tended to be my way. On the surface, Belinda could be working with Zental, but she'd literally been to hell as part of her training. Why would she want to help bring it to this realm?

"Marcy is always bringing in new items; that's what relic hunters do. Her magick draws her to them." Anne tapped her chin. "Most of the new acquisitions are pretty tame. A brooch that lets you hear through walls, a doll that absorbs psychic distress. The only other item is this necklace, but I took it with me."

Unless we spent hours going over every relic, this was a dead end. "So, what did you find out about the necklace?"

"Nothing and a lot." She pulled a plastic bag from her pocket and laid it on the desk. The teardrop necklace sparkled in the light, but nothing seemed sinister about the piece. "On the surface, it is a necklace. Good quality with a bit of residual magick clinging to it. Could have been a good luck charm or love devotary that one of the local woo sisters got lucky with."

In Asheville, people called anything new age or "magic" woo. In the magickal community, we called hacks and fakes woo since we know what magick is. A lot of tourists spent good money on "magical" Asheville. The healing vortex was extremely powerful so sometimes a woo got lucky and managed actual magick.

"But there's more to it," I guessed, not wanting to sound to eager.

Anne nodded. "There's a lot more to it. When I showed it to Marcy, her magick went nuts. As the owner of Willow's Dream, she's seen a lot of weird stuff, but this was new to her. I ended up putting it in a lead box to seal it away. When she calmed down, she said she felt compelled to kill."

"Marcy? Kill?" Marcy was a lot of things, but a murderer wasn't on the list. "I've never met a more nonviolent person in my life."

"Exactly." She picked up the bag and set it in a metal container and sealed it. Drew exhaled sharply.

We both looked at him. His skin was red and his eyes dilated. "You okay, Drew?"

He shook his head as if to clear it. "Sorry, I heard whispers telling me I was in danger and needed to kill you both. I don't know what came over me."

"I never wanted to kill anyone," I pointed out. At least not due to the necklace. "Neither did you."

"The magick seems to be attuned to only certain people or a type of magick. When I tested it in my home lab, I got no reading for hellspawn magick, but the results certainly point that way. While I can't tell what it is, I am certain it is from hell and we don't want it in circulation."

Why would a lone gunman be carrying a hellspawn necklace that encouraged killing? Or…was the influence of the necklace why the gunman had tried to kill us? I was quickly growing tired of having questions with no answers. Zental played a game, and I didn't know the rules, and if I didn't figure them out quick, we might not see tomorrow.

"Can you destroy the necklace?" Enchanted jewelry that made some people want to kill other people seemed like an item nobody needed, ever. If Belinda had gone rogue and she was after it, I really wanted it secure. Yet I still couldn't fathom Belinda working with hellspawn to destroy the coven. I couldn't fathom any of my sisters doing that. Magdalene was the one who'd been convinced it was true and now she was dead.

Anne shook her head. "Best I can do is create a pocket dimension and seal it away. It would take an enormous amount of skill to penetrate an unknown dimension to retrieve it."

"Do that then." At least that would keep it out of the way for the time being. There were nine days until the new moon. If Magdalene had been right, Zental would make his move to enter our realm physically and kick off a cataclysm of biblical proportions.

I dug into my pocket and produced the coin that Magdalene had given me, the one that she said would close any portal at a horrible expense.

Maybe I could get some ideas on how to use it more safely about it before I returned to the coven house.

Anne's eyes went wide in shock. "If you have that then the end of days is here."

Oh, good. Let's spill the beans on the apocalypse.

27

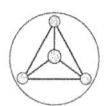

"You know what this is?" I asked in surprise. I'd figured it was a talisman that Nao had created.

"That is the *Deleo Ianua*. The angel Gabriel created seven seals to contain the demon lords of hell. He also created seven coins to destroy the corporeal form of any demon lord that tried to walk on earth, breaking the covenant between Heaven and Hell. Those coins have been lost for millennia and now you show up in my office with one."

"I warned you that there is more to the story." I tried to smile, but I don't think it worked.

Anne held up both hands. "Don't tell me. The covens have protected the nexus points since the beginning of time. I'm sure you have it under control."

I shook my head rapidly like I was racing over speed bumps. "We do. Magdalene gave this to me as a last resort. Can you tell me what to do with it?"

For a minute I thought Anne might throw me out or run screaming from the room, but she pulled herself together as her training took over. "If Satan came strolling down Broadway, toss him the coin. It will do the rest. The blast will probably level the mountains and a good part of North Carolina and Tennessee, but that would be preferable to living in Hell."

Talk about a weapon of mass destruction. In my mind's eye, I saw the devastation left in the wake of such a blast. Beautiful Asheville a smoking crater. My sisters would all be gone as would the people who, knowingly or not, depended on us to protect them from the threat that came through the portal. No one outside the coven, and now Anne and Drew, would know the truth, that we'd sacrificed everything to save them. The world would be told it was a freak nuclear accident or an underground gas explosion.

"Sounds easy enough," I remarked off-handedly, trying to sound confident even though my voice shook.

Drew placed his hand on mine. His eyes didn't hold fear or anxiety, just concern. "Throwing your life away is always easy and never the best decision. You'll find a way past this."

I could have kissed him at that moment. Instead, I said my goodbyes, pocketed the coin-op Armageddon, and headed back to the vault to find a way around dying.

Sunday morning started at the crack of noon. I rolled out of bed and got ready for another day in the vault. Fall firmed its grip on Asheville, dropping the temperatures along with my mood. I pulled on my Brew Tour sweatshirt and headed down into the basement more futile searching. As the earth spirit commanded, I was being patient and persistent and running out of time. Six days until the new moon and I wasn't any closer to finding a way to stop Zental.

I detoured to the kitchen to grab a protein bar for breakfast. Pallavi paced back and forth in the kitchen, muttering to herself. This was not normal behavior for my best friend. "Vi, is everything okay?"

She crossed the room and hugged me tightly. After which she held me at arm's length to look me over. "Jess, thank the bright goddess. I need to talk to you alone."

There aren't a lot of things that freak me out. Being stuck in a room with bad music. People actually drinking Bud Lite. And the new number one on the freak out list was… Pallavi inspecting me closely yet not commenting on my lack of style. We'd been friends for over six years, and I could count the number of times she hasn't remarked on my fashion choices on one finger. Something horrible was going on.

"Let's go." I followed her into the library where she closed the door and set wards, just like Magdalene used to do. The only difference was the lack of a teapot.

Well, there were more differences. I was Mother-in-name-mostly instead of Magdalene, and saying goodbye to first Heather and now Mags kept threatening to send me running away.

Our relationship had been complex, but I felt adrift on the sea without her being my guiding light. Since Belinda left, I'd lost the ability to even reach out to her spirit. I pushed back the tears, unwilling to break down over her loss when the fate of the world hung in the balance. I was done running. The *Deleo Ianua* in my pocket was a constant reminder that my avoidance days were over.

The long table at the side of the room looked like a woo-based Pampered Chef party had exploded. Tarot cards, iChing coins, teacups, trays of sand, and more were scattered over every available surface. In the center of a clear area sat a pile of bones that looked suspiciously like human fingers

Was this conversation going to get out of hand? I suppressed a laugh at my own joke, recognizing it for the borderline panic that Vi's anguish was inspiring in me. We couldn't both be hysterical.

She sat at the far side of the table. I pulled out a chair and sat across from her. I wondered if the bones were finger-lickin' good? Stress does wonderful things to my sense of humor. "Bones?"

Vi nodded. "None of the normal channels will yield anything. It is like the universe has been plunged into darkness. I was forced to deal with that wretch of a man to obtain the materials, but it is the first insight I've had."

For Pallavi to deal with our friendly neighborhood necromancer Sal Green spoke volumes about how deep in the shit we were. She hated him with an unholy passion. For the record, he wasn't my favorite person either. Magdalene had needed to chastise him on several occasions when his magick went too far, or his sourcing activities did. "What insight have you had?"

She frowned. "I would tell you, but I think it better you experience it yourself."

"Vi, I can't do divination. Hell, I can barely guess what I'll do next."

"I can guide you through what I divine." She bit her lip as she considered the pile of bones. "You are under severe pressure. I only get scraps of information, but I sense it's important that you experience the visions and draw your own conclusions."

"You need a second opinion?"

She nodded. "I fear that I am assigning too much importance to what the goddess is showing me."

I understood the feeling. In part, I'd asked Vada to research with me since I didn't trust my own knowledge enough to not skip over an important detail. "Do I need to prepare in some way?"

"Just take my hand, close your eyes, and open your magick to me."

I took her hand, her long, thin fingers intertwined with mine. I closed my eyes and relaxed. The magick warmed me as it flowed into Pallavi. The sensation intensified as Vi took control and pulled me into her visions. Flickering images raced past as her spell took us into the mystical realm of foretelling. Her voice caressed my brain as she chose the first bone from the pile. "This is the present situation."

The view shifted in a blur until my sight was filled by a dimly lit room. A single light bulb hung from a rusty chain where it swayed slowly back and forth. Something moved at the edge of the pool of light but it was indistinct. The walls were cut stone as was the floor. That narrowed it down to half the buildings in Asheville. "I don't see anything of use here."

"How does it make you feel?" Pallavi's voice came to me with a strange echo. "There are more senses than your eyes, Jess."

I stopped thinking and just was. The overwhelming sense of confinement hit me like a hammer. I wanted to break free and run as far and as fast as I could. "I feel trapped."

"As do I." I sensed her setting down the first bone and selecting the second. "This is the future."

The scene blurred and resolved around me. A brief flash of light and then nothing. I opened my senses but felt nothing out of the ordinary. "Something is actively blocking the future, though the flash of light is more than I've seen with other methods."

"At least it's consistent." I waited for the next prediction as she switched. Was the flash of light the coin being used? Could that be the most probable outcome for all of this, destruction of all that I loved to stop Zental's entrance onto our plane of existence?

Was she not able to see the future because there wasn't a future?

There had to be a way out, but with six days left I had no idea what. I needed a clue, even a hint of a clue. Something that would point me in the right direction.

"This is the influences that are bearing on the situation we face," Pallavi said, her voice soft as down feathers. Her calm tones soothed my jangled nerves.

The image settled on a set of giant rocks standing in a field. The largest stone, the size of an old Cadillac, sat on a series of rocks that jutted from the ground. Anger swirled around the place even though the setting was so serene. Who could be angry in such a place? I marveled at the structure, wondering how such a huge piece of rock could be raised unless you used magick.

"And this is the way forward. In this case, I am thinking that it means a path to avoid the outcome."

The image started to clear. I could make out a metal stairwell; on the top rung I saw a shoe just stepping down. Before the image came into focus, I felt a jolt shoot through me followed by a tearing sensation. The world blurred around me as the rip current of magick pulled me under. From the nauseating feel of it, it was absolutely not Pallavi's divination. I fought, steeling my mind as Magdalene had shown me so long ago. My defenses crashed into place under the psychic attack.

"The future is written in stone. Serve me and I will spare those you love." It was Zental's voice.

"Fuck you. I'm going to kick your ass back to hell."

I poured my magick into my defenses as the onslaught continued. Pallavi opened her magick to me, bolstering my ability to drive Zental off. A white light nimbused around me, breaking the attack. Magdalene stood before me. "Jess, you know what you have to do, child."

I returned to my body like I'd been shot from a cannon. I sat straight up from where I'd been slumped in the chair. Pallavi's eyes opened as the spell shattered. "Jess, are you all right?"

I nodded. The afterimage of Magdalene had been seared into my eyes. I hesitantly blinked, causing it to fade. Even in death she still protected me, my own personal Obi-Wan Kenobi. The last scene before Zental's attack, with the metal stairs, I'd recognized it. But from where?

Pallavi watched me as I rubbed at my forehead, trying to think of why a shoe would be the path out of this mess. I pictured the image again, a single shoe on a metal stair tread. Was it particular stairs? Metaphorical? Was it my shoe? I didn't own any shoes like that or know of any stairs. It was on the tip of my brain and I couldn't jog it loose.

"I do not know what happened. I did the same reading earlier and nothing happened."

"Zental is targeting me, that's why. What did you see when you did it earlier?"

She shrugged. "I had hoped you would know. I saw a black leather shoe on a stair. It meant nothing to me. The slightest trace of hope lingered there. I wish I could tell you more." Her eyes lowered to the table. She thought she'd failed me, but in reality, I'd put her in tremendous danger.

"It not your fault, Vi." I ran through the scene again in my head. "I'm obviously meant to find the person in the shoe, but who?"

Vi rubber her chin. "What if we went to see Peter at—"

Suddenly, I realized where I'd seen the shoe before. The day I was in Malaprops to see the Archivist. The shoe belonged to Gerwin Aaker, the oracle. He'd said he could no longer see the future, just like Vi. He'd also seen me die. I didn't need to hear either of those things again, so why would I need to visit him? Then again, who was I to question the universe handing me a clue I'd wished for? I hugged Vi with a whoop. "I've got it!"

Time to go see the man about a prophecy.

28

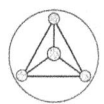

After discussing the rest of the visions with Vi and deciding what I should ask Gerwin, I headed to the Montford Historic District and the home of our millionaire investment wizard Gerwin Aaker. Unlike all the magickal community who tried to stay inconspicuous as possible, Aaker wallowed in his fame as an expert financial prognosticator. Of course, it's much easier when you can see the future to predict the next hot trends and invest early. Basically, he was a cheat. I wondered if the SEC would believe me if I told them how he had amassed so much money.

As I pulled up in front of the large gray house, I could feel the property values dropping. The stupid insurance company gave me a lime green Kia to replace my car which they totaled. From the glare I received from the neighbor, wearing a floral top, expensive jeans, and special gardening hat and gloves, she could as well. After I gave her a dirty look, she returned to pretending to weed so she could watch me enter Gerwin Aaker's house.

I climbed the porch stairs and knocked on the front door. Two metal chairs sat off to the left on the wide wrap-around porch. The stately columns proclaimed the history of the house as well the cost. After a minute, Aaker opened the door. My jaw dropped because I expected a butler or a bodyguard to answer. But there stood Aaker, wearing an ironed plaid shirt and khaki slacks. The "casual" clothes of the rich and famous.

"Why Miss Flood, to what do I owe the honor of your visit?" He looked past me to see if I was alone. "Usually, the more cultured members of your coven come calling. I will say I'm excited to hear why you are standing on my doorstep with kickoff only a few minutes away."

I pulled out the line I'd heard Magdalene use a million times when dealing with Asheville's upper crust. You really couldn't run roughshod over someone like Aaker who preferred his women pretty and quiet. "Mr. Aaker, sorry for any inconvenience, but I need to speak with you."

His eyebrows quirked. "So, you do have manners when you want to. Please come in."

He opened the door wider for me to enter. I stepped onto highly polished zebra wood floors that cost more than I'd ever made in my life. One of a kind art pieces decorated the walls lit by ornate lamps made for such displays. "If you don't mind, we can speak in the theater room. The game is about to start."

"Doesn't knowing the future ruin football for you?" I asked as we wound our way to the back of the house. We entered a three-row theater with a full wall TV showing the pre-game. He muted the announcers and indicated for me to take a seat. It was like sitting on a cloud.

He grinned at me as he placed a Carolina Panthers hat on his perfectly combed hair. "I stay away from any questions pertaining to sports. You need some mystery to keep life interesting. Now, I doubt you came to discuss my football betting skills. What may I do to assist the coven? You do represent the coven in this matter?"

I almost blurted out that I was, in fact, the leader of the coven and due the proper respect, but I bit down on it hard. No one could know that Magdalene had died or that the coven was so weak at a time when we faced the greatest threat the magickal community had ever seen. "Yes, Magdalene asked me to speak to you about a divination that one of our sisters did."

He nodded. "Then you came to the right place. What is your question?"

"To be honest, Mr. Aaker, I don't know." He started to speak, but I held up a hand. "Please, I know this sounds strange, but if you'll allow, I will explain."

He leaned back in his chair, eyes flickering to the screen. The announcers were still blabbing so I had a few more minutes. "Please do go on."

"Thank you. I experienced a vision that involved you earlier. When we spoke last, you mentioned that the future was being blocked, but you'd seen me die. I was wondering if you had had any other prophecies around the events that are unfolding?"

A frown creased Aaker's face. "Miss Flood, you are correct in your facts, but I never informed you of these things. You and I have not spoken in recent history. I am not sure how you came by this information, but the truth is, I did indeed see you die and I've not been able to pierce whatever is preventing my ability to predict the future. It has cost me a large sum of money to be sure."

What was going on? I knew for a fact that Vada, disguised as Heather, and I spent time with Anker at the bookstore. How could he forget that? "I spoke to you at Malaprops, not two weeks ago. That was when you warned me of your prediction."

"I never enter Malaprops. The idea of the Archivist recording my activities is highly unsettling to me."

I'm sure it was. Nobody wanted a record of wholesale exploitation of the financial systems for your personal gain. But he had no reason to lie to me about that conversation. If he hadn't been there then who were we talking to? There were plenty of people who could change their appearance, but they had to have inside information to pull it off. The irony that Sasha had changed Vada's appearance during that exact encounter wasn't lost on me. "If you didn't tell me these things, then how do I know them?"

The frown deepened. "I'm certain your sister would have relayed my warnings since I drove to the coven house and delivered them personally."

My stomach dropped like I was on the downhill side of a four-hundred-foot roller coaster. "Exactly who did you tell and when?"

"Sasha."

The clue I'd been waiting for had just dropped in my lap, and all I could think was I was glad it wasn't Vi.

※

I drove around for a while, thinking. Shinedown's "Enemies" played in the background as I turned into the coven's driveway. I couldn't take the chance that Sasha would flee, or worse, allow Zental to attack one of us. I parked and went directly to the workshop. Gareth wasn't there and that was good.

I entered what we termed the Armory. Gareth kept all the training

STONE COLD WITCH

weapons as well as any items used in protecting the nexus. At the rear of the room was a door. I placed my hand on the center panel and it swung open for me. Inside were the tools for stopping rogue mages, rampaging extra-dimensional monsters, and the like. I found the gauntlet without much trouble.

I stood holding it, shocked that I was about to clamp it on one of my sisters, especially one I felt so close to. Being the leader comes with a price and today the bill had come due. I returned to the house, climbing the stairs to my room as fast as possible, hoping to avoid any of my sisters.

Lucia waved as she opened the door to her room, balancing a pizza and cans of cherry Pepsi. Must be time for Warcraft. I slid into my room so I could devise the best way to get the cuff on Sasha before she could stop me or summon help. We needed to be outside, where I could use my magick to restrain her. After a while, I cobbled together a plan, put the gauntlet and my robe in a backpack, and headed out.

Gareth was in the kitchen as I passed it enroute to the front door. I paused, considering his skills could come in handy, but he'd never been involved in coven issues that directly during my time here. It wouldn't be right to involve him only a few days after becoming Mother, if Magdalene had never done it. Since Sasha could use magick and call in demonic reinforcements, Gareth wouldn't be much help. Decision made, I left the house.

I took the path through the woods to the glade. Most of the evidence of our fight had been cleared by Gareth or the weather removed it. The stone altar still lay in ruins. It was time to fix that. I unfolded my robe and slid it on. I could do the magick without wearing my robe, but somehow it seemed appropriate. I concentrated, wishing I had my earth sigil to help focus my power. I pictured the altar in my mind and pushed my will into forming it.

"*Veni*," I whispered as I let the spell go. Pieces of broken rock tumbled aside as the ground opened and shafts of fresh stone grew up to repair the broken artifact. Around the outside, nine short pillars pushed out of the ground, stopping at knee height so the coven could sit around the altar. The main thrust of solid granite speared up from the center of the circle, forming a new altar that would hold our dead when the time came and allow the leader to perform the ceremony of binding.

Long minutes passed into hours as I poured my magick into the structure. The original sculptured piece hadn't been damaged, so the faces watched as the new rose from the rubble of the old. The spell faded as the pristine white granite shone in the afternoon sun. I walked around it, my hand tracing the veining in the unpolished rock. It was beautiful in a rough, natural way. Stone lost its soul when people polished it to make kitchen counters from it. This was how it was meant to be.

I sat on one of the blocks I'd summoned and rested. It had taken more out of me than I would have liked, but I needed a reason to call the circle together. After a while, my energy returned and I made my way back to the house. Lucia met me in the foyer as I entered. "Please tell the sisters we are consecrating the new altar at sundown."

Lucia's smile brightened the room. "Sure thing, Mo…Jess." She ran back up the stairs to get the others. Having the altar restored would be a temporary morale boost, though unmasking Sasha would ensure it would be a short-lived one. I went into the kitchen and ate. My mind was a riot of thoughts and worries over how this would go down.

At six, the rest of the coven, garbed in their robes, met me at the front door. Vada beamed at me. "Jess, I am so happy to hear you have restored the altar."

I smiled back, trying to look sincere and in control. "As leader, I felt it was something the coven needed since we've no clues as to how to avert the coming darkness."

Pallavi's eyes widened at that, but her mouth stayed closed. If anyone could expose what was going on, it was her, but instead she nodded.

"Shall we, sisters?"

I opened the door and we walked together to the glade where we'd lost so many. I heard gasps from behind me as we turned the corner and they saw the new altar. Whispers of appreciation came to me as I halted at the head of the altar. I held out my hand to Sasha. "Sister, please take my hand so we may consecrate our new altar."

Tears stood in Sasha's eyes as she took my hand. Before she could react, I snapped the cuff on her wrist with a resounding clack. She collapsed into a heap on the floor as her magick ceased to flow.

It was time to get some answers.

29

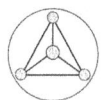

"Jess, what are you doing?" Vada's voice snapped like a whip. I'd never heard her as angry or confused as she was right now.

"The bracelet will only stun her for a few minutes, so we need to move. I'll explain everything. We need to get Sasha into the training room as fast as possible." The training room was warded so all magick stayed in and all outside magick stayed out. Since Zental, with Sasha's help, had only managed to get into the foyer and my dreams, hopefully, it would keep him from freeing Sasha before the new moon. I'd deal with her after, since if we lost it wouldn't matter.

"Jessica, I strongly object," Vada said, arms crossed and a grim expression on her face.

"Would you argue with Magdalene? This is life of death, so help or get out of the way."

Pallavi grabbed Sasha's other arm and together we dragged her into the training cell. Sasha's head lolled back and forth as the spell wore off. If she started screaming it wouldn't matter. Our closest neighbor was over five miles away, and we lived in a dome of wards that rendered us invisible to the unseers.

Gareth met us at the front door and got out of the way as we dragged the now awake and combative Sasha inside. Lucia reached out to lay her hand on Sasha, who tried to bite her. The second attempt went better as she spelled Sasha to sleep. The older woman slumped again. Pallavi and I staggered at the sudden change from feral bobcat to doorstop. Gareth swooped in and put her over his shoulder.

"I've got a lot of questions, but they can wait. Where do you want her?" Gareth asked me. The look I got meant he was serious about getting answers even though I technically outranked him.

"In the training room, please. We need her secured so she can't get out while we question her." I then turned to the others. "Meeting room, now."

I strode off expecting to be followed. I resisted the urge to look back, but I heard their footsteps behind me. I took my normal chair and waited until each had been seated. "I'm sorry for the lack of communication—"

"It is Mother's right to keep what information she feels from the coven, even if it puts the others in danger." Vada's tone couldn't have held more spite if she'd delivered it in a semi.

I held up both hands in surrender. "I will explain fully." I wanted to stick my tongue out at Vada, but restrained myself. "Magdalene knew there was a traitor in the coven but wasn't sure who. She tasked me to find out."

"And why did she pick the most junior of us to do such an important task?" Vada was in rare form today. She'd known Sasha for almost a hundred years and I assumed their bond of trust had been unbroken that whole time.

"Listen, Vada. I didn't ask for any of this. Magdalene trusted me because the demon attacked me the night Heather died and then again in my dream. Simple as that. Pallavi's divination sent me to Gerwin Aaker." I heard a nasty remark mumbled under Vada's breath and ignored it. "He told me that he came to the house one day before Heather died and told Sasha that he'd viewed a prophecy that I would die."

Vada's face fell as she realized the implications. "But he told us at Malaprops in front of the Archivist."

"Which he denied ever happened. If you remember, he also knew it was you disguised in one of Sasha's illusions. We chalked it up to foresight, but now we know different."

"Sasha set you up," Lucia said, her eyes wide with shock. "She told us she was going to the grocery store."

Pallavi shook her head. "What could Zental offer that the coven could not?"

"I don't know, but we need to find out." I caught each of their eyes.

"We need to be unified. Belinda and Nao could be alive. It would have taken nothing for Sasha to hide them after the fight if they were unconscious, claiming they ran off. We have to rescue them, if possible, or avenge them, if not."

Pallavi turned to face Vada. "It seems we chose well when we selected Jessica as our leader."

"Well is an understatement," Vada said with a toss of her magnificent hair. "We chose an excellent leader. I'm sorry I doubted you. I was confused by the events of today." She bowed her head in my direction. "Please forgive me."

"Vada, look at me." The older witch did as I asked. "I doubted me. There is nothing to forgive, but there's a whole lot to get done before the new moon. If we don't stop Zental, none of this matters."

"Agreed. Let us go speak to our lost lamb." Vada stood, waiting for me to lead. This mother crap needed to end.

I got to my feet, and we went to the basement. Gareth sat on the floor outside the training room. "She's secure. May I sit in?"

"Of course." I held out my hand and helped him to his feet. The weapon's master grinned at me. "Gonna be like old times."

"You mean being in the Marines?"

"No, the Spanish Inquisition."

I did a double-take to see if he was joking, decided he wasn't, and inwardly shuddered before opening the door. Sasha sat in a heavy metal chair, arms and legs bound to it. "Jess, why are you doing this? Have I upset you?"

"Since you betrayed the coven and helped to kill at least two of its members, I'd say yes, you've upset me. Let's start off with why are you working with Zental? What did he promise you?"

"Promise me? Nothing, child. I do not work for anyone except coven." Sasha smiled sweetly like I was a slow kid who just didn't understand. I wanted to kick her teeth in.

"Lucia, prepare a circle of inquest around the chair. We don't have time to waste with this pointless bullshit."

"Yes, Mother," Lucia answered. She left the room to fetch the articles she'd need for the spell.

The circle would force the person at the center to tell the truth, but it also would harm any spirit possessing Sasha. If she were possessed, then we could restore her, but I suspected that wasn't the case.

"Don't you think that's a bit harsh, Jess?" Gareth asked from where he leaned against the wall. "Maggie always said they were dangerous to the subject."

I spun on him. "I don't care if it makes her a fucking vegetable. She's responsible for at least two deaths and opening a portal to hell. Anything that happens isn't bad enough." I winked at him and could tell he got the message though his face never changed expression.

"I understand, Mother. I retract my objection."

"Thank you." I turned to the other two witches. "Does anyone else wish to speak for the accused?"

Neither one's expression changed, but each shook their head. I turned back to Sasha whose face had gone white. Her head dropped and her shoulders slumped. "I'll tell you what you ask. No need for the inquest."

"And why should we trust you?" Illusionist personalities tended to fracture over time, and I wondered if that had happened here.

Lucia entered carrying her ceremony kit.

I welcomed her back. "Sasha has agreed to speak freely. Can you set up an inquest circle?"

I heard a sigh of relief from Lucia. "Yes, Mother. It is much easier." Our techno witch laid out the circle with ease. Within a minute, she activated the spell and a golden shield surrounded Sasha.

"What color are my eyes?" I asked Sasha.

"Black." The golden sphere went dark at the answer before returning to gold.

"Are Belinda and Nao alive?"

"Yes, but I don't know where they are." The sphere didn't change. A huge weight lifted off my shoulders. My sisters still lived. We had to find them before the new moon, not just for their sakes but for the whole world. I felt the coin's weight in my pocket and wondered if six days was all any of us had left to live. Aaker had seen me die with a knife to the chest, not in a magickal nuclear explosion. But I couldn't ignore that an Asheville-destroying explosion would probably mean Aaker and Vi and the rest would have trouble with divination.

"Did you disguise yourself as Belinda and trying to break into Willow Dream?" I asked next. The other sisters seemed surprised by this, and I realized I'd forgotten to tell them the details in all the chaos.

"It was a handy talisman," Sasha said with a shrug, referring to the necklace that made someone want to kill others. "I thought it was worth the chance to get it back."

"Did you try to kill me and Vada that night in the woods or did you make someone else do it?"

"You are too strong and my lord wanted you turned or removed. I gave the necklace and a weapon to a homeless man and left him to ambush you," Sasha spoke like she was describing ordering a new shirt. "When he failed, I killed him and left him for the bears to eat."

"Why would you kill the poor man?" Lucia asked hand over her mouth.

"The is a price to be paid when you fail the minions of hell."

"Why did you betray us?" It wouldn't help us avert the cataclysm, but I needed to know for my own peace of mind.

She didn't answer for a moment. "Jessica, I am dying. I have pancreatic cancer. Magdalene said magick could not heal it, but I don't believe her. One of Zental's humans works at the hospital and offered everlasting life in new body if I helped the demon lord. I said no, but as I got sicker, I changed my mind. He gave me a tonic to stop being sick. Magdalene betrayed me so I returned the favor."

None of us said anything. I broke the silence. "I'm sorry, Sasha. Magdalene wasn't perfect, but I'm sure she had her reasons."

Sasha spit on the floor. "Jealousy. Since we met, she wanted what I have. Beauty. Now I wither while she stays young. She got her wish and now she's dead."

I looked at Gareth who shrugged. I didn't know what to think. If it was true that Magdalene turned her back on Sasha, it was horrible; if not, then Sasha was caught up in her own reality.

"What do you know of Zental's plan?" I asked, setting aside the accusations Sasha had leveled against Magdalene. They had no bearing on the threat Zental represented. "We need to stop him."

"His man will kill Nao or Belinda and use their blood to bind the portal. After that Zental will own reality and rule over humans forever."

Another reason we had to find our missing sisters. Without the blood for the ceremony, he wouldn't have the power to open the portal. I racked my brain for anything else I needed to ask that might help us divert the oncoming event. With the inquest circle, she would have to answer us. "Do you know how to stop him from killing everyone?"

Sasha nodded. "There is time. Join me and you will be rewarded. We will no longer hide in shadow but rule over the people who tortured and killed us. Why die to save people who hung your sisters in Salem?" Her laughter rang out as she thrashed in the chair. After a long time, she dropped off, unconscious.

I left the room and Gareth resumed his spot outside the door. As we returned to the meeting room, I pondered on how to find witches that are being held captive by a demon. "What kind of tracking options do we have?" I asked the group. "I guess it wouldn't do us any good to put out a magickal APB?"

"I could do a tracking spell but we don't have enough witches to fuel the magick," Lucia said. "I'm sorry. That would have been too easy."

I thought about how Magdalene had found me behind the Harris Teeter both easily and quickly the night all this had begun. "Maybe it could be easy. Did you install Find My Phone on everyone's phone?"

She blushed as she answered. "Yes, Mother insisted that we be able to find all the sisters in an emergency. She asked me not to tell everyone about it so it's possible Sasha doesn't know." Her eyes lit up. "I'll go check to see if I can locate them." She ran up the stairs to her tech lab. If anyone could find Belinda and Nao, it was Lucia.

We took our seats. I felt like I'd been going for a month with no sleep, but in reality, I'd only been up a handful of hours. "So, what do we do with Sasha?"

Pallavi looked me straight in the eye. "We should kill her to ensure the demon lord cannot use her to further his plans. She has witch blood that would activate the portal, same as our other sisters."

I wasn't expecting that solution. "While I understand your point, what if we need her? It's not like we can undo death." I also didn't want her dead, no matter what I'd said to Gareth in order to scare her into talking. I just wanted her to come back to us, though I had my doubts that that could happen.

"She is a traitor and should be treated as such." Pallavi's whole demeanor screamed aggression.

"I think we need to restrain her until after the new moon. We can strip her powers and her illness will finish her off. There is no need to dirty our hands with her death," Vada coolly interjected.

Pallavi softened. "If we can find a place that the demon lord will have no chance of claiming her, then I will agree."

That was the million-dollar question. Where do you stash a person Zental is looking to release? Did he know how to track iPhones, too? The first place he'd check was here. No one in the community could be put in harm's way by leaving her with them. Even Anne couldn't withstand a full assault from the demons. There had to be an answer.

Lucia charged into the room, throwing her hands up in victory. "I rock! Both their phones are at One World Brewing. They have to be there."

"You do rock, Lucia," I said with a smile. "And I know where we can put Sasha that Zental will never find her."

It was time to call on the earth spirit again and bring her a guest.

30

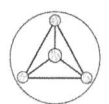

With Sasha bound and gagged, Gareth and I drove the back roads to the earth spirit's cave. He insisted on coming along in case Zental made a play to retrieve Sasha, and it wasn't that he thought he could protect me from a demon lord. I pretended not to notice he carried a pistol in a shoulder rig under his leather jacket. A bullet to the head would stop Sasha from being of use to anyone.

We reached the cave, and I hopped out of the truck, leaving Gareth to guard the unconscious woman. I hoped the earth spirit would allow me passage into the cavern so I could request that Sasha be held there to deprive the demon lord of her services. Demons were powerful but no match for a full elemental in her natural state.

I stepped into the cave and spoke into the darkness. "Earth spirit. It is I, Jessica Flood. I failed your trial but need to talk with you about an urgent matter."

"If you are to enter, you must pass the test I have laid out before you. Speak the words and survive the challenge if you would address me." The voice echoed around the cave, giving it that ominous movie effect. It worried me, so it worked.

I swallowed hard. I knew taking the test of passage was a possibility, but I had hoped the impending threat of the demon's assault might shortcut the process—not to get my sigil but just to talk to the Earth Mother. I didn't have a choice. "You set me on the path of patience and perseverance. I am here to prove myself worthy of your trust. I will accept the challenge."

"Then proceed, child of stone. Do not veer from the path less ye fail and die."

I set my shoulders and walked into the darkness. "*Sentio*." The darkness faded to twilight as the cantrip took effect. I followed the path I'd taken before to the bridge. The stone guard didn't appear this time. I crossed the bridge, waiting for the challenge to begin. Nothing. No guards, no creatures, just darkness. It put me more on edge than anything else I'd dealt with.

I stepped into the circle carved from the white marble and took a knee. "I am ready to prove my worth as a disciple of the earth."

The earth spirit flowed out of the wall, her delicate features crafted out of various stones, giving a Picasso-type appearance. I wondered what other elemental witches saw when they met the spirit. She stood before me as elegant as any queen that had ever walked the Earth. "Welcome, my child. Answer this question. Why do you bring the witch for me to guard?"

I opened my mouth to respond but closed it. The easy answer wasn't the right one. I'd rushed through my whole life, thrown caution to the winds, and played loose with the rules, and where had it gotten me? Nowhere. Magdalene had been right. I should be an initiate in all the elements by now. I needed to answer from my heart and not the first thing that popped into my head.

"Sasha is my sister in every way that matters. She has been kind and helped me when I needed it. She has taught me and counseled me and been my friend. My hope is she will return to us after we've defeated Zental, but if he takes her, she will be lost to me forever. As the leader of the coven, I should kill her to ensure she can't be used by the enemy, but I think she will be safe here."

I waited in silence as the earth spirit considered my words. I wasn't sure if they answered the question correctly, but I answered with the truth of my heart and that would have to be enough.

"Rise and don the mantle of earth initiate."

"What?" I blurted. "I thought I had to surpass the challenge of earth?"

A smile crossed the spirit's face. "That was the challenge. You were set on the path of patience and you have achieved it. Most would have rushed to end a life, not understanding the ripple effects such an event causes.

You have persevered through much and stayed true to yourself. You are a worthy initiate of the earth."

I bowed my head. "Thank you. I will not fail you again."

The spirit laughed softly. "Yes, you will, but not for rash decision-making. All things fail in time, it is part of the cycle. May I touch you to bestow a gift?"

"Yes."

"Please stand, child of earth. You need never kneel before me again." I did as she asked. She flowed across the marble floor until she was in front of me. She placed her hand gently on my shoulder. "I mark you as one of my initiates." A coolness that reminded me of entering a cave on a hot summer's day ran through me. It seeped deeply into the muscles below as her touch lingered. When she removed her hand, the coolness remained.

"The task before you will take all you have and more, I'm afraid. I have given you the boon of the sigil to help you in your struggle against the dark one. Bring Sasha to me and I will keep her until the new moon has passed."

"Thank you." I retraced my steps back to the entrance. I halted before stepping into the sunlight since I still had my enhanced vision on.

Gareth brought Sasha over, carrying her fireman style. He laid her on the ground before me. "Since you're alive, I take it that congratulations are in order?"

"Yes, they are." I couldn't keep the stupid smile off my face. I reached down and pulled my sweatshirt over my head, tossing it to Gareth. The edge of the new design poked out from under my T-shirt sleeve. I pushed my sleeve up and saw the earth sigil in perfect detail. Even Cam couldn't have done such an exact rendition. My fire sigil used red ink where this was dark but cast a faint bluish glow as I looked at it. *"Robur."*

Gareth looked puzzled, but the power of the earth flowed through me like a landslide. I'd never felt this strong before. I picked the unconscious Sasha up and cradled her like a sleeping child. I didn't see a traitor, just my sister who'd taken ill. Gareth's eyes bugged out a bit at the sight. I pulled out my best Arnold impression. "I'll be back."

With the strength flowing through me, I felt like I could carry Sasha to Charlotte and back without breaking a sweat. Her face looked so peaceful. I hoped I was making the right decision, but time would tell. All I knew is I couldn't kill her and be good with the decision afterward.

I reached the earth spirit and laid Sasha down in the center of the circle. I touched her forehead and released the spell.

Sasha's eyes shot open as soon as the spell broke. "Where am I? What have you done to me, I can't see," she screamed as she sat upright. I'd forgotten that the cavern was pitch-black without *Sentio* on.

The walls began to glow as Sasha jerked around in her panic. As the light reached a higher level, her eyes locked on me. "Jessica, you bury me in cave? I thought better of you."

"You are not to be buried, only kept safe until the new moon has passed. Will you freely stay and accept my protection?" the earth spirit asked Sasha.

Sasha whirled around, scrambling away from the new voice. "Who are you?"

I blocked the path to the bridge in case she ran.

"I am the spirit of the earth. I offer you sanctuary here until the new moon has passed. Will you accept it?"

"Nyet." Sasha spat on the ground before the spirit's rock form. "I will rule when Zental ascends from hell. Kill me or free me."

"I'm sorry you will not accept my offer." Clear quartz rose from the floor, entwining the witch's legs like a growing vine. The rock grew rapidly as Sasha swore in Russian and fought to free herself. The crystals continued until they encased her fully.

"Can she breathe in there?" Sasha looked more like a statue than a person with the thick rock surrounding her.

"She is in a type of stasis, merged with the earth to maintain her. She will be safe. I will release her after the new moon passes."

"Thank you for everything." I bowed my head to her as she melted back into the wall. It hadn't fully sunk in that I'd become an initiate. Master would be a long way off, but I'd have access to much greater magick with the sigil to connect me to the source. If I survived the new moon, I'd have to work toward my water and air sigils. Sometimes being an elemental witch reminded me of being in the Girl Scouts earning badges, but without the cookies.

I released *Sentio* and the world returned to normal as I exited the cave. Gareth held my sweatshirt as he leaned against the truck. My breath caught in my throat as I looked at him. I pushed those feelings aside.

"Usually I have dinner with a woman before she starts throwing clothes at me."

"Do you get a lot of women throwing their clothes at you?"

He laughed, but his eyes were locked on me. "Sometimes, but not the ones I really want. At least until now."

Gareth flirting with me? That was new. "Do you bed all of the coven leaders as some sort of initiation?"

"No, but I might make an exception for you." He at least had the decency to look mildly embarrassed. "This is so not where I meant to take that joke."

I cocked my head. "So, you don't want to sleep with me?"

He held up his hands in front of him. "You are my student and there are lines that shouldn't be crossed."

I'd broken a lot of rules over the years, but I saw his point. Not that a tumble with Gareth wouldn't be worth it, but now wasn't the time to complicate things. "I gotcha. We can discuss this later."

He laughed. "Yes, Mother. We should probably return to the coven. I'm sure they are worried about you."

He was right. Just trying to leave had been excruciatingly difficult. Vada meant well, but I couldn't have my sisters on my hip twenty-four hours a day. I pushed thoughts of Gareth out of my head. It was more difficult than it should have been. His smell, the feel of his hands in mine, every little detail intruded on my thoughts. I'd had a crush on him for years, but now it was different. Magdalene's death had changed everything.

As we drove back to the house, I gave him the play-by-play of my trip into the cave. More out of nervous energy than any real need to explain it. It was far less exciting than the first trial, but he listened as I told him about Sasha being encased in quartz. I wondered what he thought of all this, though he hadn't shared his story with me.

We pulled into the driveway and parked the truck. Vada appeared from the back door as I exited the garage. She practically vibrated with excitement, which was totally out of character. "You earned your initiate of the earth?"

Gareth winked at me as he returned to his realm behind the garage. Vada cleared her throat to get my attention, which had been firmly attached to watching Gareth's retreating backside.

Returning to my conversation with Vada, I pulled up my sleeve, exposing the faintly glowing sigil. "I did."

Vada clapped before throwing her arms around me in an enthusiastic hug. Basil would have paid through the nose to have her hug him like that. Come to think of it, most of the people of Asheville would.

I pulled free of her death grip. "The earth spirit will hold Sasha until after the new moon. There is no way Zental is getting her in there. One less issue to deal with."

"Agreed." She took my arm as we walked to the house. "Magdalene would have been very proud of you, Jess. She knew you would find your way one day."

If only she'd lived long enough to see it with her own eyes. "Thanks, Vada. We need to rescue Nao and Belinda before it's too late. Once they realize we've neutralized Sasha, they might kill them. We don't even know who all is in league with Zental and what to watch out for. We need a plan."

We entered the house to find Lucia and Pallavi waiting in the kitchen. After the brief celebration, it was time to get down to business. "We are going get our sisters back."

And I intended to accomplish it tonight.

31

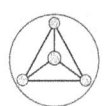

We spent the afternoon planning before heading off to rest. The Earth Mother's words buoyed my spirits, but Zental had pierced the defenses of the coven house before. Even with Sasha out of the picture, I couldn't be sure that she hadn't left behind any surprises.

I went to Sasha's door and studied it. The wards covered the basic alert and locking, but nothing nefarious. Lucia paused next to me. She was wearing a Sylvanas T-shirt and carrying a cherry Pepsi. "I'm skipping raid night. Can't concentrate on Warcraft at the moment. You want some help?"

"I was thinking of kicking the door down. Do you have a better idea?" I grinned at her, and she responded with the classic eye roll. Always a winner.

"Let me grab my kit. You are crazy."

I laughed as she left to get her ceremonial magick gear. It was easy to overlook how strong in her craft Lucia was. The gamer-girl persona masked a deep understanding of her magick and made her seem younger than she was. The way she dressed reinforced the image and many people had underestimated her to their own detriment.

She returned carrying an old medicine bag. "I can remember when I carried this bag to deliver babies back in Honduras before I was drawn to my first coven." She set the bag on the floor, opened it, and proceeded to set up her spell. She hummed as she worked. I leaned against the wall and marveled at the precision needed to create her magick.

"Do you ever wonder why your magick requires the tools you use? My magick channels elemental energy but I don't need tools to work it."

"I don't need anything to work my magick. No one does, really." She continued setting up a small brazier with pieces of a gray-green bark in it. She lit it, allowing the smoke to rise around the door. "Different people have different strengths. The pieces I use help to anchor the magick and increase its potency. I used a shield spell against the spider demon when I didn't have any tools available. With a proper setup, I could have trapped it and banished it, but controlling that much magick without the proper setup is dangerous since nothing is containing it."

The smoke wrapped around the wards that covered the door, showing them far more clearly than I could see with my eyes. Lucia studied them, bouncing a vial in her hand. She put it away and retrieved a different one instead. "The tattoos witches wear are focus points which allow us to draw a more concentrated magick than, say, a chaos mage."

Arty must be back in the picture if she was using chaos mages to illustrate her point. At heart, he was a good guy, but handling raw chaos warped you in unpredictable ways. Assuming we lived past the new moon, I'd have to keep an eye on him.

Lucia poured the vial into the brazier and the smoke turned to an angry red. More glyphs appeared, hidden under the top layer of wards. "Some nasty spells there, but I'm missing something." She pulled a leather wallet out, undid the ties, and unrolled it to display a new set of vials. "How you focus your magick is more like your personality than a statement on the magick. Magdalene's brought spirits to aid her, but it's not much different than Belinda using death energy to fuel her spells."

She took a vial with a pitch-black substance in it and dribbled it into the brazier. "Magickal theory really geeks me out. If I hadn't been drawn to a coven, I think I'd have been an Archivist." The smoke twisted in a serpentine fashion as it slithered up the door. It curled around the center, revealing a hex straight out of hell itself. "Good thing you didn't kick the door. That is a death spell. Sasha is system-crashed if she put this trap on a door for just anyone to trip."

I studied the hex. I didn't have the experience or knowledge that Lucia did, but from the little I knew, it was a nasty piece of work. "Maybe she did it more recently, after she decided she was okay with us being dead. Can you break it?"

She looked up in shock. "I can hack anything, magick or technological. I can't believe you'd even ask such a thing."

"Sorry, I don't know what came over me."

"It's okay. I figure a rock probably hit you in the head and rattled your brain loose." She packed away the leather wallet after replacing the empty vial. The next piece made my stomach clench involuntarily. She removed a metal box covered in glyphs and wards. There wasn't an empty space on it. Lucia donned on a heavy pair of leather gloves and pulled a set of tongs and a pistol from her bag. She handed me the pistol. "Point this at my head. If any part touches my skin, shoot me and keep shooting until you're certain I'm dead."

"What?"

"Jess, focus," she snapped. Gone was the fun gamer girl, replaced by a strong, knowledgeable witch. "I'm going to add a piece of the unholy crucifix to the brazier. If it touches me, evil will consume me in a matter of seconds. If you don't kill me, Zental won't be an issue for the world any longer."

I had vaguely heard of the unholy crucifix before, but not that it was instant evil to both the witch who touched it and the whole world. How had Lucia come by a piece of it? "There has to be another way to break the wards."

Lucia set the tongs down. "You're right. Kick the door in. I'll make sure we release your spirit to the universe, assuming there's anything left of you after that hex fires."

I eyed her for a long moment; she didn't flinch at all. "Anyone ever mention you can be a real bitch?"

She smiled sweetly at me. "No, I hide it well, unlike some of us."

Even at the prospect of being consumed by evil and having me blow her head off, she still could throw shade. "Right, if it touches you, fire until dead. Please be careful. I can't lose another sister." Our eyes locked for a minute, and I realized how much Lucia meant to me. The feelings were in her eyes as well, before she returned to the task at hand. I pointed the gun at her head, finger off the trigger. This was no time for an accident.

"I'm always careful. That's why I've been alive for so long." She picked up the tongs and eased the box open. The stench that filled the hallway reminded me of a fish packing plant buried in a sewer. Very slowly she eased a blackened piece of wood from the box and laid it on the brazier. She closed and sealed the box and placed the tongs in a plastic bag.

The fire burst into a raging yellow flame. Shrieks filled my ears as it burned. I kept the gun pointed at Lucia's head and would continue until she said otherwise. The smoke enveloped the hex, obscuring it from view. A loud crack rang out as the door split in two. More smoke billowed around the hex, expanding out into the hall.

"Shit," Lucia said as she frantically searched for something in her bag.

A figure manifested as the smoke grew, taking on a humanoid shape. I fired the gun into the smoke, punching holes through it. The thing screamed in agony as the shot tore away at it.

"Keep shooting," Lucia yelled as she uncapped a bottle and muttered a spell. She filled her mouth with the liquid and then sprayed it in a burst onto the demon that continued to grow from the smoke. It shrieked as the spray washed over it, shrinking it down until it vanished and the smoke cleared. Lucia fell back, panting as she lay on the floor.

I knelt next to her. "You okay?"

She nodded slowly. "Good call shooting the demon. The pistol is loaded with bullets laced with angel tears. Really messes hellions up."

"You got more of these? I think they may come in handy." I'd fired all six shots to slow the monster before it could completely enter our realm. Dumb luck on my part, but sometimes your instincts knew more than your conscious mind.

"Gareth stocks all sorts of fun in the Armory. We should visit before tonight."

"Good idea, though first I'm going to check out why Sasha left a death hex on her door." I kicked the remaining part of the door out of my way as I entered.

"I knew you'd end up kicking in the door," Lucia said with a laugh.

I did the mature thing and ignored her. As I looked around I realized I'd never been in Sasha's room before. An old-fashioned half-canopy bed sat against one wall. A white wooden rocker held a small doll. The long bureau had various bottles and photos in gilded frames. I looked at each; most were old pictures of serious-looking people dressed in traditional Russian clothing. Probably her parents or siblings, long dead. A beautiful young woman with Sasha's younger face peered back at me from one sepia tinted photograph. How young she had been? A white veil draped over her head and she held a small grouping of flowers. More things I didn't know about my sister.

I opened each drawer and poked through the contents while Lucia looked under the bed. Nothing of any use. I pulled out the drawers, checking for concealed compartments, and repeated that for the nightstands while Lucia searched the bathroom. Not a single piece of evidence to link her to the demon lord or the demon lord to his plans. I walked around the room again, pushing out my magickal senses. I couldn't detect anything, but Sasha was an accomplished illusionist. The book of the damned could be sitting under an invisibility spell and I'd never see it.

After a half-hour of fruitless searching, I was about to give up when I felt a loose board under my foot. I pulled back the carpet and there was a wide seam around a single board.

"This looks interesting."

"Good find," Lucia said as she inspected the board for any more traps. "Looks clean."

"We'll see." I levered the board free and gasped. A steel box sat in the space under the floorboard.

I pulled the box out, realizing too late it could be booby-trapped, but since it was so well hidden, she hadn't bothered. I checked the latch and didn't see anything. Lucia nodded after she checked it as well. The box opened easily. Inside was a leather wallet like Lucia's, filled with vials that held hair. Eight vials labeled with the names of my sisters. I held Magdalene's up and it was empty. A cold chill ran down my spine.

"That bitch used Magdalene's hair to summon the spider," Lucia said, anger coloring her words. "We should kill her now."

"We need to stay focused," I said, fighting to not let my emotions take over. With an effort, I shoved them aside. Revenge had to wait until we'd stopped the demon lord.

I checked each vial, and they all contained hair until I got to mine. It was empty as well. Had it already been used, or did Sasha have plans for it that we'd interrupted? Lucia shook her head as she took the vial from my fingers but said nothing.

I set the wallet on the floor. Lucia returned the empty vial and re-rolled the wallet as I brought out the next item, a ceremonial dagger. I pulled the blade free of the scabbard, revealing the runes that ran down the blade. I reversed the knife and handed it to Lucia, not trusting my translation skills.

She held the knife up and examined it. "It is dedicating the life the knife takes to its master Mammon. Well, at least we know who Zental is now." She sheathed the blade and set it aside.

Knowing we weren't facing Lucifer himself lifted a weight off my shoulders. Mammon was the Lord of Greed and one of the most powerful demons in Hell. It made sense he'd be making a play for all of the souls on this realm. Nothing ever satiated the Lord of Greed.

The last thing in the box was the necklace Heather had been wearing the night she was murdered. My heart sank as I realized that Sasha could never come back from the darkness she'd taken into herself. She'd killed in the name of hell and had damned her soul in the process. There could be no release to the universe for her. Her essence wouldn't return to the magick that had given her everything. She'd set up her sister to be murdered in exchange for immortal life.

Tears ran down my cheeks as I handed the necklace to Lucia, who sobbed openly as we held each other. There could be no truce. We were at war and the only acceptable outcome was a total victory or to die trying.

To do that, we needed Belinda and Nao back. Tonight they would return home, no matter how many people I had to go through to get them.

I needed to call in the big gun, Gareth.

32

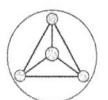

I found Gareth in his training studio behind the garage. He pummeled the heavy bag with a ferocity that bordered on manic. His shirt was off, and his body glistened with sweat. I swear his six-pack had a six-pack of its own. I pushed my thoughts away, though it wasn't easy.

I cleared my throat to get his attention, a sure sign he was distracted, given no one ever snuck up on him. He turned to face me, sweat running down his face from the intense workout. "Jess, sorry I didn't hear you come in. What can I do for you?"

"Does the bag owe you money?"

He laughed. "No, just working off my anger. Ever since Maggie died…"

I nodded, kicking myself for not checking on him more. He'd lost the woman he'd been with for over three hundred years. People forget themselves when someone they love died. What was the appropriate reaction after losing someone you'd been with for a virtual eternity? I mentally shook myself. Time for all that later. We had to beat Mammon or none of this would matter.

I handed him Heather's necklace. He stiffened as he realized what it was. "Where did you get this? It wasn't on her body."

I took a deep breath. "Sasha's room."

"I told you that you should have killed the fucking bitch." He handed back the necklace and resumed his assault on the unarmed punching bag.

"What's done is done. Sasha was in league with Mammon. They've got Nao and Belinda. We have to free them. I need your help."

He did a series of quick jabs before unleashing a vicious undercut. I'd sparred with Gareth over the years, but I'd never seen him bring this kind of fury before. It was a good reminder that our friendly neighborhood handyman was a dangerous guy. "What good am I against magick? I'm a warrior, not Harry Potter."

I shook my head. "You're a lot more than that if you've been with Magdalene for so long. We need to get into One World Brewing and free our two sisters. Tonight, before they discover that Sasha has been removed. I don't know what we'll face. It may be human thugs with weapons and no magick. I'm asking for your help and hope you won't turn me down."

He snorted, repeating the series of blows, each repetition faster until his hand blurred as he struck. "Jess, I have no doubt you could clear the room and not get blood on your Vans, but I take your point. Count me in."

I sighed with relief. Even if Gareth couldn't help us, I'd feel better with him at my back. My sisters weren't exactly the 501st. "Lucia introduced me to your angel tear bullets. They would be a good addition to your weapon, just in case."

He stopped punching and moved until he stood in front of me. I could smell him, but not in the 'gross, you've got BO' way. Sweat ran over him as he met my gaze. I swear sparks flew between us, and I didn't look away. He nodded to me. "Got it. What time are we rolling out?" The gleam in his eyes frightened me but in a good way. Gareth was ready to avenge Magdalene as much as I was.

"Place closes at midnight. Leave here at eleven, set up, and enter just before closing. After the staff leaves, it's party time."

"I like how you think. I'll have the truck ready." He turned to get his towel from the bench by the wall. That was my cue to leave before things went any further. After one last look at his sweaty body, I returned to the house for a cold shower and other preparations to get my sisters back. It was going to be a long night.

At eleven, we met in the garage as planned. Gareth wore a loose-fitting jacket over a black tee and jeans. His Agram 2000 pistol hung from a shoulder strap. He'd have three or four knives on his person somewhere. Nice to know he'd be there if anything went wrong.

He plucked one of the two small paper bags from the hood of the trunk. He tossed me one.

"A gift for me? I didn't get you anything." I pulled a new karambit with a shoulder harness out of the bag.

"I made Gabe replace the dragon claw since it melted. He guaranteed you won't be able to melt this one."

I took the blade out of the sheath. The black surface glimmered in the overhead light of the garage. The curve arced around to allow slicing on the backstroke as well. "I love it. What's it made from?"

He scratched his chin. "Gabe said it's a thunderbolt crafted from a meteor strike in Sedona. The coven there recovered it and sold part of it to him. Myriam inscribed it with runes of piercing and purity. Should do a number on any demons you come across."

Vada arrived a few minutes later wearing a long dark coat over her outfit. She looked ready for a night of clubbing, not assaulting a hostage site. "I have what I will need." She glanced at the karambit. "That is a beautiful knife. Did Gabe craft it for the occasion?"

"He did," Gareth replied, handing the second bag to Vada. She removed a long, thin stiletto blade from the bag. The blade was the sister to mine, but elegant and deadly, like Vada.

"Thank you, Gareth." She slid the knife back into the sheath then secured it inside the right knee-high boot she wore. She fastened it in place and murmured a spell over it. "Can't have it coming loose, now, can we?"

"No, that would be unladylike." I set my knife in place under my jacket, and we climbed into the truck to drive into Asheville.

Gareth parked on Patton Street to wait. Farm Burger and Salsas were already closed, which helped keep down the civilian count. Fifteen minutes before eleven, Gareth, Vada, and I strolled down the alley that led to One World. A shaggy-haired bouncer sat on a molded plastic chair outside the door. We waited as two hipsters stumbled out, almost falling on the bouncer. He pushed them off while we waited. "We're closing in fifteen, but you have time for a quick one." He didn't bother to check our IDs.

"Man, you fucking carded us," one of the hipsters yelled as we entered the brewery. Since I did day tours of the breweries, I hoped I wouldn't run into anyone I knew, but I had a skull cap, large glasses, and leather jacket to reduce the chances further.

We descended the three levels into the main taproom. There were a few last call types still at the bar, finishing off their drinks. Gareth ordered three lagers and we took a place by the thrown together stage that was empty at this point. The rest of the room consisted of a bunch of tables, the fermentation tanks, and brewing equipment behind a half wall and a couple of bathrooms. Where they had my sisters, I wasn't sure, but they had to be here.

We sipped at our beers until we weren't being watched. I triggered the spellstone that Nao had created for me a long time ago. The bartenders didn't notice that we vanished from sight. We stood next to the dartboards, invisible to anyone watching.

The taproom closed and the staff cleaned up. It took about an hour for them to finish, though we had to endure watching a vigorous make out session between the two bartenders before they left. Once the lights were off and everything was quiet, we got to work.

Gareth unholstered his Agram 2000 which he'd trained me on as part of my schooling. I had a Glock in my shoulder harness that I pulled out, just in case. I flipped off the safety but kept my finger away from the trigger. Gareth had drilled trigger discipline into my head until it hurt.

We searched the taproom in a manner of minutes but found nothing. Lucia had checked again and the phones were still here. Behind the bar, there were two sets of old stairs, but they were blocked by the HVAC ducts. Willow's Dream had a pocket dimension behind the corrugated metal "door;" my guess was they had the same here. Motioning for Gareth and Vada to follow, I took the steps up and banged my head on the pipes. I ran my hands along the area, searching for a way to open a secret door, but didn't find anything.

"Not sure what you're doing, but I didn't think you could phase through solid wood," Gareth said as I took the steps down.

"I'm not Kitty Pryde if that's what you're suggesting."

"I don't know what that means." Gareth's perplexed expression almost made me laugh, but it wasn't the time. He must not be interested in those new-fangled things called comic books.

Lucia had pinpointed the phones' position, but GPS didn't count for height. Up or down? "I'll explain later. Let's check the other side."

We rounded the bar and I took the steps up, putting my hand out in front of me this time. As I reached the third step I went through the ducts and passed into a dark room. A single light bulb swung lazily from a chain in the center of the room. This was what Pallavi had seen in her divining.

Gareth stepped in front of me, crouching as he entered the darkened space. I whispered *Sentio* and touched him, granting him the night vision along with me. The room came into focus as the spell took effect.

There were two metal beds in the back corners of the room. A table and two chairs stood at the other end along with a toilet against the far wall. A figure sat chained to the closest bed, two ponytails hanging down from her head. I scanned the other bed, but it was empty.

Gareth stalked toward the occupied bed, the Agram's barrel just below level. He swept the room as he went. I had the Glock in my hand as I brought up the rear with Vada between us. Nothing stirred in the room as we crept across it to Belinda, who was also gagged and blindfolded, presumably to make it harder for her to escape. A creak in the floorboard stopped us cold. We waited, watching the darkness, but still nothing moved. I'd expected to fight our way through humans or demons, but creeping through the poorly lit room was far more nerve-racking than any fight. I almost longed for the demons to attack.

Vada removed the stiletto blade from the boot sheath as we waited. The blade virtually glowed with radiated power under the single bulb. This place was straight out of central casting for a horror movie. I shuddered at the thought.

We reached the center of the room, Gareth holding up his hand to stop. He moved so his back was to Belinda and motioned Vada to go past him. The Agram swung back and forth as he waited for resistance, but none materialized. I turned so I held the stairwell in my field of vision, shoulder to shoulder with Gareth.

We stepped back toward Belinda, each covering a portion of the room. Vada stayed close until we reached the end of the beds. Gareth took a knee at the corner of Belinda's bed and I took the empty one. Nothing moved in the room. Vada got to Belinda and removed her blindfold then the gag from her mouth.

"What are you doing here? It's a trap."

That was when all hell broke loose, literally.

33

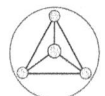

A loud crack announced the demons had arrived. "Get her free," I told Vada, who was already doing it. The ceiling in the center of the room gave way. A cloud of plaster, dust, and who knows what else billowed out from the collapse. I choked as the dust invaded my nose, mouth, and eyes. I heard the others coughing as I wiped at my eyes to clear them.

Growls came from the plaster cloud. As the silt settled, I could make out a vague shape in the center of the room. A low snarl reverberated through the space as it moved toward us. Gareth recovered enough to unleash the Agram at the thing. A series of short bursts deafened me as he fired into the hulking figure that emerged from the cloud.

The head of a crocodile balanced on a bipedal body, its jaw jutting out and full of razor-sharp teeth. Its long tail slashed back and forth as it stared at us. It was built like an Olympic bodybuilder on steroids. It growled again as I readied to fight.

"Zental offers you safe passage to discuss joining his army to conquer the humans, Jessica." Its words slurred in a mouth built for crushing prey, not discussing an offer of surrender.

"Don't you mean Mammon? We know who is behind Zental's mask." In my peripheral vision, Vada worked on freeing Belinda from the manacles that held her to the wall.

It barked a laugh. "He said you would figure it out. Took long enough." Great, I was being insulted by a crocodile. I was really looking forward to kicking its ass.

"And if I say no?" I asked, buying time for Vada to release Belinda. We might have to run for it. "What then?"

The demon snarled. "Then I am to eat you and any you brought with you. I'm hoping you agree. Humans taste awful."

"I'd hate to upset your delicate stomach," I said, though my sarcasm was lost on the thing.

"Just taste bad, no other issue," it explained. "You come with me now."

"And what about my friends? What will you do to them?" Metal clanged as one of the manacles came free, followed by the second. Belinda was clear. I glanced over my shoulder as Vada helped her to her feet.

"I do nothing, but they eat humans. Like the taste."

I searched the room with my eyes and didn't see anything until I looked up. Five ghouls clung to the tops of the wall, heads tilted toward the floor with glowing red eyes fixed on us. Their gray-green skin had a sickly molted effect that implied disease. Their faces were so taut that they had no lips to cover the rows of shark's teeth in their mouths. This was getting worse by the second. "Where is Nao? I won't agree if she's not returned to me first."

The croc grunted. "Master has her someplace else. Now you come or they eat all you." It snapped its jaw shut to emphasize the point.

"Belinda, can you take care of the ghouls?" I whispered over my shoulder.

"Answer now," the croc said, stepping closer. Its nostrils flared as it sniffed the air, head weaving back and forth.

Belinda's voice sounded off. "They gave me something to stop me from using my magick."

I whispered *Robur*, feeling the strength of the earth fill me. "I've considered and you can shove Mammon's offer up your ass."

"Aw, now I have to eat you." It lunged, jaws opening wide. Gareth unloaded the Agram directly into its gaping maw. Against the armored skin, the bullets hardly had any effect, but the angel tears striking the soft tissue was another story. The demon reared back as the bullets punched into its mouth and throat. Black ichor sprayed from the wounds.

It righted itself and moved more cautiously this time. A hiss from above warned me in time to bring the Glock up and fire two shots into the head of a ghoul that clung to the ceiling above us. It screamed in pain as it retreated back to where the others clustered behind the croc. Six on three weren't great odds. Belinda could have reduced the ghouls to ash in a matter of seconds.

The demon's tail lashed against the floor in anger. Ichor dripped over its long fangs from the bullet wounds. It charged in, ready to knock us over with its sheer size. Its arm slashed at my head, but I blocked the wrist. I wasn't a black belt like Gareth, but six years of training had taught me a thing or two.

Not enough, though. The left fist slammed into my shoulder. I spun, dropping to the floor from the force of the blow, my Glock skittering across the ground. Gareth leaped over me and opened up with the Agram. I'd thought the bullets would drop a demon in his tracks, but not this one.

Vada stood behind me, summoning. In her hands appeared a shining silver sword. As the croc circled Gareth, she lashed out, slicing it across the left shoulder. Smoke poured from the wound as the monster roared in dismay. It backed away from the invocation witch. She jumped over me, pressing her attack.

"Watch out," I yelled as a ghoul launched itself from the wall, landing on top of Vada. She collapsed in a heap on the floor. The ghoul swiped with long curving talons, tearing into her coat and leaving furrows of blood behind. I got to my feet and kicked it in the face as it attempted to bite my sister. Its head snapped back as the blow landed.

The ghoul hissed at me then launched itself, mouth wide open. The Glock went off behind me. Five bullets struck the ghoul in the face. Its head exploded in a gout of black sludge and the body fell at my feet. I turned to see Belinda holding the pistol with both hands. "Nice gun, pulls to the right a bit. I'm going to use this if you don't mind."

I smiled at her. "Welcome back, I've missed you. Consider the gun yours." I reached down and pulled Vada to her feet. The homecoming was short-lived as the croc knocked Gareth into us. "*Ignis*," I shouted, pouring my energy into the spell. My firebolt struck the massive demon in the chest, driving it back. "Kill the ghouls while I keep the lizard busy."

Belinda moved off to my right, pistol barking as she took down a creature that had gotten too close. Vada fought another with the sword, leaving rents that bled smoke when she landed a blow. Gareth circled to my left, two knives out, waiting for an opening.

"We do this wolf style," Gareth called as he dodged a swipe of croc's talons. "Whoever has its back attacks and retreats."

I shot another firebolt into the demon's head, staggering it. Gareth darted in low, slicing the backs of the monster's left leg. It would have worked perfectly except the tail lashed out and sent him spinning across the room and into the wall. Blood ran down his face from the impact. I hoped he was okay, but if we didn't beat the demons none of us would live to see tomorrow.

The Glock spit death at another ghoul before I heard the hammer strike the empty chamber. The croc took advantage of my distraction and landed a swipe across my stomach. Fire lanced through me as the skin tore and the blood ran down. The demon raised its fist for another blow. I spat out the first spell that crossed my mind. "*Rima.*"

A loud cracking preceded a scream of fury and agony from the gator. *Rima* was used to break rocks in half. I had managed smaller rocks before, but with the earth sigil, I exercised a much larger magical load. The scales up and down the demon tore apart, not just snapping in half, but crumbling like week-old bread under a sledgehammer. Ichor leaked from a million cuts as the demon's stone scales broke down to nothing.

I jumped as a shining blade emerged from the chest of the demon, black blood spewing from the wound like Old Faithful in Yosemite. Belinda knelt next to Gareth, holding a cloth to the gash in his head. The sword retracted and the croc dropped over, smoke pouring off it as it returned to the nether realms.

"Thanks, that was touch and go for a minute," I said to Vada, who was soaked with the foul blood. Somehow, she pulled it off. "I thought it had me."

"Inspired use of your earth magick. I will dispatch the other ghouls. No need leaving them for the authorities to find." Vada said, saluting me with her sword.

"It's a pocket dimension, they'll never find it." Then I heard sirens pulling up outside. Someone must have called the police after all the noise.

Vada smiled. "It's not a pocket dimension, just a hidden room. I will be a moment."

"Belinda and I will get Gareth ready to go." I started to leave when a shiny silver item caught my eye. The croc must have had it, but its body had dissolved to nothing. It was a long silver needle. I took it and slid it into my jacket pocket. Why would a demon have a needle?

Gareth had come to but looked a mess. The cut on his scalp was deep and would need Lucia's assistance since the hospital was a no go. I still held the earth's strength so I lifted him to his feet, his arm over my shoulders.

Vada returned the sword to wherever she summoned items from. "I saw a window we can exit into an alley. We should come out on Patton near the truck."

We followed her out the first-floor window and down the trash-strewn alley. It took a few minutes to get Gareth to the car since we didn't want to be seen by any upstanding citizens while covered in blood and gore. Vada drove while I sat in the back holding the cloth the Gareth's head. Belinda rode shotgun.

Vada pulled into traffic and away from the scene of the crime. Belinda looked back. "Thank you for rescuing me. I wasn't sure—"

I cut her off. "Belinda, you are my sister and I love you. I know we've not gotten along well, but things have changed. Everything else that's happened isn't important. Our coven is what matters."

She stared at me, disbelief in her eyes with a touch of hope. "I've been awful to you, blaming you for those people's deaths when we fought the hounds."

"And I've been awful back." I adjusted the makeshift bandage on Gareth's head as he stared out the window in a daze. "We are sisters now and forever."

She smiled at me for the first time I could remember. "Thanks, Jess."

Vada cleared her throat. "There have been some changes in your absence we should tell you about."

Vada's serious tone after our semi-heartfelt exchange made Belinda quit smiling. "What happened?"

"A great deal, but the significant thing is that Magdalene…" Her voice cracked. "She was lost to us."

"Oh." From the back seat, I could see Belinda's jaw working as she fought not to cry. "I think I knew. I knew it had to be bad."

"And you should know Sasha betrayed us," I said, to redirect her emotions. Not that Belinda didn't deserve time to grieve, but as much as I had fought with Belinda, she had always been a direct and to the point woman. She would not want things cushioned for her. "She is somewhere…safe. The others have asked me to serve as leader until this is over."

"What?" Belinda said, looking between us, waiting for us to laugh at the joke. It would have been ill-timed humor at best. When it didn't come, she sighed. "I guess I've got some catching up to do…Mother."

I looked to the heavens for help. "The only thing you'll call me is Jessica or Jess. When this mess is over, we are picking a new coven leader and it won't be me."

At least I hoped it wouldn't.

34

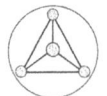

I cast *robur* again and carried Gareth into the basement. Guilt over his injuries was like a spike through my heart. Gareth was trained to fight people, not demons summoned from hell. The little voice in the back of my head told me we'd have lost if he hadn't been there, but a flood of heartache and guilt washed over it, drowning it on the spot.

Lucia and Pallavi sat at the circle since Vada had called ahead to warn them we needed healing. With Belinda back and now able to access her magick, we had a partial circle to heal Gareth. I set him in the center of the pentagram and took my place next to Lucia. Vada sat on my right and grasped my hand. Belinda completed the circle as Lucia intoned her spell.

Gareth's skin paled in the candlelight. I wondered how much blood he'd lost on the way here. Lucia would heal him, and after a few days, he'd be back to new. Witches mended faster in a circle since their own magick accelerated the process. The spell would fix the worst of the damage and we'd have to let Gareth's body do the rest. I should have never taken him against the demons.

I opened myself to the circle, feeling my magick merge with my sisters as Lucia focused our combined energies to heal Gareth. Her voice grew stronger as she wove the spell, crafting it to mend Gareth's wounds. The magic did more than that. I felt the place the croc slashed me knit back together as the spell intensified.

Lucia's fingers tightened on mine as her voice rose, a note of panic tinging her chant. Something was wrong.

Gareth lay in the circle and the blood had stopped, but his head thrashed back and forth as if he was trapped in a nightmare. He groaned loudly. His arms covered his head like he was protecting himself. Lucia ended the spell. When I looked at her, her face was flush and damp with perspiration. She caught my eye.

"The magick can't bond to him correctly. It's like something is blocking the spell from healing him fully. It sort of worked." Concern colored her face. "I've never dealt with anything like this."

This was not good. Magdalene had mentioned that he had secrets. Was this due to those secrets or some strange poison in the demon's claws?

Gareth fought to get himself to a seated position with Belinda assisting him. I stood and helped Belinda get our handyman ninja warrior upright. The blood slowly seeped from his wound, but it was mostly healed.

After a lot of wrangling, we got Gareth into his room above the garage. Lucia arrived with a first aid kit. She cleaned and bandaged the wound the human way, taking time to make sure the bleeding had stopped and checked for broken bones. After she was done, Belinda and I helped him to bed. Using a hospital always caused problems, but it would be far better than for Gareth's wound to become infected and make it worse. Hopefully Lucia's magic combined with her medic expertise would be enough for us to avoid that.

"Well, that was fun. Count me in for the next fight." All three of us crossed our arms as one. "Seriously, thank you for patching me up. I took a hard knock to the head. That croc was faster than I gave it credit for."

Belinda sniffed. "Demons are always stronger and faster than they look. I appreciate the risk you took in coming to free me." Something had changed with Belinda since she'd been captured, but I couldn't put my finger on it. I needed to talk to Gareth, but Belinda was a close second in priorities.

"Can you gather everyone in the meeting room? We still need to find Nao and catch Belinda up on the situation. I'll be there in a moment." I watched as they left together. Belinda stayed as close to Lucia as possible, as if she couldn't bear to be left alone for one second. I worried about her, but then again, I worried about all of us.

I sat on the bed next to Gareth and put my hand on his. "How are you feeling?" I studied the drawn lines of his face, the tired slump of his shoulders. A million questions raced through my head, but the last thing I needed to do was rush him.

"What happened with the demons?" His color had returned to close to normal. The tightness around his eyes betrayed the pain he was in.

I ran down the rest of the fight. He asked a couple of questions along the way but seemed satisfied with the outcome. I decided to dive in and ask, since the worst he could do was say no, at least in the condition he was in. "Lucia tried to heal you, but she said something blocked her from doing so. Any ideas why?"

He sighed, letting his chin drop to his chest. "I should have told you after Maggie died and you were selected coven leader. Probably would have told one of the others if they'd been chosen. But I just couldn't find the right moment."

I sat back, stunned. "I thought we were close. What the fuck, Gareth. I've—"

"Jess, stop." He waited for minute before he continued. "Telling one of the others would have been easier since I don't care what they think of me. I trained each of them because Maggie forced it on them. You were the only willing one."

I was confused. Wanting to learn to fight made me someone he couldn't trust with a secret? "What would that have to do with anything?"

"We are close, far closer than I should have allowed you to become. I'm afraid when I tell you my tale, you'll despise me and send me away. I could handle that from anyone else, but not you." His eyes met mine and I understood; Magdalene's death had freed him. My heart skipped a beat at the thought of us being together.

I moved farther onto the bed, pushing his legs out of the way. "Tell me. I can't promise anything, but I know who you are now which counts for a lot."

"I'll tell you, even though it may destroy anything between us." He pushed the pillow behind his back and resettled. "My name is Achan and I was born in the years before Christ. I lived in a small town in what is now Iran. Nomads raided our village on a night while I was guarding the flock. My whole family was slaughtered and my daughter was taken by slavers. The archangel Rafael came to me and offered me the power of God to wreak vengeance on the slavers, but it could only be used against the wicked. I went to the camp and killed all of the slavers, but in my bloodlust I killed my daughter and all of the slaver's families. I couldn't stop myself. By spilling the blood of a truly innocent souls, I lost everything."

"I'm so sorry, Gareth . . . or should I call you Achan?" My heart wanted to break, thinking of the horrors of killing your own child.

He shook his head slowly. "I was a monster that day and punished for it. It's been so long; I can't even see her face." He cleared his throat. "Anyway, when I was done killing, Rafael came to me again. I begged him to restore my daughter. She was all I had left. He refused and instead cursed me with everlasting life so I could properly pay for my sins."

"You're immortal?" Witches lived a long time; we eventually died of old age or willed ourselves back to the universe. But Gareth was another age altogether. He had to be over two thousand years old.

"The curse would last until I had taken enough lives of evil men to balance the scales. There was another catch. When I get old or hurt, I need to transfer bodies, taking another as my own." He held my eye as what that meant sunk in.

"What happens to the person you trade with?" I asked, but I knew. This was why he hadn't wanted to tell me.

"They die." No artifice, no excuses, just the facts. It was one of the reasons we got along so well.

"Oh."

His eyes dropped to the blankets. "For centuries, I stole bodies from the rich or from people who had what I wanted, convinced that I would never be free of the curse. Then I met Maggie. She took me in, taught me control, and loved me for who I was. When I need a new body, I take one from a truly evil person and return to the coven to help any way I can."

"What happens if you refuse to transfer to a new body?"

"The older I get, the more the hunger for a new body drives me until I can't control it and take the closest one. If I am injured severely enough to die, the same thing happens—the closest person to me becomes my new shell. Once I shot myself in the head in the middle of nowhere, trying to end it all. I took over a farmer fifty miles from where my body was. Rafael's curse is infallible."

Technically Gareth was a murderer, but he no longer had a choice, no more than a praying mantis could control eating its mate. Could I feel safe around someone that could accidentally kill me if they were injured? What of the coven's safety? Did they have the right to know the truth? Questions ricocheted through my brain, but in the end, Magdalene had trusted Gareth. That would have to be enough for me.

"This doesn't change anything as far as I'm concerned. I'd rather you tell the coven, but also understand your need for secrecy. Once I'm not the leader anymore, I will tell my replacement if you won't." I reached over and squeezed his hand.

Tears gathered in his eyes as he squeezed my hand in return. "Jess, you don't know how much this means to me. Maggie was the only one who could accept me. Everyone else I've ever told rejected or tried to kill me."

Trying to kill him seemed unwise, especially if you did it yourself and did a good job of it, because suddenly Gareth's curse would transfer him to your body.

"Here, we're all outcasts of one type or another. You belong here." I looked at his bandaged head. "Will that cause you to need a new body?"

"I don't think so, but if it does, I'll leave. I won't risk you just to stay here." He tightened his grip on my hand.

I leaned forward and kissed his forehead. "Get some rest. I need to find out where Nao is before the new moon." Only four days remained. I had to discover a way to defeat Mammon without laying waste to Asheville. Time was running out faster than the answers were coming. I wanted to stay, but my sisters needed me more than ever.

If there was a better time for an ice-cold beer, I didn't know it.

35

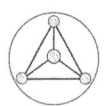

I met the sisters in the meeting room with a full glass of Hi-Wire Bed of Nails in one hand and a bag of potato chips in the other. I was tired, hungry, and ready to turn the leading over to someone who was qualified. I flopped in my chair and drank my beer. I looked up to find my sisters smiling at me.

"What?"

"If you're drinking beer, things are better than they seem," Pallavi answered.

"Or worse." I considered for a moment. "Or I'm just thirsty. So, we have a few things to discuss." I held up my hand, counting off as I went. "I'm going to guess Sasha had something to do with Belinda and Nao being captured since she lied to us about you running off." Belinda nodded. "But we still need to know where Nao is since she wasn't with Belinda. How do we stop Mammon from coming through to our realm? And finally, if he does, how do we send his greedy ass back?"

A nervous round of laughs was better than I expected. We had four days and were down three sisters. Our Spiritualist had been killed by a demon. There wasn't any calvary, just the five of us. If we could find Nao, we'd be at six, and with magick, threes were always better.

"I suggest we begin," Vada said. She'd changed from the torn clothes from the fight into a sweatshirt and leggings. "We are running out of time in which to find Nao or we will have to face whatever comes with who we have."

Belinda's hair was down and she had deep, dark circles under her eyes. "They moved her earlier when they set the trap for you. From what I overheard, they need three witches' blood to cast the spell." She pushed back her sleeve showing a scab where she'd been cut. "I'm sure Nao has one as well."

"I don't think Sasha had any cuts, so they may be one witch short," I said, stopping to sip at my beer. "Regardless, I refuse to leave Nao with them for a second longer than necessary."

"Now that we realize Lucia finding their phones was part of the trap, how do we find our lost sister without any traces of her to follow?" Pallavi said. "I doubt the demons will set another trap to lure us in."

Lucia spoke up. "I can create a finding spell to track her. It will take me at least a day to assemble the parts and ready the spell. With five of us, we have enough to fully power the magick. That's why we couldn't do it sooner."

I nodded. Lucia had turned into the bedrock of the coven since Magdalene had died or maybe she always had been and I hadn't paid enough attention. "Pallavi, stay with Lucia when she goes out, but start in the morning. Everyone needs sleep, especially Belinda. You look like you're about to fall over."

"I'm fine, Jess," she said, stifling a yawn. "I feel so stupid for not realizing Sasha was behind all of this. When the spider demon hit us, she silenced, bound, and covered us with illusions so you couldn't see us. I couldn't break free of the spell."

"Sasha's strength is vastly underrated because of her craft." Vada pushed her hair back from her face. "Even to the coven, illusions are treated as lesser magick than divination or spiritual magicks, but they can be quite deadly in the correct hands."

"She also disguised herself as Gerwin Aaker and told me and Vada I was going to die," I said, for Belinda's benefit. "And I have a suspicion she disguised herself or someone as Belinda when she attempted to break into Willow Dream a few nights ago."

"She fooled us all," Lucia said. "I thought Nao had summoned the demon lord since we found the talisman. We were all noobs."

"Let's talk about how to stop Mammon, and then everyone gets some rest. We can't rescue Nao if we are all too tired to work our magick."

For the next two hours, we discussed various ways of defeating demons and closing portals. I didn't bring up the *Deleo Ianua* because if we needed it, we'd already lost. In the end, we weren't any closer to finding an answer than when we started. I hugged each of my sisters and wished them a good night. Belinda whispered "thank you" in my ear as I hugged her. I kissed her on the cheek before she stumbled up to sleep in her own bed.

I took my glass to the kitchen and put it in the dishwasher and placed the empty bag of chips in the trash. Someone had left a light on in the garage. As I exited, I noticed the door to Gareth's bay stood open. I walked over to find him loading a couple of bags into the back of his truck.

"Leaving without saying goodbye?"

He flinched as his head came up and he saw me standing there. A guilty expression crossed his face. The bandages were gone, though the angry red of the wound remained. "I left a note upstairs for you explaining everything."

"A note? We're good, then. Far better than telling me to my face. I could see the appeal." I knew I wasn't being fair, but I was hurt, tired, and more than a little scared, and now Gareth was heading for the hills. Granted he'd been through a lot, but I didn't fucking care about being reasonable at this point. "Just when things get tough, you run off? What would Magdalene think?"

He reared back as if I'd slapped his face. "That's not fair. I lost someone I'd been with for centuries." He crossed his arms. "Maggie would have understood because she knew I needed to leave to protect the people I love."

It was my turn to be shocked. "Protect us? How?" When I moved closer to him, I could read the pain that laced his eyes. Once again, I'd jumped the gun and spoken when I should have listened. "Maybe we should start at the beginning."

"If we're going to talk, we should do it inside. You're shivering." He took my arm and led me up to his apartment. His rifle case and two other small bags sat on the bed. On the pillow sat a folded piece of paper with my name. "I thought it would be easier for both of us if I left without a scene."

"Scene?" I raised my eyebrows, challenging him to double down on the use of the word. I stepped to the bed and snatched the note. I resisted tearing it in half.

He shook his head. "Wrong word. Nothing makes sense around you."

He dropped on the bed. "I told you about my curse, but there is something else. There is something wrong with this body."

"What do you mean' wrong'?" I asked, a bit more harshly than I should have. "You're injured. It will heal."

"It's not the physical wound," Gareth started.

I cut him off before he could say more. "You live with a coven of witches. We can heal whatever the demon did to you."

Gareth stared at his feet. "The demon tainted me somehow and I can feel it growing. I have to change bodies soon or I'm not sure what will happen."

I stayed where I was, arms folded and listening. "Go on."

He sighed. "It will take a few days to find a person that won't be missed. With all the surveillance and tracking, I also have to go to a mage and get my fingerprints and appearance altered, so I'm not stuck with that person's old life. It will also take a while for me to process their existence and be fully me again. I retain a lot of their memories when I first do the transfer."

"Are you coming back?" I really didn't want that answer, but I needed to hear it. I hated how much I wanted him to say yes. I refused to react either way.

He chewed his bruised lip for a second. He closed the distance between us, sitting next to me on the bed. "Do you want me to?" Across from me sat a man who was over two thousand years old, who could take bodies at will, asking me like a scared teenage boy if I'd go to the prom with him.

"Yes."

He nodded, a grin sneaking into place, and kissed me gently on the lips. "Then I'll be back. Any requests?"

"Requests?"

He laughed. "Jess, I can take anybody I choose. I usually picked military types so I'd be ready to protect Maggie without having to bulk back up. Now…"

"No requests, I want you here for you." I paused for a second, grinning like an idiot. I kissed him before saying, "If you could keep the six-pack that would be nice."

"I'll try my best." His face went serious. "Usually I go to a war zone and a soldier goes MIA. I'll have to be extra careful this time."

"You will come back?" I kicked myself for sounding so desperate, so needy. I'd had boyfriends before, but they weren't part of my real life and fell to the side without much regret. The thought of not hiding my abilities from a partner was a powerful draw, not to mention the crush I'd had on Gareth since I'd arrived at the coven.

"I will. As soon as it's safe to do so."

He tried to stand, but I'd made my mind up. I tackled him before he was upright, pushing him back on the bed and kissing him. He kissed me back with a passion that surprised me and threatened to pull me under. His hands moved down my body as I wrapped my arms around his neck.

He pulled away. "Jess, I have to leave no matter how much I want to stay."

"I know, but I want this and if you never come back, I will remember this for the rest of my life." I resumed kissing him, and this time there was nothing stopping us. He kicked the bags off the bed and pulled me on top of him fully. I could feel the muscles through his chest tighten as his arms wrapped around me.

I unbuttoned his shirt, exposing his chest. He pulled his shirt off and removed mine. Our skin burned against each other as the rest of our clothes hit the floor. I lost track of everything. All the worry, fear, and anxiety fled under his touch.

Too bad it couldn't last.

36

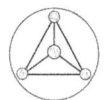

When I woke, Gareth's smell lingered around me. My skin tingled from where he'd touched me, bringing a smile to my face. As I sat up, I saw the note was propped on the dresser. Gareth and his luggage were gone, but I could still feel him on my lips and my body remembered his touch. I silently prayed he'd return soon, but if he never did, we spent our last night the way we'd wanted.

I climbed out of bed and dressed, realizing we only had three days left. On the night of the new moon, everything I knew could be gone in two different ways. I might have to burn Asheville down to prevent Mammon from entering this existence, or I'd fail and evil would destroy everything. I wished for a third option, where I stopped Mammon without using the coin, but I was out of ideas. We also didn't know if there were more people working to bring the demon lord to Earth besides Sasha, but it seemed likely. Sasha alone couldn't have kept Belinda and Nao captive at the brewery.

It was early enough that I didn't expect to have company when I went back in the house. First I passed through the garage, the bay for Gareth's truck empty. He'd be back if the universe willed it. I continued on to the house.

The lights were on in the kitchen as I entered. I became acutely aware that I wore the same clothes as last night. Vada sat at the island, sipping at a cup of coffee. "Is he gone?"

I stopped cold.

She chuckled in her low throaty way. "You could start a fire with all the sparks between you. I'm surprised it took six years."

"Did Magdalene know?"

"Jess, you wear your emotions on your sleeve. Everyone knew but him." She sipped at her coffee. "It is good that he is gone. He is very dangerous."

What did she know? "How do you mean?"

She set her cup down. "Magdalene entrusted me with his secret, thinking that I would be the next leader. I assume he told you?"

I nodded, sitting down next to her on a stool. "He did. I don't think he knew you were aware of his…ahhh… secret. He believes the lizard demon did something to his body, causing it to rot until it dies."

"Demons corrupt everything they touch. Our magick insulates us from most of the effects. If he returns, you must be wary of him."

"Why? Gareth is a good person." I didn't like the direction this was going. Vada had her opinions, but she wasn't my mother telling me who I could be with. I was a full witch and coven leader; I could make my own choices.

"Gareth is…" She lifted her cup for another drink. "Achan is angel-cursed. He is a murderer so many times over, the word has lost its meaning. Mother gave him purpose and set him on a better path, but she was careful with his involvement. She didn't want to endanger anyone. Why do you think he was a weapons coach and handyman instead of helping us in our battles? He could have killed one of us tonight, just by dying. He is the most dangerous person you will ever meet. Think on this before you resume your dalliance with him."

"Wait a minute—"

"No," Vada said, overriding my objections. "You are a grown woman and I do not seek to tell you what to do, but only a fool kisses a cobra without knowing they may die for it. Do you understand?"

"Yes, Vada." It came out far more meekly than I liked. I decided to ask the question that had bothered me since I'd been made leader. "Why didn't you take coven leader for yourself, since Magdalene wanted you to be next?"

She turned the mug around in her hands for a moment. "I am not the leader we need to best the demons. I can be honest with myself that I would like to lead the coven, but I am not a warrior, and we need you and your instincts if we are to fight."

I wished I had as much faith in me as Vada did. "I'll do my best not to let you down. I'm not sure there is a way we can win."

She placed her hand on mine. "Jessica, if we fail, we shall die as intended, wielding our magick in the defense of humanity. We have been set on a path few would willingly tread, but we must accept our fate. You should change before the others awaken."

I hugged Vada and went to my room. After a long shower and a fresh set of clothes, I felt ready to face the challenge ahead. At least as ready as I ever would. A knock on the door brought me back to reality.

I opened the door and Basil stood there. He wore a rainbow-striped shirt and dark slacks. "You were not who I was expecting," I said with a laugh.

He flashed his thousand-megawatt smile at me. "Well, then I'm so sad for you. You should always expect the best." He swept past me into my room, which was a bit messy, but I'd been busy.

"Did I miss the tornado?" He picked up a T-shirt and tossed it aside to sit on the bed. "We need to go see a man about a thing."

"A thing?" I asked, wondering why Basil had decided to grace me with his presence. I hadn't seen him with all the commotion. "Are things okay with Chip?"

He looked at me funny. "Of course they are. Frank Talos called me earlier. He found something strange about the serum we left with him. Up for a ride over to White Labs to see the alchemist?"

I groaned. The things I did to protect the human race. "Fine. If he touches me, I'm punching his fucking lights out."

"Duly noted." Basil bounced up. "You'll have to drive Buttercup. I took the fairy express."

"Should you be using your angelic powers with Heaven looking to recall you?" Basil didn't want to go back to being the strongman for God, and I didn't want that kind of guilt on my conscience. I grabbed my leather jacket, glad that the demon's talons hadn't torn through it. Then I loaded up on all the weapons I could carry since I never knew what would happen anymore—new dagger, apocalypse coin, Elixir of Theron, silencing stone, and a couple of other items.

"The wings are part of me. Using the sword or the voice would be much riskier." He put his arm around me. "Let's go see about a potion."

An hour later we stood back in Talos' lab. The noises from outside the walls grew louder as we waited for him. He pulled a folder with the reports from the serum. "It took a while to figure out what exactly was going on. When I got it down to the component parts, I found something unusual to say the least."

"Well, don't keep us waiting," Basil exclaimed. He was in full-on mode today. I usually associated that with something being wrong, but he hadn't mentioned anything.

"The serum contains Jess's DNA, but underlying it was the components of the actual healing factor. The serum was meant to react only to you, and something corrupted it. I ran some tests on the piece of glass." He flipped through a few pages, skimming over it with his finger. "Here it is. Whoever made the demon serum with your DNA probably didn't know the vial would corrupt it."

I exhaled since that cleared Lucia. The empty vial that had my name in Sasha's room made sense now. Even with Sasha working for Mammon, the possibility that another sister had turned remained, however unlikely. "Any idea where the vial came from?"

He ran over the sheet again. "There's a large concentration of bauxite in the clay. From the analysis, it looks like the vessel came from either Southern Europe or Africa. I can't be certain. Human bone was another ingredient in the glass, but there were no genetic markers to place the person."

Human bone and bauxite. What a strange combination. "Is there anything else you can tell us?"

Talos reviewed the pages again but shook his head. "Nothing that would prove anything."

Basil dove in. "Talos, at this point guesses are perfectly acceptable."

He shrugged. "If I had to guess, the potion was developed for Jess, but the vial tainted it, so it looked like a hellion serum. The container alone would have set off any angelic presence. If I didn't know any better, I'd say the bottle was built to tip you off to the hellion aspects. Just a guess, since there's no data to back it up."

Why give me a bottle that would trigger a reaction in Basil? We were jumping at shadows as Mammon pulled our strings. Would we ever catch a break or get the upper hand? So far it didn't seem likely, and none of this gave me any insight into finding Nao or defeating the Lord of Greed.

I leaned back against the workbench behind me, waiting as Basil read over the findings with Talos, peering over his shoulder like a helicopter mom. A loud warning siren made me jump out of my skin. "What the fuck was that?"

Talos scurried over and shut down the machine. "Stupid machine is always sounding the alarm when there's nothing around. I need to recalibrate it." His face flushed red. Embarrassment or something else?

"What does it detect?" I asked more out of courtesy than curiosity. Frank hadn't hit on me or gawked, so I played nice. The machine stood about two feet tall with a metal tray under a pyramid structure that had wires soldered to the four intersection sites.

He glanced at me suspiciously. "Why do you want to know?"

I held up my hands. "Just trying to take an interest in your work, Frank." That did the trick.

His eyes lit up like a kid's on Christmas morning, and I groaned inside but kept the smile plastered on my face. "This is a cosmological transducer. It reads items and determines the amount of holy or unholy energy associated with it. Give me an object and I'll show you."

I reached into the pockets of my leather jacket hoping to find loose change when something sharp stabbed into my finger. I pulled it out, a drop of blood welling from the wound. I sucked on my finger for a second.

"What happened?" Basil asked as he looked up from the paperwork. "You cut yourself."

"Yeah, I'm an idiot." I carefully reached into my pocket and retrieved the needle I found while rescuing Belinda. I held it up. "I found this and forgot I put it in my pocket."

Talos blanched. "Where did you get that?" he stuttered as his eyes grew wider.

"I found it the other night. I figured somebody would get stabbed with it and I was right."

Talos stammered out. "That's not a needle, Jess."

I looked at him like he was daft. "Of course it is. What else could it be?"

"It's a key."

Hello, break, welcome home.

37

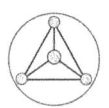

"What exactly do you mean it's a key?" I asked, holding back the happy dance that was about to explode out of me in full Saturday night rave joy.

"May I?" Talos asked, obviously taking no chances with unauthorized touching. When I nodded, he took the needle, walked down the row, and placed it in a new device. "Demon magick is based on lies. Think of this machine as a lie detector." He set the needle on the tray inside the glass enclosure and closed the door. He punched a few buttons and the needle rose and spun in midair. A minute later a solid silver key existed where the needle had been. The machine spun down, depositing the key back on the tray.

"Wow, that was cool." And it was. I liked this version of Frank, though I doubted he could contain the sleazy ladies' man persona for long.

He retrieved the key. "This is its true nature, but the hellions never leave things in their true form." He handed me the key.

It weighed a lot more than the needle had. I passed it over to Basil, who examined it closely. "Could be a key to anywhere in Asheville."

I hoped it was the key to where Nao was being held. Basil returned it to me. "Thank you, Frank."

He smiled like a puppy who'd pleased his master. Maybe I'd misjudged him after all. "If there is anything else I can help with, let me know."

"Will do." Basil followed my lead and we left, out into the cool September weather. The leaves were hitting full color and the leaf peepers were out in droves, appreciating nature before heading back to their track homes and long commutes. I dropped Basil off at his house and then proceeded back to the coven. AC/DC Highway to Hell came on the radio and I was beginning to think a demon had possessed my car stereo. Maybe it was the universe warning me. Either way, it was a good song to drive to.

I parked, not stopping to stare at Gareth's open parking spot, and strode into the house. I yelled up the stairs and Lucia popped her head around the corner. "Bring your kit and everyone meet in the training room. They made a mistake; now we have to exploit it."

Lucia whooped and started banging on doors. I headed to the basement with the key, ready to go get my sister back. Vada and Lucia were the first to arrive. Lucia set her bag down next to the summoning circle and opened it. "What are we doing, oh wise raid leader?"

"Once Belinda and Pallavi get here, I'll explain." Belinda arrived next, followed by a rather damp Pallavi.

"Sorry, I was bathing when Lucia requested our attendance."

I laughed. "We could have waited another few minutes for you to dry off. Anyway, when we found Belinda, the demon croc had a needle that I found when he disintegrated. Talos determined that it is actually a key. My guess is it unlocks where Nao is being held."

"That is wonderful," Vada said as I held up the key like a trophy. "If we can disrupt their plans, we may gain the upper hand."

"We'll need a locater spell to find where the key belongs," Lucia said as she pulled items out of her kit.

"Key?" Pallavi said, her eyes glued to it. I moved the key and she followed.

"Pallavi, you okay?" Belinda asked as she reached up to touch the other woman's forehead.

Pallavi batted her hand away and lunged. "Key. Need key." Her hand latched onto my wrist, pulling it toward her. I lost my balance and tumbled forward. The key slipped loose as I hit the floor, knocking Belinda off her feet. Pallavi dove for the key, both hands wrapping around it.

She spun around and her eyes were solid red. "Key for master," she said, though it was not her voice.

Vada stepped between her and the door. "*Insinuo*," she commanded as

Pallavi charged her. A gold medallion materialized in her hand, glowing with a light so bright it hurt my eyes to look at.

"*Reppulisti repellam te in nomine dei.*" Vada's eyes burned with anger as she held the medallion before Pallavi, who crawled into the corner of the room. She whimpered as Vada closed on her. "*Soror autem relinquo.*"

Pallavi screamed, her back arching in response to the medallion. Her arms flailed as she thrashed on the floor. Something pushed up from her chest, an amorphous blob under the skin. It pulsed red as the thing trembled under Vada's spell.

Vada loomed over our sister and her obviously demonic hitchhiker. "*Relinquit soror mea,*" she screamed, imposing her will on whatever controlled Pallavi. "*Ex turpi bestia.*"

Pallavi's body slumped to the floor unmoving as a specter floated free. The skeletal face worked soundlessly as it hovered over its victim. Energy poured into the ether as it tried to solidify.

The glow from Vada's medallion seemed to trap the entity in a state of flux, and she cast us a frantic glance. "I cannot draw it out for long. It's a leech demon. If I kill it, it could kill her."

Shit, was it worth the risk? No. But I didn't want to have to imprison Pallavi until we could figure out a way to safely remove the hitchhiker.

Magdalene could have done it. Which reminded me...

"Would the Elixir of Theron work?" I asked, presenting the vial from my pocket.

"How did you get that? No, no time to answer." Vada gave a sharp nod. "Pour it on Vi. It must make contact with her skin. But don't let the leech touch you."

Coming at Vi from the top, avoiding the writhing demon, I sprinkled the red liquid on her face.

The reaction was instant.

The thing shrieked, head back as it howled in agony. Its body began to break apart, dissolving before our eyes. I watched until the last pieces had vanished and the medallion went dark.

Lucia ran to Pallavi, checking her pulse. "She's alive. The Elixir worked."

I knew Pallavi was tough, having survived being kidnapped from her native Africa and subsequent enslavement in the pre-Civil War South. She'd escaped to follow the call to her first coven in Canada. Surviving a leech demon just added to her overall badassery. I moved to take her hand as Lucia checked her over. The scent of the Elixir was peppery, mixed with the all too familiar sulfur of the demon.

She woke as Lucia tapped her gently. "Did we lose the key?" she asked in a barely audible voice. "I'm sorry, I tried to fight it."

"You did great," Vada said as she knelt next to Pallavi. "We couldn't have rid you of it if you were not fighting the specter."

"Sasha lured me into a trap and allowed the demon to possess me. I am sorry. I have failed you."

I shook my head. "No, you have shown us that we can beat these demons. If I hadn't had the Elixir of Theron, we'd have thought of something. We need to stay together and fight them."

Vada held the medallion out before her. "Please, sisters, touch the icon. We need to know none of us are tainted."

I placed my hand on the golden disk; nothing happened. Each of my sisters did, in turn, revealing us all to be clear of the demon's touch.

Belinda ran upstairs and brought back a glass of water for Pallavi. She sat up and drank deeply. "I've been trying to break free to warn you, but the leech held me in a prison in my mind. I saw what was happening but could not control my own actions."

"When did this happen?" I asked, skimming back in my mind over my interactions with Vi the past several days. She had not seemed awkward, odd, or anything besides her usual self. Had she relayed information to Mammon that she gleaned from me?

"Three days ago, Sasha asked me to meet her at the portal. When I got there, she unleashed the leech demon on me. I wasn't ready and it took over. I steeled my mind though so Mammon couldn't know our plans."

"Sasha needs to go to the halls for what she has done," Belinda said, acid dripping from her words. "She is a traitor and should pay the price. I will execute her if you won't." The last was directed at me.

"I'd hoped that Sasha could be brought back to us, but if we survive the new moon, we will judge her and sentence her to death as is the coven's way." My heart broke at the thought of killing the woman who brought me soup when I was sick and helped me when I struggled to adapt to my new life here. Had she been beholden to Mammon the whole time? I doubted it. Greed filled Mammon's followers, forcing them to do whatever it took to accumulate more of whatever they sought. Sasha had been warm and giving almost until the end; it had taken an incurable human disease to corrupt her. Still, I'd do what I must do to protect the coven and the nexus.

Lucia returned to setting up her tracking spell for the key as Pallavi pulled herself together. We were going to need counseling after all the trauma we'd endured the past few weeks. I bet I could get us a group discount.

A half an hour later, Lucia was ready. Pallavi insisted she take her place and did, over Lucia's arguments against it. Pallavi was old enough to make her own decisions. We joined hands, the key resting on a golden plate in the center of the circle. I opened myself, allowing my power to join the others as Lucia worked her magick.

As the spell coalesced around the key, it shattered into a million fragments that rained down over the plate. Lucia slumped in defeat.

"The key had a counterspell to resist being used to find where it goes. Without something else, we'll never find Nao in time."

"Would a lock of hair work for that tracking spell you were trying to prep?" I asked, remembering Sasha's case with all the hair samples.

Lucia's head bobbed with enthusiasm. "Sympathetic magick can't be blocked. The part always wants to join the whole. Pallavi and I haven't finished collecting the materials I need, but I can be ready by sundown to cast the spell."

"Vada, take Lucia to get what she needs. Pallavi, you are on bed rest until tonight. I won't risk you overextending yourself when we'll need every ounce of magick come the new moon."

"We'll meet back here at sundown. Belinda, Vada, and I will be leaving as soon as we know where Nao is. Sisters, we'll only have one chance to get her back so let's make it count."

❧

The sun had been down for an hour when we reconvened the circle. Lucia took the vial of hair and set it in a brazier. A map of Asheville sat in the center of the circle, surrounded by the objects Lucia had bought for the spell. A small ball bearing sat on the map to indicate where Nao was being held.

"The demons will be fighting us, so the map will become obscured while I push through their counter magicks," Lucia said, reaching out her hands to both sides.

We joined hands as Lucia pulled from our reserves to channel the energy into the burning fire that contained Nao's hair. The smoke drifted in circles as Lucia fought against the demon's magick, but after an hour the ball bearing rolled around the map in concentric circles, closing in on a location gradually. The ball bearing finally spun in place over a location on Lexington Street.

We had what we needed. Belinda noted the address before she joined Vada and I as we headed toward the BMW. Fuck the Kia rental, I was the mother now. If we were going to fight our way in and out of a demon's lair, we might as well arrive in style. Magdalene would hardly have approved, but as coven leader, I made an executive decision.

The address turned out to be an upstairs loft over a tourist shop that sold all sorts of must-have crap. Pink flamingos warred with silver spinning wind chimes and a sign that said, 'my other house is the bat cave.' If there were wards around the place, none of us could detect them.

I parked the car and tapped the meter for two hours of time. If it expired, a parking ticket was the least of our worries. We strolled down Lexington as casually as possible, dodging people on their phones or lost in conversation with their significant other.

A single staircase led up into the loft which worried me, so we continued along the sidewalk. Another pass from the opposite direction revealed that the loft had a rooftop terrace. We found an alley, filled with dumpsters, debris, yet more tourists taking a shortcut to the next street, and one pissed off cat, which ran directly behind the target.

"Change in plans," I said as I pulled my sisters out of the flow of traffic. "I'm going to climb the wall up to the roof. I'll go in from there as you come in the front door."

"I hate to quote Lucia, but you never split the party," Belinda said after a particularly affectionate couple passed us.

"If they are waiting for us to come up the stairs, I'll get the drop on them. We need to rescue Nao as fast as possible."

Vada sighed. "I don't like it, but it makes sense."

It was time to unleash the witch commandos.

38

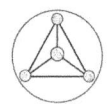

Vada and Belinda window shopped while I made my way to the back of the building. The alley gave me cover from prying eyes so I could climb to the roof unseen. Using *Veni*, I pulled spikes out of the brick and concrete walls to build a DIY ladder. There was enough stone in the building materials that it responded to the spell, and I reached the top in about five minutes. I tiptoed across the open space of the roof, but other than a solid door, nothing was up here.

I examined the door, but no wards or hexes registered. Magick flowed below me, probably the hiding spells they used to mask the location of Nao. Too much magick in one place would be a dead giveaway as to where they were keeping her. I turned the handle and the door opened to reveal a spiral staircase down into a darkened room below. Before I took the plunge, I leaned over the edge of the roof and signaled Vada and Belinda to enter.

The door bumped closed behind me while I descended the staircase. The first stair creaked as I put my weight on it, so I took my time, limiting the noise. I moved down, getting a picture of the loft. A sofa sat against the far wall, with a second parallel to it. A small table and chairs were off to the left of the staircase. A kitchen took up the back corner of the space, flanked by two doors. Glowing runes and glyphs of hiding were inscribed on the walls, illuminating the room enough to see by. Nothing stirred in the apartment.

I reached the main floor just as Vada's head peeked around from the front door. I nodded for them to join me. Vada slunk like a cat across to me. Belinda stayed by the door, her eyes darting around rapidly. Her behavior worried me since I didn't know if she was reacting to magick I couldn't detect or having a panic attack from her captivity.

"Belinda?"

She approached, still nervously scanning the room. "Do you feel it? Death is here, waiting."

"Do you think Nao is dead?" I asked, trying to pinpoint what she was feeling. Her death magick sensed things no one else could.

"I think she's here, but I can't tell if she's alive."

"Vada, check the room on the right; I'll take the left. Belinda, let us know if anything changes." They both nodded. Vada reached her door, opening it slightly. After looking in, she closed it softly. "Someone was here from all the beer cans, but they aren't here now."

Time to see what was behind door number two. I did a quick check for magick and found none. The door opened easily, revealing Nao, strapped to a hospital gurney in the center of the room. An IV drip was attached to her arm, but she was awake, though a gag had been stuffed in her mouth. The room had another door that stood open, revealing a bathroom. There were no windows, just a dresser with a single lamp and a TV on it.

Nao shook her head as I approached. Her face was bruised and her clothes were torn in places and covered in dirt. Her long, dark hair was matted with crusty blood from the cut in her scalp. Just another in the list of things Mammon would pay for when we met.

I released the gag and she coughed for a moment while I detached the bag from her arm. Her voice was rough but she could speak. "You need to leave. They want you, not me."

"Sounds like a plan. Let's leave. Can you walk?" I set to unbuckling the straps that held her in place.

"I think so," she said, anxiety thick in her voice. "Jess, they are going to enslave everyone, but they need you."

"You can tell me later. We need to get you out of here and fast." I finished undoing the last strap and got Nao up and off the gurney. She stumbled a bit as I helped her through the door. As we entered the kitchen, Vada ran over to assist me. Belinda held the door open. The stairwell barely fit one person at a time, so I had Vada lead Nao down to street level first.

Nao held the stair rail and stepped down, Vada in front of her steadying our sister as she fought to use her legs. I motioned for Belinda to follow. Instead, her hands flew over her face and she screamed in terror.

I turned in time to catch the blow on the shoulder instead of my head. I fell to the side, landing hard on the floor of the apartment. Belinda was knocked forward, out the entryway and down the stairwell. The door slammed behind her. A figure moved toward me, a man I knew far too well.

Oak stood over me, a sawed-off baseball bat in his hands. "I told Mammon you'd come for Nao, but they doubted me. Demons don't understand human emotions well."

I pushed myself up only to have Oak kick me in the side, flipping me onto my back. The air forced out of my lungs, I lay gasping and unable to cast. I heard Belinda pounding on the door, yelling my name. At least she hadn't been hurt badly. I rolled to my side, determined to shove a piece of rock through Oak's spleen. He swung the bat and the lights went out.

§●

A none-too-gentle slap woke me from my unintended nap. Oak's ugly face came into view as my eyes adjusted. I was tied to a chair and had a gag in my mouth. I struggled to move, but the ropes held tight.

Oak laughed. "You think I don't know how to tie someone up after all this time?" He pulled a chair over and sat across from me. "Sorry about the gag, but until you're sedated, I can't have you casting spells."

That was good to know. Oak had been around for centuries but hadn't spent much time with witches. Most of us used verbal triggers for spells, but Magdalene had been riding my ass for two years to learn to craft spells without it. I could barely light a candle, but I could do it, eventually. At least with the gag in my mouth, I wasn't distracted by making snappy comebacks.

"I'd hoped that it wouldn't come to this, but Mammon said that you were too strong to let live. He agreed to spare the others, so they'll be safe."

I ignored him, concentrating on crafting *Ignis* in my head. It seemed like a year ago that I'd been sitting in Vortex Donuts and sulking and failing at lighting candle wicks with my brain. If I could get the spell correct, a trickle of power would burn through the ropes. Even the mighty Green Knight couldn't block fire. I imagined all that hair bursting into flames and had to swallow a laugh. The spell fell apart.

Patience and persistence. I started over, building the scaffold of the spell in my mind. Magdalene always said lazy witches relied on verbal cues to use their magick and I fulfilled the description perfectly. The spell fell apart again as my frustration mounted.

"Jess, I'm sorry, but after centuries of being forced into servitude, I'll be free again. Since fucking Merlin cursed me, I can't touch my sword or armor. The Green Knight died that day, replaced by a peasant. I've had to kill some people, but you would have done the same in my shoes."

If my rage could burn any hotter, the ropes would incinerate and take Oak with them. "Heather?" I tried to say, but it came out as a mumble.

Oak's head dropped to his chest. "I killed Heather to prove I would obey Mammon. He wanted to torture her, but I refused. At least she had a clean death. I loved her, but I have to be free of the curse at any cost."

I gripped the gag with my teeth and barely mumbled. Without the gag I could cast, but not with it. "Fucking coward."

That one hit home, garbled or not. His head whipped up, red as Rudolph's nose. "You don't know what it's like to live under a curse." He stood up, knocking his chair over. "I should fucking tear your heart out, but Mammon wants you. Sasha lured Heather in so I could kill her. One of your precious coven turned on you." He stopped short of saying his next bit, instead stomping out of the room and slamming the door.

For once my mouth actually helped me out. With Oak out of the room, concentrating on the spell was easier, though not easy. Time after time, the spell crumbled as I fought to hold it together. I took a deep breath and tried to relax. My frustration caused most of the problems with casting the magick.

Every witch starts off learning to meditate. The practice stills the mind allowing the magick to flow freely, not tied down by the worries of correctness or fear of failure. I repeated my meditation word over and over, feeling a calmness spread through me. I continued the meditation while I built the spell in my head. One burst of flame would free me. The spell crumbled.

I thought back to the last time I'd practiced casting without words. A day or so after the Vortex Donuts incident, I'd been playing the new Halestorm album while constructing *Ignis* and it worked. Without realizing it I hummed "I am the Fire."

The melody flowed through me. The spell came together and held as I opened a trickle of magick. Sometimes all it takes is a candle.. A small flame heated up my index finger. I pointed it up and hoped it would burn through the ropes since I couldn't see. The flame burst into being, burning the hemp fibers. I smelled smoke as I felt the rope loosening. One good yank and I was free. Lucky for me he hadn't wrapped rope around me like in the old movies. I removed the gag, working my jaw to loosen it up while I untied my legs from the chair.

If I ever met Halestorm, I'd hug every one of them.

Now to find out where I was besides in a room someplace. I could blow out a wall, but without knowing what was there, I could be risking innocent lives. I'd have to go out the front door. If I got to toast Oak in the process, he had it coming. That and a lot more.

The door wasn't locked because Oak knew how to tie up people. He'd underestimated me for the last time. I opened it a crack and saw another room, with a solid wood door straight across from me. It looked like the way out to me. I stepped into the room and heard Oak. "How the fuck did you get free?"

The big man stood in the grimy kitchenette, a huge sandwich in one hand and a beer mug in the other. "You killed my sister, motherfucker."

I launched a firebolt straight into his face. It was better than I imagined. The blast drove him into the refrigerator, knocking it over with a loud crash. His face vanished for a second behind the fiery explosion. His food and beer landed on the floor as his hands slapped at the inferno that engulfed all of his hair. He looked like a giant birthday candle.

The room was clear so I made a break for it. I darted toward the door, knowing I couldn't kill the Green Knight by myself. Two steps in and a hand grabbed me by the neck. The goat demon shimmered into view as he raised me off the ground. I futilely fought to get air through my windpipe.

"Don't kill her yet." Mammon's voice came out of thin air. "I need to speak with Miss Flood."

The demon banged my head into the wall, and for the second time in a day, I was unconscious.

So much for my great escape.

39

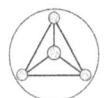

This time I woke up to the smell of brimstone, goat, and burned hair. The last one made me smile. I wished I'd done more than just set his beard on fire, but I counted it as a victory. One was all I got. I was tied and spread eagle in the center of a pentagram on a stone altar. Candles flickered at the points where the star met the circle. Unless I missed my guess, both were drawn with blood.

The goat demon stared at me and bleated when my eyes opened. Tattletale.

"Ah, you are awake," Mammon said, still in the Zental guise, as he stood over me. Correction, an image of him. As he got closer, I could see through him. He hadn't crossed over to our realm before the new moon. I still had two days if I could get out of here.

"Can I kill her now?" Oak snarled down by my feet. I lifted my head to see the now bald and shaved Oak. He was uglier than I'd believed possible. His nose was too big and his mouth was lopsided. Scars crossed in multiple places on his face and head.

Both relieved and terrified at the lack of a gag, I decided to use the only weapon left to me, my mouth. "Damn, I should have burned your head off to save the world from your ugly." Not the best rip, but I was still getting warmed up and probably had a concussion or two.

He growled and stepped forward. The goat demon's hand pushed him away from me.

"*Ignis.*" I cast a flame bolt that impacted an invisible barrier and died. Regardless, Oak leaped back and I swear he peed himself in the process. Well, at least I tried. It was good to still have access to my magick in case an opportunity showed itself.

Mammon floated in front of him, his back to me. "Are you really so stupid? If you enter the pentacle without the proper spells in place, you will free her. Do you think it will go any better than the last time you met?"

"I suppose not." The only thing missing was a full-on pout. The Green Knight had been feared in his time, but now he was an old man, screaming about the injustices done to him and blind to the ones done to others. "I just want to kill the bitch when it's time."

"And so shall you. Once she is dead, I will deliver your sword to you so that you may open the portal and allow me my entrance to the human realm. Lucifer can have hell, but I will reap the souls of the mortals."

Oak bowed his head in deference. "Yes, my lord."

"Still serving, aren't you, Oak. You're such a good lap dog. Fetch, boy." I heaped on scorn like whipped cream on a piece of apple pie. "So much for being free."

"Leave us, Bredbeddle," Mammon said with a wave of his hand. "Miss Flood is quite adept at inflicting wounds with her serpent's tongue."

Oak slunk off, the goat demon following as he left. Mammon spun in place to face me. "Miss Flood, you have proven yourself to be far more difficult to deal with than I had expected. I thought once the white witch had been dispatched, your coven would fall under the sway of my agent."

"You mean Sasha, the traitor?" I laughed harshly, trying to pull off confident, brave Jess. "I've taken care of her."

"I applaud you for your tenacity, but we have come to the end of my patience." He floated closer. I could see the brimstone fires of hell in his black eyes. Even dressed in an immaculate suit to play the part of the reasonable demon lord, he still reeked of greed and evil. "Tell me where my disciple is."

"You are the all-knowing Mammon. Can't you snap your fingers and a lackey will find her? How about the weak little phantom you placed in my sister to spy on us? Did she fight you too hard for you to find out what you needed? Looks like you'll always be Lucifer's bitch."

He snarled at me, and I was very happy to be dealing with a projection and not the real deal. "Tell me what I want to know, or I will make this very unpleasant for you."

I spit at him. "Do your worst. You may kill me, but my sisters will stop you and your kind from entering our domain."

Fire raced along every nerve in my body at the snap of his fingers. A scream ripped from my throat as the pain intensified to the point of oblivion. I thrashed against the restraints that held me to the altar as the tidal wave of agony washed over me. Then the pain stopped as suddenly as it started.

Tears flowed down my face in relief. I'd never felt anything like that and prayed to God I never would again, though I knew there was more coming. I couldn't let him know anything. My sisters relied on me to keep them safe and I refused to break that vow.

"Miss Flood, that was a mere sample of what I can do to you." He floated around to stand by my feet. I didn't bother to raise my head.

"Go fuck yourself," I said through gritted teeth. Every nerve in my body pleaded for me to tell him, but being stubborn was an art form for me. Every second I held out bought my sisters more time to plan. "I'd rather piss myself than bow to a coward like you."

"Tsk, tsk." He waved his finger at me like I was a bad child. "Your mouth will be the death of you. That I can assure you. How much you suffer in the meantime is up to you, however. Tell me, where is Sasha being held?"

I didn't say anything. Let him wonder what I was up to. I counted the seconds in my head. Each one precious to me as I knew my time was almost over. I'd never see Gareth again or share a beer with Basil. I'd miss Lucia's goofy moments and long talks with Pallavi. If I saw Magdalene when I returned to the universe, I would apologize for being weak and lazy.

"Last chance," Mammon said as he glared down at me. Raw hunger showed on his face. The greed that had driven him from Heaven explained everything the demon lord was. Conquering our realm wasn't for glory or to be worshipped, it was to claim all the souls for himself.

"Crawl back to God, maybe he'll let you lick the toilets in heaven clean." I tensed for what would come next, not that it helped. Over the next few hours, we repeated the cycle. He'd torture me with the sensations of insects tearing my flesh or drowning in a pool of piranhas or whatever his evil mind could devise that was worse than the last one. He'd ask again and I'd defy him. I don't know how long it lasted, but eventually, I broke.

"She's in the earth spirit's cave, encased in quartz until after the new moon. You can't reach her there." I laughed maniacally, my brain shattered by the constant torment he'd inflicted on me. I didn't care, just prayed I'd die, but I didn't. The rational part of me knew the torture was in my mind. It didn't make it any less terrible.

"We could have avoided this unpleasantness if you'd just told me earlier. You are correct, I can't reach her, but my associate can."

The door opened and Arty walked into the room. The chaos mage juggled three bright blue balls of energy as he approached the circle.

"Arty, what are you doing?" I sobbed at the realization that everything I'd gone through would be undone by Arty helping Mammon to retrieve Sasha. I should have listened to my sisters and killed her. The earth spirit had assured me Mammon could not take Sasha, but nobody could have predicted Arty's betrayal.

"Sowing chaos," he said matter-of-factly. "The universe thrives on chaos, and I live off the universe's energy. Humanity has become too structured; it is time for an upheaval and a new beginning."

"But he'll destroy everyone you love. He'll kill Lucia. Is that what you want?" My poor sister had loved this strange man and would die because of him. No one claimed that life was fair, but to have the people closest to you betray your trust was a knife in the back.

A shadow of doubt washed over Arty's face as he dropped one of the chaos orbs. It shattered on the floor, a brilliant flash of blue. "I want Lucia as payment for retrieving the witch."

Mammon studied the mage before saying, "Done." I saw the smile on the demon's face as Arty turned back to me. He was lying. About everything he promised everyone. Because…that's what demons do. By the time Oak and Arty figured it out, it would be too late.

He quirked a smile at me. "See, Jess? Lucia will be fine. We'll live in the chaos together, experiencing a new reality. Things will be glorious. I'm sorry you won't see it."

"You don't have to do this. There is plenty of chaos now."

The look on his face reminded me of the junkies when they spoke about getting high. "You have no idea. The levels of entropy from Mammon entering our dimension will dwarf everything since the big bang created the multiverse."

"Go retrieve the witch," Mammon commanded.

Arty looked at me first. "Should I tell Lucia anything for you?"

A million things raced through my mind. How many times had I ignored her or teased her about playing games? How many nights had she wanted to talk, and I went out instead? She'd saved us with her dedication to her craft and I failed her with my bad judgment and insufficient dedication to learning magick. "Tell her I love her and I'm sorry."

Arty pointed his finger at me like it was a gun. "You got it." He wandered out to destroy all of humanity for a cheap high.

I'd have cried more, but I was out of tears. I'd failed everyone who ever counted on me. If I had my four sigils, I'd have been strong enough to stop Mammon and save humanity. Magdalene had begged me to practice, and I'd ignored her. No. Worse. I'd been rude and dismissive. I'd argued like a child and run off to prove her wrong when it could have killed me. I didn't deserve to beat Mammon. I just prayed that my sisters would find a way to stop him and avenge those of us who died.

"So now you realize how badly you've been beaten," Mammon said over steepled fingers, enjoying the final knife to my heart. "I have controlled the game since the beginning and on the night of the new moon, Oak will open the portal to hell, and I will arrive."

"Where will you open it?" I didn't care, but the least I could do for my coven was keep him talking to buy them time. "In the middle of downtown for all to see?"

He chuckled. "No harm in telling you, since you'll be dead shortly." He moved next to me and knelt down. "Oak will open the portal at Burial. It is the perfect location, don't you think?"

I didn't answer though I had to admit, it was somehow appropriate to open a portal in a brewery with a Gothic horror theme. I closed my eyes and drifted off, hoping it would end soon.

Oak kicked my leg to rouse me from my exhausted stupor. He held a ceremonial dagger in his hand. "I've been looking forward to this. You should have taken the master's offer."

"Good boy, Fido," I mumbled, using up the last of my defiance. I welcomed the peace of being released from this broken body. I locked gazes with Oak who I'd thought was my friend. Let him see the disappointment in my eyes as he took my life.

He grinned as the knife raised over his head. "Your blood will open the portal to hell. I'm sure we'll see you there." The dagger sped toward me. Fire raced down my back as the knife plunged into my chest, piercing my heart. I looked into the smiling face of the Green Knight as he twisted the blade and ended my life.

40

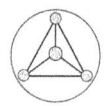

Air flooded into my lungs as I gasped. My hand flew to my chest, ready to find the knife buried in my heart, but nothing was there. The room around me blurred like I was drunk. My thoughts were muddled and disorganized. Unsteady, I pushed myself up.

When I did, a white-hot flash of pain flared down my spine. Where was I?

Oh. In the coven house. On the same table that had held Heather's dead body less than two weeks before. Lucia's candles were laid out around me in the same way we had with Heather's body.

Yet it seemed I was alive. I struggled to remember what happened, but the only memory that was clear was Oak stabbing me.

I wore my ceremonial robe over my Shinedown T-shirt and my tie-dye Vans. Something strange was afoot at the Circle K. I lowered myself until my feet reached the floor and stood. No weakness or stiffness. What was going on? I could feel the knife piercing my skin, the burning in the center of my back as the knife hit my heart.

I walked through the five chairs that had been arranged in a half circle. Was this another cruel trick by Mammon to break me? Was I in purgatory or something and he was torturing my soul? I thought I'd told him what he wanted to know, though what it was I couldn't remember. I could only remember the stabby part.

I pulled the front of my shirt forward and checked my chest to verify, but there wasn't even a scar.

The foyer was dead silent. I went to the library and the kitchen, but no one was around. My phone was gone, so I couldn't check the date and time. For all I knew, if this was real, it was the new moon and my coven was facing Mammon without me. I opened the fridge and pulled out a pile of roast beef. I sat at the island and ate the whole thing, stopping only to drink a couple of Burial Shadowclock pilsners.

Burial. For some reason, I felt like it should be important, but it eluded me. The demon lord had tortured me, but those memories were foggy at best. My back ached like I'd been burnt. I rinsed out my glass and put it in the dishwasher along with the plate the meat had been on, though I poured the blood into the sink first. Vada fussed if I left it in the dishwasher because of the smell.

I wandered out to the front door. I opened it to find a cool night, the moon not yet new. I hadn't been gone long enough to miss the fight. Assuming I wasn't in a weird afterlife or a demon's prison of delusion. I closed the door and went up the stairs to my room, but it was empty and the wards were gone. I'd moved into Magdalene's old rooms, hadn't I? I went to the large master bedroom and opened the door. The room was a mess, so that was good. A clean room would have meant I wasn't at the real coven house.

I retraced my steps and knocked on Vada's door. She'd know what was going on and could tell me why I felt stoned and disoriented and not as dead as I would have expected.

No one answered. My heart sank. I must be dead after all. I stared at the door, missing my sisters. Would Magdalene and Heather be waiting for me? How could I find them or was this the between place?

A scream returned me to some semblance of reality. Vada stood in her nightgown, her eyes wide with terror, babbling something I didn't understand. It sounded Arabic.

"Vada, can you not scream in my face? I'm having trouble enough focusing without you freaking me out."

She stopped, putting her hand on the side of my face. "Jessica, how are you alive?"

Before I could answer the hallway was filled with screams as the other four sisters ran to see what had happened. Lucia held a war ax in her hands, but the rest were unarmed and dressed for bed.

"Seriously, what is with all the screaming?" My thoughts moved at a snail's pace and all the commotion didn't help. "You act like you saw a ghost."

Lucia approached warily. "Jess, you're dead." She glanced back at Belinda whose mouth gaped, staring at me. "Is she dead?"

Belinda shook her head, her ponytails swinging back and forth. "No, she's alive. I'm not sure how. It would explain why I couldn't find her in the Halls of the Dead."

"You went looking for me?" Tears leaked down my face, though I didn't understand why. Everything was fuzzy still. I hugged Lucia. The pain down my spine intensified, but I didn't care. Someone would kill her, but who? Frustration welled as I pushed against my mental barrier to remember anything that had happened, Repeatedly, I saw the knife plunging into my chest. Saw the blood spurt from the wound. Felt the tearing and burning.

Lucia held me at arm's length. "They dumped your body at the front door with a warning not to interfere."

Pallavi hugged me hard. "I thought we had lost you forever. The wound to your heart was unrepairable. How did you return to us?"

I shook my head. "I don't know, but my back is on fire."

Lucia turned me around and tugged my shirt up so she could see. She whistled softly. "Didn't you have a tattoo on your spine? They must have burned it off your skin. Let me get something for the pain."

"Mother had me get that ink a bit ago. I don't know why."

"Did she touch it after it was done?" Lucia's eyes widened when I nodded. "I've heard of resurrection glyphs. Mother brought you back from the dead…well…the spell did."

I sent a silent prayer of thanks to Magdalene. Even beyond the veil she still protected me.

"What can you remember, Jess?" Vada asked.

I shook my head trying to clear it. "My thoughts and memories are clouded. I only see brief flashes. Oak stabbed me through the heart. What a dick."

Vada gripped my arm, before pulling me to her. "We broke down the door, but they had taken you. I'm so sorry we left you with them."

I hugged Vada, fighting to remember anything other than the stabbing sensation and the fire that shot through me. "You could never let me down."

Nao hugged me next. "I told you to leave me. Why didn't you listen? They killed you." I could feel the tears running down her face and soaking my shirt. I smoothed her hair, letting her cry. No need to remember, just being in the moment for Nao. When she finished I answered the best I could.

"You are my sister. I will always be there for you. Besides, they didn't kill me very well, it would seem." I laughed at my own joke, though I knew it wasn't funny.

"What else can you tell us?" Vada asked as Nao stepped aside. "Tomorrow is the new moon. How can we stand against the Prince of Greed when he has beaten us so soundly?"

I looked into her dark brown eyes. I knew she was scared, terrified more likely. I was the coven leader, but I couldn't remember much from the past three or four days. Destroying the phantom that was possessing Vi was the last memory I could even touch and it was indistinct.

"Nothing. I think if I sleep, the fog will lift and I'll remember what happened."

She nodded. "I will stay to guard your sleep."

"I don't need you to guard me. They don't know I'm alive."

"We've thought we held the upper hand before, only to find out we were betrayed by people we trust. Everyone here will stand with you. If you choose not to fight, we will abide by that decision as well. We will follow you, Jessica."

I started to protest. How could you follow someone with Swiss cheese for brains? She cut me off. "Sleep. We will discuss this in the morning."

I hugged each of my sisters and then Vada put me in my bed. I lay in the dark, waiting for my memories to return. In the movies, Obi-Wan's ghost would show up to point Luke in the right direction. The only ghost here was me, a shadow of my former self.

I stood up and got my headphones, turning on my playlist from my computer. I listened to the music and relaxed as the songs comforted me with the normalcy of it all. I must have gone to rescue Nao, from what she said. If she'd warned me of anything, I had no recollection of it, or how we'd found her.

I thought back to Magdalene and how she'd led the coven. Strong and determined, yet warm and caring when you needed it. Could I ever be that person? My own mother had beaten me and made my life hell until I felt the draw of the coven. My life had gotten so much better once I'd gotten away from the drugs and the crime, but I still carried some of the traits that had led me to juvie.

The song switched to Halestorm's *I am the Fire*. I hummed along until I noticed my hand sweating. I held it up and a burst of flame shot from my finger into the air. I jumped, knocking off my headphones. The flame went out.

"What happened?" Vada's voice came out of the darkness near the door. I jumped again, startled, since I thought I was alone.

The lights came on. "Sorry, I don't know what happened. I was listening to my music and I shot off a jet of flame."

Vada shook her head. "You've been through a lot. You really need to sleep." She pulled the chair next to the bed and turned off the lights. I crawled back under the covers, staying near Vada. She took my hand in hers and squeezed. "I will keep you safe. Now sleep."

I didn't say anything, just squeezed her hand back. Before long I had drifted off to a sound sleep.

The light from outside woke me, Vada still in the chair next to the bed. She woke when I sat up, checking the room before settling in on me. "How are you feeling?"

While I didn't feel as muzzy, my memories still raced away when I grasped for them. "It's all empty after we freed Vi."

Vada nodded. "All is well, it may take time."

"We are out of time," I said, climbing out of bed. I'd gone to bed dressed, too out of it to change. The sleep had helped with some of the fogginess that clouded my thinking, but not my memories and that was what we needed. A light tap on the door. "Come in," I called.

Pallavi stepped into the room. "I have an idea that may help," she said. Her hands clenched repeatedly as she stood there. Something was bothering her. "I fear that it may do more harm than good, though."

"Tell me." I would take any chance if it could restore my memories. Tonight, Mammon would enter the world of the living and consume it in his greed.

"I can enter your mind and try to unblock your memories. I fear that the blocks are there to protect you from what happened. If I am successful, they will all return at once which could damage you beyond repair. I do not offer this lightly as it is very dangerous." She looked at me and then Vada, who looked at me as well.

"How long will it take to be ready?" I didn't like the possibility of being damaged beyond repair, considering I was fresh out of resurrection tattoos, but we were out of time to defeat the demon lord and save humanity. I was sure the key was somewhere in the time I'd lost.

"I am ready now. I would suggest the training room in case things go awry." Pallavi fidgeted, her nerves getting the better of her.

"Let's go."

Ten minutes later, I sat surrounded by my remaining sisters in the healing circle. I lay on my back, my head resting on Pallavi's legs as she prepared her spell. She touched my temples lightly as the spell flowed into my mind. I could feel her thoughts as she navigated the corridors of my memories. Pieces of what she saw floated to the surface, the face of my mother, Basil drinking beer, driving with the windows open, singing along with the radio, and many more.

When she found the block, she tore it aside, and I dropped into a nightmare.

41

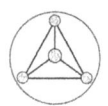

I screamed as the memories burst back into my consciousness. Mammon tormenting me hit like a tsunami as every detail returned in perfect clarity. Arty and Oak's betrayals, Mammon's final words to me, all back, but the torture threatened to drown me in its intensity.

I felt hands grasping me as I relived the previous days at fast forward. I fought to break free of the pain and suffering, but there was so much. Pallavi's voice echoed in my head but couldn't understand her words. Then I heard the demon lord's final statement. They would open the portal at Burial.

I grabbed ahold and clung to it like a life preserver against the rush of agonizing pain. I don't know how long I lay there, curled in a ball, but eventually, I restored control over the pain and fear and returned to reality. Pallavi helped me to sit up, tears pouring out of her eyes. It took me a moment to realize she'd experienced all of those memories with me.

I pulled her in tight. "I'm so sorry," I whispered over and over again. If I had known she'd have to live through them, I don't know if I'd have changed my mind, but that didn't mean I wasn't sorry. Time would tell if we'd made the right decision.

Belinda handed us each a glass of water that I drank down as if I'd been days without. "We're gonna need something stronger." I led my sisters into the kitchen and pulled Gareth's bourbon out of the cabinet. I poured a shot each for Pallavi and me and we drank. The clock read eight twenty-two a.m. It was good enough for me. We both had a second. Then it was time to talk.

I skipped the torture. No sense subjecting them to what Pallavi had already endured, and if I tried to tell them, I might not ever stop crying. I might become too afraid to move forward and that just wouldn't do. So, I described Oak's betrayal and his reasons behind it and that they would open the portal at Burial. I left off the part about Arty until I could decide how to broach it to Lucia.

"Fitting place for a demon portal," Belinda remarked. "All that goth stuff probably helps put them in the mood."

"The beer is good," I replied, earning a chuckle of relief from the group. "There's one more thing. Mammon had another disciple, someone we know, and that person was going to try to get Sasha out of the cave. Lucia, I'm really sorry, but it was Arty."

"Oh," Lucia said, her eyes blinking rapidly. "I hadn't seen him in a few weeks, but we'd been talking and…" Her voice cracked before she took a deep breath. "It doesn't matter. The question is, how do we stop them?"

"We are no closer now than before," Nao said, pushing her hair back over her shoulder.

Vada rubbed her face; she was probably exhausted from watching over me all night. "Let's start with who will be there?"

I ticked off the who's who of demon lovers. "Sasha, Oak, Arty, probably a couple of demons, and if we don't close the portal, Mammon." I didn't let them see me flinch on that last one. The memories of the torture were nibbling at my composure, and I couldn't afford any weakness.

"If Sasha is going to be there, I have glasses that see through illusions," Nao said. "I owe that bitch for kidnapping Belinda and me. Mother had me build enough for all of us." She stopped and looked wide-eyed at me. "Sorry, I meant Magdalene."

"You haven't gotten the 411 that no one is to call me anything but Jess. When this is over, Vada will be taking charge as Magdalene intended." Time to change the subject. "We can neutralize Sasha. What about Arty? I can't go toe-to-toe with a chaos mage."

Lucia cleared her throat. "Arty's my problem." Her eyes held a haunted look as she spoke. I know she loved him, and in a weird way, he loved her back. But he'd never love anyone as much as he loved power.

"He refused to free Sasha unless you were spared. He did want to save you," I said, hoping it would help and not make it worse.

She sighed. "Mammon's greed has infected him if he is trying to generate chaos. His order believes in maintaining it and balancing it, not increasing it. I've got an idea on how to deal with him."

"If Pallavi is up to it, we can take care of Oak," Vada said. I glanced at Vi's face, noting the tremble in her lip. I'd lived through those memories, but they were new to her. She nodded her agreement. "We can't kill him, but between us, we should be able to take him out of the fight so you can concentrate on closing the portal if they open it."

"You'll need me," Belinda said awkwardly. "That is, if you'll let me."

"Belinda, I need you more than you'll ever know. We can't do this without you."

She smiled at me. We had a long way to go to repair our relationship, but we were on the right track. If tonight went south, none of it would matter. "Put together whatever you need to fight. I can add my strength to yours or just protect your back."

"I'll be ready." Belinda stood a bit straighter. Sometimes, a little faith paid huge dividends.

"My guess is they'll open the portal at midnight. We need to be there by eleven so that we miss the staff. I don't want innocents in the line of fire. Be ready to move out at ten."

"What are you going to do?" asked Belinda.

I couldn't get blackout drunk, so I picked the next best thing. "I'm going to grab a shower and a nap. Bang on the door if you need me."

I walked up to my room, closed the door, and locked it. And the minute I was alone, I fell into my bed and sobbed as the intense memories of being broken pushed back into my thoughts. I cried until I got control of myself. I didn't know if I'd ever be right again, but I planned to make them pay for what they had done to me. I only wished Gareth was here to help, but I didn't need him to finish this.

Getting up, I made my way to the shower, where I stood in the hot water for a long time, letting it soak into my tired muscles while ignoring the pain from the abraded skin on my back. Tonight, we all might die, so I intended to enjoy my last day. I toweled off and returned to my room to get dressed. A white plastic sack sat on the floor next to the door. I opened the bag and closed it immediately, gagging at the smell.

My jeans. Right. I'd had the *Deleo Ianua* in my pocket when they kidnapped me. Taking the clothes into the bathroom, I turned the hot water back on. I upended the bag's contents into the bottom of the walk-in shower for a quick rinse. I picked up the jeans with two fingers and heard the metallic ping of the coin striking the shower's tile floor. I tossed the jeans back into the water to rinse and retrieved the coin.

They had missed it when I was captured. I flipped the coin over in my hands, feeling the etched texture of the crucifix and the crown of thorns. Powerful symbols for a devastating piece of magick. At least I had my nuclear option should things go wrong tonight.

I pulled out clean clothes and dressed. All black again. I was turning goth, though my black high-top Vans would make up for the less than fashionable clothing options. My bed looked comfy, but I doubted I'd have peaceful sleep with all the shit floating around in my head. I turned on my computer and looked up tour dates for my favorite bands, watched videos, and generally wasted time while I waited for the coming event. After some deliberation, I emailed Basil and gave him the run down since I didn't have my phone. He didn't respond, but that was normal for him.

I grabbed a couple of beers while I watched Star Wars. Might as well enjoy what could be my last day on Earth.

*

I met the coven in the kitchen at ten as planned. Lucia held her case in front of her while the others wore magickal pieces from their collections. I needed the elements to be with me for my part of the fight.

"Wear these," Nao said as she handed us each a pair of square-framed glasses. "If Sasha is casting illusions, you won't see them."

Pallavi held them out to look at them. "Couldn't you at least have made them stylish?" She put them on, and they looked horrible on her long, thin face. I put mine on without comment, as Nao appeared fairly irritated.

The drive into Asheville was uneventful. We parked on the far side of a row of manufacturing shops and warehouses. After a quick spell to unlock the place, what was left of the coven entered Reid's metal fabricator through the front door. We locked up and moved into the rear shop space. The back door had a window that overlooked the front of Burial with a full view of the Sloth and Tom Selleck mural on the side.

Around eleven-fifteen, a truck pulled up, and Oak, Sasha, and Arty got out. Sasha concealed the truck with an illusion as they entered the taproom. "Belinda and I will enter through the front. Everyone else will go in through the side," I told them. "The only thing that matters tonight is keeping the portal from opening. If one of us drops, keep going."

Nods all around. We broke into our groups and went in. Belinda and I stopped behind the truck they'd so nicely left in place to use as cover. Vada led the rest to the side entrance. I counted to fifty and we moved out.

Burial's front door had scythes for handles. Belinda's power absorbed the hexes they'd trapped the door with. Lucia had prepared something to handle them on her side. *"Robur,"* I whispered, feeling the earth's strength surge into me. My anger fueled my magick, making it even stronger than normal. They'd fucked with the wrong witch.

I pulled the door open, and it came free in my hand. So much for making a quiet entrance. Two toughs in skull caps ran to stop us. I threw the door at them like a Frisbee. It struck them full in the chest, throwing them into the bar before coming to a stop.

Another ran in from our left. *"Obfoco,"* Belinda said with a flick of her wrist. He dropped to the ground clutching his throat. We stormed into the taproom. Just past the bar, the tables had been set to the side and a large pentagram had been drawn with blood and bones. In the center of the circle rested a silver plate, three feet in diameter.

Over it shimmered the beginnings of the portal to hell. The human flunkies had been busy. Two bodies lay next to the plate, their throats cut to add the element of death needed for the spell. More grunts charged in to attack Belinda and me. With cooperation we didn't have to fake, we employed some of the team fighting strategies Gareth had worked so hard to teach us. Her magick dropped most of them while I pummeled the ones that got too close.

Oak strode across the room, a sword out and ready to join the fight. "I killed you," he bellowed as he reached the stairs on the left side of the taproom.

That was as close as he got.

Vada, coming in from the side, leapt and cleared the rail while swinging her silver sword. The blade sliced through the big man's right hand. He bellowed as his weapon fell to the ground along with the hand that still held it. He whipped his off-hand fist at Vada, but missed, punching the wooden keg to the side. Pallavi intoned a spell, fighting to control the Green Knight, as Oak jerked back and forth. He swung wildly at Vada who darted in, delivering slashing blows. He couldn't be killed, but he could be taken out of the fight.

A ball of blue chaos energy erupted in the center of the struggle, throwing Pallavi and Vada sprawling along with a toppling Oak.

Arty strolled in, two more orbs dancing over his outstretched hand. He laughed at his handiwork, not even glancing at Oak who was flailing on his side. Sasha followed him, calling up illusions that we couldn't see. Illusions only worked when the viewer was tricked by them. The glasses nullified Sasha's magick.

Lucia charged down the stairs and into view, and Arty cursed when he noticed her. "Lucia, Mammon will kill you if you're here. Get out while you can."

Sasha screamed. "Kill her, Arty, she can break the portal." She closed in on the pair who stood staring at each other in the middle of the fight.

Nao seized the opportunity to pounce. Dressed all in black, she dove down the stairs, over Oak as he struggled to rise, and tackled the traitor witch. Sasha thrashed as Nao clamped a manacle on her wrist, cutting off her magick. Oak batted Nao as he rose, knocking her toward Belinda and me, where we were finishing off the grunts.

Lucia reached out and touched Arty's face. "I'm sorry."

The chaos mage pulled her arm as if to flee with her, but she abruptly drove a sharpened steel rod into his chest. Arty stared at it for a second before he realized what she'd done. Lucia had constructed the spike out of order, the enemy of chaos. As it pierced the mage, the order flowed into his body, destroying the chaos within. His magick went wild with the introduction of so much order.

He burst into blue flames as the chaos engulfed his body. "Lucia," he cried as he reached for her. She leaned back and kicked him in the stomach, directly into Oak, his clothes bursting into flames as they collided. I grabbed Belinda and ran past the engulfed mage and the enraged Green Knight.

I reached the edge of the pentagram and stopped. We were too late. Mammon stood on the ground, the portal fully open as his demons milled behind him ready to destroy humanity.

"Miss Flood, you certainly are persistent. It will be a pleasure to kill you again, this time permanently."

We were too late, and we had no chance at all against a demon lord who had fully entered the realm. My stomach hollowed and my heart stopped. I reached out, grabbing Belinda's hand as the startled witch squeezed my fingers, but I didn't tell her what I was about to do.

I dug into my pocket, pulled the *Deleo Ianua*. The coin glittered in my hand as I made my choice. We would all die to save humanity but we wouldn't die alone. I threw it at the feet of the demon lord.

Nothing happened.

42

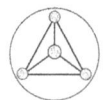

Mammon laughed as the coin bounced harmlessly at his feet. He placed one wingtip-shod foot over the silver piece. "Sasha replaced the real coin with a fabricated one. I didn't realize you still had it in your possession."

My sisters joined me at the pentagram, ready to fight a losing battle. Pallavi had Oak under control; Sasha was nowhere to be seen. After all of this, I'd kill her if she ever crossed my path again.

"Return to Hell before we seal the portal or I'll kick your sorry ass back through it and let Lucifer deal with you." My anger grew as I stared at the Lord of Greed. He'd killed two of my sisters, tortured me, and turned Sasha against us. Add to it my issues with authority, and I was beyond pissed.

"You think I'm done? You cannot match the power of Mammon." He flicked his wrist and the side of Burial exploded outward, throwing debris into the night. The picnic tables next to the building scattered like Legos thrown by a child having a major hissy fit. The roof above the taproom burst in a maelstrom of debris settling alarms off in cars and buildings up and down the street.

My earth sigil grew hot as the ground began to shake. A rock structure forced its way through the debris until it stood twenty feet high and just as wide. The silver portal behind Mammon rippled as the tremor continued. The minions of hell itself clustered closer and closer on the other side for the opening to finish widening.

"*Rima*," I yelled, directing the spell at the doorway into Hell, attempting to shatter the rock and block it. The energy ricocheted and struck me, knocking me back into the bar.

"You think I would let an elemental witch destroy my creation? Miss Flood, don't think me stupid," Mammon taunted over the noise of the demon army as they waited for their chance to invade Earth. The silver faded as the entryway into Hell opened completely, going as transparent as air. "Kill them."

A flood of demons poured into the space around the portal. I climbed to my feet and cast *Rima* again. This time I directed the spell at the ground under the demons. Gnarled and scabbed demon hands grasped me as my power tore into the earth, creating a crevice that ran ten feet across and the width of the portal.

Every animal noise imaginable filled the air as the demons fell into the pit. More came leaping into the gap. Some made it; others fell.

Lucia shouted over the noise. "They are climbing the walls, Jess."

I gathered my magick. "*Phoca*," I said, letting my power seal the crevice, trapping the demons and silencing the shrieks of the dying hellions. More poured out of the portal; their screams were the stuff of nightmares and horror movies.

"Time to kick some ass, ladies." I unleashed a firebolt into the lead demon, a horned monstrosity with a shark's mouth and talons the size of machetes. It flew back into the horde, bowling them over as it went.

Vada's sword was out, slashing through demons as fast as they came at her. Streams of black wove around a group of charging imps that withered and died under the touch of Belinda's magick.

We'd barely dented the oncoming masses. I dodged the attack of a bird-headed demon who drove its serrated beak at me with a squawk. My fist caved in its head. Lucia stood behind me, a pistol in her grip, blasting anything that tried to flank me. If I didn't think of something soon, we'd be overrun by sheer numbers.

"Surrender and I will kill you quickly," Mammon yelled from his vantage point atop a huge overturned fermentation tank.

I flipped him off as Lucia's shot tore a nasty-looking hellion's head in half. A roar sounded from my left. I stole a glance and my mouth dropped. Oak waded into the fight, swinging a broken two-by-four with his remaining hand. He swept through the flank smashing anything that got in his way.

Lucia yelled from behind me. "Pallavi's got him." She dispatched two more imps carrying sharpened rocks as daggers. The angel tear bullets tore through the lesser demons like shit through a goose.

"Back up," I yelled. Once my sisters were clear I said, *"Nivis Casus Ignis."* The last time I'd cast the spell was during my earth sigil test. This time, burning stones the size of softballs rained down on the hellions. A few hit Oak, but I didn't care as long as it didn't break Vi's control of the big man. He continued his assault on the demons as they were pummeled from above. The wave faltered as the casualties piled up. The spell finished with over half of the demons dead or close enough that they couldn't fight.

"I've had enough of this," Mammon shouted at me. He hurled a ball of black smoke that knocked Pallavi over. She hit the ground hard and didn't move. Lucia turned to run, but I grabbed her. "Stay together. Never split the party."

She nodded, reloading the Glock with a fresh clip. Oak shook his head and turned on us. He had fresh welts where the stones had hit him, burning his skin. "I'll fucking kill you," he roared as he charged at us.

"Ignis," I said and the two-by-four in his hand burst into flames. He kept coming. I renewed my strength spell and met him at the edge of our circle. Lucia pumped two shots into the Knight before he swung at me. I slipped under the blow and kidney-punched him hard. He grunted and unleashed a massive backhand. I got away from the worst of it, but he clipped the side of my head and sent me sprawling.

Two goblinesque demons pounced on me, their teeth tearing at my reinforced jacket. I punched one in the face, splattering it all over me. I'd owe the dry cleaner a fortune to get all the shit off my jacket. The other one ran away.

Oak reached down and grabbed my throat. "I'm going to enjoy killing you, bitch. Look what you've done to me."

One of his ears dangled from a strap of skin, and his scalp had been torn in multiple places and scorched in others. He looked more demon than man. "You are one ugly motherfucker."

His grip tightened. Stars swam before my eyes as I fought for breath. What was the deal with everyone choking me? I kicked at him, but that didn't phase him at all. Imps leaped on my legs, climbing and biting through my jeans into the skin. Blood trickled down as they tore into me.

A light appeared above me. Was it my time to rejoin the universe? It intensified, causing the demons to mewl as they tried to avoid the brightness. The pressure let up on my windpipe and air flowed in.

I looked down and saw a golden sword sticking out of Oak's chest. He staggered, dropping me to the ground. Lucia and Vada pulled me away as the sword retracted. Oak toppled over and Basil stood behind him.

Not my Basil, but God's holy seraphim, Barchiel. His wings were full, and he was robed in white with a golden torc around his neck. A crown of green leaves perched on his golden hair. He looked down at me.

"Sorry I'm late, I had to get some friends." He turned, holding the burning sword over his head. "*Angelis ad contritionem.*"

Out of the light emerged hundreds of angels all dressed like Basil with swords of their own. The demons howled and the fight was on. The hellions fought in packs, overwhelming angels with numbers though their losses were high. Everywhere their swords slashed, demon ichor flew in great arcs.

Basil helped me to my feet. "You never answered my email," I accused without any anger in my voice.

"Vada called me. It took a bit to get help arranged." He touched my throat, and I felt healing warm the skin. "I am forbidden from touching Mammon. You'll have to defeat him in order to rid the world of his presence. The angels will buy you time."

I nodded. "But this means—"

He touched my lips. "We all pay a price to protect the ones we love. Don't waste it."

He shot up and dove at a giant hellion with a frog's head and razor-sharp horns. He whooped as he fought, slashing right and left with his sword. Leave it to Basil to show off.

"Sisters, we have to take down Mammon," I said. Pallavi limped slowly toward me, but blood trickled from her nose. She wasn't up to fighting. "Lucia, protect Vi." I marched across what was left of the taproom toward Mammon, who screamed insults at Basil as the angel hacked apart another giant demon. I sent a firebolt at Mammon's head to get his attention. I managed to mess up his over-gelled hair.

He dropped from the top of the fermentation tank, landing in front of us. "Miss Flood, you certainly have become a major inconvenience to me. I will enjoy ridding the world of you and the rest of your ilk. I agree with the Almighty on one count."

"Which is?" I couldn't resist asking since he so nicely set it up. Vada,

Nao, and Belinda shifted so he was the center of our half circle. Vada held her sword ready on my right. Nao, armed with an ivory dagger, was to my left, and Belinda just past her.

"Never suffer a witch to live." He held out his hand and a black spear appeared in his hand. I recognized the head, thanks to the research we'd done in two weeks about stopping demons, as the Spear of Destiny.

I pulled the karambit from its sheath and prepared myself. "Brought the good silverware, did you?"

He swung the spear down and thrust, but I sidestepped the obvious attack and slashed his arm as I slid under his guard. Black ichor dripped from the wound. I'd have to thank Gareth the next time I saw him. The dagger's runes glowed a dull red.

Mammon's eyes widened in surprise. Had he forgotten one important factor of being earthly? In hell he was invincible, but on this plane, he had a physical body that could be hurt. Belinda cast a spell that wrapped around his torso, but he shrugged it off. His counter spell pushed her back to where two demons latched on to her, trying to pull her to the ground.

Nao leaped to her defense. She drove the point of the ivory dagger into the closest demon. Smoke poured out of the puncture wound. Within seconds the demon had drifted away on the wind. Belinda dispatched the second with a spell that disintegrated it on the spot.

Mammon spun the spear and swung at Vada, who neatly blocked it and countered with a quick riposte. All those years training with Gareth had served us well. He pivoted and thrust the spear at my head. It sliced a lock of hair off, but I managed to avoid the point.

I cast a firebolt at him, forcing him to step back. The cut in his arm had made him wary. That worked to our advantage. Nao ducked under the butt of the spear and stabbed with the ivory dagger. It snapped as it struck just under his ribs, leaving a large fragment embedded in his side. He quickly backhanded her, knocking her into the downed tank.

Belinda cast a swarm of beetles at him. They attacked him, tearing pieces of clothing and then flesh from him. He flipped the spear around, forcing Belinda's spell to falter as she stepped out of reach of the blade. I struck while he was distracted. The edge of the karambit tore into his leg which spewed more ichor across the floor. I danced out of range as he spun the spear like a quarterstaff.

Vada stabbed at his exposed back as he whirled, trying to cut me. We were fighting like a pack of wolves taking down a grizzly bear. His swings grew wilder as he took damage from the four of us now that Nao had returned to the melee.

I dove in to slice as he attacked Nao and slipped in a patch of ichor on the floor. I lost my balance completely and fell flat on my ass. He turned, a huge smile showing his fangs, and stabbed down as I played flipped turtle. A nimbus of blue encased me right before the spear landed, throwing white sparks into the air. Lucia stood a few feet behind me, holding hands with Pallavi. The shield cracked from the force but diverted the blade into the ground. I rolled to my left, getting enough distance so I could regain my feet.

Vada stabbed from the side, opening him up more. He bled from numerous spots, but he didn't slow. He fought with an unholy determination to kill us. He thrust the spear again, missing me by a mile, but too late I realized his plan. Instead of missing me, he stabbed directly at Lucia, who was defenseless. The blade shot out toward her. At the last instance, Pallavi pushed Lucia clear, but the spear rammed through her stomach with a sickening tear. Vi's face went ashen as she crumpled to the ground.

"No," I screamed, launching myself at Mammon. He blocked the knife and kicked me away from him. Lucia pulled me to my feet. Vada retreated under a series of fast attacks. Nao and Belinda struck from behind, but nothing worked. Vada's strength was flagging. I had to do something.

I screamed *"Veni."* The ground erupted into a solid stone wall between Mammon and Vada. The spear chipped the stone as it struck, but it would take a month to break through the granite.

I glanced at my fallen sister, my closest sister, as Lucia fought to save her life. I'd had enough. I strode toward the demon lord, knife ready. The battle between the forces of Heaven and Hell raged on as we'd been fighting the demon lord. Bodies from both sides were scattered around the demolished taproom. So much pain and death, all for Mammon's eternal greed.

He leveled his spear at me. "You can't beat me, witch," he snarled. His fangs were more pronounced as were the ridges in his face as his true aspect came forth.

"This is over, Lord of Greed. Go back through the portal and be done." I knew his insatiability wouldn't let him accept, but it was worth trying. "If you're defeated here, Lucifer will own you in hell."

His eyes betrayed his fear.

"Leave, Mammon. Take your minions and go while you can. The seraphim can dispatch you if I fail and you know it."

His gaze flickered to where Basil hovered overhead, watching the showdown, flaming sword in hand and ready to use it. Mammon licked his lips. He knew as well as I did that angelic weapons could harm him in a way our earthly, witch magick couldn't, not quickly, and perhaps not in time. He probably also knew that Basil wasn't the most rule-following seraphim in the Almighty's ranks. "He is forbidden to interfere in matters of mortal men."

With that, he launched his attack. I stood still, waiting for the blade. At the last instant, I pivoted to my right and grabbed the spear by the shaft. I cast *Robur*, renewing my strength so I could keep Mammon from yanking the weapon free. Now came the biggest gamble I'd ever made.

"Basil!"

43

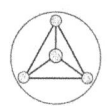

Basil's eyes locked on mine. I held out my hand. An eternity went by as I waited for his answer. He reached back and threw the blade down to me. I caught the sword by the grip. The blade burst forth with white-hot fire.

Mammon's eyes widened. "You can't." His voice went shrill with fear. "He can't interfere."

"You fucked with the wrong witch." I slammed the blade into his chest with every ounce of strength I possessed. Mammon released the spear as his hands smacked at the pommel of the sword. Rivulets of white fire expanded from the wound like rivers from a lake. His external form crumbled, leaving the true demon lord in its place.

Mammon's curved horns grew as his skin turned red and rolls of fat appeared up and down his body. He ballooned outward as the fire burned its way through whatever passed for his bones and nerves. A third eye appeared in the middle of his forehead as his chin elongated to account for a massive set of pointed teeth and huge fangs.

Pieces of him cracked and fell off as the fire consumed him from the inside. His talons raked at his chest, feebly attempting to dislodge the sword, but it was no use.

A shimmer appeared next to me, revealing a tall, darkly handsome man with solid black eyes. Lucifer, ruler of hell, stood virtually next to me in an Armani suit, holding a demon-headed walking stick. "Why, brother, you seem to have gone and gotten yourself killed."

"Lucifer, avenge me," Mammon pleaded as more of his parts fell off, including one I wished I'd never seen.

"Avenge you? Why would I do that?" He nodded to me. "As Miss Flood so eloquently pointed out, you fucked with the wrong witch."

I gawked like a first-time tourist at Lucifer. It wasn't every day the Prince of Lies quoted you. I took a step back.

"Well, I can't have you cluttering up the place." With a snap of his fingers, what was left of Mammon disappeared, leaving behind many detached demon parts. Seriously, you can't unsee these things.

Lucifer turned to me. "Miss Flood, admirable job. You do your coven proud. You shan't have anything to worry about from Mammon or any other Prince after this. Good day." He faded from view.

Basil landed and retrieved his sword. The demon horde disappeared with Lucifer, leaving the dull gray of the portal behind. We'd won, but I turned to find my sisters gathered around Pallavi. Her head was propped in Lucia's lap. Her eyes were open though her skin had the pallor of death.

I ran to her, knelt, and took her hand. I glanced up at Basil. "Can you heal her?"

He shook his head, tears spilling down his cheeks. "The Spear of Destiny killed Christ. The wounds dealt with it are beyond our ability to heal. I'm sorry."

Pallavi gripped my hand tighter. "Jessica, do not mourn me. I saw what was to come. If Lucia died, we all would fail. I gladly exchanged my life for all and will set down the burden of my memories and reunite with the universe."

I looked to Lucia and she shook her head. If Basil couldn't cure it with angelic power, what chance did a mortal witch have? "I love you. I will miss you every day of my life."

Pallavi coughed, blood spattering her chest. "I love you, too. Take care of my sisters or I will kick your butt."

"I will. Rest now, my friend."

Pallavi closed her eyes and her breathing slowed. We huddled around her until it stopped completely. To my surprise, motes of light danced around her body, streaming up into the night sky. Her spirit rose from her body, beautiful and perfect. She touched each of our heads and I heard her words.

"Jessica, I could not bear any more. You are much stronger than I to live with the hurt Mammon did to you. I love you, sister, never forget that. I will await you until your watch is done."

I stared at her, imprinting the sight into my memories. My best friend had gone and I'd have to find a way to move on and live my life, protecting the nexus and my coven. Pallavi faded into mist and returned to the universe.

I felt a presence behind me. When I looked, another angel stood watching over us. He had long golden hair that matched his robes. A blue cape hung between wings that stood at least two feet past his head. "I know you normally handle such duties, but I wanted to ease her suffering."

Lucia was the first to recover. "Archangel Michael?"

He nodded. "I've come to shepherd home one of our own. Know that you all have done well today. I am sorry for your loss, but humanity has been saved through your sacrifices."

I stood and faced him. "If you'd have stepped in to stop Mammon's plans, none of us would have had to make a sacrifice. My sisters are dead because the Lord of Greed wanted to feast on human souls. Isn't that your domain to take care of?"

Michael's perfect brow furrowed. "Humans are such fickle beings. You want the free will that the Almighty has granted you, then you want us to protect you. You can't enjoy the freedom without being willing to pay the price when it comes due. The Green Knight set this in motion along with one of your coven. How is that our responsibility?"

My mouth opened and nothing came out. A first in my lifetime, to be sure. "It's not." I could feel my cheeks flushing as I realized I'd just yelled at a very powerful angel. "Can you leave Basil with us as a deterrent to other demons?"

He shook his head. "As the Prince of Lies rightly said, you, Jessica Flood, and your coven are the deterrent you are seeking. Barchiel requested aid in exchange for returning to his rightful place among the Almighty's host. It is not for me to free him from his solemn oath."

I sighed, defeated. I'd lost Heather. I'd lost Magdalene. Now I'd lost Pallavi and Basil in this mess. "May I say goodbye?"

"Of course, child." His beautiful smile warmed me, and it also pissed me off. Authority figures get under my skin. "I am not so cruel as to separate you without time to say farewell."

"Thank you." I bowed my head in respect. I saw Basil across the room and started to go to him.

"May I make an observation before I leave?" Michael asked. His features reminded me of Magdalene when she knew I needed a friend, not a leader. I nodded. "Jessica, there is a tenacity in you which makes you strong. Do not cast it away because of social conventions or to please others. A weaker person would have run from this fight. Remember that as you go forward in life."

"I will." I returned to Basil, head down. He'd given up his life on Earth to help save it. To save me, and Chip, and Asheville. How could I ever repay such a debt? I wasn't sure I would make the same decision in his shoes. "Thank you for saving us."

He lifted my chin. A big smile was plastered on his face. He wore his normal street clothes, the sword and wings put away for now. "Mammon is the Prince of Greed. Mortals couldn't beat him without a bit of angelic help. Makes us look bad."

I laughed. "That outfit makes you look bad. You look like a circus clown." He wore a red and white horizontal striped shirt and aqua pants. "All you need is the big shoes and red nose."

"And I should take fashion advice from Miss Rock tee? Puhlease." He cocked his head at me. Tears flowed down his face. "I always knew this wasn't permanent and I'd be required to return to an eternity of service."

"What about Chip? Did you leave him a note?" After everything else, Gareth trying to leave without telling me to my face still hurt, and I hadn't been married to him for years. "What will he do without you? For that matter, what will I?"

"He will move on as will you. My time here is over." He pulled me into a rough embrace. I returned it, though I resisted adding to my strength to crush him to a pulp.

A bright light illuminated him as he stepped back. His tears turned to muffled sobs. Why did I feel like I was losing more than everyone else? The unseers would never know the price we paid to keep them safe.

It wasn't just. Or fair. It wasn't right. And wasn't the Almighty supposed to respect some sort of fairness and balance? We'd saved the planet with only a little tiny bit of help from Basil. Imagine if we hadn't saved the Earth from Mammon. Without us humans down here living and messing up and struggling and praying and loving and dying, the Almighty wouldn't have anything left to do.

I knew all this as surely as I knew I didn't care about the consequences for what I was about to do. The Archangel himself had just told me how strong I was, and letting their friends sacrifice everything for them was not how strong people acted. Why was I giving up without a fight? I wheeled around and stormed over to the Archangel.

"Listen, I don't care what Basil promised to who. The truth is he belongs here. His husband loves him, I love him, and we are all better people for knowing him. Why would you take that from us after we have just saved the entire world so that you still have a world to worry about? Shut off the damned light show, take your holier than thou attitude, and shove it up your ass. Now does he stay or what?"

Vada grabbed my arm, her eyes as big as hubcaps. "Jessica, he is an Archangel, show some respect."

I jerked my arm away. "I did. I didn't kick his ass first."

Michael laughed. Not a hee-hee or a chuckle. He full-on roared with laughter. After a minute of him cracking up, he caught his breath. "There is that fight I spoke of." He wiped his eyes with the sleeve of his robes. "Do you know how long it's been since someone told me off?"

"A long time?" I guessed, not sure what exactly was going on. I'd expected fire and brimstone, not a laugh track.

"Far longer than you'd guess, Jessica." He shook his head, still laughing. His eyes glowed white for an instant before he spoke again. "The Almighty being moved by your impassioned plea has decreed Barchiel may stay." He waved his hand and the lights vanished and Basil thumped to the floor.

I grabbed Michael and hugged him hard, causing a couple of feathers to pull free of his wings. "Thank you."

After I let him go, he spoke to Basil. "You are forbidden from summoning your angelic vestiges while with the humans. If you summon them, you will be returned immediately to your proper place. Agreed?"

Basil nodded, still in shock. "Agreed."

Michael winked at me. "Shove it up your ass. Wait 'til Saint Peter hears this one." He faded into mist, leaving me with my sisters and Basil.

"You will make an old woman of me, Jessica," Vada said, staring at where Michael had been. "You've stood up to the Prince of Greed and an Archangel. What's next, the Almighty himself?"

"Maybe." I hugged my sister. "Depends on how pissed I am."

44

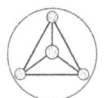

It had been six weeks since the fight with Mammon and the demons. Basil and Chip reconsecrated their marriage the previous weekend and I was their best man. Life had settled back into as normal as living in a coven could be. We severed Sasha from the group, denying her access to our magick, since being part of a coven wasn't like being a lone witch. Apparently covens had enough trouble with members going bad over the years that coven membership had strings and ways of dealing with malcontents. I'd tried to abdicate the coven leadership, suggesting that Vada was well suited and Magdalene's hand-chosen successor. They refused. I did like having the bigger room.

I'd returned to working the brew tours on the weekends. Magdalene had left instructions to transfer her extensive holdings to the next leader, so technically I was wealthy. Far wealthier than Gerwin Aaker, but he'd never hear it from me.

I'd gotten into a rhythm. Study in the morning, go to the local dojo to train in the afternoon, and dinner with my sisters each evening. Vada was an amazing chef, so we ate well. At night, we talked about our missing sisters, wondered when the universe would send replacements, and cried occasionally.

The magickal community was not pleased to have been kept in the dark about Mammon and the coven's losses. Vada did most of the speaking though I stepped in from time to time to reinforce my role as coven leader, a fact more than one person was not happy about. Saturday nights I spent with Chip and Basil, drinking beer and playing games in whichever brewery we ended up at. Life was dull without people trying to kill you, but I'd manage.

I'd avoided Vortex Donuts after Arty's betrayal. Today, I decided that was stupid and I was also craving a yeast donut. My iPhone in hand, I got a chocolate donut and sat at the same table where Arty had given me the vial of chaos magick. I was flipping through text messages from various community members when a tall man sat down next to me.

"That seat's taken," I said without a second glance. "Plenty of room elsewhere."

"Sorry, mate" he said with a soft Australian tone. "I'd heard there was a position open for a handyman at your place. I must be mistaken." He tipped his brown suede cowboy hat at me as he stood. "Ma'am."

I watched him walk across to the counter. Suzy flirted with him, but he just ordered a donut and coffee. He had dark hair and a cute dimple when he smiled. He must have been six-two in his work boots. His build was lean and muscular like a swimmer, but he carried himself like a fighter.

He carried himself in a way that looked…familiar.

He nodded as he took his food and headed for the door. "Hey, bud" I called. "Take a seat."

He obliged me, taking off his hat to set on the table next to him. "How did you hear about the job?"

He shrugged. "Some blond dude I met on the road. Looked in bad shape, but he gave me a tip on work. Told me you hung out here. I've been stopping in every day for the past couple of weeks. You're a hard woman to track down."

I nodded. Nobody who hadn't been given permission, or whose current body hadn't been given permission, could find the coven house. "You ex-military?"

"Yes, ma'am."

"Knock off the 'ma'am' crap."

"Yes, Ma…Jess." He smiled at me. "He told me it was a good job and I'd fit in right fine."

"I'm pretty sure you'll fit in." I pulled the karambit from its sheath. "What type of blade is that?"

"Karambit. Must be high-end with all those funny markings."

I slid the knife back, not wanting the locals to freak out.

"Can you fix a toilet?"

"Yep."

"Glock or Sig?"

"Glock 19 to be specific."

"How do I kiss?"

"Great… crikey. What gave it away?"

"Nothing, just a hunch. What do I call you now? Can't call you Gareth, unless you are telling the coven."

"Name is Angus so I'll stick with that. Do I get the job?"

"Nope. But I do have an opening for a domestic partner. Interested?"

He smiled and everything was right with the world.

For now.

ACKNOWLEDGMENTS

WOW!

When Darin and John asked me to join the New Year, New Books campaign, I leapt at the chance to be grouped with two talented authors and great friends. The outpouring of support from fans and other authors was amazing to behold. We had everyone from NYT bestselling authors to fans who were posting links. And it worked! You are holding the product of that campaign, and I couldn't be more proud of this book. I'd especially like to thank April Baker, Dennis Meyer, and Alec Christensen for buying the tuckerizations in the book. Alec bought one for his sister Katy who is now the a librarian in fiction. You can find their names if you look.

Our daughter, Emily, came into my office and asked for a witch book with no love triangles in it. I told her to write it on my whiteboard. About a month later, I had just finished Never Steal from Dragons and the story hit me like a bolt from above. A while later, Stone Cold Witch was born (though it started life as Welcome to the Cataclysm).

The decision to place this book in Asheville, NC was an easy one. The town is wonderful with thriving arts and brewery businesses. We love to take long weekends in Asheville to unwind and recharge. The people are always friendly, and the coven does a great job of controlling any rogue magick. All of the places mentioned in the book are real and, hopefully, still open after the pandemic. You can wander through Malaprops (please don't open the fire door like Jess does), have a beer at Burial or Green Man, and go check out the stairways to nowhere at One World Brewing Downtown. The only things made up (as far as you know) are the coven house and the Nexus Portal. A lot of the bit players are inspired by actual people we've met on our many trips to Asheville. If the chamber of commerce is reading this, I'd love to do a Nexus Witch Tour of Asheville!

This book has gone through the wringer to publication. Needless to say, Jess and her sisters are too strong to give up and now here they are. The world of publishing is ever-changing and fickle as hell. The move to Indie presses or self-publishing has really opened the market up to stories that would never be seen otherwise. The reader truly benefits from new voices being able to find their platform.

As usual, a book doesn't come into the world solely by my efforts. My partner-in-crime Jody Wallace does the developmental edits that take the roughly written story I've completed into the readable gem you now have. Emily Leverett does the copy/proof-reading to eliminate as many typos and grammar issues as possible. With every book I've written or read there are typos that slip through. I figure they deserve to live on if they made it past all the edits. Natania Barron did the amazing cover for the book. She really captured the mood I was going for. James Tuck created the Mytorian Circle art and did it as a tattoo on my right forearm, just like Jess has. John Hartness did the formatting, so it is ready for printing.

Those are people who make the book possible, but I have a host of friends and family that came out to support the Kickstarter campaign and pledge their hard-earned money to support us. I couldn't be more grateful or humbled by the support. Others are the people I depend on to keep me sane and having fun. My con family is ever-growing and incredibly wonderful.

My family is the true rock that keeps me stable and happy. Our kids are both healthy and moving on with their lives now that they are adults. Blaze keeps me company while I'm writing and is always good to enforcing treat breaks. And most importantly, my wife Hope. She who puts up with far more than she ever should have to, but for some odd reason still loves me. Some things are stranger than fiction, but I am thankful every day for her.

And finally, a thanks to you for taking a chance on Stone Cold Witch. If you love it, please leave a review, or tell your friends, or both. There are two more Nexus Witch books coming to you soon!

Until next book,
Patrick
January 2024

SPECIAL THANKS

A special thank you to all our Kickstarter Backers!
You helped make this happen, and these books are for you!

Sheryl R. Hayes, Kiersten Keipper, Bill Feero, Chuck Teal, Beth Wojiski, Kerney Williams, Dino Hicks, Jessica Bay, Rowan Stone, Josh Minchew, V. Hartman DiSanto, Hope Griffin Diaz, April Baker, Princess Donut, Allison Charlesworth, Shanda, maileguy, Joelle Reizes, Alexandra Corrsin, Joseph Procopio, Kevin A. Davis, Robert S. Evans, Eric P. Kurniawan, Amber Derpinghaus, Andy Bartalone, R. David Grimes, Patti & Joan Holland, Scott Casey, Asha Jade Goodwin, Chuck & Colleen Parker, Jessica Nettles, Sarah J. Sover, Joe Compton, Brendan Lonehawk, Tera, James & Hannah Fulbright, Chris Fletemier, Carol B, A. L. Kaplan, Joey & Matt Starnes, Wanda Harward, Dennis M. Myers, Evelyn M, Nick Crook, Bob!, Bill Bibo Jr., Karen Palmer, Dina Barron, Charlie "Kaiju Mapping" Kaufman, Nancy E. Dunne, Rachel A. Brune, Noella Handley, Sara T. Bond, SM Hillman, C Keeley, John L. French, Anthony Martin, Lynn K, Fay Shlanda, Cristov Russell, Candice N. Carp, Samuel Montgomery-Blinn, Susan Griffith, Vee Luvian, Randy Cantrell, Gail Z. Martin, Tawni Muon, Caryn S, Jimmy Liang, Preacher Todd, Casey & Travis Schilling, The King of Rhye, Ruth Brazell, Melisa Todd, Vic Chase, Tom Sink, Nicholas Ahlhelm, Donna Berryman, Richard Novak, Liz Lamb, Angie Ross, Jonathan Casas, Christy Wilhelm, Robert Claney, Carol Gyzander, Ollie Oxxenfree, Ángel González, Caitlin Wright, Michelle Botwinick, Ashley & Cody, Amelia Sides, Nicole Rich, Ardinzul, Scott Valeri, Richard Dansky, Josh Bluestein, K.H. DeNeen, David Price, Mair Clan, Leonard Rosenthol, Vikki Perry, RHR, Jennifer & Benjamin Adelman, Everette Beach, Charlie Hawkins, Zeb Berryman, Julia Benson-Slaughter, Jesse Adams, Ash Peeples, Susan Ragsdale, Tina Hoffmann, Robert Osborne, A.M. Giddings, Michelle LeBlanc, Amanda, Ken St Clair, J. T. Arralle, Alec

Christensen, hemisphire, Marian Gosling, Zack Keedy, Dee Kennedy, Andrea Fornero, Allison Finch, Sandy Reece, Maya Barb, Shirley Kohl, Ronald H. Miller, Adrianne McDonald, James Ball III, Louise K, Elyse M Grasso, Steve Ryder, Debbie Yerkes, Brendon Towle, LB Clark, Jenn Huerta, Emily L, Eric Guy, Reverend Trevor Curtis, Jim Reader, Shauna Kantes, Stephanie Taylor, Kyla M, Micah Cash, Eric R. Asher, Cindy & Scott Kuntzelman, Avery Wild, Wes "nothing clever to say" Smith, Tamsin Silver, Steve Saffel, phoenix17, Mike Dubost, M.C. Jordan, Sarah Thompson, Cursed Dragon Ship Publishing, Venessa Giunta, Drew Bailey, Sue Phillips, LaZrus66, Scott M. Williams, William C. Tracy, Larissa Lichty, David Scoggins, Mari Mancusi, Jim Ryan, Seth Keipper, Marc Alan Edelheit, Dr. William Alexander Graham IV, Perry Harward, Liam Fisher, Jessica Glanville, Susan Roddey, Regina Kirby, Jeremy Bredeson & Leon Moses, Misty Massey, Janet Iannantuono, Regis Murphy, "Yes That Mark" Wilcox, Berta Platas, Kristen Clark, Matt, B. Y., Theresa Glover, Carol Malcolm, Dr. Keith Hunter Nelson, Adam, Leigh A. Boros & Robert A. Hilliard Jr., Aysha Rehm, Gary Phillips, Tom Savola, Audrey Hackett, Michael J. Sullivan, Annarose Mitchell, Karen M, Patrick J. Blanchard, Kayleigh Osborne, Chris Oakley, Andrea Judy, Casey, Helen Gassaway, J. Matthew Saunders, Carol Mammano, Danielle Ackley-McPhail & eSpec Books, and Jared Nelson.

ABOUT THE AUTHOR

Patrick is the author of the award-winning Darkest Storm Series published by Falstaff Books. Other titles include Never Steal From Dragons and Watchers of Astaria series from Distracted Dragon Press. Other publications include Fairy Films: Wee Folk on the Big Screen, a collection of fairy essays. Patrick is a member of SFWA.

An avid gadget user, Patrick is also the Director of Technology Services for Author's Essentials LLC providing solutions and advice for writing professionals. Patrick writings delve into software, hardware, social media, and all things web-related. The primary focus of Author's Essentials is how and when to employ technology to enhance your writing process.

Patrick resides in Charlotte, NC with his wife and two children. In his spare time, he's a PC gamer, homebrewer, 3D printer enthusiast, and DIYer. You can usually find him in the Hearthstone Tavern or wandering Azeroth as a Blood Elf Warlock in the evenings.

You can find out more at https://linktr.ee/patrickdugan

ALSO BY PATRICK DUGAN

The Shadow Blade Series

The Ashen Orb Bounty

The Dragon's Wrath Bounty

The Wayward Mage Bounty

Pixiepunk Series

Never Steal from Dragons

Watchers of Astaria Series

Fate & Flux – Prequel

Of Cogs & Conjuring

Pistols & Potions

Machines & Monsters

The Darkest Storm Series

Storm Forged

Unbreakable Storm

Storm Shattered